P_i

MW01246053

"WOW! What a great read. If you thought renting a $55,000 a month beach house in Southampton Long Island is what dreams are made of, think again. At least not for this new to be married couple. It starts on a beautiful summer's evening with a jog down the beach but soon takes a drastic turn. And things keep getting darker and darker and more and more mysterious.

"You just can't imagine where this heart pounding read is all going to go, which just increases the dread. Anyone who loves a who-dun-it is going to suck this one right up. Miller does us all a favor by giving us something new and original with heart pounding reality. I highly recommend *JoggerKill*."

Robert Pine
Hollywood Actor, stared in Enola Gay, Wish Man, CHIPS, Independence Day and many others; Father of actor Chris Pine, staring in Wonder Woman

"This is the perfect novel to scare yourself silly . . . and to devour in one sitting. You will slingshot from the possibly shark-infested beaches of Southampton to secret tunnels under the surrounding woods. Meet werewolves, wolves, wild dogs, and serial killers who all want to up the body count. There is a smart police chief and his somewhat annoying, drone-flying, techie son, who team up with a by-the-book FBI profiler to catch a bloody and mystifying killer. Spooky and satisfying."

Michele Mazzola
Former Special Projects Editor, Harper's Bazaar magazine

"What could be nicer than a run on a beautiful beach? Just imagine the brisk wind in your hair, the salty smell of the ocean breeze, and the sound of your feet hitting the hard sand. But, after reading *JoggerKill*, I'll always be looking over my shoulder at the beach or when out alone! The action was gripping, and the suspense had my stomach tied up in knots wondering what would happen next.

"Great read Jock Miller! I've been looking forward to a second novel from you after enjoying Fossil River. I strongly recommend *JoggerKill* as a good read in a comfortable chair with a glass of wine . . . better make that a glass of scotch because you'll need it!"

Janet Zollar, *Consultant*

"The brilliant and well written story of *JoggerKill* will immerse your head and heart and utterly consume you until the very last page. What could be more fun and twisted than a murder in the swanky Hamptons? A must read!"

Ellen Steiner, *President, Matterhorn Partners, L.P.*

"Jock Miller, a seasoned writer of such incredible books as *Fossil River*, has written a nail biting, edge of the seat thriller in *JoggerKill*. Early on, one asks, is it a pack of dogs, a wronged high school student getting revenge, or one directed by the other? An exciting road to travel, this story will have you reassessing and wondering along the way, who or what is causing such havoc in the usually quiet and peaceful Hamptons, home of the wealthy and sometimes eccentric villagers. You will love the twists and turns right up until the end. Can you solve the mystery?"

Mark Miller, *Retired Executive Vice President and General Manager, Hearst Magazines, Currently serving on the Hearst Corporation Board of Directors as Life Member*

"It was with great interest that I read and enjoyed *JoggerKill*. As a former criminal defense attorney, I was impressed by the author's knowledge and understanding of the criminal justice system. When my children were in school, I worked with several committees and groups involved in school activities and know bullying is a very serious problem. I look forward to purchasing copies and sharing them with family members, friends, and colleagues that include defense attorneys, prosecutors, judges, teachers, and school administrators."

Clark Dove

"Reading *JoggerKill* by Jock Miller was both horrifying and heartbreaking! Horrifying to read about someone who basically is a werewolf and has all the killer instincts and uses them. And at the same time heartbreaking to read about this kid getting horribly bullied and–*spoiler alert*–manipulated by someone he trusts! A great scary read! Impossible to put down! Kept me captured right through the final page."

Jamie Craig

"*Jogger Kill* grips you fast and holds your attention . . . a real page-turner . . . characters are real . . . lots of suspense and mystery, all the way to the end. If you like psychological thrillers this book is for you."

Michael Zollar

Jogger Kill

A Psychological Thriller

Jock Miller

DocUmeant Publishing *Diversified*
244 5th Avenue
Suite G-200
NY, NY 10001
646-233-4366
www.DocUmeantPublishing.com

Published by
DP Diversified
an imprint of DocUmeant Publishing
244 5th Ave, Suite G-200
NY, NY 10001
646-233-4366

This is a work of fiction. Names, characters, businesses, places, events and incidents are either the products of the author's imagination or used in a fictitious manner. Any resemblance to actual persons, living or dead, or actual events is purely coincidental.

Permission should be addressed in writing to the publisher at publisher@DocUmeantPublishing.com

Edited by Philip S Marks

Cover Design by Patti Knoles, www.virtualgraphicartsdepartment.com

Dangerous Dog Vectors by Vecteezy

Printed in the United States of America

10 9 8 7 6 5 4 3 2 1

Library of Congress Cataloging-in-Publication Data

Names: Miller, Jock, author.
Title: JoggerKill : a psychological thriller / Jock Miller.
Other titles: Jogger kill
Description: NY, NY : DP Diversified, 2023. | Summary: "A pack of wild attack dogs are tracking down and killing joggers. After the fourth victim is slaughtered, the Police Chief of Southampton, Long Island, whose daughter was the first victim, is determined to avenge her death. He suspects there is a serial killer behind these tragic killings. But it is the Chief's son and girlfriend who discover a horrifying fact.. Someone from a Long Island high school is purposely tracking and hunting down students from their class causing the largest manhunt in the northeast by the FBI and police"-- Provided by publisher.
Identifiers: LCCN 2022057244 | ISBN 9781950075850 (trade paperback) | ISBN 9781950075867 (epub)
Subjects: LCGFT: Thrillers (Fiction) | Novels.
Classification: LCC PS3613.I5385 J64 2023 | DDC 813/.6--dc23/eng/20221219
LC record available at https://lccn.loc.gov/2022057244

For my wife, Kay Zollar Miller, who has always encouraged me to pursue my dreams and promote my interests. Thank you for 58 years of connubial bliss and a family of 28 strong!

Contents

Prologue   xi

PART I
The Hunt

Chapter 1 1

Chapter 2 9

Chapter 3 15

Chapter 4 28

Chapter 5 32

Chapter 6 41

Chapter 7 49

Chapter 8 53

Chapter 9 61

Chapter 10 67

Chapter 11 77

Chapter 12 81

PART II
The Tracking

Chapter 13 88

Chapter 14 93

Chapter 15 101

Chapter 16 108

Chapter 17 116

Chapter 18 122

Chapter 19 125

Chapter 20 130

Chapter 21 138

Chapter 22 147

Chapter 23 153

Chapter 24 160

Chapter 25 162

PART III
The Confrontation

Chapter 26 168

Chapter 27 171

Chapter 28 174

Chapter 29 179

Chapter 30 186

Chapter 31 192

Chapter 32 195

Chapter 33 203

Chapter 34 208

Chapter 35 212

Chapter 36 218

Chapter 37 224

Chapter 38 228

Chapter 39 232

Chapter 40 237

Chapter 41 244

Chapter 42 247

Chapter 43 250

Chapter 44 256

Chapter 45 259

Chapter 46 263

Chapter 47 267

Chapter 48 273

Chapter 49 277

Chapter 50 280

Chapter 51 286

Chapter 52 288

Chapter 53 290

Chapter 54 296

Chapter 55 299

Chapter 56 305

Chapter 57 312

Chapter 58 316

Chapter 59 320

Chapter 60 325

Chapter 61 335

Chapter 62 343

Chapter 63 346

Chapter 64 351

Chapter 65 355

Acknowledgments 359

About the Author 361

Other Works by Jock Miller 363

PROLOGUE

IT IS KNOWN that 91 million people swim in the United States every year. Of those swimmers, 84 are gruesomely attacked by sharks, and six of them die.

It is also known that 110 million people jog annually, and 4.5 million people are viciously attacked and bitten by dogs, requiring 13 thousand of them to be hospitalized. Of those, 51 died last year according to Atlanta's Center for Disease Control.

This much is historical fact. What follows is fiction. Yet, one suspects what you are about to read could be happening at this very moment . . .

PART I
THE HUNT

CHAPTER 1

THE BEACH HOUSE was perched atop ten-foot pilings located behind gust swept sand dunes off Dune Road in Southampton, Long Island. The young couple had paid $55,000 to rent the cottage for the month of July. It was one of three outbuildings on three acres of pristine beachfront property on the Atlantic Ocean. The vast twelve-thousand square foot manor home on the property had unobstructed views of the shimmering Atlantic ocean from its living room and seven bedrooms. The owners were in Tuscany staying at their villa for five weeks. "Call us only in an emergency," they had told them.

A large pot of boiling water hissed atop a bed of hot coals just behind the mound of dunes outside their cottage. The dunes, held together by clumps of beach grass, partially sheltered the warm summer breezes blowing sparks into the air from the fire as the setting sun illuminated a path across the water that seemed to touch Ireland's Cliffs of Moher. It was 8:39 PM, July 2nd, Saturday night, and a slice of moon shone brightly off to the northeast.

A maroon blanket with a Harvard logo lay on the sand. Two brown paper bags sat on its edge. One contained seven live blue claw crabs that the couple had caught in the morning from the

Shinnecock canal. They had used a wire coat hanger skewered through chicken wings from last night's dinner attached to a spinning rod as bait. The bag quivered with movement. The other bag contained four freshly husked ears of golden sweet corn from Taskey's farm stand. A half-empty bottle of Chopin potato Vodka was wedged into the sand next to the blanket along with a small bottle of vermouth. The couple looked forward to having sex on the beach after dinner.

The screen door to the cottage swung open, and Judy Bennack, in her late twenties, scampered down the steps onto the beach. She wore a fire engine red halter top and blue spandex shorts. Her strawberry blonde hair was tied in a ponytail poking out from beneath a Lehman Brothers baseball cap. She had taken the cap along with the rest of her boxed belongings after the company collapsed in 2008. As she looked back over her shoulder she shouted into the cottage, her voice trailing off as she topped the dune, "Be back in thirty."

Sam Wade leaned out the second-floor window. "Love you," he waved cheerfully.

"Love you too," she yelled back as she sprang into a slow jog toward the water.

She jogged down to the seaweed line, then headed north along the water's edge. The saltwater felt good on her feet, and she could still see detail in the dunes to her left and the advancing tide to her right. She passed a lone fisherman who was hurling a Rebel plug beyond the breaking surf into a night run of striped bass and blue fish. She waved to him as she passed then quickened her pace.

Bennack was a disciplined jogger, averaging five miles a day, but it was not for fitness that the five-foot five-inch woman exercised. It was for competition. She had placed eighth in the ten-kilometer run out of Easthampton and fourteenth in her first 26.2-mile marathon to Montauk Point. She had read and studied

James Fixx's, *The Complete Book of Running*. Competition excited her and, she believed, jogging was essential to maintaining her competitive edge in the male dominated world of investment banking. She worked in the financial sponsors group at Barclay's Capital Bank after Lehman Brothers collapsed and was acquired. Running helped diffuse the pressure at work and silence the constant vibrations of emails and phone calls that streamed over her iPhone 11.

She quickened her pace, now running through the white wash from advancing waves that slid up the beach swirling around her calves as she jogged with increased effort. As the water raced back toward the breaking surf, she was surprised at the power of the undertow. But this was good, she told herself, for it made it more difficult to jog on wet sand that seemed to fall away with the passing of each stride and the cool water felt good on her bare feet. She felt the acid build up in her legs now, and the subtle pain reminded her that she was almost half way there before she would turn around and high kick on her return back to the cottage completing her thirty minute warm up for tomorrow's 10K.

A sliver of the setting sun vanished and darkness fell upon the beach. The half moon off to the northeast gave a dusky glow as an eerie light shone upon the large mansions and smaller outbuildings on her left. Lights flicked on in distant houses, and this sign of life gave the young woman confidence she was not alone. She jogged another hundred yards through the wash then spun around for the return home. The tide had come in faster than she thought, and the next wave enveloped her waste sucking her back toward the breakers. She struggled to free herself from the undertow, and her powerful legs propelled her in an angle leading closer to the shoreline. In the white wash, she thought she saw a dark object streak through the water toward her, but she was not sure. At first, it looked like a big piece of floating driftwood, dark gray or black, but it moved quickly in the wash then vanished in the darkness behind her.

Sam Wade had just come out of the cottage to check on the fire. He missed the last porch step and twisted sideways to his knees somehow managing to spill precious little of his extra dry martini. "What the hell?" he slurred laughingly then stood up and ambled over to the fire lifting the lid on the black crab pot. The water boiled over onto the hot coals with a loud sputtering hiss. "Perfect," Wade snorted aloud then poured the bag of live crabs into the boiling pot. He took a long sip of his martini, swallowed one olive, then leaned over to grab the bottle of vodka to replenish his drink. He hesitated, then wedged the bottle back into the sand. He was into his third martini and promised himself that it would be his last for the evening. To have a fourth would deny him sex. It happened last night after he half finished his fourth. When he rolled over atop Bennack, legs entwined in urgent ardor, he had passed out in a stupor, flaccid.

Tonight would be different, he reassured himself with a thin smile. They had been dating for ten months now, and they had rented the summer cottage as a test. But it was more than that. Tonight was going to be special. Wade climbed atop the dune and peered off to the left, knowing that Bennack was now on her way back home jogging to the finish line that promised blue claw crabs, fresh corn on the cob, and great sex on the beach, and, he smiled yet again, something else.

Wade reached deep into his pocket and pulled out a small turquoise box with a white ribbon neatly wrapped around it. He had opened the box three times to check the contents mounted neatly inside a black velvet box. It was a 2.3 carrot perfect blue-white diamond that he had purchased two months ago from Tiffany's. His heart skipped a beat as he rehearsed what he would say. He had asked her father, Tom Bennack, for permission last weekend, and he thought he might vomit before the words spilled out. "Yes," the father had said somewhat formally. "She's a strong woman, Sam. You think you can handle her?" Wade didn't hesitate. "Yes, sir," he affirmed, his heart pounding in his chest as if it would burst.

Wade leaned toward the ocean, the gentle onshore breeze tickling the back of his head. "Will you marry me, Judy?" he said aloud. No, he decided, too trite. Every guy says that, he guessed. It's got to be different. Not good enough. "I fell in love with you the moment I saw you at Barclay's." Trite, yet true. Still not good enough. He took a long pull on his martini, looked out across the Atlantic Ocean, squinted, and the edge of a thought pierced his mind. "Judy," his heart fluttered yet again, and he coughed. "Shit," he told himself aloud. "Suck it up, Wade." Again, "Judy, how do I love thee, let me count the ways. I love thee to the depth and breadth my soul to keep." She's too smart and she'll catch it immediately. "Plagiarized from Elizabeth Barrett Browning," she'll say. I'll feel like a shit, he decided. Then it came to him in one simple, delightful thought: Just give her the fucking box, and the ring will say it all.

He smiled into the warm summer breeze checking the box again, then sipped the last of his martini while listening to the faint sounds of Picnic's Moonglow drifting from the open cottage window. He descended the dune toward the water, waiting for her return. When he reached the water's edge, Wade stood rigid and peed into the white foam of the incoming tide trying to scroll the initials SW and JB atop the froth. He wrote a wobbling SWJ and ran empty on the "B." The gentle onshore breeze felt good, and he quivered a warm response, then looked south squinting to see Bennack in the distance. He thought he saw a silhouette of something moving toward him maybe a half-mile away but wasn't sure.

Bennack had advanced toward the seaweed line now, and her pace quickened. Another strong wave slid up the beach beyond her, and white wash now covered her knees. She saw another dark flash of movement in the water in front of her, and spun out to the left to avoid it, deeper in the water now, her heart pounding. Something was wrong. She could not see detail, but it was dark and thick, and it moved sideways within the surf. She had only one thought: *get the hell out of the water . . . now*! The undertow pulled at her powerful lunging pace, and she seemed to be running in place without any forward movement.

Suddenly, from behind her, she felt a searing pain clench the calf of her left leg, and she fell forward collapsing beneath the next advancing wave. She struggled to stand, but something grabbed her right leg, pulling her down under yet again. She felt a sharp bite and knew that something terrible was happening to her. She reached down to touch her left calf and felt bone and strings of flesh. Then she felt something else: powerful jaws of something that had her in a death grip. Desperately thrusting her head above water, she threw her head back and screamed a guttural bubbling cry of terror, thrashing urgently in the white wash which was turning red. Now she was on all fours desperately clawing at the sand for purchase in an effort to pull herself up the beach out of water towards safety, but yet another wave crashed behind her propelling the powerful surf beyond her. She swallowed salt water and coughed violently screaming beneath the surf in muted terror.

Her mind exploded with the knowledge that she was being attacked and eaten alive by a shark, maybe several of them. It was all happening too fast. Confused, panic now gripped her mind, and she rose to her knees and screamed yet again, arms thrashing, as something exploded out of the water in front of her, hurling itself at her with such speed and force that her body bent over backwards in a painful arc of splashing blood and sinew. When she fell beneath the white wash yet again, her trachea and esophagus had vanished, and the white froth of the advancing tide was now a sanguine circle of death that grew with the ebb and flow of each passing wave. The beat of her heart gave its last convulsive quiver of dread and her lifeless body rolled over and over toward the breaking surf, sucked out to sea by the powerful undertow where it would sink slowly to the sandy bottom before being consumed by ocean predators. Her Lehman Brothers hat, like the company she once worked for, floated helplessly in the turbulent surf, then vanished into the murky depths of the sea.

Sam Wade stood on the beach for another twenty-three minutes trying to clear his head from the last martini. She would be back soon, he kept telling himself. He tried to remember what time it was when she left the cottage. Then, he was trying to remember how long she had said she would be jogging. Was it fifteen or twenty minutes? Maybe thirty? He couldn't remember. He started to walk north along the shoreline hoping to meet her on the return, but after walking the better part of a mile, he turned back toward the cottage, his mind filled with angst and a slur of unsettling thoughts. It was not like her to be late. He knew she would return soon, but when? Now it was 8:40 PM and the coals on the fire were white, the crabs day-glow red, and the water not boiling. He leaned over and picked up the Chopin bottle of vodka and filled his martini glass to the brim, no vermouth this time. He inhaled a long swig of the drink and, for the first time, the thought that something might be terribly wrong entered his mind with a searing punch of reality.

CHAPTER 2

PATROL SERGEANT ANDY Johnson was leaning against the wall urinal in the South Hampton police station peeing. He was admiring Playboy's Miss July calendar, affixed to the wall in front of him with green duck-tape. He mused with furrowed brow if her breasts were real. Something sucked about bogus tits, he thought gloomily. His father once told him what authentic breasts were like forty years ago before the rage of plastic surgeons swarmed over less endowed women like knife wielding predators convincing them that large breasts attracted men of promise. "Soft and velvety to the touch," his father had said of real breasts.

Johnson heard the phone chirp twice through the thin bathroom door. He shouted, "Could you get that, Chief . . . taking a leak." Johnson flushed the urinal, flipped the *Playboy* calendar to take a quick peek at Miss August. His mouth gaped in astonishment. "Mother of God," he gasped.

Twenty-five minutes had passed since Police Chief Tom Bennack finished his Big Whopper and fries. He sensed a tightening in his chest and couldn't quite catch his breath. Maybe it was the uncooked onions, he thought. He gave a bubbling belch as he picked up the phone hoping it was not yet another DWI or head-on collision on Dune Road. Night duty always sucked he had told Johnson, and it wasn't for the faint hearted. That's why the chief always assigned the more seasoned patrolmen to night duty, Johnson had told the younger patrolmen.

The South Hampton Police Department was split into three divisions: Communications, Detective, and Patrol. It was the Patrol Division that got all the action, and each of the five squads were commanded by a Patrol Sergeant. Chief Bennack oversaw the entire operation. Behind his back, his staff bitched and moaned about his pain-in-the-ass attention to detail. "The goddamn guy never lets up," croaked Patrol Sergeant Johnson to Nate Futterman, a seasoned Marine vet on the force. "He's fucking obsessed," Johnson concluded in a bitching Brooklyn twang.

South Hampton was in full summer party mode, and distress calls had been coming in for the past three weeks, with increasing intensity: a house maid raped by an Hispanic gardener from Guatemala; a butler accused of molesting his employer's twelve year old daughter; a Prince Charles Spaniel impaled on the end of a trident eel spear leaned against a waterfront mansion front door with a note on the forked spear prong that read, "*The last bark! It got what it deserved, the yapping mennace*", and three complaints of disturbing the peace from oversized mansions built more to make a statement of extravagant opulence, than to accommodate large bustling families of genuine purpose.

South Hampton had succeeded in attracting many well-moneyed people who could easily afford waterfront homes . . . movie producers, actors and actresses, literary agents, investment bankers from Wall Street, real estate moguls, CEOs of blue-chip companies, and novelists who had made the New York Times Best Selling list in hardcover, paperback, Kindle, and Nook, and had sold their books to movie producers. The balance of the population surrounding the wealth consisted of wannabe financially less fortunate folk who rented the mansion outbuildings and gate houses just so they could tell their friends elsewhere that they spent the summers in South Hampton. Financially hocked to the hilt, of course, without anybody knowing they were worried sick about affording the next meal. They were far below the next tier of wealth, the Nuevo Riche. South Hampton, like Telluride and Aspen Colorado, was a magnet for people with unfulfilled dreams hoping that somehow living amidst genuine wealth would rub off on them.

"Southampton Police, Chief Bennack here."

"Tom?"

"Yes. Who's this?" Bennack responded crisply.

"Sam."

"Hey, Sam. Did you ask her yet?"

The question hung in the air.

"No," Wade said flatly.

"Why not?" he said, eyebrows furrowed. Bennack heard an unsettling silence on the phone. "Sam?"

"Something's wrong, Tom," Wade said, his voice barely above a slurred whisper.

Bennack leaned toward his desk and sat up, his heart skipping a beat. "Talk to me."

"It's your daughter," Wade said.

"What's wrong, Sam?" he said, his face taut with concern.

Wade cleared his throat. Bennack heard a slur in his words. "She went jogging on the beach about an hour and a half ago and isn't back yet. You know your daughter. That's not like her."

Bennack breathed in deeply, and his chest tightened again. He knew it wasn't from the onions this time. "She has a 10K tomorrow, doesn't she?" he said trying to convince himself she was okay.

"Yeah," Wade managed, "but . . ."

"She's probably pushing herself, Sam. You know how competitive she is. I wouldn't sweat it. She'll be back soon enough." Bennack stood up, phone pressed to his right ear, staring around his small office, fidgeting with a #10 pencil. His eyes fixed on a silver framed picture of his daughter in her Columbia Business School cap and gown accepting her diploma from the dean of the business school, along with a Beta Gamma Sigma Honor Society certificate. Bennack studied his daughter's face proudly, then walked a half circle around his desk. Next to her picture was a larger framed photo of his wife Andrea and their son Grady. "It's safe on Dune Road. She didn't go swimming, did she?" said the Chief, lips tightly curled.

Sergeant Johnson burst breathlessly into Bennack's office. "Did you see Miss August?"

Bennack held up his hand in a shushing motion. He cupped the phone and said, "You're unbelievable, Johnson. Zip it."

Johnson saw the look on the chief's face, and spun on his heel, walking swiftly out of the office, cursing himself for the intrusion. "Stupid asshole," he muttered aloud.

"You there, Tom?"

"I'm here. Go ahead."

"She went jogging, unless . . ."

"Unless what?" pressed Bennack, his voice like ice.

"She told me she'd be back, Tom. I think she said thirty minutes.

That was almost two hours ago. Something's wrong. I know it."

Bennack sensed concern in Wade's voice, but he also knew something else. Bennack raised his two children never to be late. 'A lack of responsibility if you're not on time,' he had told them. He felt the first rush of concern sweep over him like a bad dream and snapped the pencil in his hand in half. "Did you try her cell?" he said with a controlled voice.

"Left it at the cottage. We were about to eat dinner. You know how much I love your daughter, sir. Tonight's the night, for Chrissakes. I have the ring in my pocket, and she . . ." Wade burst into tears.

Bennack felt a cool shiver skitter across his shoulders and sweep down his spine like a hot ice pick. The thought of something happening to his only daughter made him feel sick to his stomach. Possibly losing her gripped him with stinging reality. "Stay there, Sam. I'm on my way. Keep looking." He put the phone back on the cradle with a hard smack.

He spun on his heel and walked briskly into Patrolman Johnson's office. "There haven't been any shark attacks yet, right?"

"No. Not that I know of," Johnson said. "What's up?"

"My daughter's missing. She went jogging on the beach about two hours ago. That was Sam Wade. She's not back yet and he's panicked."

"That's not a long time, chief. She'll be back soon enough. I wouldn't sweat it." Johnson hesitated a brief moment then added, "Wasn't the guy going to ask your daughter to marry him tonight?"

"Yeah. I gave him permission last week."

"She's okay, chief. Let it go . . ."

"Maybe so, Andy, But I'm not sure. Something doesn't sound right. She's not one to ever be late," Bennack said, his eyes leveling on him.

Johnson twitched in his chair, staring back at him. "Not on the same subject, but I always wanted to ask you something."

"Not now, Andy," Bennack said holding up his hand in a stopping motion. "Hold the fort. I'll call if I need backup. Alert the patrolmen in the field just in case we have a problem."

Johnson made another feeble attempt to assuage his boss. He wanted to apologize for bursting into his office. Instead, he said, "She's okay, chief, seriously."

"Easy for you to say, Andy," and Bennack vanished out the side door before Johnson could respond.

Chief Bennack never used his siren unless he had proof something was imminently wrong. Johnson's eyes widened when he heard its wail fill his office. He looked out the window and saw the chief's patrol car pull away, tires screeching, red lights flashing.

CHAPTER 3

A S BENNACK'S PATROL car pulled into the Hobbs estate off Dune Road, he expected to see his daughter's car and Sam Wade waiting out front. Instead, he saw nobody, and the circular drive was pitch dark and empty.

Bennack pulled up in front of the house, exited the patrol car and pushed his way toward the left side of the estate manor home, following a slate path. He entered a small courtyard and could see the guest cottage in the distance, hear the breaking surf of a rising tide. The lights were on, and he was relieved to see Wade sitting in a porch rocker. He assumed his daughter would be sitting beside him, because her German Shepherd, Helka, protectively sat next to the cane chair as she always did when she was there. Bennack had given the K-9 attack dog to his daughter as a gift when she got her MBA at Columbia. But the real reason for the gift was that Bennack felt uneasy that his daughter was no longer under his watchful and protective charge. Helka had been trained by Bennack in his K-9 unit to protect, guard, and attack on command before he became chief of the South Hampton Police Department. Helka seemed nervous sensing something was wrong.

The dog gave a guttural warning growl, teeth bared, until Bennack extinguished the threat with one command, "Sitz." The dog silenced, its tail acknowledging her friend with a gentle wag. The word was one of many that Bennack had used in his Shutzhund German training of K-9 police dogs used to locate drugs and human predators.

"Where is she?" said Bennack looking at his watch as if it had the answer.

"She's in trouble. I know it, sir," Wade frowned fretfully.

"You walked the beach?"

"Yes, sir."

"How far?"

"A mile. At least a mile, maybe more. She went north." Wade pointed feebly to his left.

"How long ago?"

Wade stood up and put his left hand atop his head. "I don't remember, sir. Christ." Wade never said, "Sir," unless he felt uncomfortable or intimidated. This was his future father-in-law. When he asked for Judy Bennack's hand every other word to Bennack was, "Sir."

"Guess," persisted Bennack, his voice low and demanding as if he had met Wade for the first time and was in the midst of a serious cop probe.

"I can't think, sir," Wade offered, his arms hanging limply at his sides.

"What was she wearing?"

"Jesus, sir. Shorts and a top, I think. How's that going to matter? She's missing," Wade said in a mournful monotone not thinking about mustering any details except his future wife had vanished and that's all that seemed to matter.

"What color? I need the details, Sam. Details."

The words seemed to spin around in Wade's head like a pair of sneakers inside a dryer in full cycle.

Bennack grabbed Wade's shoulders and shook him. "Think, goddamn it. It's important."

"Red and I think blue, sir. Maybe her Lehman hat, and . . ."

"Did she take Helka with her?"

"No."

"Why not?"

"I don't know."

"What else?"

Wade buried his face in his hands, bursting into tears, falling backward where he thought the chair was. He misjudged and collapsed onto the floor like a deck of cards in 52 pickup.

Bennack picked him up and slumped him back into the chair. Helka gave a whine of empathy, licking Wade's hand that hung limply over the chair's arm like a cooked noodle. Bennack leaned down a foot from Wade's face and snapped his fingers. "Sam, listen to me. I know this is tough for you. Sucks for me too . . . When she left you, did she tell you where she was jogging?"

Wade looked up at Bennack's face. It was blurry and Wade shook his head to clear the image. "No, sir."

"Think!"

"She didn't say, sir, except she'd be back in thirty minutes, or was it twenty? I can't remember."

Bennack stood up and faced the ocean, shaking his head in frustration. He flipped open his two-way and punched a button. "Chief to headquarters."

"Yeah, chief. Go ahead," Johnson said officially.

"I want three squad cars at the Hobb's house on Dune Road in five, sirens on."

"Roger that, chief. Done." Johnson swallowed hard to clear the lump in his throat, dreading the answer to his question when he heard, 'sirens on.'

"Did you find her?"

"Stupid question, Johnson. No, for chrissake," Bennack responded sharply. Johnson knew the chief well, and his voice was obsessively crisp, all business. But, he sensed, for the first time, that the chief's words were laced in unsettled panic. He hoped he was wrong.

Johnson heard the chief ring off with a sharp click. He cursed himself for asking the question.

In less than ten minutes, the chief had three South Hampton patrolmen canvassing the beach with him, north of Wade's cottage. The fourth cop was Nate Futterman, the Marine vet, who was still in the back seat of his Chevy patrol car when he got the call. His car was stationed at the far end of the Maidstone Golf Club Parking lot, hidden behind two rows of retired golf carts.

It was his night off, but he always kept his squawk box on to keep track of night calls if the Chief needed backup in case of emergency. Francine Weatherby, one of three Maidstone Golf Club pros, had just removed her pink laced panties and was in the process of mounting Futterman. The car radio was playing Johnny Mathis '*Up, Up, and Away*' when Futterman pulled out and said, "What was that?"

Weatherby said, "Jesus Nate. What was what?"

It sounded like Andy Johnson's voice." said Futterman. "From headquarters."

"What the hell are you talking about? Forget it," she demanded as she grabbed his buttocks and shoved him onto her yet again, her angry cry splitting the silence.

Futterman popped out and said, "Wait Francine. I gotta check something," and he thrust his upper body up and over the front seat, his bare ass glowing from the light of a half-moon that shown through the rear window in a golden eerie glow.

He fumbled for the hand mike, but Weatherby, a large muscular woman with dyed red hair known to drive a golf ball three hundred yards, grabbed him again pulling him back from the front seat. She slid sideways flipping Futterman around as if he were a toy manikin and found him, arching upward, unrelenting. The patrolman grunted, stole a labored breath, and found his hand mike punching the talk button to speak. His voice pitched an octave higher when he said, "Andy, Futterman here. What's up?"

"Scramble to Hobb's estate, Nate. Dune Road. Chief just called for backup, all hands on deck. His daughter's missing. Went jogging on the beach a couple of hours ago. Not back yet. He thinks . . ."

Johnson heard what sounded like a woman's voice screaming, but he knew it wasn't out of pain. What drifted over the South Hampton Police Station speaker phone, Johnson thought he heard a crescendo of pulsating sounds, definitely female. He grinned into the phone.

"What the hell's that?" he said with a half chortle. "It sounded like . . ."

Futterman slapped a cupped hand over Weatherby's mouth as she climaxed, and garbled a response, "Nothing, Andy. Just the radio. I turned it down," he lied. "I'll be there in five."

When Futterman arrived at the Hobb's estate, the driveway was a glut of cop cars. He got out and rearranged himself. When he walked around to the surf-side cottage, it was empty. Futterman punched his two-way on and said, "Hey, Chief . . . Nate here. I'm at the Hobb's house. Where the hell are you guys?"

"About a mile and a half north of the cottage. Get your search light and air horn. If you see anything, give us three blasts. Nothing out here yet," the chief said in a controlled voice.

"Roger that, Chief. On my way," Futterman said, his groin aching from Weatherby's unrelenting thrusts.

Three patrolmen, Chief Bennack, and Sam Wade searched purposely along the water's edge, zig-zagging the beach up to the dunes then down to the water's edge, lights piercing the darkened night. Patrolman Rick Huntley saw a light beam flash southward and knew Futterman had begun his search. Chief Bennack commanded Helka with sharp calls, "Voraust" for run out, go forward and, "Such," for track. The dog ranged back and forth, nosing the sand, snorting for scent. Bennack heard barking in the distance then a deep guttural growl. Maybe the dog found something, thought the chief hopefully, but the distant barks faded confirming the dog was ranging farther north toward the dunes. The more Bennack pressed on, the less hopeful he became confirming that something had happened to his daughter. He pushed it out of his mind forcing himself to focus on the search.

Two hours passed and the patrol had canvassed three and a half miles of coastline. Patrolman Futterman brought up the rear and was ambling slowly behind, checking every clump of seaweed and drift wood on the beach. He found a washed-up lobster pot buoy, cut lines, plastic bottles, and a splintered piece of planking that had probably came from the hull of a small boat, but no signs of the chief's daughter.

At 12:46 AM, Chief Bennack's voice broke the air. "Spread out. Futterman, you're closer to the cottage than us. Maybe she circled back onto Dune Road and jogged back home, rather than using the beach. She might be back at the cottage now. Check it out and get back to me. Over."

"Roger that Chief. Ten four," Futterman said with a gaping yawn, his groin still inflamed as if he had been kicked in the balls.

The chief ambled farther north passing Sam Wade who now sat on the beach bent over dry heaving. "You okay?"

Wade did not respond and the chief decided to leave him alone, knowing he was lost in grief and probably nursing a hangover.

The pungent odor of low tide was beginning to mix with the refreshing smell of the ocean. Futterman turned and slowly ambled back toward the cottage, his eyes following the scanning beam of his powerful search light. He approached a lone fisherman who had waded out into the breaking surf casting a large plug of some sort beyond the waves. On the beach, where the fisherman had been standing, Futterman's light illuminated two blue fish and a striped bass the fisherman had caught. The bass was still alive and flopped lazily in the sand, gasping for its last few waterless breaths. Futterman watched the bass expire and thought of the chief's daughter wondering if she was still alive. He pressed on heading south, back down the beach.

Helka, the German Shepherd, found a small pile of jetsam and was sniffing the contents, barking at the assemblage of washed-up litter. Bennack shone his light along the seaweed line and found a pink bra, too small to be his daughter's, a small rubber doll with a few strands of blonde hair still attached to the head, countless plastic water bottles, one blue sneaker, an assortment of tampons, a plastic bag filled with surgical needles and syringes, three condoms, and varying sizes of drift wood covered with tar. It was a shredded blue spandex halter top that sent Bennack's heart into a spasm of despair. Helka nuzzled the halter top and whined as if confirming his master's thoughts. His daughter used similar attire for jogging, Wade had told him, and his heart skipped a beat. He tucked the damp fabric into his black leather jacket pocket, and continued his search, Helka leading the search tracking back and forth nose to the ground.

In the distance, Patrolman Futterman could see the faint profile of another fisherman. He had already passed two other fishermen as he headed back to the cottage, but he decided to pause and watch for a few minutes. The fisherman was working the surf within fifty feet of Futterman, his powerful beam now lighting up the surf encircling the fisherman. He heard the man yell, "fish on," and watched him land a large fish. The man trudged back through the surf dragging a gaffed stripped bass behind him. As the man approached, Futterman said, "Congratulations. Mind if I ask you a few questions?"

The fisherman emptied his gaff and the striper flopped on the beach beside them. "Sure. What?"

"We're looking for a woman. Blonde, late twenties, five-foot fourish. Went jogging earlier tonight about seven o'clock. See anybody jog by here with that description?"

"Nope," said the man. "I didn't get here until nine o'clock. She go swimming? Bad undertow if she did."

"Far as we know," Futterman said, "she was jogging. I don't think she went swimming. Keep an eye out for her. If you see anything suspicious, call us . . . South Hampton Police."

"Will do, officer. Be easier searching for her once the sun's up. Good luck. Sorry, I've got to get back out there. There's a school of cow bass, thirty to forty pounders. This one's a pup, only twenty." The man waded back into the surf and hurled a silver spoon with a strip of squid attached to a large treble hook out beyond the second wave.

On his third cast, Futterman saw the rod bend over in an arc touching the water. He suspected the fish was large just by the way it was fighting. Twelve minutes passed and Futterman couldn't resist watching as the fisherman seemed to be gaining on the fish. He guessed the fish was now somewhere in the white wash. The fisherman urgently walked toward the fish, reeling in fast, his gaff at the ready. In the beam of Futterman's light, he could see that the fish was just beyond the first breaking wave. The light beam followed the line, and he thought he saw a large dorsal fin and the bulk of the fish rise to the surface then submerge. The man reeled the fish in closer, then he held his gaff high in the air and arched it down into the bass. The man felt the weight of the fish and hoisted his catch partially out of the water only to collapse under the next wave beneath the surf.

Futterman stood rigid. "What the bloody hell?" The patrolman walked toward the water hesitatingly. "Hey," he shouted. "Hey." But the fisherman had vanished.

Then it happened. The fisherman's head rose above the frothy white wash, and Futterman heard a blood curdling scream, "Help," and he vanished yet again beneath a crashing wave. Futterman frantically stripped his shoes, socks, jacket, and gun holster off bursting into a dash thrusting himself into the surf. The fisherman suddenly bobbed up atop the water yet again screaming a guttural cry for help. Futterman lunged toward him, water above his belt. He knew from the man's cry something was terribly wrong, and it happened so fast he didn't give thought that maybe the fisherman was being attacked by a shark.

The patrolman reached the fisherman and raised his head above the water, but the weight of the man surprised Futterman as he desperately tried to pull him toward shore. Futterman finally reached the edge of the surf, and stood to drag the man and his catch ashore. As they reached the tide line, Futterman collapsed in a tidal pool of salt water left behind from a receding tide.

The fisherman's breath came in short spasms and his eyes were closed. Futterman unsnapped the gaff from the man's waders and looked down at the fish. It was pitch black, and he could not see detail. He rose to his knees and fumbled for his search light. He turned it on and shone it on the large fish. It was then he realized it was not a fish. It was a bloody miasma. A shriveled mutilated corpse of some kind, crabs crawling in and out of two gutted eye sockets from something so hideous that Futterman leaned over and puked from the sight of it. The upper torso of a nude body, shriveled breasts as flat as pancakes, and stringy blonde hair twisted in sandy knots, was all wrapped in seaweed entangled by a yellow nylon rope and red lobster buoy. Somehow, thought Futterman, this shriveled alien-like corpse was probably the chief's daughter, Judy Bennack. The fish hook from the silver lure had snagged on what was left of the woman's left upper thigh.

The fisherman's eyes blinked open and his look of fear in his eyes was palpable. "What the hell is it?" the man pushed out of his mouth.

"A body," Futterman somehow gasped, tasting bile in his mouth.

The fisherman lay back, his head touching the edge of the tidal pool. He turned his head sideways and joined Futterman retching into the shallow pool. "I don't fucking believe it," he sputtered wiping his mouth with a grizzled hand. "Who the hell is it?"

"I think you caught the woman we've been looking for," Futterman said in utter disbelief thinking it was a one in a million cast.

"Jesus fucking Christ," the man said, his eyes staring blankly at the gaffed corpse. Then he rolled over again and puked until his guts wrenched in pain.

Futterman, retrieving his clothes, pulled out the air horn from his jacket and said, "Hold your ears." He gave three long blasts into the damp night air. He waited thirty seconds, gave three more blasts, and then a final three.

In less than eight minutes, Futterman saw lights hurrying along the beach toward him. Patrol Sergeant Johnson arrived first. Two more patrolmen arrived before the chief.

Chief Bennack knew it was bad news when he heard three horn blasts repeated. When he arrived, he did not say a word. He looked down at what lay twisted in the center of three light beams. He poked his left boot at the head and his daughter's face bobbled up at the night sky, eye sockets gaping at him like empty saucers. Her mouth gave birth to small crabs darting in and out of the opening in a horrifying mask of pain. It did not resemble the face of Judy Bennack, his daughter, nor any human. It looked more like a monster from another planet. A split second passed while the chief stood silently in denial, his mind refusing to register the site. It couldn't be his daughter, he tried to convince himself. Her left breast had enough of a bulge left in it to confirm that it was the body of a woman. In spite of the swollen face, the throat torn out, and the blonde hair twisted in sand-filled knots, he knew it was his daughter. The only piece of clothing that still clung to her ravaged body was a pair of pink panties exposing bone, and there was a large gash below her left breast as if a knife blade had been drawn across her sternum. Her German Shepherd, Helka, sniffed the corpse and gave a deep guttural protective growl, baring its teeth as it sniffed and snorted around the face and shriveled remains. Then it looked up at Chief Bennack and howled a prolonged cry, realizing that what lay on the beach in a sod of gristle, torn flesh and bone was the remains of its master.

Sam Wade stood beside the chief, both of them in silence. Then Wade burst into tears, collapsing in grief to his knees. Chief Bennack seemed dazed, his mind trying to comprehend the gruesome loss. He wanted to run away from the scene and scream in an agonizing burst of utter despair. Instead, he checked a heave of emotion from his chest, put his right hand on Wade's shoulder and squeezed softly as if to convince both of them that it was all a bad dream and nothing had happened at all.

The fisherman was now standing in a circle of dazed men. "Did she drown?" he offered in astonishment.

Futterman was the first to say it. "A shark got her," his voice resolute.

Chief Bennack released his grip on Wade and turned to face what was left of his daughter. He stared at the gash that streaked across her chest. "I'm not convinced it was a shark," he hissed between clenched teeth.

Sam Wade wiped a damp sleeve across his tear-streaked face and rose to his feet. "She was jogging. How could it be a shark?"

Futterman said, "Look at the mangled body. If it wasn't a shark, whatever killed her did one hell of a job." He pointed the toe of his boot at what was left of the woman. "Looks like a set of powerful jaws to me. Had to be a shark."

Bennack shook his head hard trying to jar his mind back to reality forcing himself, reluctantly, back to his role as chief of the

South Hampton Police Department. He took his police jacket off and carefully draped it over what remained of his daughter's body. He looked at Sergeant Johnson and said, "Call an ambulance. Tell them we have a DOA on the beach north of the Hobbs estate. Tell them . . ." Bennack paused, catching another convulsive sob before it surfaced, "she's my . . ."

The chief could not finish the sentence prompting his three policemen to move in closer, encircling him. There was nothing else to say that would comfort Bennack. Sam Wade managed to stagger toward the circle now surrounding Bennack. Seven minutes passed and the men stood in silence not breaking the circle, arms around each other comforting, trying to comprehend what had happened. In the distance the faint sound of a siren broke the still of the night and a tint of first light shown faintly in the distance across a vast shimmering sea, due east.

CHAPTER 4

AS FIRST LIGHT swept over the landscape giving shape and detail to beachfront mansions and the shore line, two emergency medical technicians arrived on the scene and carefully placed the corpse into a body bag, lifting the remains back to the ambulance. Chief Bennack watched the process in disbelief knowing only one thing: He promised himself he would find out how his daughter died. If it wasn't a shark, he had told his squad of patrolman, he would track down the predator who took his daughter's life and even the score.

The one unsettling thought that crept into his mind now was that if she was killed by human hands, Bennack was not sure he would be capable of letting the son of a bitch go through due process alive. Bennack's only career quest was to be a top cop dedicating himself to righting wrong with law and order. Incessantly, he watched every TV cop drama and live cop profile in his quest to emulate those officers he held as heroes protecting a society. Increasingly, far left liberal politicians promoting their politically correct ways infiltrated and undermined every cop's duty with the requirement of having video cameras strapped to their body filming every arrest and encounter. To every force in the nation, the process confirmed a growing mistrust between police and the public at large. To Bennack and his force, Black lives did matter, but as Futterman, the ex-Marine cop, protested, "Screw the liberals. All lives matter."

Bennack did not frequent bars as a teenager or participate in smoking weed or quaffing beers. He took hell from his peers, of course: pansy, goody two shoes, ass wipe, and copper were handles bestowed on him, but he shrugged it all off as typical teenage bull shit. It wasn't his parents that disciplined him to know the difference between right and wrong. His father was a high school graduate and Brooklyn fireman, Engine House 84, who, when he wasn't putting out fires, was drinking away his paycheck. His mother, a second-grade school teacher, was loving and protective, and to Bennack seemed to always be putting out fires within their own home when his father came home too drunk to find the bathroom, pissing on the walls and floor of their home.

Bennack's visceral instincts made him return pocket change found in pay phones back to the operator or pick up a street penny and give it to a homeless person plus whatever loose pocket change he had. But now, entrenched in his career, Bennack faced the searing reality that his own daughter had died on his beat, and he knew it would take all the courage and conviction he could muster to solve a case that landed painfully on his own doorstep. To that extent, Bennack hoped his daughter was killed by a shark, not by human hands.

Andrea Bennack lay in bed twitching from a dark dream she had had before many times. This time she was being chased by someone into a dead-end chamber. No way out, high walls surrounding her. Then someone appeared in a beam of white light walking toward her calling her name. She felt a warm flush of heat spreading over her body as the image got closer, but it always had no face, no sex. She wasn't even sure it was human. At least no face that she recognized, but it was something familiar to her and she always awakened in a cold sweat after the dream. Her eyes opened and she rolled over in bed, her left arm reaching out to embrace her husband in an early morning snuggle before he awakened to start his day. He was not there, and she rose up in bed to a sitting position looking around the room, squinting to see detail. Faint light filtered into the room through both sides of a dark shade. She rubbed her eyes and opened them wide. A shadow stood by the bedroom door in silence. She started. "Tom?"

"Yes. Is Grady home?" His voice was hollow.

"Yes. I think so. Why? Something wrong?"

Bennack let out a painful gasp of grief and burst into tears.

"Oh my God, Tom. What is it?" The woman sprang from the bed turning on a bedside lamp.

Andrea had seen her husband cry before when she gave birth to their son. "Tears of joy," he had told her. But when their golden retriever got run over by the garbage truck, he had wailed as if it were one of his own children. This time, it scared her. "Tom?"

All he could say was, "Judy."

Andrea thought about Sam Wade, the proposal. "What happened, Tom? Speak to me."

Bennack pushed the words out of his mouth in one paralyzing moment of grief as if another voice spoke through him. "She's dead," the voice said. Andrea did not scream or say a word. Her head turned slowly toward the ceiling, her eyes rolled up into her head, and her body fell forward. In one agonizing motion, Bennack leaped toward her catching her in his arms before she hit the floor. It brought him back to reality and the fact that their daughter was gone, and there was nothing he could do to bring her back. The only thing that remained in their lives as a painful reminder of their daughter Judy was Helka who now sat at their opened bedroom door watching Bennack catch his wife before she hit the floor, his head tilting to the left trying to comprehend what had happened. Eyes wide, Helka looked up at both of them locked in an embrace and, from its throat, a melancholy soft cry broke the silence.

CHAPTER 5

THE POPULATION OF South Hampton, Long Island, is 6,500 during winter months, swelling to 35,000 during the summer. The average personal income is $69,547, and the housing market's median selling price is $1,068,199. Tom Bennack made $103,500 a year as Chief of Police, and Andrea, his wife, cleared $65,000 as an RN at South Hampton's Spielberg Memorial Hospital. They bought a small ranch house eleven years ago on Salt Marsh Creek for $429,000 at the end of the great recession. Their meager assets convinced the conservative South Hampton Community Bank to finance the mortgage, with twenty percent down, at $343,200, but only if Andrea's father agreed to collateralize the mortgage with a pledge of stock. As a result, Tom Bennack had to borrow $28,000 from his father-in-law to make up the balance for the down payment of $85,800. It left them a balance in their joint savings account of $2,386.63. "Not enough to cover PB&Js for a year, for Christsakes," Bennack had moaned to his wife over his third extra dry martini, trying desperately to salvage his pride.

"It doesn't matter, Tom," Andrea had told her husband. "Dad's rich and I'm the only heir." The comment didn't assuage

Bennack's guilt. It only amplified the class difference between them. Now, twenty-eight years later, Andrea was feeling the class difference between them, but to Bennack he was happy to be a class level above how he was raised. She was raised in an upper-class family on the Gold Coast of the North Shore of Long Island in Lattingtown. Private elementary school at Portledge at $45,000 a year, then boarding school at Friends Academy at $55,000 a year, and Vassar College at $72,000 a year, all paid for including the 560LI azure Beamer convertible given to her as a gift when she graduated from Friends.

Living in a small middle-class section, flanking the western border of South Hampton, was beginning to wear on Andrea's once disciplined resolve to remain faithful to her plight in life. It was the constant subtle glances and comments from Dave Pritchard, the owner of South Hampton's elite Cobblestone Restaurant, that began to erode Andrea's commitment to her husband. Pritchard's most recent comment about how they could couple in some discreet way teased her imagination and curiosity of what it might be like to have an affair. At first, she had totally dismissed his comments as playfully harmless, but as her life scrolled out confirming that financially she was trapped, at least until her parents died, the $15,000 Christmas gift checks to her and Bennack, $30,000 total, never quite seemed to make a dent in their social life and ability to afford the unaffordable. For now, there was no financial upside, and the thought of dismissing Pritchard's comments began to take on a dimension that offered a possibility of adding excitement to her life. But the death of her daughter now punctured the thought and put a hold on everything.

The South Hampton morgue was an eighth of a mile from
Spielberg Memorial, and it looked more like a Quonset hut on
a college campus than a momentary resting place for the dead.
A mid-twenties blonde receptionist, wearing thin rimmed tortoise
shell glasses was reading the June issue of *Cosmopolitan* magazine
entitled, *Ten ways to seduce your married boss*, when Tom Bennack
walked through the front door.

Bennack walked past the receptionist. He had frequented the
morgue only six times in ten years to bear witness to a corpse, and
each time the downstairs smell of formaldehyde and compromised
bodies from car crashes or occasional gunshot wounds always left
him mute and empty. He turned around facing the receptionist.
"I'm here to view a body," he managed

She motioned Bennack to the sign-in sheet, and he signed the
form and printed his name.

"Downstairs, through two doors, turn right," the young
woman said.

"I know."

The woman stared at his face briefly then peered at the sign-in
sheet. "I'm sorry, Chief Bennack. I didn't realize it was you." She
nodded to the aluminum doors and said, "Who's it this time?"

Bennack looked away, not answering her. He turned on his
heel and vanished behind the doors, mending his way toward the
morgue's lab room.

When he entered the lab, the pathologist, Dr. Kay Roberts,
was bending over a gurney plucking at a cadaver who had died
the night before from a ruptured aortic heart valve during a triple
bypass operation. The large room was sealed by thick windowless

aluminum doors, and the room temperature was 58 degrees, the constant temperature of good sommelier wine cellars, the pathologist had told the chief the last time he visited. "I prefer cool temperatures because it keeps the smell down to tolerable levels when the bodies are being dissected, especially the intestines," she said without a grin as if she were reading a passage from the bible, or some medical journal.

Gurneys lined both walls. At the end of the room was a bank of thirty-six cadaver drawers. She looked up as Bennack entered the room and said, "I'm so sorry, Tom. I was hoping they mislabeled the name when they brought her in. What a tragedy."

Bennack avoided her eyes, struggling to keep his composure, and Roberts picked up on it. She quickly covered the cadaver with a green plastic sheath and rolled the gurney back to the refrigerated vault and slid the corpse back into the unit. She checked her clipboard and walked over to vault fourteen pulling the body out of the chamber and sliding it onto the awaiting gurney. She rolled it beneath the neon lights in the center of the room. "I'll make this quick, Tom," she said, her eyes conveying sadness.

"We still can't believe it, Kay. It doesn't seem real," he managed in a shallow voice.

Feeling his pain, she offered, "Why don't you pull up that tall chair, Tom. Make it easier for you. You don't have to watch. I can email the report to you."

"I'll stand, Kay. Thanks." He thought he might cry, but he desperately sought to control himself. "I prefer to stand."

"Ready?"

Bennack nodded, reluctantly, sucking in a deep breath and exhaling slowly through clenched teeth.

She pulled the plastic cover back from the cadaver lying on its stomach and Bennack winced, tears filling his eyes. The pathologist's experienced hands slid over the body as if she were reading

Braille, stopping only to examine each wound, then moving on to the next laceration. The body was riddled with puncture wounds. She looked up at Bennack. "You don't have to watch this, Tom. I can call you later with the results," she repeated as if he hadn't heard her the first time.

"No, Kay. I have to know what killed her. They think it was a shark."

"They?"

"The patrolmen who were with me on the beach when she was found. Some fisherman foul hooked the body. Thought he had a striped bass," Bennack said in a mournful whisper.

"Was she swimming?"

"No, jogging."

"How did she wind up in the surf then?"

"We don't know."

"Maybe she jogged into the water to cool off," offered Roberts. "Makes more sense to me."

"Maybe."

"How close to the shore do sharks feed?" Roberts questioned, probing the cadaver.

"This time of year, when the Gulf Stream comes close to Montauk Point, the water heats up, and they've been known to come in pretty close to shore. They feed on bait fish, blues, and stripers."

"So," said Roberts with purpose, "it's possible that when your daughter jogged into the surf to cool down, she was attacked by a shark feeding close to shore. Is that possible?"

"Yes," Bennack said. "I've seen blue sharks chase a school of bluefish into the white water. When I was surf fishing for stripers two years ago, a blue shark chased the blue fish out of the water onto the beach, the shark right behind them . . . waiting for them to wash back into the water." For a moment, Bennack seemed to forget the remains that were lying on the gurney in front of him. He told the story with agitated fervor until he looked away from Roberts' gaze onto the mutilated body of his daughter. His eyes filled with tears again and the room fell silent.

Roberts looked away, eyebrows furrowed in thought, as she continued examining the corpse. "No question your daughter was viciously attacked by a predator with sharp teeth."

"Looks like a shark attacked her legs," Bennack said shaking his head. "Maybe pulled her under."

Roberts continued to study the remains of the body, carefully examining each wound. They were deep and jagged. She took waxed imprints of the bite wounds.

Bennack stood rigidly defiant, tears now streaming down his face. He motioned her to continue with a nod without speaking a word.

Roberts examined the torso using a hemostat to spread a thin gash that ran ten inches across her left torso, looking up at Bennack. "This looks like a knife wound, Tom, but I'm not sure. It could have been made by a rusty nail from a piece of drift wood."

"I thought the same thing when I saw it, but it might be from the fisherman's gaff when he hooked her . . . thinking it was a fish."

"He used a gaff?" Roberts queried, eyes wide.

"Yes."

"Probably what it was then," she concluded, rolling the cadaver onto its back. Her eyes widened. The pathologist stared at the upper body, then the cadaver's face. She was startled by the look of terror. "Whatever it was, the look on her face confirms she didn't drown. She was attacked viciously, and something scared the hell out of her before she took her last breath."

Roberts pulled the chin up and examined the neck. "Jesus, Tom. This is what killed her. The throat and esophagus are missing. Whatever it was had sharp teeth and strong jaws." She frantically scribbled notes into her log book.

Bennack's hands were trembling and sweaty. He felt light-headed. "So, what do you think?"

Roberts was silent in deep thought, writing into her log with long sweeping conclusions. She walked away from the gurney over to a lab table and held the bite imprints she had just made next to other imprints on file. Only two matched the imprints she had just taken, and they were both made by shark teeth.

She walked back to the gurney. "Because your daughter was running through the water, the extent of bite marks and mutilation, my prognosis would be a shark attack. The puncture wounds to her body confirm that something with a six- to eight-inch jaw span attacked her, but only two of the jaw imprints match other sharks. If it was a shark, it wasn't a big shark. The ten-inch gash across her torso is either from a nail in a piece of driftwood, the gaff, or from a jagged knife. But the confusing issue is not just with the gash across her torso, Tom. It's with her throat. Something locked onto her throat and esophagus and ripped it clean from her body. Very strange, because with that kind of lethal attack, it almost seems purposeful or pre-meditated as if the predator knew what it was doing. A shark attack on its prey would be random . . . legs, arms, head. Whatever first crossed its path of attack." She looked up at Bennack, her face screwed up in a mask of doubt. "Tom, I'm totally baffled by this case. I've never before been at a loss for cause. I'm sorry I can't be more decisive."

"So, you're saying she could have been murdered?"

"I'm saying I'm not totally convinced that her death was caused only by a shark. Some of the jaw marks on her body were definitely made by sharks, but I'm not certain that's what killed her. She might have been attacked by other predators once her body was sucked out to sea. I just don't know for sure. It's a tough call," Roberts concluded with frustration in her voice. She leaned over the cadaver's chest and studied a very thin slice below the left breast. Her fingers ran along the thin red line, and she took a small knife and probed the cut. It didn't seem deep. She studied it closely then stood up.

"If the gash is from a knife," Bennack said soberly trying to piece it together, "then somebody killed her. Right? Sounds like a stupid question."

"This is not a fatal wound, Tom. But a human didn't inflict the wounds to the legs. That was done by a shark, probably more than one because of the jaw marks. But her throat and esophagus are a different story. A shark wouldn't have gone for the throat. I think something else did it, but I have no clue what it might be." The pathologist hovered over what was left of the neck. Again, she peered at the strings of flesh that were still hanging loosely from where the throat and esophagus once attached. She shook her head. "Fuck it. I just can't tell."

Bennack turned his back to the pathologist and lunged toward a trash bucket. He pitched forward and puked into the container in a wretch-torn convulsion that pulled on the pathologist's gut. She almost joined him but forced herself back to the hideous job at hand.

The Chief acknowledged her comments with a simple nod. He took a deep labored breath opening the log book. Roberts watched the soft expression on the Chief's face dissolve into a knot of tension, his jaw muscles tightening.

Name of deceased: Judith Foster Bennack
Date of Birth: 7/27/1986. Age at time of death: 27.
Height: 5'5". Weight: Estimated before attack: 122 pounds.
Hair: Blonde. Eyes: Blue. Blood Type: B- DOA: 6:30 AM.
Saturday, July 2.

Cause of death: *Trachea, esophagus, and larynx torn from subject's throat causing massive blood loss and immediate asphyxiation and trauma to the body. Puncture wounds from jaw imprints taken match two sets of jaw imprints from a shark, possibly two different species: Blue or Lemon.*

Wounds to both legs caused massive blood loss due to severing both femoral arteries. Large ten-inch gash across torso, not lethal, but deep cut through muscle tissue and tendons . . . possibly executed by a sharp object of unknown origin.

Conclusion: *Subject D.O.A. Possible shark attack. Numerous puncture wounds from jaw span of 6 to 8 inches. Massive attack to neck area, trachea and esophagus torn from body. While it appears to be a shark, if the ten-inch gash across subject's upper torso was caused by a knife, then murder cannot be ruled out.*

Dr. Kay Roberts, ACF, FACS.

Chief Bennack finished reading the report and looked up at Roberts, an icy chill spreading through his body and down his spine. He started to say something, but nothing came out of his mouth but a faint rasp of despair. An expression hung on his face like he was about to take his last breath. Kay Roberts did not say a word. She closed the lab report and escorted the chief to the double doors, her intuition confirming that the case of Judy Foster Bennack's death was far from over. It was just beginning, she told herself. Something haunted her about the different jaw imprints on the cadaver . . . one in particular.

CHAPTER 6

A WARM FRONT swept in off the ocean on Sunday night giving throngs of South Hampton residents the feeling summer had arrived and was here to stay. People in swimsuits lay on pristine white sandy beaches atop a patchwork of colorful towels, music wafting through the air as if it were all contained within a bubble of surrealistic life lived and protected only by the opulent.

The memorial service for Judy Foster Bennack occurred on Wednesday of the following week at 10:00 AM at Our Lady of Mercy Roman Catholic Church. The sanctuary was packed leaving standing room only. Judy Bennack's Investment Banking team from Barclays Capital had rented the South Hampton Jitney bus for the memorial. The eulogy was given by Chief Bennack, and he managed to get through the speech with only one wrenching emotional pause when talking about their loss of the daughter that brought them so much happiness and pride. The Klonopin Bennack had taken seemed to suck every emotion out of his mind leaving him with the dull feeling that the world around him was moving in slow motion. But the pill worked its purpose and his wife Andrea sat in the first pew wearing dark glasses and a small black hat with a thin veil covering her face.

From the packed pews behind her, her shoulders betrayed her emotion. She was in the same mental state as her husband, subdued with the wonder drug that left her mind without purpose and worry.

Grady Bennack, Judy's seventeen-year-old brother, wanted to share his memories of the sister who always protected and encouraged him. Grady insisted he did not need a Klonopin so when he started reflecting on his love for his sister and how much he would miss her, his voice was calm and resolute, seemingly nonchalant as if he had pushed the tragedy into another world. But, beneath his words lay anger, and it was building. As he talked about their times together, he seemed unflappable until he mentioned that she had asked only a week ago if he would accept being an usher at her wedding if Sam Wade asked him. He would accept in a moment he had told his sister. Grady looked up from his notes staring out at the congregation trying to find Sam Wade. Their eyes met and Grady said, "Sam, I know my sister really . . ."

Wade pulled a handkerchief to his face. Grady hesitated, stuttering to push the words out of his mouth to finish the sentence, but he could not speak. Instead, the teenager took a deep breath, stepped away from the podium, and his knees buckled. He fell to the floor, hitting his head on the marble christening bowl on the way down. Bennack leaped up three steps toward his son and knelt down embracing him.

"I miss her, Dad," and he burst into a wail of grief that echoed through the church into the narthex.

After the service, Grady approached his father. "Do you think a shark really killed her, Dad?"

Bennack came into his son's space. "Yes. The pathologist confirmed it."

"If someone killed her, Dad, they'll wish she never had a brother."

"It was a shark. We've got to let it go, son," he said. "That's what the pathologist concluded."

"I'll never let it go, Dad . . . never."

Bennack wanted to agree with his son. He put his arm around him and pulled him close. "I understand," but he was not sure he did. It just seemed like the right thing to say to assuage their devastating loss.

The only light in Bennack's den came from two laptops. Grady Bennack was punching keys as if his life depended on it. When he paused in thought, another laptop next to him was streaming images and text with incessant input. Grady's parents were out to dinner with two couples from South Hampton, friends who, during the reception after the memorial service, convinced them they had to get away from the house.

Grady Bennack leaned over his Toshiba laptop squinting to read the small print on shark profiles: how many attacks and deaths from shark attacks. His girlfriend of seven months, Julie Harned, sitting next to him, was surfing the net for shark feeding habits. She had turned seventeen three weeks ago, and Grady knew she was still a virgin because she told him when he first kissed her. "I'm saving it for marriage," she had told him. Grady said, "That's cool, but I'm not. I've already had sex." He lied. Harned had strawberry blonde hair raining down her shoulders to the small of her back and a cute pixie nose that wrinkled when she smiled.

What he found in his Google search was alarming: the top ten shark species had inflicted 326 attacks on humans last year.

"This doesn't add up, Julie. Of the top ten shark attacks on humans, 134 out of 326 victims were killed. I can't see how my sister, jogging in shallow water, could have been killed by a shark. Dad says several sharks attacked her."

Harned stared at the data on her screen, eyes wide. "I haven't found any data confirming a shark attack in our South Hampton waters or Montauk Point. But it says Blue sharks and Great Whites are off Montauk Point and along our north and south shores."

Grady scanned the data. "Blue sharks attacked eighty-two people and killed twenty-six. Great Whites attacked 237 swimmers and killed sixty-five."

Julie leaned close to her screen. "But there're no reports any-where that confirm a swimmer was attacked or killed by a shark in our waters. It confirms that sharks do come in close to shore feeding on striped bass and bluefish, but no human attacks or fatalities yet."

"There was a run of striped bass the other night. It could have brought sharks in close to shore on a feeding frenzy, but . . . ," Grady hesitated in thought.

"What?" pressed Julie.

"My sister wasn't swimming. She was jogging."

"But if she was jogging in the water to cool off, an incoming tide . . . if sharks were feeding on stripers close to shore, one could have attacked her," Grady frowned in thought.

"Your dad said it was more than one shark," Julie said. "According to all the records, sharks don't run in schools. They're predators and hunt alone."

"Unless there was blood in the water," Grady said.

"That could bring more than one shark in close to shore, maybe several as your Dad suggested," Julie offered.

Grady shrugged his shoulders and looked up from the glowing screen. "I don't think she was killed by a shark." He stared into Julie's questioning eyes.

"What does your dad say?"

"He says sharks killed her. He told me to let it go."

"What did you say?"

Grady looked back at her shaking his head. "I can't let it go."

Julie leaned close enough to Grady for him to smell some kind of perfume. It was sweet like lavender, he thought. He leaned toward her and his lips brushed hers in a soft kiss. Grady thought he heard a sigh but wasn't sure.

Chief Bennack had spent Thursday morning filling out the police report. At 9:10 AM, he got a panicked call from the South Hampton Mayor, Jacques Atchity. "You've got to help me quash these goddamned reporters, Tom. They're going to force us to shut the beaches down. Rumors about the shark attack are out of control."

Newsday called Bennack at 10:45 AM to confirm the story about his daughter's death telling him that he had read about her passing in the South Hampton Ledger. He claimed he was doing a surf fishing story about the blue fish and striped bass run, and one of the fishermen had told him about the woman who was attacked and killed by a shark. Bennack urged the reporter not to start false rumors about shark attacks. "It'll freak out the entire South Hampton community," he told the reporter, "and we're not totally convinced it was a shark."

"What do you mean?" the reporter pressed. "What else could it be?"

"Just what I said," Bennack shot back. "It's not totally conclusive so don't print anything."

"Free press, Mr. Bennack. Forget it. I'll follow up with the coroner," and the reporter rang off.

Bennack slammed the phone back on the cradle and said, "Shit."

News of the attack appeared on page six of *Newsday*'s Friday edition and the *New York Times* picked up the story and ran it on page two in Saturday's edition.

Mayor Atchity called the chief the moment he got *Newsday*. Bennack had just read it in the *New York Times*. "Thank God there's no pictures," he screamed into the phone, "but the bastard screwed us with the headline." Brady read it over the phone.

"WOMAN KILLED BY SHARK JOGGER RAN INTO THE SOUTH HAMPTON SURF AND MET JAWS!"

By Saturday morning, two of seven beaches were closed, and by Sunday morning at ten o'clock, the South Hampton beach, all lots, were completely shut down, cordoned off with yellow '*no trespassing*' tape and no access. Mayor Atchity called an urgent Board of Directors town meeting inviting the South Hampton populace to attend. "It was a random shark attack," Pathologist Dr. Kay Roberts said, prompted to attend the meeting by Chief Bennack. "But we can't rule out the possibility it won't happen again."

The meeting room came alive with debate. A man stood up in the back of the room. "You can't keep the beaches closed," he said angrily." It'll ruin our businesses for the summer," said Charlie Lott, owner of Hampton Real Estate, LLC.

"I agree with Charlie," said Barbara Smith, manager of the Tiffany retail store. "Our very existence relies on summer residents. No swimming, no business. You've got to reopen the beaches now. Our livelihood depends on it. You'll kill the summer for all of us."

Chief Bennack, sitting at the front of the room, stood up and the room fell silent. "I don't know how many in this room have ever lost a child, but it's the most painful loss one can imagine. I know the pain." Bennack hesitated for an awkward minute before continuing. "My first priority, as your police chief, is to protect your lives and property. Beyond that, it's to ensure that everybody in this community is safe and can enjoy all that this beautiful surf-side community has to offer. Our daughter's death was a tragedy, but I believe that Judy's passing was a very rare occurrence. The likelihood of another shark attack is remote. There have not been any shark sightings this summer."

"So open the beaches," someone shouted.

The room of 178 people burst into applause.

Mayor Atchity stood up and faced the dissenting crowd. "I'm prepared to make a motion to the Board of Directors. I propose we open the beaches within forty-eight hours."

"Twenty-four hours," a woman yelled out.

Another applause broke the silence.

The mayor turned to the Board of Directors sitting on either side of him and said, "Do I have a second?"

"I second the motion for forty-eight hours," said Walter Stackler, owner of South Hampton's Pour House, a popular bar and restaurant.

"All in favor?"

Collectively, the Board passed the motion and the meeting room at Town Hall emptied with the chatter of pleased residents and retailers.

By Tuesday morning, all beaches were open again, and the summer pace in South Hampton resumed its frenzy.

CHAPTER 7

FRIDAY OF THAT week, July 5th, a rain storm swept across eastern Long Island with thunderous lightning and gale force thirty knot winds. The Ten-K run scheduled for Saturday was postponed to the following Saturday.

It was 10:50 AM, driving rain pelting the windows of Andrea Bennack's bedroom. The curtains were still drawn, She had taken the week off trying to will away depression. She slipped out of bed and went into the kitchen, fixing herself a cup of hot water and lemon and returned to the bedroom lying atop a green chaise lounge. Her mind drifted back over time trying to recapture glimpses of her daughter's past: Judy's first steps, her first birthday, kindergarten, elementary school, high school, first boyfriend, first kiss, then college. Her MBA, graduating with honors from Columbia Business School. How could God let this happen? Life seemed so unfair, Andrea thought with a painful punch of reality. She was angry and there didn't seem to be any easy answers to assuage her feelings. Dead at twenty-seven, her daughter's life snuffed out like a candle.

The proposal from Sam Wade, which was supposed to happen a week ago, then a wedding with the promise of grandchildren, all of it vanished in a painful blink of an eye. Life, Tom had said countless times, really did suck, and we were all helpless victims clawing our way through it to control the outcome.

Tears streamed down her face now as she thought of her daughter and how much she had been robbed of promise. Her mind drifted into her own life: her first kiss, first prom date, the first time she had sex at fifteen, and what it was like. It was awful, she remembered, and it hurt. What she had read in books and been promised in movies seemed so much better than the grim reality of the physical act. She thought of her daughter again, and the many times she tried to advise her through her teenage years about protection, caution, and the fact that boys could care less about whom they violated as long as they scored and could brag to friends. Those were the words Andrea had used with her daughter because she wanted to make harsh points about the realities of what all boys and men wanted. Sex, sex, and more sex, Andrea remembered telling her daughter. "Guys just love to get laid. And those who don't get laid lie about it just to save face. It's all about testosterone and the male ego, she had told Judy. So, be careful, she had warned her daughter, and be very selective. But she delivered the message repeatedly to Judy because she did not want the same thing that happened to her to happen to her daughter.

Andrea allowed herself to steal back in time when she had sex the second time. It was with a different boy than the first, Thanksgiving of her sophomore year in college. She lay still on the lounge trying to remember the details of the second date with the third guy. She remembered that the sex was better than the first time, even better with the third boy when she climaxed for the first time. It happened in mid-July behind a dune on South Hampton beach, two months after she graduated from Vassar. The man was confident and purposeful with a broad grin, perfect teeth, a deep dimple punctuating a square chin, and a shock of wavy blonde hair. Handsome for sure. He was two years older than she was, maybe three. She guessed twenty-four or five. They had been drinking Gilby's gin and grapefruit juice, and he kept coaxing her to have another one. It seemed like a good idea because she could not taste the gin, so she assumed there was not much of it in her drink except, after the third drink, she was surprised to find that she lay on a blanket stark naked with this man beside her who was also naked. It all seemed so natural, no guilt, no worry, no panic about being caught. They coupled, legs entwined, writhing on the beach with urgent ardor. Her first orgasm came in a slow, building tingle of heat that rose up in her body and seemed to touch every nerve ending at the far reaches of every extremity of her body. She didn't moan. She didn't scream. Instead, she rose up beneath him arching in a wild gyrating trembling moment of utter joy and sensation then collapsed back onto the beach with an exhale. Without thinking, she uttered the word, "Fuck."

"Indeed," the man chortled in her ear which she remembered thinking later was rather cool. She was so absorbed in her own climax, that she wasn't even sure if he climaxed. It was the voice of Tom Bennack and three months later, missing her second period, she discovered she was pregnant with a daughter, Judy Foster Bennack. The flashback laced her mind with guilt, but she knew why she allowed herself the fleeting memory. She was bored with her life, and had met someone seven weeks ago who flirted with her, enough to tease her conscience into considering an affair for the first time in their marriage. His name was Dave Pritchard, and he owned a popular South Hampton Restaurant on Main Street, The Cobblestone.

The rain had stopped, and she could see a slice of light piercing the drawn shade, confirming the storm had passed and the sun was out. But still she continued to lie on the lounge for another fifteen minutes wondering if she would dare break the trust of her twenty-eight-year marriage with the Police Chief of South Hampton. She knew she loved Tom Bennack for who he was: a trusting and loving husband who was a good father, lover, and friend. Maybe having some good sex with another man, without any commitment to a relationship, might not be a bad thing, she asked herself in the silence of her room. Maybe it might even be good for their relationship, strengthening their bond of friendship and sex. I will take it a day at a time, she promised herself. When she finished the thought, she realized that her heart was beating fast, and she was out of breath. She wasn't even sure why: guilt or hopeful promise, but for now it lessoned her grief and seemed a welcomed distraction.

CHAPTER 8

SIX DAYS PASSED and the weather was hot and sticky. Beachfront parking lots were packed to capacity by 9:30 AM and people lay beneath the midmorning sun head to toe, beach umbrellas and towels covering the hot sand.

Chief Bennack was busy coordinating three shifts at the South Hampton Police Station thankful they had only made two arrests since the July 4th holiday: one for a nineteen-year-old Hispanic girl who was a summer nanny on her day off. On a fifty-dollar bet, she guzzled two six packs of Corona with a chaser of scotch then meandered nude on the beach in front of the South Hampton bathing crowd. Patrolman Futterman made the arrest, waiting three minutes before telling the girl to put her clothes on. He told patrolman Johnson later that her breasts were bigger than Playboy's Miss August. "Whatever you do," Futterman pleaded, "Don't tell the chief I said that." Johnson wet himself in laughter.

The second arrest was for a DWI owner of a Blue Bentley Continental GTC convertible that was weaving down Dune Road on the opposite side of the street at 2:15 AM. When patrolman Johnson pulled the car over and asked the driver to step out of the car, a twenty-year-old man fumbled for the door handle and fell out of the car doing a face plant on the asphalt road, breaking an eye tooth. He could not stand up, even when Johnson hoisted him and tried propping him against the rear door. He just slid off the side of the car onto the ground like a deflating rubber doll. Johnson withdrew the man's wallet checking the license. He recognized the name immediately: George D. Thornton, IV. Johnson shook his head knowing that at the age of seventeen the young man founded DiamondMind, the search engine company that had taken away thirty-five percent of Google's market share in less than two years. At the age of twenty, the patrolman had read in the *New York Times*, Thornton had sold his company to Microsoft for four billion dollars. "Only in South Hampton do you find this shit," Johnson told the chief.

Randy Zand was a disciplined jogger averaging five to eight miles a day on the macadam streets that wove in and out of a dense stand of trees in his neighborhood of Amityville, Long Island. His nightly jogging course took him by an inlet canal lined with small boats, and the smell of salt water always cleared his head from the pressures of work as the head buyer of Macy's apparel division at 34th and Broadway, New York City.

There was another section of his routine jogging route he liked because it led him off the streets into a narrow dirt path meandering around the Amityville water tower rising above the dense maple and oak tree pack in a figure eight. Ten-foot black letters on the water tower announced the small town with, "Amityville." Four years ago, two teenagers from Amityville high school climbed the tower on a dare and painted large red letters, "SUCKS," after the town's 'E'.

Zand liked the path because, at the center of the loop, the dirt path led through a tight tunnel of small birch trees making it barely passable. During snowfalls, he would take his two children along the dirt path to play within the birch forest because the birch bows formed beautiful white archways leading into interconnecting compartments forming igloos of snow laden branches.

It was 6:38 PM when Zand's train pulled into the Amityville station. A twelve-minute walk took him home to his four bedroom split-level ranch, and to his wife Nancy and two children, Seth and Elizabeth.

He greeted his wife with a kiss. "What's for dinner?"

"Thought we'd cook out tonight. Burgers and dogs," she said. "Why don't you skip the run tonight," she added. "Make us a couple of vodka tonics." The corners of her mouth turned up in a wisp of a smile.

Zand thought for a moment and said, "Sounds good, honey, but I had a tough day today. Buyers in from China. Big line of new stuff and the trade talks are still not resolved. Jog will do me good. Clear the mind."

"So would a vodka tonic and . . ."

"And?"

Maybe some action," she added playfully.

He pulled her into a brief hug and their son broke the silence with, "Dad." Seth charged his father's legs and pushed him sideways away from their embrace.

"Hey son," Zand said, and he leaned down kissing the boy on his forehead. "Loving you," he said affectionately.

Zand looked back at his wife. "I won't be long, honey. Give me fifteen, twenty tops, and I'll do the burgers. I'll put the coals on now so the fire's ready when I return. Then I'll have that vodka tonic with you."

Nancy Zand looked back at her husband and hesitated. A thought entered her mind, unbidden, and two words slipped out of her mouth, "Be careful."

Zand flinched at the words. She had never before told him to be careful and he paused in thought. "It's safe,' he offered. "Same route. Why did you say that?"

"I don't know," she said. "Back in fifteen?"

"Back in fifteen."

Zand changed into his jogging clothes and vanished out the front door in a slow jog. His wife watched him from the living room window circle the cul-de-sac twice then jog to the corner and turn right. Zand had a spring in his step for a good reason. On his return he looked forward to telling his wife that he had gotten the promotion today to Vice President of Macy's apparel division promising a thirty percent raise and a corner office. It would enable them to buy a larger home and the twenty-five-foot I-O Sea Ray boat they had both dreamed of when they had moved to Amityville four years ago. Today was a good day, Zand thought, as he saw the Amityville water tower rise up, blocking the view of a setting sun in the distance.

He jogged toward a thin dirt path at the end of the street and vanished into a thicket of forsythia and wild vines choking the trees arching over the pathway. Zand always enjoyed this part of the jog because it was silent, save for the sound of his feet softly hitting the pathway in a muted rhythm that kept his stride. He advanced deeper into the thicket now aware of the sweet smell of wild honeysuckle. His mind filled with the successes of his life: his wife, two healthy children, a promising career, and Nancy and he had just chatted about the possibility of a third child. What Zand did not know was that his wife was already pregnant and was planning to tell him over the weekend, maybe sooner.

Zand took a sharp right turn and the water tower loomed in the distance. He looked at his watch: 7:08 PM Almost halfway there, he told himself. He saw the birch forest up ahead and quickened his pace. The sun was setting, and it cast moving shadows along the path. As he jogged forward, his senses heightened, aware of the rhythm of his own breathing and the sound of his jogging shoes softly hitting the dirt path in a staccato shuffle of forward motion. He thought he heard something off to his right but wasn't sure. Maybe it was another jogger, maybe not. Then the brief sound vanished as quickly as it came, and Zand was alone in thought. Moments passed and he heard something again, off to his left this time. It sounded like breathing—or was it panting. His head snapped to the left and he jogged in place, eyes darting left to right, right to left, peering in and out of thick pockets of dense shrubs and thick clumps of overgrown forsythia and tangled choke vines. He knew something was moving through the thickets flanking him. His pace quickened and he vanished into the birch forest. The moment he entered the thick tree pack, he sensed movement again, broken twigs off to his right, now a sharp breaking branch behind him. He burst into a fast run, dodging, weaving, in and out of the thick birch forest. For a brief undisciplined moment, he told himself there was nothing to fear for this was his turf, his neighborhood and there was no wild creature that could possibly harm him. His heart was now pulsing dread through his body and the thick canopy above him seemed to block all light. He cursed himself for not bringing a flashlight. Still, he held to the path that cut back and forth through the forest believing that he could make it to the perimeter in time. In time for what, he thought. Stupid thoughts, he scolded himself. Nothing could harm him, especially not now, he told himself.

As he approached the end of the birch forest, he heard branches snapping yet again, and heavy breathing that seemed to surround him on all sides. When he looked over his shoulder, he saw another flash of movement through the forest to his left. He squinted to see detail. It was moving fast, but then so was he, for chrissake. Then he saw more movement to the right. It was closer to him than he first thought. Get to the clearing, his brain commanded. Fast, faster. Zand exploded into a wild dash, but as he quickened his pace, whatever was tracking him kept his pace. Up ahead two more dark images emerged from the thick birch forest and were coming at him. At first, he thought he saw a dog, but if it was canine, it was big and it was cutting him off. Then he saw another dark image. Maybe another dog, maybe not. It was loping along with the dog coming at him, if that's what it was. Instinctively, he looked for a stick, a branch, anything to defend himself. Zand left the well-worn path of security and lunged through another section of the forest. He had no idea where it led, but he knew he had to escape. If he could get to the water tower, he could climb up the ladder and be safe, but how to get there? Was he circling, doubling back on himself? Whatever it was had encircled him and he saw a lighter section of the forest up ahead. Zand ran as fast as he could, zigzagging through the thick rural forest and then it happened. From the right side a large, dark predator lunged at him. Zand was relieved to see it was a dog, but his relief quickly sank into an utter panic of helplessness when two more dogs charged his left flank. He felt a searing pain on his left calf and realized the beast had its jaws locked onto him, fangs cutting through skin and sinew, deep into muscle and bone. Another animal attacked his right leg, clenched onto his upper thigh. It was the third dog that leaped onto his back and forced Zand to collapse to the ground. The sound of guttural snarls ripped through the air. Zand kicked and screamed, arms and legs flailing in all directions. These were only dogs, for God's sake, his mind raced. Get the hell up. Find a club, a stick, a branch. The sound of the wild pack snarling, biting, ripping flesh, and tearing into him was more than horrifying. For the first time, the thought that he might not escape alive coursed through his mind. He knew in one paralyzing moment that his life was at stake. They were eating him alive. He had to get to his feet.

Zand rolled over to protect his vital organs, now on his hands and knees, clutching for purchase anything on the ground that would enable him to rise through fir and fury to his feet, but the power and aggressiveness of the dogs pulled him down again. He screamed for help, punching, and kicking again, gyrating in a tight arc of his own blood and sinew. He got one of the dogs with a hard kick to its face, a black Rottweiler, he thought, but the beast was so fast and powerful that it grabbed his ankle and shook it like a rag doll.

Zand hobbled to his feet and was surrounded by four, no five dogs. Another dog joined the circle in a leaping arc. He lashed out at them in a wild effort to grab the large dead tree branch five feet in front of him. He staggered toward it and picked it up, leaving a trail of dark blood behind him. Now he had the advantage, he told himself, but the action was fleeting at best, swinging in all directions, hitting two of them, but it only drove the fury to a new level. When he faced the pack in front of him, the dogs behind him charged and sank their jaws into his calves yet again. He tried to run out of the circle but then it happened. A different sound uttered from one of the dogs—or was it human. Zand's heart surged. The moment he heard the sound, a deep and guttural command, alien like, all the dogs attacked him in unison bringing him down in one urgent thrash to the ground like wolves taking down a stag. Once down, they tore at his flesh ripping strings of muscle and tendon sending a shower of blood into the air. The biggest one sank its jaws into Zand's throat with a growling snort, its piercing eyes meeting Zand's before his eyes shut in a searing shot of pain that caused Zand to take his last breath before his trachea and esophagus were ripped savagely away from his limp body. What he saw standing atop his body, before he took his last sputtering breath of life, was a unclear movement that caused his heart to seize. His mind registered one last thought of terror: This was not a dog, not a wolf, perhaps not human. It looked like a mutant of some kind with piercing vivid eyes. Yet in the blur of motion there might have been two images of something hovering even closer, watching as Zand's body twitched back and forth, as if he were still trying to escape, but his heart had already beat its last surge of blood. The pack was ripping Zand's body apart now, only bone, gristle and sinew remaining amid the miasma of red that oozed over the ground in a sanguine ten-foot blanket of horror.

Nancy Zand walked out to the cooker to check on the hot coals. They were now white hot. She looked at her watch and her eyebrows furrowed. It was 7:48 PM, and it was getting dark. Nancy walked through the home and out the front door. She stood motionless for five minutes. Then . . . ten, fifteen. Waiting . . . Nothing. Twenty-five minutes passed and she knew that something was terribly wrong. He should be home by now. He had been jogging for more than forty minutes.

She walked back inside and picked up the phone. Her heart was pounding when the Amityville police officer answered the call.

CHAPTER 9

S OUTH HAMPTON'S MAYOR Atchity finished his plate of scrambled eggs and extra crisp bacon then paused briefly, sipping a cup of café de Costa Rica, extra dark, he had just poured into a colador. He finished reading *Newsday*'s headlines then slowly scanned each page for articles in the news of particular interest. On page three, something caught his eye and he squinted, leaning forward. His eyebrows furrowed in questioning thought as he read, **"JOGGER MAULED TO DEATH BY PACK OF WILD DOGS."**

Atchity finished the article, scanned the rest of page three and was about to turn to the next page when he hesitated. He took another sip of coffee and looked up, staring out the window. His golden retriever, Misty, was chasing a tennis ball thrown by his eleven-year-old son, Ben. The mayor looked back at the headline and reread the news item. It described the attack as vicious and unprovoked, leaving the body ripped and torn in unrecognizable shreds. The Mayor looked out the window again. Misty sat obediently at his son's feet and gave the ball back to Ben, tail wagging for another toss. Man's best friend, thought Atchity, looking at the headline again shaking his head.

At first, the mayor didn't make any connection. The recent shark attack that took place in South Hampton waters close to shore involved Bennack's daughter who made the fatal mistake of jogging into the water to cool off. This jogger was attacked inland and killed by dogs. Besides, thought Atchity, Amityville was fifty-eight miles to the west of Southampton, an hour poke on 27A and the expressway. Still, the mayor was puzzled enough to pick up the phone and dial Chief Bennack's cell phone. He took a long pull on his coffee and swirled it around in his mouth, thinking this was a long shot at any link between the two deaths. They were both joggers, yes, but nothing more. The mayor let the phone ring twice in his ear then leaned over and put the phone back on the cradle. Why bring more angst to his police chief, he thought.

Atchity shook his head. "No way there's any connection," he said aloud. He flipped the page of *Newsday* to a Macy's two-page full color ad promoting a new line of summer swimsuits. The ad copy read, "Summer fun at the beach."

Atchity's phone chirped, and he leaned over picking it up.

"You just call me?" Bennack queried.

Atchity gritted his teeth and took in a short gasp of breath, stalling for thought. "Yeah, ah . . ."

"What's up?"

"Did you read *Newsday* this morning?"

"No, *New York Times*, Why?"

The Mayor flipped the paper back to the article. He stared at the headlines yet again.

"You there, Jacques?" Bennack said, his voice flat.

"Yeah, Tom."

Atchity seemed distant. "So, what did you call about?"

"Page three, *Newsday* . . ."

"What about it?"

"Another jogger killed."

The silence from Bennack was stark, and Atchity swallowed hard. Finally, a one-word response knifed the air, "Where?"

"Amityville."

Bennack curled his lower lip in thought. "That's an hour drive to the east, Jacques. What killed the jogger?"

"Dogs."

"Man or woman?"

"Man. They tore his body apart, Chief . . . beyond recognition."

"Why are you telling me this, Jacques? Judy was killed by a shark attack in the water. I'm assuming the jogger was killed on land."

"Yes."

"There's no connection. Not even a remote chance. Andrea and I are desperate to put this tragedy behind us, for chrissake. Please . . ."

"I'm sorry. I shouldn't have called," Achity said cursing himself, and he heard a hard click of the phone confirming Bennack was pissed.

Bennack sat in silence staring at the color photo of his daughter. Helka sat faithfully by Bennack's desk occasionally nuzzling the chief's leg for attention. Having the dog near him seemed to ease the constant mental anguish of losing his daughter. Helka was, to Bennack, helping keep Judy's spirit alive and he now had the dog with him on his calls and in the office. He stood up and walked into patrolman Johnson's office. "Can I borrow your copy of *Newsday*?"

Julie Harned had just finished her last homework assignment for English: writing a book review on Wuthering Heights by Emily

Bronte. She was ruminating about Heathcliff's character flaws when her cell phone chirped.

"Julie . . ."

"Grady. You okay? Your voice . . ."

"Dad brought home a copy of today's *Newsday*. It was on his desk and opened to an article about another jogger attack. The guy was mauled to death, eaten alive, it said."

"How?"

"He was jogging in Amityville. Attacked by wild dogs. Ripped to shreds. Same as my sister."

"I don't see a connection. Your sister was killed by sharks in the water, Grady. And Amityville's . . ."

Grady's voice was high pitched and agitated. "I know, I know. But only two weeks apart, two joggers killed. Our research confirmed how rare it was for sharks to come in that close to the beach and kill a swimmer. I have to believe it's just as rare for a jogger to be killed by a pack of wild dogs. But maybe not. Help me, Julie."

"Like what, Grady?" Julie yawned into the phone, her hand gently patting the soft velvety head of a mocha-colored dog, its tongue lolling, her family pet, Scout, a sinewy pit bull.

"How many dog attacks on humans?" Grady queried.

"There's no connection, Grady. Give it up. Your father told you to let it go. He's right."

"What if you lost your brother, Julie? What if this happened to Max? Would you let it go?"

"Not fair. Don't go there, Grady. Please . . ."

"So how many people have been attacked by dogs? How many killed?"

The phone went silent.

"Julie . . . you there?"

Harned was lost in thought: what if her brother was attacked and killed like Grady's sister?" It prompted a response, her voice laced with angst.

"Lots, I guess. Mailmen maybe . . . I have no idea."

"What kind of breeds attack people the most?" Grady persisted.

Harned thought about Scout killing someone and smiled. "Scout wouldn't hurt a flea," she said into the phone.

"Maybe," Grady said, "Maybe not. Newsday says at least four dogs slaughtered the jogger. What kind of dog breeds would kill a human like that and how many people are killed by dogs each year?"

"You actually think your sister was killed by dogs, Grady?" Julie asked, her voice trailing off in disbelief. "Come on . . . Judy was jogging in the water, not onshore when it happened."

"We don't know that, Julie. I don't know what I think. It's possible, I guess."

"Did you speak to your dad about this?"

"Yes."

"And?"

"He was ticked, told me to let it go. There's no connection, he said."

"So let it go, Grady. Jesus. It's up to the cops, certainly not us. We're teenagers, not detectives. Let your dad do the work."

Julie leaned toward her laptop computer and punched a question into Google: *How many people killed by dogs annually?*

"What are you doing, Julie?" Grady pressed. What he heard startled him.

"God," Julie gasped into the phone.

"What's wrong?"

"You won't believe this," Harned said.

"Believe what? Talk to me, Julie."

"I'll help you, Grady, but if your sister was killed by dogs and not sharks, and the two jogger killings are somehow connected, something horrible is happening."

"Come over," Grady said. "We've got work to do" and he clicked off his cell phone.

Harned stared down at her pet dog, Scout, and for the first time looked carefully into the animal's mouth, questioning man's best friend. Its sharp fangs shown menacingly in the lamplight. Harned fixed a studied gaze into her pet's eyes. They were liquid brown, almost hollow, and the dog cocked its head to the right, studying Harned with a questioning glance. "Good dog," Harned offered as the thought about what she had just read on the internet seeped back into her mind like a bad dream. She leaned closer to her pet's face, eyes still fixed unaware of the challenge she had just made to the dog. She did not notice the dog's lips flare displaying its very serious set of teeth, but what frightened her for the first time was the guttural challenging growl deep within the animal's throat that broke the room's silence with a hint of dread.

Harned pulled back from the dog's muzzle and said, "Bad dog. Bad dog."

Scout ran out of the bedroom, tail between his legs.

Harned's mind was spinning as she closed her front door and hopped down three steps. She broke into a slow jog heading for Grady's house, her laptop tucked beneath her left arm. When she turned the corner, she looked back over her shoulder and it occurred to her that she was alone. Across the street she saw a large black dog, but it was chained to a small dogwood tree. It barked and lunged as she passed causing her to break into a full run, her heart pounding in her chest. What if it happened to her brother Max? What if it happened to Grady? What if it happened to her right this moment? As she turned left at the next corner, another dog barked in the distance then another, still another.

CHAPTER 10

C HIEF BENNACK SAT restlessly in his office chair biting his lower lip in troubled thought. In front of him was a copy of today's New York Times. On page three, four columns across, the headline read,

Another Jogger found dead in less than two weeks.

SHARKS, WILD DOGS, OR FOUL PLAY?

July 7th, Amityville, New York. According to Nancy Zand, wife of the late Randy Zand, head buyer of Macy's Apparel Division, her husband had just arrived home and, as was his nightly custom, went out for an evening jog. That was the last time she saw him alive before she placed a frantic call to the Amityville Police Department.

Randy Zand, twenty-eight years old, was found the next morning by another jogger in the heavily wooded section near the Amityville water tower. According to Police Chief Treverton Clark of the Amityville Police Department, Zand's body was dismembered in a gruesome miasma of body parts strewn in a ten foot section within a thick clump of overgrown bushes and vines.

According to the coroner's report, Zand was attacked by a pack of wild dogs. Three of the animals were identified as dogs, but a troubling question remained about the identity of the fourth animal, and there might have been a fifth predator, but the coroner's report was not conclusive about the identity of dog breeds.

Less than two weeks ago, another jogger, Judy Bennack, was killed by a shark attack as she jogged along South Hampton beach apparently in the water of an incoming tide. While there is no proof that these two jogger attacks are related, it is worth noting that all joggers should be careful when jogging alone. Be aware of your surroundings at all times, and carry a club with you, just in case a dog threatens you.

Bennack sat rigid staring at the headlines. How could it be foul play, he thought. His daughter was killed by a shark and the second jogger attack was by wild dogs. He shook his head willing away any other option other than it was pure coincidence. Still, he cut the article out of the Times and stuffed it into his shirt pocket. He picked up the phone and called home.

"Hello."

"I love you."

"I love you too, darling. What's up?"

"How about a romantic dinner for two tonight at the Cobblestone?" Bennack said hopefully, wanting to clear his mind.

Andrea hesitated a brief moment, but it was long enough for Bennack to pick up on it. "Problem?"

"No, not at all. I was thinking I might have bridge tonight," she lied. The thought of seeing Dave Pritchard, the owner, along with her husband made her nervous "No . . . Tom. No, that would be nice."

"Good. I'll look forward to it."

"Me too," she shot back, trying to be casual.

Bennack placed the phone back on the cradle and tried to focus on last night's police reports.

"What are you out of breath for, Julie?" Grady said as Harned entered the front door of his home.

"The thought of that dog attack spooked me out. There seemed to be dogs barking everywhere on my way over here."

Grady laughed aloud.

"It's not funny, especially when you're alone and jogging."

"We're in the den, mom. On the computer," Grady said trying to change the subject.

"I'll be going out with your dad tonight for dinner at the Cobblestone. Dinner's in the microwave. There's enough for Julie. Two chicken pot pies."

"Thanks, Mom."

Grady opened his laptop and Julie plugged hers into the outlet next to the desk. They both began searching the Internet for dog attacks and copying their results to print.

Grady's fingers flew across the keys with purpose as he began to list the facts. "This is incredible Julie."

"What?"

"Dogs were domesticated 15,000 years ago from grey wolves."

"They came from wolves?"

"Yes," Grady said, "and you won't believe this. Forty-three million households have seventy-two million pet dogs in the United States."

Julie shook her head when she said, "There are over 400 million dogs in the world. Unbelievable."

"No wonder there're so many dog attacks," Grady said. "The Center for Disease Control reports 386,000 people are attacked by dogs annually. Over 1,000 per day, half of them children."

"No way," Julie said in disbelief.

"And wait until you hear about pit bulls."

"I don't want to know."

"Over the past two years, pit bulls killed . . ."

"Grady, I said I don't want to know. Scout wouldn't hurt anybody."

"Fifty-two people, Julie."

"Grady," she shouted. "Stop it."

"It's true."

Julie looked back at her screen and began copying data. Finally, she said, "There're a lot more breeds that kill than just Pit Bulls," she said defensively. "Last year the Rottweiler killed seventy-three, German Shepherds killed nine, Siberian Huskies killed twenty-one, Alaskan Malamutes, four, Doberman Pinchers, six, Chow Chows, seven, Presa Canarios, nine, Boxers, four, and wolf hybrids, nineteen."

"But the Pit Bull tops them all at 166 people killed globally," Grady persisted. Grady scanned the internet data on dogs and said, "Get this. March 13th, 1942, the Quartermaster Corps (QMC) of the United States Army began training dogs for the newly established War Dog Program, the K-9 Corps. Over a million dogs served on both sides during WW1, carrying messages along the complex network of trenches and providing psychological comfort to soldiers. The most famous dog to emerge from the war was

Rin-Tin-Tin, an abandoned German war dog found in France in 1918 by American soldier, Lee Duncan, and taken to the United States. Duncan nicknamed the dog, 'Rinty'. When the United States entered World War II, a group called Dogs for Defense began a movement to mobilize dog owners to donate healthy and capable animals to the U.S. Army. Members of the K-9 Corps were trained for a total of eight to ten weeks. After basic obedience training, they were sent through one of four specialized programs to prepare them for work as sentry dogs, scout or patrol dogs, or mine-detection dogs."

"Why are you telling me this, Grady? It's irrelevant."

"No it's not, Julie. If somebody has trained dogs to attack joggers, it's vital for us to understand how they are doing it and why."

"This is for your dad, Grady, not us."

Grady ignored her plea and kept reading. He was lost in the subject and said, "This stuff is amazing, Julie. In active combat duty, scout dogs proved especially important by alerting patrols to the approach of the enemy and preventing surprise attacks. The top canine hero of World War II was Chips, a German Shepherd who served with the Army's 3rd Infantry Division. Trained as a sentry dog, Chips broke away from his handlers and attacked an enemy machine gun nest in Italy, forcing the entire enemy crew to surrender. The wounded Chips was awarded the Distinguished Service Cross, Silver Star, and the Purple Heart all of which were later revoked due to an Army policy preventing official commendation of animals. See, Julie. They trained dogs to attack and kill in the war. Somebody could easily do the same with attacking joggers."

"I doubt it. You're guessing on all of this, Grady, and it's a wild guess at best. Why are you telling me all of this?"

"Because I don't want you to get hurt by your dog."

Julie looked back at her screen grimacing, prompting Grady to say,

"What?"

"It says seventy-seven percent of dog attacks are committed by family pets; twenty-five percent of all deaths caused by dogs on chains. But this proves nothing, Grady. Your sister was killed by a shark. Why are we even researching all of this stuff?"

"Because I'm not convinced my sister was killed by sharks, Julie. That's why. And because of this recent jogger attack by dogs."

"Maybe, but maybe not," Julie said. "You don't know for sure. You're barking up the wrong tree."

"Very funny," Grady said. "Nobody knows for sure. Not yet anyway. So, what are the chances my sister was killed by dogs? I've found only sixteen shark attacks per year, only one person killed every two years," Grady said, his voice laced with purpose. "It means the chances my sister was killed by sharks versus a pack of wild dogs statistically favors dogs by a very wide margin."

"So, print out all this data and give it to your dad. Let him decide. It's up to him to pursue this, Grady, not us. He's the police chief and we're two teenagers. Let it go."

Grady printed out the data and stacked it neatly on his dad's desk with a note that read: '*Dad, please study this information. I think dogs killed Judy, not sharks. Love, Grady.*'

Grady heard his mother exit the front door with a quick, "Goodbye kids," and the house was silent. Grady dimmed the light in the den and shut down his computer. He slid onto the couch next to Julie and kissed her on the lips, smelling that sweet smell of lavender. He put his arm around her and pulled her close. She kissed him back and Grady slowly slid his hand up under her blouse feeling the outline of her bra. He French kissed her for the first time, and she undulated toward him. He tried pinching her bra-strap to unclip it with his left hand. It did not budge. He tried again and it gave way. She did not resist. Grady felt, for the first time, the velvety flesh of her supple breasts. He thought he heard the soft whisper of a moan.

Julie's mind was whirling in thoughts. Her mom had told her about birth control, the importance of saving herself for the right man. Was Grady the right man? Hell, she thought in an impassioned embrace, he was only a teenager as was she. How would she know? How would he know? And yet, she found herself lusting in the moment, lost in a flood of staggering new temptations urging her to proceed . . . maybe out of curiosity, maybe not. Yet the thought of saving herself for marriage kept creeping into her mind with renewed guilt. In the heat of the moment, Grady wondered how long he had until his parents returned. Was there enough time?

The Cobblestone was partially full, and Tom and Andrea Bennack sat in the back corner of the dimly lit restaurant chatting about the day. A flickering candle dimly lit the table cloth. Cobblestone's owner, Dave Prichard, knew their drink order and brought it to the table. It consisted of an extra dry martini, two olives, Chopin Vodka, and a Budweiser®. Tom picked up the Budweiser before it hit the table and guzzled a large swig and belched. Andrea Bennack thought, *For God's sake, Tom.*

The police chief wiped his mouth with the back of his hand and looked up at Pritchard with a shit eating grin on his face.

"Nothing like a cold beer, huh Tom?" Pritchard smiled as if nothing happened.

"You bet, Dave."

Another round of drinks came to the table and the food soon arrived. Bennack was so engrossed in his medium rare New York strip steak, forking a cut of meat into his mouth without switching utensils, that he didn't see the wax from the lit candle dripping on his police chief hat. Andrea blew out the candle and tried to scrape the wax from his hat., Bennack's head was pointed down in his food unaware. It just renewed for Andrea the differences between their backgrounds. Fuck, she thought, his napkin wasn't even on his lap, he chewed with his mouth open, both elbows were on the table, and he always belched after each meal without covering his mouth or apologizing. This was the Tom Bennack whom she had fallen in love with, the South Hampton head cop who never seemed to her to do wrong or be uncomfortable for who he was, with no excuses. What you saw in him is what you got, and she liked that resolve. Behavior like this from her husband had never mattered before; but lately, everything he did seemed to annoy her and reinforce their class difference. They subtly reminding her, or justified to her, that just maybe there would be nothing wrong if she entertained having a fling. The loss of their daughter seemed to heighten that feeling and change everything. She was now on a course without a rudder. But, she reasoned, or maybe rationalized, being in limbo for now might be okay . . . maybe a good thing for the moment.

She was hearing her husband's every other word, something about patrolman Futterman arresting a Hispanic woman on the beach yesterday for nudity. Her eyes scanned over her husband's left shoulder at Dave Pritchard who, as their host, was walking table-to-table warmly welcoming everyone. Andrea focused on the man's smile, dimpled square chin, and light blonde hair curling a couple of inches over the white color of his blue Brooks Brothers shirt. As Pritchard approached their table, Andrea's heart fluttered but she was conscious of not appearing to care. Her eyes stared down at the floor and she took in Pritchard's Stubbs and Wootten embroidered black velvet shoes. An embroidered anchor appeared on the left shoe and a yard arm and burgee on the right. Classy, she thought.

"Hey Dave," Bennack said. "Steak's perfect as usual. How you been?"

Pritchard extended his hand and pumped Bennack's in a firm shake. He stared into Andrea's liquid brown eyes with purposeful intensity. Andrea shifted uncomfortably in her seat noticing Pritchard's dark green initials, DCP, IV, neatly embroidered on his well starched shirt.

He leaned over and whispered softly, "So sorry about Judy, Andrea. My sincere condolences to you both again."

"It's been tough, Dave. Thanks. Day at a time," Andrea nodded.

Pritchard returned the nod as if subtly implying . . . to be continued, Andrea hoped. Silly thoughts for a married woman, she chided herself.

Bennack resumed eating his steak, not switching hands. Andrea stared at her husband's head, his face buried in a plate of food. Her life seemed to be going nowhere in slow motion, and she looked up staring into Prichard's eyes, a mesmerizing Navajo turquoise blue. *Who has eyes like that,* she wondered. *Nobody,* she told herself. *Only Dave C. Pritchard, IV.* She teased herself with guessing what the C stood for.

She couldn't help herself. "What does the 'C' stand for?"

Pritchard looked down at the initials on his shirt. "Very observant," he said. This time it was definitely a wink. "Charles."

"Of course. Charles the fourth." She felt immediately comfortable with the class reference. He just stared at her, studying her face then she felt his eyes scanning her body, her husband's face still buried in his plate.

Bennack looked up and said, "Good food, Dave."

"Thanks, Chief. Always good to see you," and Pritchard moved to the next table. He looked over his shoulder back at Andrea and smiled. She nodded a subtle acknowledgement, feeling out of breath as she did.

They finished dinner, no dessert, ordering two decaf cappuccinos. When Bennack motioned the waitress to bring the check, she said, "Dinner's compliments of Mr. Pritchard."

When Andrea looked across the dining room, Pritchard was smiling at her. Andrea nodded with an appreciative smile. *Did she just see Pritchard wink yet again?*

CHAPTER 11

HARNED GRABBED GRADY'S right hand just as he cupped the V of her inner thighs. Suddenly the sound of a car door slam broke the moment and they scurried from the couch adjusting their clothing.

All Grady could say was, "Jesus."

"We shouldn't have done that," Julie blurted out, her breath coming in a short spasm of effort. "I've got to get home."

"I love you, Julie Harned."

Julie looked back at him, not sure if she was embarrassed for what she just let him do, or relieved that they had both crossed over a bridge for her, at least, that had never before been breached. Grady promised himself he would never tell her that this was the first time he'd ever violated a girl's privacy. When she had shown him her promise ring and explained that it was her pledge to herself to be a virgin until she got married, Grady shrugged his shoulders hoping at some point he could break through the pledge. Tonight was a beginning, he told himself, and that seemed a good omen.

As Bennack walked past his den to retire for the night, he saw the light on his desk glowing atop a stack of papers. He entered the den to extinguish the light and read the top note from Grady attached to seven pages of notes that read:

'Dad . . . I saw the article in Newsday about another jogger attack. Julie and I researched shark and dog attacks. I think you should follow up with this second attack. We think there might be a connection. Love, Grady.'

Bennack shook his head knowing his son wanted to follow a similar career path, but Grady insisted he did not want to be a police chief like his father, but a detective or an FBI agent. Bennack, trying to be supportive, encouraged him to study criminology, but there were times like this that his son pushed the envelope of his patience to the brink. Bennack reached for the lamp switch and flicked it off. As he walked out of the den, he hesitated in step and stood rigid in thought. Something forced him to return to his desk and flip the light back on. He sat down pulling himself closer to the desk and picked up the first page. He read the second page, then the third, now into the statistics comparing shark to dog attacks. Bennack finished the last page and stared across the den at a picture hanging on the far wall. It was one of his favorite photos taken with his K-9 attack dog team when he was out on patrol in his early twenties. Two K-9 attack dogs, a German shepherd and a Rottweiler, had sniffed out and taken down a suspect who had just killed a young mother and her eight-year-old daughter with a 38 Berretta for a pair of diamond earrings and a Tissot watch. Bennack was standing over the suspect who lay on his stomach, the Rottweiler's jaws clamped on the nape of the predator's neck, the German shepherd hovering over the top of the suspect, its jaws tearing at the man's left buttock. Bennack's mind seemed to freeze in thought as the flashback brought back the vicious guttural sounds emanating from his attack dogs as they held the predator down. Bennack took in a deep labored breath as he recalled the man's unrelenting blood curdling screams for help as the dogs pulled and tore at his flesh.

Bennack looked down at the picture of Judy on his desk staring at her with a gasp of memories of the daughter that brought him and Andrea such joy. Then, in one terrifying thought, Bennack pictured what it might have been like for his daughter alone and jogging on the beach at sunset to have been tracked down and attacked by a pack of wild dogs. The sounds of the attack, the tearing of flesh into bone as he stared back at the K-9 attack dog scene across the room, brought him back to a sudden searing feeling of dread. Bennack knew from experience that the raging guttural sounds of attacking dogs promised to paralyze its victim even before jaws sank into flesh, and it was his incessant fear of dogs. As a child he had been attacked by a German Shepherd who leaped over his back yard fence and took Bennack by the throat. His father saved his life with a baseball bat. But Bennack was determined to get over his fear of dogs which was why he forced himself to manage the K-9 unit of attack dogs for the police force at the age of twenty-three.

He extinguished the desk lamp and exited the den. In the morning, he promised himself, he would call Dr. Kay Roberts, the pathologist who had performed his daughter's autopsy, and ask her to contact the coroner in Amityville who performed the autopsy on the second jogger. If anything, Bennack sighed in a tired yawn, this would put to bed any notion that there was any connection between both jogger attacks.

Bennack believed there was no connection between the two joggers slaughtered within the last two weeks because the killings were fifty miles apart. Yet, something triggered a troubling thought in his mind. What if Grady was right? What if it was a pack of wild dogs that managed to cover that distance and kill both joggers? If it was, Bennack knew that the pack now had the scent and taste of human flesh, and he knew from his K-9 experience, it wouldn't be long until they attacked again.

CHAPTER 12

THE POLICE CHIEF lay in bed troubled by flashbacks of the vast research he had done in an effort to understand what made dogs eat, drink, hunt, attack, track down prey, and kill. Making dogs subservient to a trainer came fairly easy, he remembered from his German Schutzhund training, but there were breeds that were bred and trained only to stalk, track down, and kill people.

The light in Bennack's den flicked back on at 3:35 AM and he quietly got out of bed and went into his office. He began rummaging through old file drawers containing training facts from his K-9 days. He pulled out the *Dogs in War* file and scanned his notes dating back twelve years. Dogs were used as scouts, sentries, and trackers from 1943 to 1945. The US Marine Corps used dogs, donated by American owners, to help take back the islands occupied by the Japanese. Doberman Pinschers became the official war dog for the US Marine Corps. They were trained to infiltrate hidden bunkers on the islands and attack and kill the occupants. Bennack looked up and yawned, remembering the potential ferocity of the dogs he trained. He turned the page and read that from 1966 to 1975, over 5,000 United States war dogs were used in Vietnam for the same purpose. Over 10,000 US servicemen were trained as K-9 handlers, and it was estimated they saved over 13,000 soldier's lives.

Bennack scanned the last page and a yellow sticky note had been attached to the last page. It read, '*In 2011, US Navy Seals used a Belgian Malinois war dog, named Cairo, in Operation Neptune Spear. The dog participated in the tracking and killing of Osama bin Laden.*' Beneath the note was another sticky note dated October 26, 2019 which read, '*ISIS leader, Abu Bakr Al-Baghdadi, the founder and leader of ISIS was tracked down by a U.S. Special Forces raid and a canine tracking dog was sent into the tunnel to entrap the terrorist and was injured in an explosion when it chased Al-Baghdadi into the back of a dead end tunnel forcing the world's most sought after terrorist to self-implode.*' He closed the file and went back to bed, his mind filled with angst, eyes open in the darkness of his room, his wife lying next to him in a deep sleep.

What if his daughter was killed by dogs and not sharks. His mind raced. Were the dogs wild, or assembled as a pack and released by their owners at the end of a summer's stay, or was it something else? He rolled over and fell into a fitful sleep.

At 9:07 AM, Bennack placed a call to Dr. Kay Roberts, the pathologist at Spielberg Memorial Hospital. Roberts was in the midst of sawing a hole through the cranial cap of a female corpse. As her scalpel probed the medulla oblongata, she heard the phone chirp twice. She left the gurney, scalpel poking from the small hole like a straw from a rum drink in a coconut shell and answered the phone.

"Dr. Roberts here."

"Good morning, Kay. Tom Bennack."

"Hi, Tom."

"I need a favor."

"Sure."

"Did you read about another jogger killed this week?"

"No."

"Killed by a pack of wild dogs."

"Jesus, where?"

"Amityville."

"What's the favor?"

"Could you call the pathologist at Amityville Hospital and share the details of Judy's autopsy?"

"I don't understand, Tom."

"To see if there's any remote connection between the jogger killings."

The phone silenced.

"Kay?"

"I'm thinking, Tom. Amityville's an hour drive west from South Hampton. Judy was killed by sharks, and the attack was on land, right?"

"Correct."

"There can't be any connection."

"I know. It doesn't make sense. Just make the call and speak to them. Please. Maybe there's a thread . . ."

"Okay. I'll make the call, but . . ."

Bennack interrupted her, "Thanks Kay. Just need closure on this."

"I understand, Tom. Might not be until later today. I've got three more autopsies."

"Call me if you find anything."

"Of course."

Roberts finished her last autopsy at 4:20 p.m. and connected with Dr. Ronald Greenberg, pathologist at Amityville Hospital. After reviewing the purpose of the call, Roberts probed deeper into the two jogger killings.

"Judy Bennack was killed by shark attack, but there were some inconclusive jaw marks on the cadaver."

"Inconclusive?" Greenberg queried.

"No match for two of the jaw imprints."

"Not shark?"

"Clearly not shark, but there were enough lethal shark jaw imprints to conclude the cause of death was shark attack."

Greenberg hesitated. "Any idea what the other two jaw marks were?"

"Smaller than shark jaws, but large enough to be a dangerous predator to joggers, or anybody else."

"Could those jaw marks` have been from dogs?" Greenberg said. "Zand's body was ripped apart by dogs, jaw marks clearly canine. But there were four jaw marks I couldn't identify, the others done by the same predators. There were dog hairs all over the cadaver. I got positive matches from Rottweiler, Doberman Pinscher, and German Shepherd. There might have been a fourth dog, but no hair sample match."

Roberts stared at the wall of cadaver vaults, her mind trying to sort out the inventory of possibilities. "How big were the four bite marks you couldn't identify?"

"Smaller than the other jaw marks made by the dogs."

A spiking chill of fear shot across Roberts' shoulders and arced down her spine. "Could they have been made by a human?"

Greenberg stuttered a response, "Christ, I don't think so. The bites were bigger than a human imprint, and . . ."

Roberts couldn't wait for the answer. "The eye teeth . . . any size or differentiation?"

"Yes," Greenberg said, an edge of fear now lacing his words. "They were bigger than human, fang like, but not as big as dog jaws."

"This is creepy stuff," said pathologist Roberts almost confirming that she didn't want to know the answer.

"There's one more thing worth mentioning. It's a postscript on my report, but there were several hair samples that didn't match dog hair," Greenberg said, almost whispering into the phone for fear someone was tapping the call.

The phone went dead for thirty seconds, maybe a minute. Roberts broke the silence.

"Was it human hair?"

"I don't think so," Greenberg said with a troubled voice. "At first, that's what I thought it might be . . ."

"Did you check the DNA?"

"Yes."

"And?"

The phone silenced yet again. Roberts heard Greenberg's labored breathing. She inhaled deeply. On the exhale, she said, "Any match . . . to anything?"

Greenberg puffed a response. "Yes, but nothing I've ever seen before . . . at least no matches for any animal on Long Island."

"But it was an animal, right?"

"As opposed to what?"

"Human."

"I'm not sure," Greenberg croaked, his voice laced with doubt. "The DNA strands were not clearly human or canine, some broken chains."

"Troubling," Roberts said. "Sounds like a mutant of some kind," she said, staring at the last sentence written in her pathology log on Judy Bennack's cadaver. It read, *'Cause of death: shark attack.'*

"Very troubling," Greenberg agreed.

"Enough to send the DNA sample to CDC in Atlanta. They've got a DNA data bank of every known species and disease on the planet," Roberts offered reluctantly.

"Already done."

"Good for you," Roberts said. "Now it's a waiting game."

"We'll know soon enough," Greenberg said.

"Thanks, Doctor. Good job."

"I'll let you know the moment I hear anything."

"Please do," Roberts said. "One last thought . . ."

"Yes?"

"I think we should keep this discussion below radar . . . at least until we know something definitively. For now, your jogger was killed by a pack of wild dogs, mine by a shark attack."

"I agree," said Greenberg . "To be continued."

"Let's pray this is the end of it. A random attack and no connection with joggers Bennack and Zand."

Greenberg didn't respond. His mind trailed off and he hung up the phone in utter silence.

Roberts waited a moment longer, the phone still clutched in her hand. A vivid image of Bennack desperately jogging through the water to escape filled her mind and she wondered, for the first time, if sharks really did kill her or was it something else. Something she suddenly realized she might never identify. The thought snapped her back to the present and she realized she hadn't yet hung up the phone.

PART II
THE TRACKING

CHAPTER 13

ANDREA BENNACK STOOD in the kitchen peering out the window at a male red cardinal perched atop the bird feeder hanging down from the gutter pipe outside her bay window. She could hear its melodious song through the window, and it filled her mind with the first moment of peace since the funeral. It was Tuesday, July 17, the third week since her daughter's death and the weather had turned unusually warm, 91 degrees yesterday at noon.

She was collecting her husband's uniform shirts and pants for the cleaners and, as was her habit, checked each pocket for anything forgotten. In one of his shirts, she removed a blue pen, and a paper clip from a pants pocket.

She collected her own clothes, two skirts, three blouses, and a blue blazer and stuffed them into a wicker laundry basket. As she hoisted the basket into the trunk of her four-year-old Lexus 350SE, her blue blazer fell onto the driveway. She leaned over and picked it up realizing she had forgotten to check her own pockets. She reached into the left pocket, nothing. Reached into the right pocket and felt a piece of paper. She extracted it and realized it was a note. She opened it up and read it. Her eyebrows furrowed and her liquid brown eyes stared fixedly at the note. In a subconscious moment of unchecked thought, she ran her right hand through a strand of her light brown wavy hair as if primping for a date.

'Sorry about your loss. Call me sometime. Lunch is on me.'

There was no phone number and no signature, but she knew it was Dave Pritchard, Cobblestone Restaurant. How did he get the note in my blazer pocket? Then she remembered. He came up behind her when she was sitting at the table, leaned over and whispered a sympathetic offering, "Sorry about Judy." Across the table, her husband's head was buried in his food: fork, mouth, fork, mouth. Pritchard was standing on her right side, she remembered. He must have placed the note in my pocket then. But why? He could have called her, could have extended an invitation to both of them, but this was a personal note to her alone. She looked up and scanned the street, the homes on the other side of the street, then the neighbors on either side of their home as if someone was watching her to see what she would do next.

A car turned the corner and came toward her, and she felt her heart pounding in her chest. Foolish thoughts for a middle-aged women. She hadn't done anything wrong, for God's sake, but it was the implication, just the thought of the possibilities. She scolded herself for the thought of Pritchard and her alone behind a closed door somewhere, somehow. It was that thought that triggered her heart to skip a beat.

The car passed, and she was relieved to see two small children in the back seat, one in a child's seat, the other sitting at the window. The girl with blonde hair in pigtails, waved at her. Andrea waved back and smiled then slid into the driver's seat and closed the door. She started the Lexus and the familiar plush interior and quiet purr of the engine soothed her anxiety. She inhaled a long overdue breath, relaxed back in her seat, and pushed the Sirius Satellite radio button for songs of the sixties. The velvety voice of

Johnny Mathis came on singing, '*Chances Are.*' Now, in the security of the cabin, Andrea wondered if she could ever have an affair. Ever be alone with another man with such temptation. What would it be like? How could she keep it from Tom? It didn't help, she thought, that Pritchard was over six feet tall, blonde curly hair pouring over his shirt collar, wearing an ascot, with a seersucker sport jacket that made his Navajo turquoise blue eyes dance in the setting sun light shining through Cobblestone's picture window. Was this note found in her blazer a harbinger of something more than just a casual lunch invitation? And what would Tom think? Could she dare follow up with a call? She swallowed hard, putting the car in reverse, then pulled out onto the street, her mind awash with temptation. She held her cell phone in her hand, thinking . . .

Chief Bennack had just completed a slow U-turn on Dune Road when his radio crackled to life. "Chief, Futterman here. Over."

"Go ahead, Nate."

"Just got a call from Halstead at the beach. They spotted a shark fin in the surf. A big one, moments ago."

Bennack gripped the steering wheel, tension coursing through his body. "Everybody out of the water?"

"Yes."

"I'm on my way."

"Roger that. Ten Four."

"Ten four."

The light atop Bennack's patrol car came to life and the siren sounded an ebb and flow blare. The patrol car skittered over loose gravel back onto the macadam road and Bennack headed to the Southampton beach parking lot. His car peeled into the lot and pulled in between a blue Rolls Royce Silver Cloud and a green Bentley coupe convertible. The chief ran atop a dune and scanned the beach. A long line of swimmers stood at the edge of the water looking out beyond the breaking surf. The water was empty of swimmers and Bennack jogged down to the gathering crowd, a bull horn clutched in his left hand.

"Could I have your attention please," Bennack barked into the bull horn.

The swimmers turned to face the chief.

"Please do not go back into the water until . . ."

Someone on the left pointed out beyond the surf and shouted, "Shark."

"Shark," another swimmer said, and everyone turned away from the water and ran back up the beach to higher ground.

Bennack's eyes squinted at the surf and then he saw it. A large dorsal fin cutting swiftly through the water. It moved inshore between two large swells, and everyone screamed. The shape of the massive predator then reappeared in a large wave that rose to crest in a white froth and the shark emerged chasing a school of bluefish that exploded out of the water in front of it in an effort to escape, but the shark came in fast, engulfing bluefish in its gaping jaws. The beach crowd gasped as half of the massive body of the shark was now out of water rolling sideways, jaws snapping at bluefish that flew out of the water in front of it onto the beach. In one thrashing, undulating motion, the fourteen-foot shark moved forward up the beach. It thrust its jaws at a frantic bluefish engulfing it in one bloody chomp.

Bennack ran down toward the water, his 38 special at the ready and the beach crowd parting in front of him. At thirty feet from the shark his safety was off. At twenty feet, Bennack began firing. His first two shots thumping into the predator's side, with little effect. After the fifth shot, a large wave broke and slid up the beach. The shark, riding with it, made a violent u-turn, and disappeared with the receding wave back into deeper water. Bennack had stood at the water's edge firing his pistol as the large shadow sunk beneath the surface. When his gun clicked empty on the fifteenth round, Bennack stared out to sea, his body trembling. In one paralyzing thought, the chief knew that his daughter, Judy Bennack, was killed by a shark and he wondered if this was the bastard that killed her.

CHAPTER 14

CHIEF BENNACK ANNOUNCED that the beach was closed for the day and ordered two of his officers to deploy yellow hazard tape closing off the beach parking lot after the last car pulled out. He heard bathers talking about the terrifying sight of seeing the shark come out of the water on a killing spree, but Bennack had seen it before when he was surf fishing. When he heard a teenager ask his mother if it was the same shark that killed the woman jogger, tears came to his eyes. If this was the same shark that killed his daughter, it was wounded, and he wondered if it would die, or attack again.

As he slipped into his patrol car, his radio crackled to life. It was Futterman.

"Just got a call from a woman at 22 Dumont. Husband being attacked by a dog. I'm on it. Over."

"Is it one dog or a pack?"

"She didn't say. I heard the man screaming in the background."

"I'm on my way."

"You don't have to come over, Chief. Got it covered."

"Ten four," the chief said without answering Futterman's comment. He spun out of the parking lot, lights flashing and siren on. When he pulled onto Dumont, he saw Futterman's patrol car in front of the house and Futterman running up to the home. Bennack pulled up behind the patrol car and opened the car door. He heard a loud guttural barking, grabbed a club from under the seat and bounded up to the front door. He heard screams from the back yard and Futterman had already vanished around the left side of the house. Bennack ran to the right. When Bennack ran through the gated fence into the back yard, he saw a Rottweiler in full attack atop a man. His clothes were bloodied, and his legs covered in gashes, streams of blood gushing out of them. The dog had its jaws clamped on the man's throat, and he gasped in pain, arms flailing at his sides.

Futterman kicked the dog's hind quarters hard and the animal spun around and attacked the patrolman's right leg, its teeth slashing through his pants into flesh, snarling as it yanked Futterman's leg side to side. Futterman lost his balance and fell down, now on all fours. The dog tore into the patrolman's left buttock and shook its head in a death grip. The patrolman tried to roll to the side punching the dog's head with his fists, but it only agitated the animal into a more frenzied attack, its jaws clamping down harder.

Bennack ran up to the attacking dog and crammed his club between the dog's collar and its neck. He gave a fast snapping upward twist to the left and the dog gave a deafening yelp of pain and its body fell limp. The Chief dragged the hundred twenty-pound body over to a chain attaching it to the backyard fence post and snapped it onto the dog's collar.

Futterman lay on the ground next to the owner nursing his wounds as the owner was groaning and clutching the wounds on his legs. He said, "What the hell did you do to that bastard?"

"K-9 training. He'll awaken soon. A defensive chokehold," the chief said wiping the sweat from his forehead.

The back screen door opened and a woman stood on the doorstep sobbing, staring at her pet dog lying still on its side. "You killed my Zeus."

Futterman could not check a sudden burst of emotion. He said, "Your fucking dog tried to kill us. You need to gas the bastard."

The woman wailed hysterically but the dog suddenly sprang to life and charged both men who were still on the ground.

"Here, Zeus," the woman cried. "Here boy. Come to momma."

Bennack had his gun at the ready. The woman screamed as Zeus launched its body through the air directly at Futterman. Four feet away from the patrolman's face, the chain snapped taught, the dog's body was yanked to a sudden stop in midair as if it had just hit a cement wall. It fell to the ground and its eyes met Futterman in a stare of rage, its throat issuing a guttural growl filled with rage.

The woman screamed, "Don't shoot."

Bennack slipped his revolver back into his holster and said to the man on the ground, "You need to get to the hospital and have those wounds treated. You might need rabies shots. You want us to take you?"

The man said, "No thanks, officer. My wife will take me."

Futterman got up off the ground and said, "Christ. That's all I need is rabies shots."

The man said, "Thanks for saving my life. Zeus has never attacked anybody. I don't understand."

"Sometimes, domestic dogs forget about all that training and revert back to their roots," Bennack said.

"What does that mean," queried the woman, tears still in her eyes.

"It means that before we domesticated dogs, they were predators that hunted and killed to survive. Your husband is damn lucky to be alive."

Silence fell on the small backyard except for the low guttural growl that sounded from the dog as its dark eyes focused on Futterman's ass.

Patrolman Futterman received seven stitches and rabies shots at Spielberg Memorial. When the chief returned to headquarters, Johnson called out, "You got a call. Said it was urgent. I put the note on your phone."

Bennack plucked the message slip off his phone. It read, '*Call Doctor Kay Roberts at Spielberg Memorial. URGENT.*'

Bennack dialed the phone number on the message slip and the phone rang busy. He got up from his desk and opened up a bottom file drawer withdrawing several hanging folders labeled DOG ATTACK STATISTICS. The contents were on faded legal yellow notebook paper, and he dumped the folders atop his desk.

He picked up the phone and dialed the number again. On the fourth ring, a woman's voice said, "Dr. Roberts here."

"Tom Bennack."

"Tom. Thanks for calling back."

"Did they find anything?"

Roberts hesitated for a moment. "Yes."

"What was it?"

"Animal."

"Could they identify it?"

"No. I mean not exactly. The DNA had human strands in it. That's the troubling part."

"I don't understand," Bennack said, his voice hollow of emotion.

"I don't understand either, Tom."

"What else?"

"The blood sample we provided to CDC was not the best."

"Not conclusive?"

"Correct."

"That's it?"

"No."

"There's more?"

"Yes."

"What?" Bennack said impatiently. "Just give me the bottom line, Kay."

"It's not canine. That's conclusive."

"So, it's human then, right?"

Roberts did not respond.

"Kay?"

"Yes."

"Was it human?"

Kay's voice was troubled, almost a tremor in her response, thought Bennack.

"Kay . . . read the report."

"You won't understand it, Tom. It's medical language."

"Then just give me your take on it. What do you think we're dealing with here?"

"Net, net? We're dealing with some kind of mutant. Not an alien as in outer space stuff, but maybe some freak of nature. They don't know yet."

"So, if it's some kind of mutant, why the hell do you think it's interacting with a pack of wild dogs?"

"Honestly, I have no clue. It's scary stuff, Tom. So scary that CDC's sending a team up to see if they can get a handle on whatever it is. They're very concerned we keep a lid on all information from the public. They don't want panic to set in especially when it might be connected to man's best friend . . . and who knows what else."

"In the meantime, we hope we don't lose another jogger."

"For sure, Kay. Let's stay close on this."

"We have no choice, Tom," and she rang off.

Futterman walked into the Chief's office just as he placed the phone back on the cradle. He was wincing in pain, clutching his left buttock.

"Rabies shots suck the big one, Chief. Hurts like hell."

"Don't clutch your ass then," Bennack grinned. "Sorry I didn't get there in time."

"I should sue the bastards for keeping that fucking predator," Futterman grimaced. "The son of a bitch took a chunk out of my ass the size of a silver dollar. The doc says I have to wear Depends because I won't be able to sit on a toilet seat for two weeks." A stab of pain shot through his ass, and he grimaced in pain, hopping in place. "Shit, that hurts!"

Bennack pulled out a filing cabinet and extracted a folder. "Read this. You might get a couple of hundred thousand for that sore ass."

Futterman looked down at the folder. In black magic marker, it read, "**DOG BITE INSURANCE CLAIMS**".

He flipped the file open and read the first paragraph aloud.

Dog bites accounted for more than one third of homeowners insurance liability claims paid in 2013, costing nearly $479 million *in the U.S., according to the Insurance Information Institute. It has risen 48% since 2003. State Farm, the largest writer of home owners insurance in the US paid more than $109 million on nearly 3800 dog bite claims in 2011.*

Futterman looked up from the folder.

"Thanks, Chief. Looks like this silver dollar's going to net me some serious payback."

He flipped through three more pages in the file and said, "The average cost of dog bite claims in the US was $29,396 in 2013, up 53.4% from $19,162 in 2004. This is happening because more people own dogs today and live closer to one another. There are 78.2 million dogs in the US according to American Pet Products Association, one dog for every four people in the US."

Patrolman Johnson walked into his space and flipped another file open. He looked up and said, "This is some serious shit, Chief. Futterman has a claim for sure. I should have filed years ago. I got bitten by a Fox Terrier three years ago when I was walking my Dachshund. The bastard took a chunk out of my right arm when I tried to break them up. It was down to the bone."

Johnson looked down at the file again and said, "A dog's nose contains 220 million olfactory receptor sites to smell anything around it as a protective alarm. A dog's bite is 450 pounds per square inch, a lion's bite is 691 *psi*, a shark is 669 *psi*, but get this . . . the pit bull is 2,000 *psi*. Shit. That's enough to sever an arm or leg."

"Shit happens," the chief said.

Bennack stood up and walked around his desk to face his two patrolmen. His face was taught and filled with concern. He said, "I want you guys to be aware of all dog activity in South Hampton. Anything unusual, I want to hear about it."

"What's up, Chief?" Futterman asked.

"You onto something?" Johnson followed.

"Not yet," Bennack said. "Not yet," he repeated with angst.

A silence fell over the small office and Bennack walked past both patrolmen and exited the building. Johnson and Futterman watched the chief walk twenty paces away from the building, and stand rigid, staring off into the distance.

Futterman broke the silence. "Spooky. Something's wrong. He's holding back on something."

"For sure," Johnson answered.

CHAPTER 15

ANDREA BENNACK PULLED into the parking space across from Chu's Neat and Clean Laundry store and fed the meter a quarter. She crossed the street, laundry bundled under her right arm, entering the shop. Moments later she exited, stood scanning the street for traffic then walked back to her car starting the engine.

As she backed up, she heard a thump on the trunk of her car and suddenly braked, thinking she had hit something. Dave Prichard poked his head through the car window and smiled. "Hi."

Andrea stared at him in silence and before she could utter a word, he opened the front side door and sat next to her in the front seat. Her hands white knuckled the steering wheel.

"You startled me."

"Didn't mean too."

"The note," she said her eyes darting nervously about the cabin not quite meeting his.

"You found it?"

"Yes."

"How about today?"

Andrea stared into his eyes and her heart fluttered. "I'm not sure what to say, Dave. I mean it was a nice gesture, but . . ."

"But what?"

Pritchard leaned over and touched her right hand on the steering wheel. It was warm and it gave her goose bumps which she hoped he didn't see.

"Relax, Andrea. We haven't done anything wrong. I just thought after your loss, it might be nice for you to take a break. We're all good friends. I'm very fond of you and Tom. We've known each other . . ."

She finished his sentence, "Since Tom and I moved to South Hampton."

"Right. A long time. So let me treat you to lunch."

"Cobblestone?"

"No."

"Where?"

"My place."

Andrea smiled. "Your place? I don't even know where you live."

"Let me show you."

"In my car?"

"Why not."

Andrea sat rigid in thought staring out the front window. Pritchard broke the silence. "Let's go." Andrea backed out of the parking space. "Go to Dune Road and take a right."

"You live on Dune?"

"Yes."

As she drove, Bennack convinced herself that Pritchard's offer was heartfelt and she was moved by his sensitivity. Accepting his offer for lunch was absolutely harmless, she thought, and she convinced herself that nothing could possibly happen. The Lexus pulled into an entrance hidden by ten-foot hedge rows and as the car pulled up to the front door, Andrea had only one thought: if a police car drove by the entrance to Pritchard's house, they would not see her Lexus from the road.

Andrea Bennack walked through the front door, Pritchard behind her. They walked across the room to a massive picture window. She was transfixed by the spectacular view of the ocean from forty feet above the waves and not a trace of humans as far as her eye could see.

"How long have you lived here?"

"About twenty years."

"Spectacular view, Dave."

Pritchard walked around her and motioned her to have a seat facing the ocean. He walked over to the bar, dolphins etched into the glass mirror, and fixed two drinks then returned.

"The usual, not too dry, two olives."

Andrea crossing her legs, staring at the sea, accepted the drink. "You remembered," she said smiling.

"Indeed," Pritchard said, touching his Martini with hers. "To you, Andrea. May you always have peace and," he hesitated, "excitement in your life."

Andrea took a long sip and looked into his eyes, aware that he was studying her body. She quivered noticeably hoping to disguise the rise of emotion coursing through her body by shifting in her seat. She took another long pull on the martini and rested her head on the sofa back pillow.

"Thanks, Dave. I appreciate this. I needed it. It's been a tough month."

"I'm sure," Pritchard said staring at her tailored plumb colored pants suit, a white frilly blouse highlighting her high cheekbones and liquid brown eyes. Her auburn hair cascaded down the right side of her face hiding the outline of a well-defined breast.

Without thinking, Andrea said, "Have you ever been married before?"

"Twice. First one lasted a year and a half. No children."

"Why did you split?"

"She was transgender. I had no clue. I'm not even sure today what it's all about, but after enough bed time together, it became obvious she wanted to be a he."

Andrea sighed. "Sorry for both of you it didn't work. I'm uncomfortable with the whole transgender bathroom thing, but since I can't relate to the challenge, the torment must be awful."

"For the person, I guess, it must be agony." Pritchard said, and he rose to take her empty glass returning to the bar.

Andrea thought about telling Pritchard to hold on the second martini, but she checked the fleeting thought concluding she had been through enough torment and her mind was starting to feel the effect of the first drink. Pritchard returned with two martinis. "Here."

"Tell me about the second wife."

"She was beautiful," he paused. "A lot like you."

He smiled and Andrea wriggled in her chair uncomfortably. She looked down at her drink and her eyes caught the shine of her diamond wedding ring in the late morning sun. She raised the martini and whispered, "Thanks," then consumed a third of her second drink.

"Not much to tell," Pritchard said, his voice soft and polished. "We connected at the Oyster Bar at The Plaza. Dated for six months and decided we had more fun together than apart. We got married three months later. Another nine months and I found out she was shacking up with a host of young men including a mid-twenties waiter at my restaurant. It was a quick divorce. Been single ever since."

"No children?"

"Thankfully, none."

Pritchard stood up, somewhat suddenly, and said, "Lunch time." He walked to the Viking refrigerator pulling out the makings for two Waldorf salads.

"You like caviar?"

"I adore it."

Pritchard placed a plate of six Triscuits topped with caviar in front of her.

"Enjoy." He nodded at her glass which was empty. "Another."

"I better not, Dave." She felt warm and unusually relaxed. Her mind wandered unchecked from her husband, Tom, the loss of Judy, her son Grady, then she held out her glass and said, "Maybe a half."

She reached for a Triscuit and bit down on half of it. "Hmmm. This is delicious, Dave. Where did you get it?"

"From Iran. I get a great discount through Cobblestone. It's called Almas. Produced from the eggs of a rare albino sturgeon. Sixty to a hundred years old and swims in the southern Caspian Sea."

Andrea leaned her head back against the sofa pillow again only this time her mind floated through unbidden thoughts. "That must have cost a fortune," she said, a slight slur in '*fortune*.'

"One kilogram, two pounds three ounces, costs 20,000 Euros."

"Dear God, Dave."

Pritchard returned with the half martini and Bennack's head was still resting on the pillow. She was relishing the caviar and slow to swallow. She reached for the glass and took a long pull on the drink before finishing the caviar. Her head rested motionless against the sofa pillow, and she closed her eyes. Pritchard leaned over and kissed her softly on the lips. She started and her eyes flickered open as she smelled his cologne. Her mind froze in thought, but her lips opened without pulling away and Pritchard leaned down beside her holding the kiss, embracing her shoulders.

She mumbled something and Prichard said, "What?"

"What's the name of that cologne?"

He pulled away maybe six inches from her face and smiled. "*Blue*. It's called *Blue* by Ralph Lauren."

Pritchard leaned in again only this time he held her face with both hands and kissed her again. Suddenly, she broke the embrace and said, "No."

Pritchard said, "What do you mean?"

"I can't do this, Dave. I just can't."

"Why not?"

"Because . . . because I love Tom. And . . . because I'm married."

"So? . . . Lots of people do it who are married."

"That doesn't make it right, Dave. I'm sorry if I . . ."

"Yes . . ."

"Forget it. I just can't do it."

She rose from the couch and said, "Thanks for the drinks," and walked toward the front door.

"You want me to drive you home?"

"No thank you. I'm okay." She hesitated. "Dave?"

"Yes?"

"I don't want this to ruin our friendship."

"You have my word it won't."

Andrea reached the front door and exited not looking back. She got into her Lexus, turned on the engine and burst into tears, her mind flooding with thoughts of losing her daughter and love for her husband, Tom. She knew he would never cheat on her and now her intentions of coming so close to having an affair angered her for the lack of self-discipline. At that moment, she promised herself never to put herself in this situation again. She drove slowly out of Pritchard's driveway, tears streaming down her face, both hands gripping the steering wheel with new found resolve.

CHAPTER 16

WEDNESDAY, JULY 25, was cloudy with a sixty percent chance of thunderstorms across Long Island. It was 6:14 AM when Rance Matthews opened the front door of his English Tudor home on Wellington Road in Garden City, Long Island. He wore matching light blue jogging attire and new Adidas running shoes he had purchased three weeks ago, his seventh pair since he started jogging nine years ago.

Matthews turned right on Chester Avenue and jogged due east toward the Adelphi University campus. When he crossed Nassau Boulevard, he heard a dog barking in the distance. Matthews had read in Newsday about the jogger killed by a pack of wild dogs in Amityville recently, but that small town was a forty-five-minute drive from Garden City so the man was at ease, his mind filled with the success of his life: his career, District Sales Manager in the Packaged Soap Division of Procter & Gamble, his newborn son, Rance L. Matthews, III, and his wife Jill whom he had known since his junior year at Garden City High School.

Jogging had become a way of life for Matthews, seven days a week, three to four miles a day. It was his way to rid himself of the pressure of constantly being challenged to make his sales budget by pushing his three Unit Sales Managers to pressure their seventeen salesmen to sell more soap.

Matthews crossed Brixton Road, then Whitehall Boulevard. Another dog barked upon hearing the staccato sound of his running shoes hit the pavement. When he entered the western border of Adelphi University, three more dogs announced his presence, but Matthews looked over his shoulder to confirm that the dogs were all confined behind backyard fences. He was safe. Since this was his normal jogging route, he knew most of the dogs by their bark and made a game out of guessing the breed. One was a German Shepherd, a deep guttural growl, another a Golden Retriever, a more friendly high-pitched bark, then a Black Labrador Retriever, higher pitched than the golden, but not as threatening as the German Shepherd. Another bark he wasn't sure of . . . either a Poodle or Boxer, he thought. He laughed at himself for the diversion.

He jogged cross campus to Cherry Valley Road, saw the Cathedral of Incarnation spire above the treetops, then spun on his heel and headed due west. He crossed Whitehall Boulevard and Brixton Road again, then jogged toward Roxbury Road. He hopped the small, wooded border fence that announced the seventh fairway of the Garden City Country Club which he and his wife had joined eight months ago. Matthews took in a gulp of fresh morning air, smelling the freshly cut grass on the pristine course. In the distance, he saw the gradual slope of Superman Hill which he had used for sleigh riding during winter snows as a child. Warm memories of growing up in Garden City filled his mind and he smiled in peaceful reflection. Today was his day and being alone in the rhythm of his daily jog made him thankful for the discipline he had acquired during his career at Procter & Gamble.

He jogged over to the eastern slope of Superman Hill and began a slow arduous run up to the top of the hill. When he reached the top, jogging in place, he looked east to see the sun peak over the horizon in a shimmering golden glow bringing warmth to his body. He turned to face the west, still running in place, over the small lake below the hill, he saw the faint misty outline of the new Towers built to pay respect for the 3,213 who lost their lives on 911. Matthews, who lost a close personal friend, Bill Godshawk, wanted to believe that it was rebuilt to promote America's determination and defiance to the Taliban and ISIS, returning respect and power to his great nation.

Matthews began his descent at a slow pace. Halfway down the large hill, he thought he saw a speck of movement in the distance off to the northeast, maybe two fairways away, he thought. Again, he jogged in place, stopping all forward movement. Whatever it was, it was moving toward him at a fast clip. He continued jogging downhill, his eyes riveted on whatever was moving toward him. He looked to his left and didn't see anything. But wait . . . movement off to the northwest. He looked right and saw two dogs ranging back and forth, noses pressed to the ground as if following a scent. Was it his scent? The thought forced a rush of adrenalin through his body. Suddenly, he stopped all motion and crouched down low to the ground. There was nothing to hide behind, and he had nothing to defend himself with except his cell phone. He pulled it out of his jogging shorts pocket. Three bars. Enough to make a call. But to whom? Dial 911? His wife? His mind raced. He looked to his left and something was on the other side of the lake dashing on the path along the water's edge toward him. He squinted and he could now see three dogs. Or at least he thought they were dogs. He rubbed his eyes to clear his vision. Two dogs on his right, three on his left. No humans in sight. Was he imagining this or was it real? Maybe they were friendly, but maybe not. How long should he wait before making a call. If they were tracking him, Matthews knew he had to make a decision and fast.

The dogs on the right had already reached the base of Superman Hill and were lunging up the incline toward him, the others about to join them. A feeling of terror now coursed through his body and a flashback of the Newsday jogger attack came to him in one paralyzing moment. He knew he had only one choice.

The 6:58 Long Island commuter train had just left Nassau Boulevard two minutes ago heading west toward Penn Station. The jogger knew the train schedule like the back of his hand because he had taken the train for four years before being promoted to District Sales Manager. The 6:58 was going fifteen miles an hour, now twenty, into thirty approaching forty miles per hour, and soon it would be up to sixty. Matthews heard the train's whistle as it left Nassau Boulevard. On the other side of the lake that flanked Superman Hill was a large drainage pipe, six feet in circumference. There was a path to the left of the drainage pipe that led to the train tracks. As the pack of dogs ascended Superman Hill, the jogger jumped to his feet and bounded down the west side of the hill toward the water, his cell phone at the ready.

As he hit the bottom of the hill, he could hear the distant diesel engine of the Long Island 6:58 train in the distance. He raced toward the train tracks and the large six-foot drainage pipe with the lake on his left. Across the lake, he saw a golfer teeing up on the third hole, a par three with the green adjacent to the tracks. Mathews was in a full run now. He shouted across the lake, "Hey . . . Hey. Help. Help me."

The golfer was on the tee box addressing his ball. He looked up and over toward Matthews across the lake and took two steps toward the lake to get a better look.

"Over here. Help me."

"What?" the golfer shouted back.

The dogs were one hundred yards behind Matthews and gaining. The golfer across the lake now saw the dogs chasing the jogger. He ran toward his golf cart and hopped in putting the cart in gear and driving at full speed around the west side of the lake, but Matthews was only fifty yards in front of the dogs, the golf cart now at the end of the lake near the drainage pipe.

The jogger was looking over his shoulder shouting, "Help, help." Forty yards behind him, now thirty, then twenty-five. Matthews had his cell phone out and had called 911. He was half way through a panicked call.

"Operator. 911. Rance Matthews. I'm being attacked by dogs. Help me. Garden City Country Club. Superman Hill. Across from third hole near lake. Send the police. Hurry, please."

Twenty yards . . .

"Being attacked by dogs, you said?" the operator repeated.

Fifteen yards . . .

Looking over his shoulder, Matthews shouted desperately, "Yes. Call the police. Now. Hurry, please. Superman Hill. Garden City Country Club."

The golf cart was now approaching the jogger head on. The driver was shouting at the dogs, "Hey . . . you bastards. Hey. Go home." He was swinging a 3 wood golf club in circles above his head and then banging it on the side of his golf cart to make as much noise as possible.

Ten yards.

Ten yards, eight yards, six, five, three yards. The jogger was running as fast as he could trying to meet up with the golf cart coming at him to get a golf club to defend himself. Matthews saw a shadow, cast by the rising sun, over his right shoulder, and he knew the lead dog was already in the air lunging at him. He saw the reflection of jaws spread wide. As he felt the paws of the dog touch his back, the jogger urgently swerved to the left and dove into the lake. Two dogs followed, leaping out into the water with a resounding splash and wild guttural barks filling the air with dread. The three remaining dogs headed directly toward the encroaching golf cart. But, seeing what was happening, the driver suddenly swerved away from the lake and headed across the seventh hole fairway at full speed. One dog, a Rottweiler, leapt in hot pursuit of the golf cart, but the two other dogs did not follow the Rottweiler. Instead, they ranged along the east side of the lake watching the jogger now swimming toward the drainage pipe, Matthews desperately swimming ahead of the two dogs in pursuit. The Rottweiler was gaining on the cart and the golfer was racing looking behind him in terror, a two iron in his hand at the ready. Now twenty yards behind the cart, then fifteen, its guttural growls sending a jolt of fear through the escaping golfer. As the Rottweiler was poised to attack, a piercing, high-pitched sound echoed across the golf course and the dog spun around and sped back toward the lake to join the rest of its pack now rounding the end of the lake approaching the drainage pipe.

The drainage pipe extended out into the lake fifteen feet beyond the shoreline, two feet above the water, so Matthews, swimming frantically, had already calculated that the pipe was his best and only chance to escape for he knew where the pipe ended and he knew that the dogs could not enter the pipe because of its height above the water.

The man in the golf cart had stopped halfway across the fairway now, holding a cell phone to his ear. In the distance he heard a siren, then another, still another. One of the police cars was already onto the golf course skittering across the fairway. Matthews had fifty yards to go to reach the drainage pipe, but he was losing his strength, exhausted from the morning jog and the desperate swim to save his life. He had kicked his new Adidas jogging sneakers off sixty yards ago, but the two dogs in the water were gaining. Forty yards, thirty, twenty, now ten. He saw the other dogs rounding the end of the lake and heard the loud panting of the two dogs swimming after him in the water. His legs were churning desperately to escape, but they were closing the distance between prey and predator, now only ten feet behind him and gaining. Matthews heard the sirens, saw the dogs gaining on him and the gaping mouth of the drainage pipe now within reach. In one desperate lunge, the jogger, now swimmer, thrust his body weight up and out of the water in one thrashing attempt to grab hold of the lip of the pipe and hoist himself out of danger. His fingers grasped purchase of the pipe's edge, and his finger nails dug in for a life grip. His gut now wriggled over the edge, and he wormed his body into the darkness of the pipe's innards. Matthews staggered to his feet and sloshed through the shallow drainage of a yellowish sludge heading deeper into the pipe.

The pipe walls suddenly vibrated, the water trembled, and the jogger knew the 6:58 AM Long Island Railroad commuter train was now rumbling overhead towards New York City. For the first time, Matthews stopped in his tracks and listened to the train pass. He was safe. He had made it out alive.

But the feeling was short lived.

He thought he heard shots ring out at the end of the tunnel. But he heard something else. Something was splashing through the tunnel toward him. He knew it wasn't human . . . and then he heard the most terrifying sound of his life: panting, and a collective guttural growling of a pack of dogs in hot pursuit, the hollow pipe magnifying the sound.

Matthews spun around and vanished deep within the drainage pipe system. On the run, he fumbled for his cell phone, wildly punched in some numbers in his iPhone and it came to life, blinked thrice and extinguished. The water had shorted his phone. It seemed dead. He tried it again. Behind him the splashing was louder, the panting now filled the pipe with utter terror, Matthews' legs churning like pistons, but the acid build up arched shooting pains through his legs and spiked up though his back. A voice said, "Hello?"

"I love you," Matthews said in a desperate voice. "I love the kids."

"Rance?"

"Yes."

"What's wrong," his wife said, her voice trailing off.

"I'm being . . ."

Out of the darkness, jaws clamped down on the jogger's left thigh. Another dog chewed into flesh and bone of his right buttock and still another lunged upward and clenched Matthews' throat crunching his windpipe in one chomp. Matthews fell to his left and, as he went down, he heard his wife's screams coming from the cell phone that was still clutched in his hand until his pounding heart pumped its last beat.

A shot rang out inside the tunnel and flashlights showed the eerie, darting glows of a search in progress. Three patrolmen were running through the pipe, as terrifying barks and guttural growls were heard in the distance. Then there was silence.

As the first patrolman reached the clump of flesh that lay still in the sludge of the pipe, his light shone down on a body. Seconds later, two more patrolmen arrived on the scene. He said, "Jesus, Mother of God. What the hell just happened?"

CHAPTER 17

PATROLMAN JEFF FOX remembered standing at the gaping drainage pipe entrance he had just exited. He was trying to gather his thoughts as he stared at the empty page of his log book back at the Garden City police precinct. His mind was a blur. Two patrolmen, who were on duty with him when he heard the 911 call, had been standing near his desk. Police Chief Tom Bennack of the Southampton Police Department had received an all-points bulletin and had sped westward, lights flashing, siren blaring on US 495. He sat at the opposite side of the table in a small dimly lit interrogation room at the Garden City police precinct.

Fox was telling the assembled group he had viewed three corpses during his fourteen years of service, one of them he had shot in the face in self-defense when the man lunged at him with a meat cleaver; but this one, he told them, was gruesomely different.

"I've responded to many dog attack victims, mostly postmen delivering mail, but those canine attacks were mostly bite marks on butts and legs requiring stitches and rabies shots, nothing like this. From my car crossing the fairway, I saw the chase, witnessed the victim swim for his life then he vanished into the drainage pipe pursued by a pack of four dogs. The three of us followed them into the pipe," Fox said, out of breath.

"Are you sure they were all dogs?" asked Bennack.

"As opposed to what? A dog is a dog. Four legs, a tail and yapping snout," barked Fox.

"Describe them. Were they together in a pack or separate from each other?" Bennack persisted.

Fox hesitated in thought. "Two were in the lake swimming after the victim, one on the west bank running toward the drainage pipe, and the fourth one . . ." Fox paused, closing his eyes, teeth clenched in reflection.

"Yes?" said patrolman Buzz Pine, hanging on Fox's words.

"The fourth was running away from the lake across the fairway chasing a golf cart heading east," Fox added. "But there might have been a fifth."

"Typical of any dog," said patrolman Laurie Cohen. "Natural tendency to chase anything in motion. Hunting instincts."

Bennack nodded in agreement. "So, what happened?"

"Halfway across the fairway, the dog stopped chasing the golf cart, turned around suddenly running back towards the drainage pipe following the others," Cohen said, dark bushy eyebrows furrowed in thought.

"Did you see anybody standing anywhere around the lake or hear any loud noise before the dog turned back?" Bennack queried.

Cohen said, "Like what?"

"A noise. Any noise."

Cohen pursed his lips, hesitating. "Yes, I think."

"Describe it," Bennack pressed.

"A high-pitched whistle," Cohen said curiously.

Patrolman Pine, peered at this watch. "About what time do you think it was when the fourth dog turned around and joined the pack?"

Cohen hesitated again, staring at this watch. "Maybe about 7:00 o'clock this morning."

"It was the whistle from the 6:58 commuter train leaving the Nassau Boulevard train station," Pine said assuredly.

Cohen nodded affirmatively.

"Maybe," said Bennack. "Maybe not."

"What else could it be," Cohen grumbled.

"A command."

"Command?" Pine questioned, catching his breath in hesitant thought.

"Something controlling the pack," Bennack said intensely, his words hanging in the air.

Cohen managed, "How's that possible? We didn't see anybody but the four dogs . . . and the guy in the golf cart was trying to escape a dog chasing him."

"Gentlemen," Bennack added crisply, "I drove here from South Hampton because something's not right. Three joggers have been killed in less than a month. The first one was my daughter," Bennack paused, biting his lip.

"I'm sorry, Chief," said Fox. "This is obviously tough for you."

"It sucks. Supposedly she was killed by a shark, but it's not conclusive.

Now this. At least two bodies mutilated by a pack of dogs, maybe a third. Coincidence? I'm not sure if all three might be related, but I'm going to have the same pathologist who performed the autopsies on the first two review this corpse."

"If they're related, we've got one hell of a problem," Cohen added with a frown of concern.

Bennack said, "Did you guys chase after the dogs after finding the body to see where they escaped?"

"Yes," said Pine. "The drainage pipe forked about fifty yards after we found the body. Cohen and I split. He took the tunnel to the right; I took the pipe to the left. Fox followed me with his dog."

"About a hundred yards in, I took a third fork that goes beneath the Nassau Country Club house," Fox said. "My K9 German Shepherd was tracking the scent, going crazy."

Bennack stiffened in his chair. "You had a dog with you? I ran the Mineola K9 unit for eight years."

"Then you know the ability of these trackers. Sarge was going nuts. Sniffing the hell out of everything, tunnel walls, sludge, winning, barking, locked onto their scent. Relentless."

The four officers hovered over a map of the underground drainage tunnel system. Bennack was tracing their path within the forking tunnels as he spoke.

"How the hell could they have gotten out? You guys had all three tunnels covered. So, they should've been trapped. The tunnels all dead-end into sewer traps leading to Stewart Avenue. All storm water drains from the streets into the tunnel system and washes out into the lake on the seventh hole of the golf course."

"Exactly," Fox said.

"Were any of the storm drainage cover grates on Stewart Avenue missing or ajar? Bennack said, his right hand fumbling with a #10 pencil pointing to the end of one of the tunnels on Stewart Avenue.

"No. They were all in place," Pine said, Cohen nodding.

"Then how the hell did the dogs escape?" Bennack said. "I'm assuming the drainage grates at the end of the tunnel system are too high for any dog to push out and escape, right?"

Fox said, "That's the baffling part. There's a seven-foot ladder leading up to the street grate at the end of each tunnel. That's what stumps us. And the grates are heavy to lift."

Bennack leaned forward toward the table facing the assembled group. "What's the angle of the storm ladder?"

Pine said, "About forty to forty-five degrees."

Fox stood up, his six-foot seven-inch height almost poking the ceiling. He looked down at Pine and Cohen, then stared fixedly at Bennack. "Are you thinking what I'm thinking?"

"It can't be," Cohen said.

"It better not be," Pine managed staring across the table at Bennack.

Bennack took a long pause, looked slowly around the room then locked eyes with Fox who leaned down and said, "We might have a serial killer out there."

"I'm telling you, Pine and I saw only four dogs. There was no human standing anywhere near them," Cohen said convincingly, "except for the golfer in the runaway cart and he was scared shitless."

Fox stared across the table at Bennack. His voice had a twinge of angst when he said, "I ran the K-9 Unit in Mineola."

Bennack said, "And I managed the K-9 unit in Suffolk County, fifteen years ago. We both know it's possible to control a pack of dogs from a distance to attack and kill on command." Unflinchingly, Bennack said, "That's how the Germans won the ground war by using dogs to attack and kill soldiers behind enemy lines."

Cohen said, "Shit. Those bastards."

The silence in the room was palpable.

"You think a human's behind the attacks?" Pine said looking across the table at Bennack, eyes wide.

"Whatever it is behind these attacks, I'm not convinced it's human."

"What else could it be?" Fox added.

"I'm not sure," Bennack said, his voice laced with concern.

CHAPTER 18

GRADY BENNACK STARED at his Apple watch waiting. Julie Harned had just rung off her cell phone and told him she'd be there in ten minutes. That was twenty-eight minutes ago, and Grady had told her he thought he might be on to something big. While she pressed him for an answer over the phone, he insisted that the matter was urgent and refused to tell her over the phone. "Get here as soon as you can," he pressed.

The knock at the door sent Grady to his feet and he walked swiftly to greet her.

"Is your mom here?"

"No. She's at work."

"I thought she had Thursdays off."

"Whatever. I forgot."

"Where is she?"

"I don't know."

"So, what's so urgent?"

He walked over to his laptop and said, "I have a hunch."

"About what?"

"About the joggers and the dogs."

Harned sat down next to him staring at his laptop screen.

"Who's that?"

"It's Randy Zand."

"Who's he?"

"The second jogger killed after my sister."

Grady punched some more keys and another picture appeared.

"Yeah. Who's he?"

"Rance Matthews.

"So . . . ?"

"The third jogger killed on Wednesday."

"What's the connection, Grady. This is stuff your dad should be doing, not us."

"I found them all on Facebook."

"So what, Grady. We're all on Facebook." She stopped to Google something. "They have 1.86 billion active users monthly."

Grady looked at her hesitating then said, "I know that, but here's the big surprise. All three joggers are the same age, twenty-seven, twenty-eight, and here's the scary part . . . They all went to the same high school, Freeport High, in the same class."

Harned's eyes widened and she let out a gasp. "Oh my God, Grady. Your kidding, I hope. Does your dad know this?"

"No. Not yet."

"Did Judy have a Freeport high school yearbook?"

"Great idea, Julie." Grady leaped off the couch and ran toward his sister's room. He searched frantically three shelves pulling out two high school yearbooks from Freeport High and dashed back into the living room.

They scoured each yearbook for pictures and class photos. "Here's Judy's class picture." She counted quickly and said, "There's hundreds of graduates, Grady."

"And three of them are dead, killed by dogs while jogging."

They studied the class photos and Grady circled his sister Judy and two other classmates.

"What if somebody's out to kill their entire class?" Harned said.

"What are the chances of that?" Grady said. "I don't think so."

"This is way too big for us, Grady," Harned said. "I'd call your dad now. I know you want to be a detective someday, but this is very big league. It's scary."

"Maybe, maybe not, Julie. This is very exciting."

"Grady. Listen to me. This is sick stuff. If there's some loonie out there killing joggers. I'm out of here. This is way over our heads."

"Maybe not," Grady repeated again. "The killer might be somewhere in this yearbook, Julie. We can do the research. Maybe interview some of the classmates."

"What if the killer's not in the yearbook," Harned said.

Grady paused, taking a deep breath. "What do you mean?"

"Just what I said. It could be anybody, maybe not connected with the school."

The front door opened, and Andrea Bennack entered the living room, standing against the hallway wall. "Hi there."

"Hi, Mom. How was your day?"

Bennack hesitated, yawned, and replied, "Good, Thank you. Good," she repeated.

"Hi, Mrs. Bennack," Harned said.

"Have you seen dad, mom?"

"No. Why?"

"I want to tell him something important."

"What about?" Bennack said.

"It's about the dead joggers," Grady said.

"What about them?"

"I don't think Judy was killed by a shark. I think she was murdered."

CHAPTER 19

CHIEF BENNACK ARRIVED home at 5:20 pm and when he opened the front door, Grady stood there to greet him.

"Dad. I've discovered something very important."

"What, son?"

"The three joggers killed all graduated from Freeport High School. Same as Judy. All the same age, same class."

Bennack stood rigid staring at his son. He didn't say anything at first then said, "If it's true, that's very significant."

Grady opened up the Freeport High School yearbook and showed his father circled pictures of the three victims. "So, they were all in the same class?" Bennack said, his voice serious and probing.

"Yes," Grady said proudly.

Bennack stared at the photos, then focused on his daughter. "I think you're onto something big, Grady. Well done. With three in the same class, it can't be a mere coincidence. I think we have a serial killer out there."

The Centers for Disease Control and Prevention, headquartered in Atlanta, Georgia, is a federal agency under the Department of Health and Human Services. It employs 15,000 people whose mission is to save lives and protect people from health threats. A team of three CDC scientists arrived at Spielberg Memorial Hospital in South Hampton, Long Island on Tuesday, greeted by Dr. Kay Roberts and Chief Bennack.

Three files lay atop a conference table within the hospital's administrative section and a short, pert woman of substance in her mid-forties, Dr. Nancy Bowe, Phi Beta Kappa, looked up from one of the files. "From the samples you sent us, there's a strain of unidentified origin. We have no other matching strains except one. We're here to get answers."

Bennack and Roberts leaned in staring into Bowe's bright amber eyes, searching for an answer. "What's the match?" pressed Roberts.

"It's not a perfect match, but it's very troubling."

Bennack's words were laced with concern and hung in the air. "What are you trying to tell us?"

Dr Pedigrew shared, "That whom or whatever killed these joggers might be part human and part . . ."

"Part what," interrupted Bennack impatiently. "Jesus. Cut to the chase. Three joggers have been killed including my daughter."

"I'm sorry Chief. From the samples you sent us, we think we're dealing with Ambrose syndrome or something close to it, a very rare disease." Bowe said.

"What the hell's that?" Bennack queried.

"It's a form of hypertrichosis called werewolf syndrome," Bowe said as she pulled out a full color photo from her briefcase.

"You're kidding, right?" Bennack said staring at the photo shaking his head in disbelief. "What the hell is it?"

Roberts studied the photo. A mask of horror swept across her face as she examined the photo of something so covered in thick brown hair that she could barely see the eyes. Her voice was barely audible. "You're implying a werewolf is behind the jogger killings?"

"Impossible," Bennack said.

Pedigrew stepped back pulling out a document and said, "That's why we flew up here. We've reviewed cases like this before, but never one involving murder. It sounds preposterous, I know. But the DNA proves there are threads of the syndrome in the blood samples tying it to the werewolf syndrome. There're only nineteen humans alive today with it and one in 340 million ever get it. The gene controlling hair growth is missing and thick hair grows all over the body, hands, face, feet, everywhere."

Dr. Roberts stood rigid, shaking her head. Bennack blurted out, "Mother of God. Why would it kill joggers or anybody for that matter?"

Dr. Bowe leaned over the table peering over her bifocals and said, "The problem is very complex and it's only a hypothesis at this point. The few who have developed the syndrome in the past, late 1800s to early 1900s, joined circuses to support themselves as freaks of nature. Some of those inflicted with the syndrome develop Lycanthropy, a psychotic schizophrenic disorder. If your killer has this disorder, he may be dealing with hallucinations, delusions, hearing voices, and possibly seeing things."

"Schizophrenia?" Offered Dr. Roberts. "Multiple personalities? So, it could think it's a dog? An alpha male?"

Pedigrew said, "No. Not exactly. If it has multiple personalities, it's not schizophrenia. It's what we call DID, Dissociative Identity Disorder. Patients with this disorder have multiple identities, each with its own voice."

"It's a trauma-based illness," said Bowe, "normally occurring before the age of five."

"So, what do you think we're dealing with here?" pressed Bennack.

"At this point, we don't know," Bowe said. "From the blood samples Dr. Roberts sent us, we're certain our killer has Ambrose syndrome that's morphed into some form of Lycanthropy. So, if our hypothesis is correct, the killer thinks it's part dog and part wolf. It attaches itself by bonding with a pack of wild dogs. It becomes the alpha male of the pack directing its lethal hunting and stalking instincts to prey on humans in motion—like Joggers."

Still shaking her head in disbelief, Roberts said, "This is utterly insane. How could it train other dogs to attack humans?"

Bennack didn't hesitate. "Wild dogs hunt in packs and there's always an alpha male leading the pack. I'm guessing these were all once domestic dogs, turned loose by their owners who wanted to get rid of them at the end of the summer without having them euthanized. So, there's no guilt. Once out in the wild, they scavenge and over time they're forced to lose all domestic training and revert to do what the first wild dog was born to do instinctively which is to hunt, kill, and eat its prey."

Pedigrew nodded in agreement. "Attracted by the instinct to pursue anything in motion, our psychotic schizophrenic killer goes on a terrorizing killing spree. Remember, with hypertrichosis that has developed into lycanthropy, our alpha male thinks it's a dog or wolf with all of the attributes that go with the animal— smell, taste, and attraction to anything in motion."

Bennack took out his iPhone and Googled 'How many joggers in the United States?' The response was "Fifty-nine million people jog in the U.S."

Roberts said, "Jesus. That's a hell of a lot of moving targets."

"There are 74,400,000 swimmers in the United States and that's a hell of a lot of targets for sharks."

"I would guess there are thousands more dogs on land than sharks in the water," Bowe said with furrowed brow.

"A *Jaws* on land," Roberts said emphatically. "While not as big as shark jaws, dog jaws are equally dangerous as the statistics confirm."

Bennack arose from his chair and walked slowly around the conference table in thought. When he approached the end of the table, he looked at the assembled group and said, "What concerns me is that my son just informed me that the three jogger victims all went to the same high school and were within a year of the same age. If that's true, then we're not just dealing with mindless, wild dog attacks, but purposeful serial murderer that appears to be well-planned and executed."

The four people sitting at the table stared back at Bennack, processing what they had just heard. Pedigrew was the first to speak. "If that's true, Chief, we better damned well get a list of everybody in that high school class."

"What the hell could be the motive?" Bowe asked.

"I have no idea," said Bennack, "but I'm going to find out who murdered my daughter. It has killed three people from the same class, so it knows what it's doing—and why."

"Not if it's dealing with Dissociative Identity Disorder that's morphed into Lycanthropy," said Bowe.

"How many personalities could it have?" asked Bennack.

Pedigrew said, "In the cases CDC has studied, normally between two or three to fifteen, but we had one D.I.D. case with over 100 personalities."

Dr. Roberts' voice was unmistakably filled with concern. "How could that be possible?"

Silence filled the room. Bennack and Roberts stood rigid, staring at each other in disbelief.

CHAPTER 20

GRADY BENNACK WAS flipping the pages of his sister's high school yearbook, back and forth frantically studying the faces of her graduating class while his girlfriend, Julie Harned, read the inscription messages signed by Judy Bennack's classmates. Grady had encircled all three Freeport High School graduates who were killed while jogging over the past two months.

"There are 2,186 students, grades nine through twelve, enrolled in Freeport High," said Harned. "How are we going to identify the killer, who might not even have been a student?"

"Does it say how many graduated in Judy's class?" Grady probed.

She flipped to the front of the high school yearbook. "Yes," Julie said. "Four hundred and two, the book says. Let me Google current statistics." She looked up and said, "In the graduating class, six percent White, nine percent Asian, thirty-two percent Black, and fifty-three percent Hispanic."

"There has to be a clue," Grady said. "Something enabling us to zero in on why someone would kill three graduates. What's the motive?" Grady looked up from his laptop in perplexed thought.

He studied the figures that he had just typed into his computer then looked at Harned, eyes wide.

"Julie," his voice high pitched. "All three joggers killed were white. Look at the percentages of graduates. Only six percent are currently white so if we apply the same percentages to Judy's class, there were only twenty-four in her graduating class who were white. That leaves twenty-one white graduates left in the class who should be still alive."

"Scary, Grady. So, you think the jogger killings might be hate crimes? Some Black or Hispanic murdering the White graduates in their class out of prejudice? If that's the motive, we've got twenty-one white people out there in danger."

"A serial killer for sure," Grady said as he circled all the White graduates remaining in his sister's yearbook.

Harned said, "Is there any alphabetical order to the killings or something they have in common?"

Grady studied the profiles of the three joggers killed including his sister.

"No. They appear to be random."

"Okay, if race is the motive, Grady, what do you think triggered the killings? Hate? Revenge? Or something else?"

"I don't know, Julie. My sister was very popular. A good student. I was ten years younger than she was, so not too close. I didn't know too much about her school activities or her friends."

"What do we know about Freeport High School?" Harned said.

Grady Googled the query and said, "Mascot is the Red Devil, the high school colors are red and black, eighty-seven percent of the graduates go on to higher education, the school borders the Long Island town of Baldwin and the school sits beside the Milburn Duck Pond. The high school newspaper is called, *The*

Flashings, founded in 1920 and is the oldest school paper on Long Island."

"I don't like the name of the school mascot, '*Red Devil*'. Three white graduates killed with twenty-one still alive. We've got to somehow warn them, Grady," Harned pressed, "but how?"

"The principal at Freeport High School has to have the alumni addresses, right?"

"I would think so," Harned said. "Did Judy keep in touch with anyone of her high school classmates after graduating?"

Grady hesitated in thought. "Yes. Eileen Langley was one. And Frank something. Can't remember his last name. I know she kept in touch with both of them. Saw each of them sometime over the past three years. Eileen came out to the house over one weekend to spend a couple of days on the beach. I can't remember if Judy saw Frank, but I know she saw Eileen because I met her."

"Can you find her phone number?" Julie said urgently.

Grady sprang off the couch and ran into his sister's room. Julie heard him rustling through papers and opening drawers. Grady returned holding a small book. "I think this is Judy's address book," he said. He flipped through it and said, "Eileen Langley. Her phone number's here." His heart raced and he looked up at Julie and said, "We've got a lead."

Julie said, "How about the Frank guy? Is he listed?"

Grady flipped urgently through the small address book then stopped, looked up, his eyes wide. "No Frank."
Call her," Julie pressed.

Grady picked up his cell phone, his hands trembling, and dialed the number.

Andrea Bennack stared out the kitchen window in troubled thought as her husband shuffled through files in his office trying to make sense of the jogger killings searching for a plausible motive. Andrea allowed herself to reflect on her marriage and the faithfulness she had mustered without incident until yesterday when she let Dave Prtichard kiss her on the mouth. She had never before been moved to kiss any man once married. The question that kept hammering at her mind was, why did she let him do it. Was she happy in her marriage? Yes. Was her husband a good father? Yes. Was he loyal? Yes, as far as she knew. Was he fun to be with? Yes. But the key question for justification of her actions seemed to be over her life in general which she knew might be the reason. It was boredom. Her life was just not exciting anymore, especially since her daughter's tragic death. So maybe that one kiss, and almost another, was the great prompter of her actions and she reasoned with some justification that this one incident might be almost justifiable. Now she was dealing with the slow trickle of guilt as to why she even allowed herself to go to his home alone.

A voice from behind her broke the thought and she jumped, "Are you okay?" Bennack asked.

"Yes," she said. "You startled me."

"You seemed in deep thought? Everything okay?"

Andrea looked into his eyes and moved toward him embracing him warmly and kissed him on the lips. "I love you, Tom Bennack."

Bennak returned the kiss and then said, "Whew. That was nice . . . and unexpected. Where did that come from? You haven't kissed me like that in a long time. You sure you're okay?"

"Does there have to be a reason? Yes, in fact, I'm more than okay. We've been through a lot lately and I've missed you." She was fumbling for the right words to say but nothing came forth except the thought that her husband was a good man, an honest man, and despite his upbringing, unlike hers, he was filled with well-meaning and his recent passion for finding the killer of their daughter filled her with a renewed fondness for the man she had married.

Bennack stepped back and held her shoulders, somewhat perplexed. "I've missed you too," he said. "You have something you want to tell me?"

Andrea's heart skipped a beat and she stared into his eyes trying to search for why he would question her. Did he know about her clandestine meeting with Pritchard, she thought. How could he know, her mind raced. Her face wrinkled into a query of confusion. "No. Why would you say that, Tom?"

"Only because you haven't kissed me like that for a long time."

Andrea blushed in thought. She approached him again only this time slowly. Both hands enveloped his face, and she gently kissed him again holding the embrace. She pulled back slowly and said, "I love you."

Bennack took in a deep breath and said, "I love you too, Andrea. That was nice."

"Too long," she purred. "It's time we started living life again, Tom."

"Agreed," he said. "Nice to be back."

"Yes," she said. "Together," and her mind drifted off into an unbidden thought. Maybe, she allowed herself, that kiss with Pritchard would have a positive effect on their marriage. Andrea stared into her husband's eyes with peace and renewed hope that everything would be okay. For now, she was enormously relieved that it was nothing more than a kiss. As for Pritchard and their future, she promised herself that she was done with him and that it was only an isolated accidental encounter. Still, the thought that she came so close to allowing herself to have unbidden thoughts of sex with Pritchard left a cold unsettled chill on her mind.

Grady and his girlfriend walked into the kitchen. He said, "Julie and I have some very important facts we've uncovered. Can we talk with you in the den?"

"Sure, son."

They walked into the den and sat down, Grady clutching his sister's Freeport High School yearbook. Grady opened up the yearbook and told his father what he and Julie had discovered. Grady's voice was excited yet filled with questions. Julie expressed fear that everybody could be at risk jogging as she reported the statistics she and Grady had found.

"We think it could be a hate crime, Dad. Somebody's killing White graduates in Judy's class," Grady said.

Bennack looked at the yearbook and said, "This is a very serious crime. We've got people on it now. We'll find out soon who it is. In the meantime, you two both have done good investigative work and it sounds like you're on track to resolving the crime. But no more, Grady . . . and Julie. I'm proud of you both. Well done, but it's time to let go. I'll handle it as I should. As I said, this is a very serious crime. The police and FBI will be all over it."

"But Dad, Julie and I have some good leads."

"What kind of leads."

"I just spoke to one of Judy's class mates, Eileen Langley."

"I remember her. Good friend of Judy's. What did she say?"

"Of course, she was at Judy's funeral so when I told her about the other two people in her class who were killed, she was shocked."

"Did she have any thoughts about anybody unusual in her class?"

"She said it was a very diversified class. Blacks, Whites, and a lot of Hispanic students. Some were rough kids. She called them hoods. Lots of swearing, pushing, intimidating, and a few knife fights. Some of the kids, she remembered, were called to the principal's office and given detention."

"Did she remember anybody strange, or had ever threaten her?" Bennack said.

"I asked her that and she couldn't remember anybody who threatened her. But she did say there were several strange or different students in the class."

"How different?" Bennack said. "In looks or personality?"

"She didn't say. Just that they were different.»

Bennack said, "You guys did great. Now let the police handle the rest. You've both given me good information to follow up on and I'm confident we'll find the killer soon enough."

Bennack stood up and left the room. Grady looked at Harned, his face lit up with enthusiasm. He said, "You and I are going to find the killer, Julie, before the police do."

"I think we should listen to your father. There's a serious killer out there and God forbid we should ever get close to whoever it is," said Harned. "Our lives would be at stake, Grady. I admit the thought of it is exciting, but I'd be scared stiff if we ever found the killer."

Grady smiled affectionately. "I'll protect you, Julie. Don't worry." He leaned over and kissed her on the lips, impressed by her attention to detail and her inquisitive mind. Yes, she was very cute, Grady thought, and that was the initial attraction to her, but now this research project that both of them were steeped in had brought them closer together. Grady had developed more positive thoughts about her total being rather than just an initial physical attraction.

CHAPTER 21

THREE PATROL CARS rounded Duck Pond Road and pulled up to Freeport High School, Chief Bennack in the lead car. Three officers disappeared through the front door and entered Chevon Williams' office. The sign on the glass door read, *Principal's Office*.

Pleasantries were exchanged and Williams motioned the three officers to have a seat encircling a large intimidating walnut executive desk. The wall behind Williams flanking either side of a large palladium window showed portraits of previous Freeport High School principals. The flanking wall had a portrait of President Barack Hussein Obama. On the principal's desk was a sign that read, 'BLACK LIVES MATTER & ALL LIVES MATTER." Bennack eyed Williams with careful inspection. He was a large Black man with huge intense dark brown eyes, kinky hair sweeping back somewhat unruly, sporting a grey shark skin three peace suit, and a day glow red and black bow tie with small images of some sort of imprint, too small for Bennack to see.

"Nice bow tie, Mr. Williams. What are the images on it?"

Williams studied Bennack as well, observing that of the three officers, he was slightly more disheveled compared to the other two. In a deep, gravelly voice, Williams said, "Thanks for noticing. Red and black are the school colors and the image is the red devil, our school mascot."

"Must scare the hell out of those unfortunate students who enter your office," Bennack said leaning toward Williams on the other side of the desk with his elbows on the edge . "The devil, I mean."

"Your opinion," growled Williams, not flinching. "Now why are you here? I have a busy schedule today."

Unflappable, Bennack said, "I'm sure you do. We have a problem, Mr. Williams."

Williams stared across the desk, his huge eyes glowing ominously without blink. "Problem?"

Bennack studied Chevon Williams' hands resting on his desk. They were thick and muscular, each the size of an outfielder mitt. He snapped the thought and said, "Are you aware that three of your Freeport High School graduates, all from the same class, have been murdered? One of them was my daughter."

Williams didn't flinch as if this was a normal occurrence, nor did he offer condolences to Bennack for his daughter's loss. It was obvious Williams didn't like cops. He'd had his fill of impromptu cop calls many times before breaking up school fights between races involving unruly unloved kids. The school was replete with diversity, Hispanics outweighing Blacks in numbers, with Whites the true minority. "No, I'm not aware. Who and what class?"

"The three killed were twenty-seven years old, one twenty-eight, all in the same graduating class ten years ago." Bennack opened up the Freeport High School yearbook he had tucked under his left arm showing three circled photos of the graduates killed. He shoved the book across the desk into Williams' outfielder gloved hands. "Note the three killed were all white."

"Implying what?" Williams snarled.

"It's obvious what he's implying," said Officer Jorge Gonzalez, sitting next to Bennack.

"It's a hate crime," said Officer Ebony Jackson, an attractive tall Black Woman of lean and mean stature sitting to the right of Gonzalez. Chevon Williams flinched at the profile of her body when the three officers entered his office. "Somebody's out to kill your white graduates from ten years ago and we need your help."

Williams' brown eyes darted briefly across Jackson's chest enough to see the press of her large breasts pressing against her uniform blouse. He hoped she didn't notice as he studied the three photos. She did.

"We need to urgently connect with everybody in that class and any teacher or staffer who might provide us with a lead," Bennack said. "How many years have you been Principal?"

"Why?" Williams said defensively.

Jackson looked Williams in the eyes, and he shifted in his seat. "Don't get defensive, Chevon. We're here trying to solve a murder case involving your high school graduates. Answer the question." Jackson sat bolt upright in her seat and Chevon registered she was pissed.

"Ten years ago . . . so this happened before my time," Williams said uncomfortably realizing that this could be very bad press for his school. He opened a desk drawer and extracted a file. Flipping through some pages in a folder, he looked up and said, "Juan Ortega was the principal before me during that time. Unfortunately, he's dead. Heart attack. Died at this desk."

Bennack followed with, "So we need the addresses, phone numbers and emails for all the alumni students in this book. How do we get them?"

Williams picked up his phone and dialed a number. "Marshawn. Chevon here. We have an urgent request. Need all the names, phone numbers, emails of all our alumni graduates from the class of 2011. You got 'em?"

"Shouldn't be a problem," Marshawn said. "I'll email the file to you."

"Thanks."

"Who was the principal for that class?" Bennack said.

"I told you. Juan Ortega. He's dead. Heart attack," Chevon said.

"So, who's still here that might remember the class? We need specifics. Need to know the profiles for each student. Names of the teachers, guidance counselors, school nurse, and anybody else who can help us. I want to meet with them now, all together, so I don't have to repeat myself."

"That was ten years ago, Officer." said Chevon. "Out of a class of 400 high school graduates you really think you can find the killer? Could be anybody in the school, or outside the school who didn't like . . ."

Bennack interrupted Chevon mid-sentence, "White people."

"Maybe, maybe not."

The principal made calls summoning selective faculty staff to his office. Within ten minutes, a diversity of seven people stood in the office: three Black, two Hispanic, an Asian and one White.

Chevon Williams turned to Bennack and said, "You've got the floor, Officer."

Bennack stepped out of the circle and faced the assembled faculty.

"I'll try to be brief. First, thanks for being here on short notice. We have three murder cases on our hands involving three of your high school graduates from the class of 2011. They were all White, leading us to believe that it might be a hate crime. Two men and one woman, my daughter."

There was an audible gasp from the group.

"All three were jogging when they were attacked by a pack of dogs," Bennack continued.

A woman from the assembled faculty said, "You just said dogs killed the joggers, yet you said they were murdered. So, you think that because all three killings were students from our high school that someone murdered them?"

"Yes, and here's why," Bennack said. "We've had the CDC examine blood stains from one of the killing scenes and what they found was very concerning. Enough so that three CDC specialist flew up here yesterday to explore the murders. They're saying that the blood stains examined confirmed that the person who committed these crimes has Ambrose which is a form of Lycanthropy. Cutting to the chase, the killer thinks it's a werewolf and is using dogs to carry out murder."

Someone said, "Jesus."

"What is Ambrose ?" Said a Black man with a thick black trimmed beard.

Bennack opened up his file and extracted a full color photo of a man who was covered in thick brown hair covering his entire body. "We don't know if it's a man or a woman, but we're looking for one of your students who had this syndrome. CDC also thinks this person might have multiple personalities and so they think it thinks it's a wolf and has bonded with a pack of wild dogs.

"You can't make this shit up," said an Hispanic teacher standing to the right of Bennack. "What do you think the motive is for killing three of our students?"

"We don't know yet," officer Jackson said. "We're hoping one of you might remember a student who might have had this syndrome."

The face of a woman in her mid-fifties twisted into a knot of concern, mouth open, eyes wide as if she had just seen a ghost. Chevon Williams saw her face and said, "Maria?"

Maria Morales was the school nurse and had been with Freeport High School for twenty-nine years. "There was a boy, I think he was in the ninth grade when he came to the school. His parents brought him to the school and spent a lot of time with Juan Ortega, the Principal back then. They met with the counselor and then with me telling us about their special needs child. When I first met him with his parents, I was shocked. I didn't think he was human. He looked like a wolf. They told us their son had this rare genetic syndrome, hair covering his entire body, and that there was nothing he could do to shave it off because it would immediately grow back. Anyway, they were very concerned about our students making fun of him and asked for our help to try and educate them about the disorder."

Bennack said, "Did he ever display any aggression toward the other students?"

"No, not that I'm aware of," Morales said. "He was a very docile child. Shy and withdrawn. But it was tragic. The first day he came to school, immediately the kids started teasing him, laughing at him, calling him names. They called him Chewbacca, that Star Wars character, on his first day. We tried to educate the students about the disease, but it was no use. Some of the kids were ruthless. Bullying him, pushing him, laughing, and pointing at him. One of the kids actually brought a dog leash to school and tried to collar him. Another brought dog biscuits and threw them at him. He spent a lot of time in my office sobbing about how mean the students were. It tore at my heart. He was such a bright and gifted child. His test scores were well above average. We tried everything, but it didn't work. So, we finally agreed to set up a special class for him. Didn't cost his parents anything. We have to take affirmative action under The Individuals With Disabilities Act, IDEA, Section 503, to educate students with special needs. But the moment he got out of his special classes, the kids would start all over again with name calling and bullying."

Chevon Williams looked around the room shaking his head. "Sad commentary on our human race." Williams looked at the faces assembled in his office and said, "Sound familiar? How many times have we all been called names? Nigger, Spic, Gringo, Wop, Chink, Jap, or Cop. Seems everybody needs a punching bag to make themselves feel more important than the next kid."

Bennack said, "We need to find the killer ASAP before it kills its next victim." He looked at Maria Morales. "Do you remember the boy's name?"

"No. Had to be at least ten to fifteen years ago," Morales said. "But I can check our records and find out."

"Please," Bennack said. "The description you gave matches the profile given to us by CDC."

"Dear God," nurse Morales said. "How awful."

"I need that name now," pressed Bennack. Morales left the office.

An Hispanic teacher said, "If it's the same boy Maria described, I feel for the kid. What they do to each other today is tragic. Social media's the killer today. Cyber bullying is up dramatically, and a number of young victims have committed suicide because of it. We lost two of our kids last year, a boy and a girl."

"It's the sad truth," said another teacher.

Bennack snapped everybody back to reality. "There's nothing sad about this if it's the same bastard that killed my daughter. It's called murder and we'll find the son of a bitch."

Nurse Morales entered the office holding a file.

Bennack stared at her and nodded. "You have a name?"

"Yes."

"What is it?" Bennack pressed.

"Hector Anguilera," Morales said. "Hispanic family."

"What's the address?" Said Officer Jackson. "And what does the file say about the family?"

Morales flipped pages in the file then looked at Bennack. "There's a problem. The family moved in 2009."

"Where?" Bennack said impatiently.

"No record."

"Did Hector ever graduate?" Jackson probed.

Principal Williams flipped open the 2011 yearbook scanning for the name Aguilera. He looked up and said, "Nothing."

Nurse Morales was deep into studying the file. She hesitated, studying a note in the file. "There's a note in the file saying the family changed the boy's name to protect his identity. There's another problem. The boy had a twin brother, Mauricio. I vaguely remember he had a brother, but he didn't have this syndrome. We focused on Hector, but I remember his brother being very upset about others teasing him."

"Why the hell would they change his name? Willams queried. "If the guy's covered in hair head to toe, changing his name wouldn't change his identity, especially to his classmates."

"Unless they changed that too," Jackson said, a tinge of dread in her voice.

Nurse Morales asked, "What do you mean?"

Williams stepped out from behind his desk holding the yearbook. "If Hector Aguilera changed his name and his appearance, who would know if it was the same kid. The only people that would know would be his parents and his twin brother." Williams held up the book and said, "His picture might be in this yearbook as a graduate."

"If that's the case, all we have to do is check the enrollment of new kids entering the school after 2009 when the family moved," said Bennack.

"Easy to do," said Williams picking up the office phone. He spoke quietly to Marshawn ordering a list of all new enlisted students for the three year period, 2009 through 2011.

Bennack said to the two officers, "We need to check out the Aguilera home before they moved. Find out where they moved."

"On it," said Jackson.

The office phone chirped and Williams picked it up. He listened intently, making notes then placed the phone back on the cradle. "We just got our answer. Fourteen new students came in during that period. Nine of them girls, five boys. Only one of the boys Hispanic and he was in eighth grade."

"They changed his name. And we're guessing they changed his appearance," Bennack offered. "What about the twin brother?"

"We don't know. Maybe they both took on non-Hispanic names," the nurse said.

"Or Hector changed his sex," Officer Jackson said. "Today it could be anything. Maybe he was one of those nine new girls who registered. Under the diversity of Lesbian, Gay, Bisexual, Transgender, Queer, Intersex and Asexual, the LGBTQIA acronym covers everybody. He was bullied and made fun of everyday of his school life, this might have been his only way out."

Bennack looked at Nurse Morales. "One more question. In your student health records, is it possible you might have a blood sample taken from Hector Aguilera when he was a student here?"

Nurse Morales' eyes widened. She hesitated, "Yes. We draw blood samples on all students in case of emergency."

Bennack pulled out his cell phone and punched in a number. He said, "Dr. Arch Pedigrew?"

"Who's that?" Said Officer Jackson.

"The doctor with CDC. He did the blood work on the last victim."

The silence in the office was palpable.

CHAPTER 22

THE PHONE CALL that Grady Bennack made to his sister's friend, Eileen Langley, lingered in his mind because something Langley had said filled him with worry. He decided not to share it with his father because it gave him an advantage on the case which he desperately wanted to solve without his father's help. Besides, he told himself, he and Harned were old enough to handle anything together without police involvement. Because they both could drive, Harned had a used Ford Mustang her father gave her when she turned sixteen so they had mobility.

This real-world experience of his investigation, Grady told himself, would enhance his college application and his career goal of being a detective. Just the thought of solving a murder case, especially this one added to his excitement. He had been researching colleges and Strayer University was at the top of his list because their curriculum offered an in-depth understanding of criminal behavior and its impact on society. In addition, it was conveniently located in Cherry Hill, New Jersey, not far from Long Island.

When Eileen Langley asked Grady why he was asking her so many questions, especially about someone in her class that she felt

stood out as different from the rest, he responded by telling her
that he was, 'Just gathering facts for my dad about the killing of
his sister and that it might be a murder case.' He lied, of course, as
any facts obtained were for his use only. In Grady's phone call to
Eileen Langley, he learned there was one student who all the other
students teased relentlessly. She remembered trying to protect
him from the other students and that he cried to her incessantly
about how mean the students were to him. She befriended him
and told Grady that he sat next to her in algebra class and that he
had hair covering his entire body and that he looked like a circus
freak to all the students except to her. Langley told Grady that he
was so desperate for friends that she was drawn to him half out of
compassion, the other due to curiosity about his uniqueness. She
also said that seeing the torture he was experiencing convinced her
ultimately to pursue a career in psychiatry. Her memory of him
was so vivid, she told Grady, that she still remembered his name as
Hector Anguilera, where he lived, and that he had a twin brother
whom she remembered as being very strange and defensive. She
told Grady that she felt horribly sad for Hector. Then, Langley
told him, upon his prodding, what happened next. One day he
and his brother just vanished. Hector wasn't in school for a week
and when she drove by his home, a moving truck was parked
in front. When Grady pressed her for her thoughts of where his
family might have moved, she said, "I don't know. But then out of
the blue I got an email from him asking her to meet him."

"When did this happen?"

"Maybe a year ago. Year and a half."

"Where did you meet him?"

"That was the troubling thing. It was about forty-five minutes
from here. Somewhere in Long Island's Central Pine Barrens. He
gave me a street address near East Quogue and told me he would

be at the end of the street but the street became a dirt road and I followed it until it dead ended.

Grady held the receiver tight to his ear. "Did you meet him."

"I had to use my GPS. I drove to the end of the road where he told me to meet him and I waited about a half-hour, but then something happened that scared the hell out of me and I drove away."

"What scared you?"

"I got out of the car and walked up to a stand of pine trees where he told me to meet him at the end of a cul-de-sac. The pine trees were thick."

"Can you give me the address?"

"Yes."

Grady heard her flipping through pages of something and then she read the address to him. It's barren alright, thick pine trees everywhere, but there were a few dirt paths leading into the barrens.

Grady was typing on his laptop as fast as his fingers could move. "What scared you?" he repeated.

"I was about a hundred yards from my car. I started to walk up a dirt path, an incline, in the field at the end of the cul-de-sac. A hill. At the top of the hill was a vast stand of pines. Very thick. Suddenly, I saw a pack of dogs coming toward me, fast, out of the trees from nowhere."

Grady said, "God. You didn't stay, did you?"

His probing question angered Langley. "Why the hell would I stay for God's sake. I thought if I stayed I wouldn't be talking to you now."

"Were they barking at you?"

"What kind of question is that, Grady," Langley snapped almost punching the call button off. "They were running at me.

I had no choice but to run down the path back to my car. Thank God I made it back to my car alive."

"Did you hear anybody yell at you?"

"No." She hesitated in thought.

"See anybody near the dogs?"

"No."

"When you got to the car, what did you see when you looked back?"

"Four dogs standing at the edge of the pine forest."

"And you didn't see anybody near them?"

"I said, No . . ." Langley thought for a brief moment then added, "But then when I started the car, I thought I heard somebody shout something."

Grady's heart was beating as fast as he was typing. "What did you say?"

"I said I thought I heard a voice."

"From where?"

"From the edge of the pine forest where the dogs were standing."

"And you said you didn't see any person in the area, near the dogs?"

"No."

"What do you think you heard?" Grady said, his voice hesitant.

"Maybe my name. I don't know."

Grady stared into the phone in silence afraid he couldn't ask the next question. He took in a long pull of air and sputtered, "You think it was Hector?"

"Maybe. I don't know. I looked everywhere and couldn't see him. I thought my heart would burst."

"Did you call out his name?"

"Yes."

"Did he answer?"

"No. Not that I heard. But maybe. I was so panicked that I . . ."

"What were the dogs doing?"

"Just standing at the edge of the pine forest staring at me. The thought of being alone and defenseless anywhere with dogs like that freaked me out."

"And that was it?"

"Yes. I drove away without looking back."

"Did you ever hear from him again?"

"No. I sent him an email telling him I tried to meet him where he told me he would be, and the experience of seeing those dogs scared me to death. But I never heard from him again."

"Do you still have his email address?"

There was a brief silence then she said, "Yes," and she relayed the email address to Grady.

"Thanks, Eileen."

"Please keep me posted. I miss your sister terribly."

"So do I," Grady said. Without check, his eyes filled with tears.

"I hope Hector's not responsible for any of those killings," Langley anguished.

"Why would you say that?" Grady said curiously. "What if he is?"

"Because he was such a sensitive person and so lonely. The pain and anguish he suffered was awful. I don't think he was capable of hurting anybody. Nobody wanted to be near him. They made fun of him constantly. The poor soul desperately wanted friends. I think I was his only friend."

Grady couldn't find words to respond. Silence filled the void forcing closure to the call and they rang off together.

Tom Bennack pulled away from Freeport High School with renewed purpose, but troubled about one comment the nurse made about Hector Anguilera. He had a twin brother, Mauricio Anguilera and that might complicate the search, Bennack thought. Was Hector the sole killer or was his brother Mauricio involved? Maybe both together, or possibly someone else. For now, he knew the next step was to locate the Anguilera family and he wondered if three officers on the case were enough. He thought about making a call to the FBI but decided to wait until they completed the search.

When Bennack returned to his South Hampton office, he sat down at his computer and punched in Anguilera's old address into his GPS locator and an image of the Anguilera home appeared. He studied the photo and then, on his police locator device, plugged in a tracer on the Anguilera move. Within two minutes, he had his answer. Bennack typed into his GPS locator 1036 Atlantic Street, Baldwin, New York 11510. Four beds, two baths, 1188 square feet purchased for $380,000 in 2012. He studied the home from atop the house then to a street drive-by view. There was a Chevrolet Sonic parked in the driveway. Bennack zoomed in on the car's license plate and read New York SNL4783, Empire State. He did a quick license plate search and Santiago Anguilera popped into the center of his screen.

He rose from his chair and said, "Bingo."

CHAPTER 23

A THICK FOG hugged the ground, shrouding bushes and spidering up trees across 840 acres of Central Park, New York City. The cool front swept in off the Atlantic Ocean at about four o'clock in the afternoon on Tuesday, July 17th.

Alejandro Garcia left his fifth-floor apartment on Central Park West between 68th and 69th street entering the Park just north of Tavern On the Green at 6:43 p.m. His daily walk normally lasted from forty to sixty minutes depending on the route and the weather. Garcia was one of three children whose parents moved to the United States from Cuba in 1981. He graduated from Hofstra College cum laude majoring in math with a minor in computer science. Through the college placement office he landed a job with Google working at their New York City facility in Chelsea on 8th Avenue and 16th Street. Seven weeks ago, he was promoted to Project Manager of Social Media.

Garcia had his first date seven months ago with Luciana Ortez who worked as a computer programmer in the same department. Her hair was prettier than her face, thought Garcia, but she was very social with brown hair curling down her back like a waterfall. The two spoke fluent Spanish to each other only when alone;

otherwise, English was their public communication. Garcia liked the fact that Luciana was born in Mexico because he had never been to the country. They had talked with excitement of possibly taking a trip to Tulum on the Caribbean coast of the Yucatan Peninsula.

Garcia admitted to a friend on his fourth margarita that he was more infatuated with Luciana's long flowing hair then with her acne cratered face caused by pigging out on White Stick suckers and Snickers bars as a teenager. At her worst, she weighed in at 247 pounds. But now at twenty-six, Luciana, religiously devoted to Weight Watchers, weighed a svelte 123 pounds and Garcia loved her personality and easy way with people. For Garcia, she was comfortable to be with and grounded with similar priorities in life.

About four months ago, Ortez mentioned marriage to Garcia and the word made him feel sick to his stomach. But last week a slow-moving warmth began capturing his mind about the possibility of spending the rest of his life with the woman. Luciana had a wonderful sense of humor and made light of herself easily making Garcia relax and feel good about himself. She had a quirky giggle that Garcia found funny even if the substance of their talks were not humorous. Yes, Garcia decided, Luciana Ortez was growing on him with a goose bump fondness. Maybe, he had concluded three days ago, he might even ask her to marry him when they travelled to Tulum.

The fog thickened and Garcia had trouble making out objects ahead of him as he walked briskly east along the path that cut through Sheep Meadow to get his heartbeat up to a monitored 120 BPM. Garcia had been a jogger four years ago but flogging the pavement and hard worn paths of Central Park had taken a toll on his flat feet and back. So, he decided swift walks at a fast clip would serve the same purpose of maintaining his health and strengthening his heart. Two joggers, both women, came toward him and the fog swirled around them as they passed. He approached the Literary Walk where Garcia had studied all the well-known author statues that stared down at him as he passed Sir Walter Scott, Robert Burns, and Shakespeare. He walked up to Balto and stopped to study the famous dog.

Garcia was passionate about the lore of the Central Park statues. Balto was his favorite because he saved so many lives. A Siberian husky and sled dog, born in 1919 and died March 14, 1933, Balto led the team on the final leg of the 1925 serum run to Nome, Alaska where the serum was desperately needed to fight an outbreak of diphtheria. Balto was named after the Samiu explorer Samuel Balto. The hero dog was transferred to the Cleveland Zoo until he died at the age of 14 in 1933. Garcia stared at Balto as his mind reviewed the dog's profile that he had read. His body was stuffed by a taxidermist and given to the Cleveland Museum of Natural History where it remains today. Now, face to face, Garcia stared at the bronze statue sculptured by Frederick Roth and erected on December 17, 1925. Garcia discovered in his research that Balto became the hero because he led the sled dog pack for the final fifty-five miles of a 260-mile run from Anchorage to Nome.

As Garcia finished ruminating about Balto's fame he remembered reading about Conan, named after the comedian Conan O'Brien, the male Belgian Malinois military attack dog who chased the ISS terrorist leader, AbuBakr al-Baghdadadi, to his death, in a dead-end tunnel compound in Seria.

The fog surrounded him, and his face felt moist. What had started as a thinly vailed mist was now a thick moisture laden fog with minimal visibility. Daylight diffused into dusk within minutes. When Garcia turned left, away from Balto now facing east, it happened. He thought he heard something. Whatever it was, he heard breathing and he thought he saw a swiftly moving object. His pace quickened into a slow jog, and he cut sharply to his right. He pressed forward cutting through Dene Slope heading to what he thought was the Tisch Children Zoo, but the fog was so thick he wasn't sure. He looked over his right shoulder to make sure nothing was following him. Another jogger, a young woman, was coming toward him and he felt a modicum of relief. The jogger passed him. He felt the pain in his back building and his flat feet throb with each stride, so he slowed down to a fast walk—his routine.

As he approached the children's zoo, he noticed that there was still construction in the pathway, so he cut around a fence and wound his way around the detour. Then saw the small tunnel leading into the Central Park Zoo. Twenty yards to the tunnel, he heard it again only this time it was louder, closer. It was breathing, or was it panting? What startled him was that it seemed to be coming from all directions. To his right, now from his left, then behind him. He guessed that whatever was out there was maybe thirty to fifty yards away from his position. He was wrong. The sound was moving, encircling him and now, for the first time, his heart skipped a beat and fear seized his being with a punch of dread. He sprang into a fast run, not aware of the pain in his back nor the shooting nerves plaguing his feet. He ran under the bridge, looked up at the Delacorte Clock and a flash of memory, as if to soothe his distressed mind, he reflected on the fact that the publishing magnate, George Delacorte, founder of Delacorte Press that became Dell Publishing, created the clock in 1965. As he passed beneath the spectacular structure, the giant bell had just clanged its seventh gong and the magical glockenspiel-style nursery music began to play in a fog-muted eerie sound as the animals began their circular motion around the arcade above him. As he coursed beneath the arch, he looked over his shoulder yet again and saw something that petrified him. Four dogs were chasing him, and the lead dog was now twenty yards away and gaining!

As he passed the Central Park Zoo on his right, he had but one choice. He vaulted over the fence and ran to the right around the seal aquarium then launched a sprint up the steps toward the polar bear cage, the fog swirling behind him. Fifteen yards behind him, now ten, the pack was closing. He had already developed an escape plan. But could he make it in time? The zoo lights shown a dim glow through the fog and Garcia focused on his last-ditch effort to reach his targeted escape. It was a large, enclosed cage containing what once held Patty Cake, a female western lowland gorilla born in captivity at the Central Park Zoo in 1972. Patty Cake's parents were Lulu and Kongo. In 1982, Patty Cake was put into the Bronx Zoo but had spent half her life at the Central Park Zoo. In 2009, a 526-pound Lowland gorilla named Tito filled the cage with its six foot two inch massive height.

As Garcia approached the cage, the fog thickened air was filled with the raging sound of a pack of dogs on the hunt with one purpose in mind. If he could just make it to the cage, he could be safe. If . . . He lunged into a desperate leap against the iron bars of Tito's cage and grabbed for his life, desperately crabbing his body upward.

The first dog threw itself onto the cage with a high snarling leap and grasped Garcia's left foot. He screamed in agony trying to kick the attacking dog off him. It worked and he pulled himself higher, still higher out of the range of four wildly leaping dogs. Then something happened and Garcia almost let go out of sheer terror. Something had climbed higher than the dogs and had a firm clasp on his right ankle. Garcia held onto the bars with renewed strength, and he screamed a blood curdling, throated shout to whatever was now hanging onto his ankle. He looked down and through a fog swirling miasma, Garcia thought he saw a dark, human figure. It was enough of an adrenalin shock to enable him to haul his body up and over the cage causing whatever had grabbed Garcia to let go and fall to the ground. Now centered atop the cage, Garcia laid motionless arms outstretched, legs splayed seemingly without life. His chest rose and fell with the deep thumping of his heart. In that very moment, he thought he might die . Below him, just outside the cage, he heard the breathing. He listened to the snarls of vicious dogs and realized something far worse than the dogs was attacking him. Something that defied description—waiting for him.

Below Garcia, Tito, sitting on a large tree stump, looked up with a deeply curious dark eyed stare. A human being was atop his cage. He stood up and moved slowly on all fours until he was directly below the intruder. Garcia lay rigid, listening. He could hear his heart thumping in his chest. But the sounds below him were commanding. The heavy breathing he now knew was panting. He heard something else. A low gurgling snarl as if half-human. Some kind of communication or command, he thought. As he lay atop the cage, he tried to distract his thinking. He thought of Luciana Ortez, her long waterfall flowing brown hair, her quirky giggle, and her soothing personality all helping him forget about her acned face which heavy blotches of rouge hid without blemish. His quick daydream was suddenly jarred to reality when the cage shook with a sudden vibration. The panting suddenly stopped. Had they gone? Garcia sat up atop the cage trying desperately to see in the dark. Nothing but blind fog laden blackness. But not hearing any sound bothered him even more. What was happening? Maybe they vanished into the fog. The stillness of the silence was deafening. And then it happened.

Something grabbed Garcia's left wrist through the cage bars with such strength and force that he thought it might be that unknown beast he had seen moments ago had gotten into the cage. With wide eyed hysteria, Garcia realized that Tito, the massive lowland Gorilla, had climbed up the side of the cage and stealthily worked his way across the caged roof directly beneath Garcia. Now, all 526 pounds of this massive primate hung from Garcia's left arm as if it were some jungle vine he had discovered. Back and forth, yanking, pulling as if it were some kind of game. Garcia let forth a blood curdling scream of terror and pain. Suddenly, Tito fell to the ground landing erect. He looked upward as a gush of Garcia's blood sprayed down upon the primate in a gaudy sanguine shower, its face curious with surprise as it discovered the left arm of Alejandro Garcia clutched in its massive hand.

Garcia lay on his back as his body drained blood from the severed brachial artery like a hose had been turned on full force sending a gaudy shower of blood upon the cage floor. Garcia's five liters of blood drained from his body in four minutes. His last thought before his heart ceased was the vacation that he and Luciana had planned to take to Tulum, Mexico.

CHAPTER 24

CHRISTOPHER NZINGA, THE Central Park Zoo keeper, arrived at Tito's cage eight minutes before seven o'clock in the morning to clean the cage and feed the massive Lowland gorilla, Tito. Nzinga got the job at the Zoo because he had trained under Jane Goodall, the British primatologist and anthropologist who Nzinga watched in amazement as she held and cuddled wild gorillas in Tanzania. But after two years of training, Nzinga went back to his native country in Huambo, Angola.

When he read a news item on the BBC website that the Central Park Zoo in New York City had just welcomed a male lowland Gorilla named Tito to the Zoo, Nzinga called the Zoo and spoke to the curator requesting a job working with the gorilla. When he gave the woman his training credentials with Lowland Gorillas in Tanzania and that he studied under Dr. Jane Goodall, the curator offered him the job pending an emailed copy of his curriculum vitae.

As Nzinga approached Tito's cage, he made his usual greeting sound which was a belch vocalization letting Tito know he was approaching the cage. The massive gorilla stood up and Nzinga's eyes became saucers of concern. Something was terribly wrong.

Nzinga stared at the ape. Clutched in Tito's right hand was a human arm that Tito was banging atop objects as if extending the ape's reach for items to grasp.

"Tito. Come here," Nzinga commanded. "Give me that." He looked at the massive circle of blood that had stained the caged floor then looked around the cage for anything that would explain the horror of the arm that Tito was now holding. The gorilla held the arm up to its face and Garcia's once live hand tickled the ape's chin hairs. Nzinga urgently looked up at the top of the cage and said in his native Bantu language, "Oh mango wangu," *(Oh my God)*.

Alejandro Garcia's lifeless body, legs splayed, one arm still clutching an iron ceiling bar, lay face down, a look of horror staring blindly down at Nzinga who was frantically dialing 911. Dazed in shock, Christopher Nzinga fell back from Tito's cage into a sitting position staring up the at the man's face, — eyes still open, mouth agape as if Garcia was desperately trying to let out one last gasp for help.

CHAPTER 25

O N PAGE FOUR of the *New York Times*, Wednesday, July 17, along with a photo of a gorilla and Alejandro Garcia, the headline in boldface type read:

GORILLA IN CENTRAL PARK ZOO KILLS MAN ATOP ITS CAGE

Zookeeper Christopher Nzinga made a gruesome discovery on his 7:00 AM, July 16th morning rounds at New York City's Central Park Zoo. When he looked into the gorilla's cage, Nzinga noticed with horror that the massive ape was holding in his hand a human arm.

When the zoo keeper looked around the cage, he discovered a body lying atop the lowland Gorilla's fifteen-foot high cage. The massive female ape, named Tito and weighing 526 pounds, was a gift to the zoo in 2009 by the Susan and Jerry Neumann Foundation.

The body of twenty-seven-year-old Alejandro Garcia apparently bled to death after Tito yanked his arm off at the shoulder from atop its cage.

How or why Alejandro got atop the massive ape's cage is a mystery. The New York City Police Department speculates that

Alejandro was out for an evening stroll or jog through Central Park and was either chased by somebody or something that forced him to climb up the gorilla's cage.

An autopsy is being performed by Lenox Hill Hospital. Alejandro Garcia was the son of illegal Cuban immigrant parents, Rosita and Rolando Garcia, and became a U.S. Citizen after Congress passed a bill to grant US Citizenship to all children of illegal immigrants.

The article drew little attention from the readership except from Animal Rights groups who picketed the Central Park Zoo after a rumor was circulated suggesting that the gorilla was going to be euthanized for killing a human. The Zoo quickly extinguished the rumor sending out a press release confirming that Tito would be spared; however, the Zoo constructed a protective border fence with barbed wire to prevent intruders from climbing the cage.

When Bennack's patrol car pulled up to 1036 Atlantic Street, Baldwin, Long Island, the Chevrolet Sonic was still parked in the driveway, New York license plate SNL4783, Empire State. He got out of his car and approached the front door of the four bedroom colonial. He rang the doorbell twice and waited. Nothing. He rang thrice more. Still nothing so he turned and started to walk toward the left side of the house when the front door suddenly opened.

A short woman in a smock appeared at the door and said, "Yes?"

"Are you Camila Anguilera?"

"Yes."

"I'm officer Bennack and I'm looking for your son Hector."

The woman stepped back and started to close the door, but Bennack kept it open with his right foot. "Where is he," persisted Bennack.

"He's not here."

"Where is he?"

"I said he's not here. What do you want with him. He's done nothing wrong."

"I didn't say he's done anything wrong. I just want to ask him a few questions."

"Like what?"

Bennack was losing patience. He thrust a picture in front of the woman. "This is him, right?" It was a photo of the boy covered in hair, the face not recognizable.

"Yes."

"When was the last time you saw him?"

"A long time ago."

"How long."

"You tell me what you want to talk to him about and I'll tell you."

"Some people have been murdered and we think your son might know something about it."

The woman tried to shove the front door closed again, but Bennack blocked her effort with a left foot in the doorway and he shouldered the door open. "You resist anymore and I'll have a warrant. You don't want that."

"Two years, maybe two and a half."

"Where?"

"I don't know. He just vanished."

"He has a twin brother, yes?"

"Yes."

"Where is he?"

"Don't know either. They left together. Hector's whole life has been a tragedy. Kids have made fun of him and bullied him all his life because of his condition. My husband and I think he just gave up on life and checked out. Just to get away from here."

"We know all about it. Any idea where he might have gone?"

"No."

"Relatives nearby?"

"None close. All in Mexico."

"Did he have a car?"

"No." She lied.

"His twin brother . . . How close were they?"

"Close. Mauricio tried to protect him. He was bigger than Hector so he beat up on some of the bullies but there were too many of them. He was overwhelmed. Now please leave."

Bennack backed up and said, "Thank you, Mrs. Aguilera. I appreciate your time. Sorry to bother you."

The woman closed the door and quickstepped to the kitchen. She picked up her cell phone and texted an urgent message.

Bennack fell into the front seat of his patrol car and drove off not looking back. The pain across his shoulders reminded him of the anxiety building over not getting a solid lead on his daughter's killer. In a fit of frustration, he pounded the steering wheel with a tight fist and screamed, "shit!"

PART III
THE CONFRONTATION

CHAPTER 26

GRADY SAT MOTIONLESS at his bedroom desk staring at his laptop computer in search of unearthing more information on hypertrichosis, the werewolves syndrome. He typed in the information on Google and Ambrose flashed across his screen. He knew it was a rare disease and his notes confirmed that only one in 340 million got it and only nineteen in the world were known to have the syndrome today.

What troubled Grady the most was trying to determine what would cause a person with this genetic abnormality to kill people and why only joggers. He had secretly read through his father's file. Nothing indicated a motive for the killings except one driving possibility that suddenly raced through his mind. His sister's best friend, Eileen Langley, had mentioned that Hector Anguilera was a very sensitive person and was teased and tormented by his classmates. Grady punched into Google, *'How many recent jogger attacks have occurred in New York?'*

Grady punched *enter* and his computer screen lit up as it sorted through data faster than a nanosecond. The first item that popped up on his screen read . . .

Dog Bites. According to the Centers For Disease Control (CDC), approximately 4.5 million dog bites occur in the United States every year, and 900,000 of those bites become infected. The U.S. population was approximately 325.8 million people as of 2017. That means a dog bites one out of every seventy-two people. Twenty to thirty of these attacks result in death.

Grady looked up from the screen and he thought about his sister, Judy, and two others killed while jogging. But he told himself, the killings were not random. They were purposeful, all of them graduating from Freeport High School the same year. He accessed his notes labeled under ***Jogger Kills*** and typed, MOTIVE and numbered the possibilities:

1. Revenge. Getting even with those who made fun of him. 2. Jogger motion triggering dog attacks. 3. Discrimination. (All people were White.) 4. Hate crime. 5. Lycanthropy, a psychotic schizophrenic disorder. (Copied from Dad's notes). 6. Bonding with dogs because he thinks he's one of the pack, and unlike humans, they accept him.

Aware that he got sidetracked on his original query, Grady Googled yet again, *'Dog attacks in New York.'* Four items appeared on his computer screen. The first took place in Queens four days ago and described a postwoman delivering mail to a home. The woman reported that she was feeding the mail through the letter slot in the front door and that a dog was snarling on the other side of the door pulling the letters from her hand as she fed them thorough the slot when suddenly the owner opened the door and a large German Shepherd with flared teeth lunged at her as she ran toward the owner's car in the driveway. She told the reporter that she leaped onto the top of the car leaving her butt within range of the dog's leap that latched onto her ass causing fourteen stitches and rabies shots. Grady read two more dog attacks: a blonde lab ate the middle finger off a four-year-old boy who was teasing the animal with a dog biscuit, and a nineteen-year-old boy got mad at his pit bull and smacked it with a rolled newspaper. As he bent over to wack the dog, the pit bull jumped up at the boy's face lacerating the left side of his cheek and taking a chunk of his nose off.

The last item caught Grady's attention because there was no mention of dogs in the attack. It was a gorilla at Central Park Zoo that had killed a man found atop the ape's enclosure. Grady leaned in toward the screen and read with intense interest. How and why did the man get on top of the gorilla's enclosure, thought Grady. He read the victim's name and wrote it down on a post-it note—Alejandro Garcia. Grady remembered that the notes in his father's file indicated that dogs killing joggers could be a hate crime against White people since all three victims were White. But, thought Grady, this victim, Garcia, was Hispanic so no connection, Grady reasoned. Just to make sure, he checked his sister's high school yearbook. He flipped the pages to the graduating class and scanned the photos before him. His heart suddenly skipped a beat, and his breath came in one short spasm. Alejandro Garcia's photo appeared on the fifth page of the graduating class photos at Freeport High School. He looked at the photo appearing in the New York Times. Ten years older, but Alejandro Garcia was clearly the same man in the yearbook. Grady Bennack knew he had discovered something big that would put this case on the national map. Four people now killed by a serial killer who was murdering people in the same Freeport High School class. He now knew it was not a racial plot to only kill White people. Garcia was Hispanic so there had to be another reason other than race. But what? Grady's mind raced trying to find some logic to the killing pattern, but nothing made sense. Grady stood up, his hands shaking, his heart pounding in his chest. He had to tell his father immediately, but maybe not yet. He forced himself to pick up his cell phone and he dialed Julie Harned.

CHAPTER 27

J ulie answered the call on the third ring.

"Hi, Grady. Missing you. What's up?"

Grady skipped a quick hello and cut to the chase. "Another man has been killed, Julie."

"You are kidding, right?"

"No. A man was found dead on top of a gorilla enclosure in the Central Park Zoo.

The gorilla tore the man's arm off and he bled to death."

"Grady, are you sure? You can't make this stuff up. Anything about dogs attacking him?"

"No."

"Then it can't be related to the same killer," Julie said. "How do you know the killing was related to the other three joggers?"

"Because he graduated in the same class as my sister. Freeport High School."

"Call your father, Grady. This is scary. I'm done with it. There's a lunatic out there and I don't want to be involved. We'll both get killed."

"You are involved, Julie. With me. We're both involved."

"No, we're not. The police have to handle this, not us. Please call your dad now. Don't wait. The killer's striking every couple of weeks, Grady."

"Remember the notes in my dad's file about it possibly being a hate crime against Whites."

"Yes."

"The victim was Hispanic, so he's killing for another reason."

"For what?"

"I don't know yet."

"What do you mean, yet? Grady, call your father now. If you don't call him now, I will."

"Okay, okay, Julie. I'll call him."

Grady picked up the house phone, putting it on speaker and dialed his father. Bennack picked up on the second chirp and said, "Grady?"

"Yes. Dad . . . there's been a fourth murder."

There was a pregnant silence on Bennack's end of the call. Then, urgently, Bennack said, "Go ahead."

"You mentioned the killer was only killing White people."

"That's right."

"Two days ago, Central Park, a body was found on top of a gorilla enclosure at the Central Park Zoo. He was Hispanic, Dad. Not White."

"Why was he on top of the cage?"

"I don't know. I was Googling jogger killings in New York State, and an article popped up in the New York Times. His name was Alejandro Garcia. The article didn't say if he was walking in Central Park or jogging. Out of curiosity, I checked Judy's high school yearbook. Garcia graduated from Freeport High School, dad, same class as Judy and the other two."

Bennack said, "Dear God, Grady. Now I want you to listen to me carefully, son. We have a very dangerous serial killer on our hands, and I want you to stay the hell away from it. No more. You understand me, son? I've told you a number of times."

Listening to the call on speaker, Julie interrupted his response in mid-sentence. "Mr. Bennack. It's Julie. I've been trying to tell him to leave the case alone. I'm scared, Mr. Bennack. He won't listen to me. Please tell him to stop."

Grady got pissed and said, "I get it, Dad." But he lied. Determined resolve now spread across his face and he stared into the house phone with a glowering look at Julie shaking his head.

Bennack pounced on the moment with, "Grady, I'm calling the FBI to handle the case with me so you must let it go. Some of the Freeport High graduates now live out of state so it's going to involve the FBI. It's too dangerous and the FBI has to get involved. Someday, son, you'll make an excellent detective, but you can't pursue this case. It's lethal and beyond our ability to handle it alone. Nobody wants to find the killer more than I do and I know you feel the same way but with four dead, we have a vicious serial killer on our hands and the FBI will help us find the killer. You hear me, son?"

Grady stared at the telephone, not answering, his mind unplugged from his father's voice, not aware that his father had asked him yet again. It was Julie's third plea and she commanded, "Grady. Grady. Your father's talking to you and he's right. Leave the case alone."

Grady did not answer her, and his silence sent a jolt of fear through her body.

Bennack rested the phone on the cradle, his eyes wide as he realized the killer had struck again. He lifted the phone to his ear and dialed the FBI.

CHAPTER 28

U NDER THE U.S. Department of Justice, the Federal
Bureau of Investigation was established on July 26th, 1908.
As a federal law enforcement agency, the FBI employs
35,104 including special agents and support professionals and
operates fifty-six field offices in major cities throughout the United
States and San Juan, Puerto Rico. The Long Island FBI resident
agency is located at 135 Pinelawn Road in Melville, New York.

The FBI method of profiling is a system created to detect and
classify the major personality and behavioral characteristics of a
person based on the crime analysis. When Special Agent Greer
Hayes received the profile assignment of finding a serial killer who
could be a werewolf, Hayes shook his head in disbelief. As that
thought seeped into Greer's overactive mind, he wasn't even conscious of the fact that his right hand palmed his Glock 38 in his
shoulder holster as the thought of confronting a werewolf caused
his heart to skip a beat.

Agent Hayes had a sterling career with the FBI lasting through
James Comey, former FBI Director. Hayes was one of the Agency's
top field agents. He helped interview Judge Kavanaugh's witnesses
and issued the third of seven reports indicating no corroboration

against the accused. Now he was free to pursue his next assignment and his tenacious and purposeful work ethic confirmed to the FBI Agency that Greer Hughes was the right candidate for this assignment. It helped that Hughes knew the geography of Long Island thoroughly and operating out of the Pinelawn Road office in Melville Long Island was a convenient focal point from which to begin his mission. Hughes was particularly excited about this case because he knew if he was successful in finding the killer, it promised him a promotion. An FBI field office manager position was his next aspiration and ultimately, he had confided to his live-in significant other, Wendy Morrison, that his ultimate quest was to be FBI Director, the office held by his former boss, James Comey, who had been fired by President Trump.

Greer sat motionless in his Pinelawn office studying a stack of papers amassed in six separate folders, one on each of the four victims who had been mauled to death by dogs. The fifth file contained information on Hector Anguilera, the suspected serial killer, and a sixth CDC file that highlighted the Center for Disease Control findings on Anguilera's genetic profile. It was the CDC file that troubled Hughes. Their conclusion was that Anguilera's blood type matched that of a rare genetic disorder found in human beings that made them look like werewolves, with hair covering their entire bodies.

Greer looked up from the file and studied the black and white photos of each of the bodies of the victims who had been massacred. He placed the photos on the table in front of him. The photos confirmed how vicious each attack was, except for the last victim who had bled to death atop a gorilla enclosure at the Central Park Zoo. The victim's arm had been torn off by a gorilla and there was no apparent dog attack but, to Greer, something had obviously chased the fourth victim to scramble up atop the gorilla cage to escape. Hughes penciled into his FBI logbook, *'Premise:*

Since the victim was linked to the other three victims through the same high school class, we can assume that dogs were involved in the chase as they had been for three other victims.'

Greer placed a large map of Long Island and New York City on the wall in front of him and marked each attack with a large, circular, red sticker pinpointing the exact location. The agent studied each file, memorizing the details. Thoroughness was one of his many assets, tenacity coupled with a compulsive desire to crack each case. Greer's six-foot three-inch body sat rigid in his chair while he tried to establish a reason behind the killings. He penciled into his log a sketch profile summary of the killer. What was motivating the killer to murder people who had been in his high school class. Hatred? Jealousy? Envy? A woman was the first victim followed by a man so sex, Greer concluded, was not a motivating factor. Some emotional reaction or attachment to each victim by the killer was driving the person to get even for something that was done to them. The interviews conducted at Freeport High School by police Chief Bennack and two other officers confirmed that Hector Anguilera, because of his appearance and genetic disorder, had been tormented by his classmates. Greer highlighted in his notes *bullying, name calling, belittling,* and *tormenting* as possible reasons for the killer's revenge Greer wrote in caps, '*DOES THE KILLER HAVE A LIST OF VICTIMS? IF SO, IS THERE A COMMONALITY OF THE VICTIMS?*' Greer pushed his chair away from his desk and studied the map. He then flipped open the Freeport High School yearbook that he had obtained from the school principal. He had circled the victims, studied the yearbook comments of the four murdered victims and read each profile of all the graduates looking for some thread of evidence tying the victims together. Nothing popped out at him that was telling except a few sarcastic comments about each of the victims which seemed normal for teenage kids, Hughes thought. There had to be something else, Greer reasoned. Something was driving the killer to kill its victims purposefully. The biggest mystery to Greer was that the murderer was using dogs to attack and kill his victims. The FBI agent wrote, 'WHY', in his logbook. The CDC file, Greer believed, had the answer. If the killer was, as CDC concluded, psychotic and delusional, he would take on the personality of the animal he believed he was, and try to control the dogs.

Greer wrote, ALPHA MALE, in the log then added, CONTROLLING THE PACK OF DOGS TO ATTACK AND KILL. Was **JOGGING** the commonality with all victims. Hughes wrote in his log, or was it the dogs instinct to attack something running away, triggering the urge to chase down and kill?

Greer's heart skipped a beat and he coughed. 'This is spooky shit,' the agent said aloud. He looked up again at the map with the four red circles. From the distances between the red circles on the map, Greer concluded that the killer was driving its pack of attack dogs to the area of each killing so the killer had to be studying each victim's life habits to know where they lived, when they went outside and when they jogged or walked. But, Greer puzzled, the fourth victim was not a jogger so Greer noted that jogging might not be the obvious reason for each killing. The four victims obviously had done something to the killer in high school, Greer concluded, to snap the murderer's mind into stalking, tracking, and killing its victims. The FBI agent stood up and suddenly snapped his fingers. He knew what he had to do, and he had to act fast. This was a wildly insane one-of-a-kind case, Hughes concluded, and he promised himself he would be the one to crack it. Regardless of the consequences, Greer Hughes was determined to get that promotion.

Hughes was excited about the case, but something else laced his mind: fear of the unknown. He had never before dealt with a

case involving a psychotic killer. Somebody with multiple personalities gave Hughes a sense of foreboding that he had never before
dealt with and coming face to face with someone who thought
he was a werewolf seemed impossible to even comprehend so he
wrote in caps in his logbook, '*PROCEED CAUTIOUSLY*'.

CHAPTER 29

THE LONG ISLAND Pine Barrens is a large area of publicly protected pine forest in Long Island's Suffolk County covering more than 50,000 acres. The Trail office is located in Manorville, New York. It is Long Island's last remaining wilderness. Almost all of the Peconic and Carmans Rivers are in the Long Island watersheds within the Pine Barrens touching East Hampton and Southhampton.

It was Grady Bennack's idea, based on his discussion with his sister Judy's best friend, Eileen Langley, to explore the Pine Barrens with his drone rather than use his girlfriend's used Mustang to drive around the perimeter of the 50,000 acres. There were no roadways leading into the heart of the Barrens, only thick wooded paths. The question he asked Julie was where should they park to strategically capture the Barrens landscape with his drone, a GoPro Karma Quadcopter HERO6.

Grady had received the super drone as a Christmas gift from his sister Judy five months before she was killed. He was determined to use the drone to find his sister's killer. Revenge and payback, he had told Julie.

The sweet smell of her lavender lipstick distracted Grady when he kissed her hello at her front door. However, her mother was in the kitchen, so there was no room for more aggressive behavior. That would have to come later, he promised himself. Being a virgin at seventeen bothered him, but it was a secret he believed he kept well-hidden from his male friends who constantly bragged about their conquests. Grady was convinced most of them were lying including himself. Julie's promise ring that she wore on her ring finger was a constant reminder to him that she intended to remain a virgin until she married. She knew Grady's desires were strong. That made her more determined, than Grady knew, to remain a virgin.

Grady sat in the front seat of Julie's red Mustang studying a map of the Barrens. He had circled the place that Eileen Langley had driven to in hopes of meeting Hector. Langley had said she saw four dogs moving through the pine barrens and thought she heard a voice but was not sure. This to Grady was enough of a lead to begin a drone search at the sighting.

"I'm not leaving the car, Grady," Julie said. "You can run the drone from the car, can't you?"

"Maybe."

"Maybe?"

"Grady, your dad told you not to get involved in this murder case. The only reason I'm going this far is that you needed a car and I'm willing to be your driver, but only to get us to the pine barrens so you can fly this thing. But I'm not getting out of the car."

"Fine, Julie. I'm not asking you to do anything dangerous."

"That's not the point, Grady. I'm doing this because I love you and . . . ," she paused in mid-sentence, "for Judy. I miss her."

Julie kept her eyes on the road ahead which was now narrowing into a washboard dirt road, the Mustang skidding right to left forcing Julie to slow down. They passed a white sign with green print, '*PINE BARRENS AHEAD 1.3 MILES.*'

"Have you thought about what you would do if you actually confronted the killer?" Julie said not taking her eyes off the road.

"Not yet," Grady said hesitatingly.

Julie did not respond, but it was a purposeful query that she hoped Grady would rethink the situation.

The Mustang pulled up to a massive stand of pine trees and Julie pulled over on the right side of the dirt road stopping about thirty yards from the trees. She kept the car engine running and sat rigidly staring at the thick pine barrens ahead of her.

"Are you nervous?" Grady asked, looking at her with the drone on his lap.

"No," Harned said turning to face Grady. "I'm scared to death and that's why I'm leaving the car engine running."

"No need to be scared, Julie. We're safe here and I'm with you," Grady said but his voice betrayed him. His heart was racing. He tried to disguise how he really felt with a lower voice, but it squeaked on the last word.

"What are you smiling about. This is serious stuff we're doing, Julie."

"I'm smiling because I know you're scared shitless and won't admit it."

"Okay," Grady said guiltily. "Maybe a little."

"Thank you for admitting it," Julie said and leaned over and kissed Grady on the lips. When they broke the kiss she said, "Promise me something, Grady."

"What?"

"That if you get close to the killer you will not confront him."

"It could be female."

"Promise me you will call the cops and not engage."

Grady opened the door and stepped out clutching the drone in his left hand. He did not answer her question. Instead, he blew her a kiss and walked away from the car toward the pine barrens.

Greer Hughes put down his last file of photos of the murder victims and stood up studying the map of red circles marking the killings. Hughes had interviewed Hector Anguilera's mother and discovered the father had left the family when Hector was eight years old. The mother told Hughes that he could not take any more of the constant belittling and making fun of his son so on a Friday night in June, eight years ago, the man vanished. Greer noted in his log that the mother was very protective and shared little information with him. His notes about Hector and his brother Mauricio were very sketchy but the mother indicated they had always been very close and protective of each other.

So Special Agent Hughes wrote in his log book, '*Both brothers very close. One might be an accomplice to the other, or one could be acting on his own without the other brother's knowledge. Either way,*' Hughes noted, '*both brothers must be found.*'

Greer tapped into the woman's home phone and cell and put an FBI agent stake-out on her home to watch where the woman went when she left her home for a three-week period. When done, he checked it off his list.

He had studied the details of each killing and was now ready to execute his plan out in the field. He left his office and entered an unmarked black Ford sedan and the engine roared to life. Hughes adjusted his bullet proof vest, palmed his Glock, and pulled away from his FBI Melville office.

Grady Bennack approached the shroud of pine trees and stopped at the edge of the tree pack. He looked back at Julie's car and flashed a thumbs up.

He saw her staring at him through the windshield with a worried expression. He studied the distance between his location and the car. If something suddenly rushed out of the woods toward him, he thought he could make it back to the car safely, but he wasn't sure.

He knelt down and prepared for his first drone flight over the pine barrens, adjusting the camera lens, focus, and distance, then checking the drone control instrument panel. Something cracked in the forest. He looked up with a jerk, to the right, then left, now center. No movement. His heart skipped a beat. He looked back at Julie, then stood up with the drone control panel clutched tightly in his hands and pressed the flight lift button. Dust below the drone puffed out in an inverted mushroom and the drone lifted into the air holding its height at eye level with Grady. The camera stared at him, as if it were human, then rose higher and zoomed over to Julie's car leveling out five feet in front of the windshield. Grady could see the concerned look on Julie's face in the screen on his instrument panel as the drone hovered in place. Grady had mastered the art of drone flying and prided himself in his ability to zoom down on an object and hold the drone steady to get close-up views from a distance. He could hide behind trees, peak out for a quick photo op then fly back to cover. What made his flying machine unique was that the mother drone had a special compartment that held a miniature drone, the dragonfly, life size, about three inches long.

The drone suddenly rose vertically 300 feet above Julie's Mustang and vanished out of site. Only Grady knew where the drone was headed. He studied an aerial photo he had printed out from Google's GPS map. Now, he was flying over the pine barren treetops at forty-one MPH, pausing to hover in place over less dense areas so he could later review in detail the land below. He had twenty-six minutes of drone flying time at full throttle, so he cut the speed back to thirty MPH.

Now he was viewing the northeast quadrant of the pine barrens and his eyes were riveted on the screen in front of him. As the drone passed over into the southeast quadrant, Grady thought he saw through the thick tree pack some kind of wooden shack. The drone circled back to the area, dropped down under the thick tree cover, and hovered. Grady stared at the photos he was recording, and the drone moved purposely in slow motion from tree to tree. In the distance was a wooden shack, the roof was somewhat damaged, but the walls seemed to be solid.

The drone moved above the shack, then encircled it. There were two windows in the shack. One in the front, the other on the left side. The drone approached the side window first and peered inside. It was dark, nothing visible at least not on Grady's screen. The drone flew around to the front window and hovered in place, Grady desperately trying to see inside. Nothing. Grady would have to study the photos later. The drone rose up over the treetops and continued its aerial mission. It swooped down four more times through the thick pine trees and Grady discovered another hidden hut. This one was bigger. The drone studied the rooftop and the sides of the structure. Something was different about this shack. It looked as if somebody might be living in it.

Grady flew the drone around the dwelling capturing many angle shots. Then it hovered close to the ground and Grady could see empty tin cans scattered around the shack. The drone flew within a foot of one of the tin cans hovering above it. Grady saw the tin can label and his heart fluttered, the drone suddenly soared above the pine trees and flew full speed back to its owner.

Grady stood looking skyward as his drone appeared about 500 feet above him then descended to land at his feet. He picked up the drone and walked briskly back to Julie's car. As he approached the car, he heard something behind him that made him freeze in place. Deep within the pine barrens, Grady heard a dog barking. It was not a friendly bark. It was an angry, deep, guttural growl and it was answered by another call, one that sent a shiver of terror through Grady's being. He lept toward the car door and thrust it open jumping into the passenger seat.

"Get the hell out of here! Floor it!"

CHAPTER 30

F BI AGENT GREER Hughes pulled his black sedan over
to the right curb on Roxbury Road across from the Garden
City Country Club's seventh fairway. It was the last of the
four murder victim sites he had visited trying to make sense of
whether or not geography had anything to do with the serial killer's victims. He wrote in his log, '*Geography not relevant to killings.
There has to be a more compelling reason.*'

In the morning, Hughes had again interviewed the principal
at Freeport High School and the nurse who remembered Hector
Anguilera. This helped him flesh out the human profile of the pro-
spective killer. But the interview he had with Anguilera's mother
added a new dimension to the case.

When Hughes asked the mother about Hector's twin brother
'how close they were?' She responded, "Very close. Mauricio
tried to protect him. He was bigger than Hector, so he beat up
on some of the bullies, but there were too many of them. He was
overwhelmed and they ganged up on both of the brothers. Once
Mauricio came home after school with a black eye and broken
nose. Four kids beat him up. Everything changed after that,"
she told Hughes. When the FBI agent pressed for an answer, the

mother said they stopped talking to me or anyone. I told their high school principal about the attacks, the ridicule, the bullying, but they were not able to stop the students.

Hughes put his car in drive and pulled away from the curb. As he did, he saw a leashed Rottweiler pull away from its owner and chase after his car. It ran out in front of the black sedan and Hughes slammed on his brakes just missing the animal. It circled the car then pounced against the FBI agents front door, its teeth gnashing against the window, saliva now dripping down the glass. The guttural sound of the attack sent a jolt of fear through the agent. Hughes watched the owner chase after the dog, demanding it come back to its owner. The dog slid down from the door and ran back to its owner. A haunting vision flashed through the agent's mind. He imagined how helpless the four victims must have been to be out alone with nothing to defend themselves from an attack. A bead of sweat slowly ran down Hughes' forehead into his left eye and it stung, reminding him how vicious each attack was from the bloody photos he had examined. It was now mid-August and the killer was averaging a victim every two weeks. Hughes knew his time on the case would have to be limited because each week he failed to get close to the killer, he was risking the death of another victim.

Hughes was hoping that the tail he put on the mother would somehow link her sons back to her with some clue, but nothing had yet happened. He had issued an APB on any suspicious van driving within the circle of death on his map with the four red circles. In his effort to understand the criminal mind of the assailant, Hughes had interviewed each of the four families of the dead victims for some thread of evidence tying them all together, but to his frustration nothing linked. Officer Bennack gave Hughes a host of reasons behind using dogs to track down and kill each victim, each of the dogs controlled to attack each victim on command, but who was controlling the pack of dogs and why? To the FBI agent, it seemed like displaced aggression. Mother spanks baby and baby hits doll, but nothing logical formed any kind of consistent explanation for the vicious murders so he concluded that the killings must be due to a personal vendetta. Hector Anguilera certainly had every motivation to punish those who made fun of him in high school, but to resort to killing the victims was beyond justification and vindication. It was now shear and gripping murder motivated by a sick mind and the thought of confrontation with the killer was slowly beginning to permeate fear in the mind of the top FBI special agent in the northeast. Coupled with a growing determination that sooner or later agent Hughes was confident he would hunt down the killer and entrap him.

Hughes' satellite cell phone chirped, the sharp ring bringing the agent back to reality. He punched the button and an angered voice said, "You'll never find me," there was a sudden click then silence. Hughes frantically punched numbers into his cell phone in an effort to track the call, and triangulate the location, but the caller's signal had vanished. "Shit!" Greer voiced, and he frantically called the FBI Washington, DC tracking headquarters to enlist aid. He shared vital information regarding the call and said, "I'll wait. Put a tracker on the call immediately."

Hughes fidgeted with his cell phone while staring at his digital Apple watch, counting the minutes. One, two, then three minutes passed. Hughes barked into his phone, "What's the status?" No answer. Four, five, six, then seven minutes passed, when a woman's voice finally came on the line. "Nothing. Not even a trace. Somebody's smart enough to know the system. From your cell we tracked your signal source to your last received call. Whoever made the call knew the exact timing of when to exit—thirty seconds."

"Fuck," said Hughes. "Not even a trace?"

"Nothing. How do you think they got your cell?

"I have no idea."

"Make sure you follow all in and out calls on my cell."

"We're on it. We read the case profile you're working on. It's unnerving that the killer has your cell and can track you. We think you should close out your cell number and get a burner phone. Tough to track."

Hughes thought for a moment and said, "No. I'm going to keep it live. My guess is that he'll try and contact me again. At least we know he's out there somewhere and knows we're on his case. Maybe this is a sign."

"A sign of what?" asked the tracking agent.

"A sign that he wants me to know that he's out there and that we won't ever find him."

"So, it's a man?"

"Yes, a masculine voice. Angry voice."

"Disguised?"

"I don't know."

"So, it could be a woman?"

"I don't know. The voice was powerful and firm without flinch. Definitely masculine. No hint of an accent."

"He's Hispanic according to the file."

There was a silence on the phone for a brief but agonizing moment then the woman FBI agent said, "Be careful."

Greer Hughes did not respond. Instead, he pressed the kill button on his cell and sat rigid in his FBI sedan. Suddenly, his cell phone became alive again with a loud shrill chirp. The agent's heart skipped a beat.

A different voice sounded. It was a woman's voice, and Hughes stared without blink at his satellite cell phone.

Hughes knew the FBI tracker was on it and he said, "Yes."

The voice said, "Greer Hughes."

Hughes stared at the second hand of his wrist watch. He needed thirty seconds more to triangulate the call. "Yes," said Hughes slowly trying to stall the caller. Fifteen seconds, twenty seconds, twenty-five seconds. The FBI agent thought the greeting was almost like a command. The voice came on again, "Greer Hughes." It was a high-pitched singsong voice. Haunting, thought Hughes and he promised to indicate the inflection in his log book.

Female concluded Hughes. He heard deep breathing over his phone. In the background he thought he heard a guttural growling sound. "Hello," Greer said. Five seconds. "Hello. Who's there?" Four, then three seconds. The breathing continued.

"Hello, goddamn it. Who is this?" Hughes demanded firmly.

More deep breathing than the phone silenced. "Shit," said Hughes, his heart pounding in his chest.

"They're playing with me," Hughes said aloud. The agent's phone came alive yet again and he jumped in place. A voice said, "They hung up a second before we could get a fix. They know what they're doing, Greer," the FBI headquarters tracking agent said. "Sounded like a woman's voice. Strange sound. Snarling in the background. Dogs, maybe."

"Yes," said Hughes. "Did you hear the snarl? How the hell did they get my number?"

The woman FBI agent, Latisha Brown, said, "Yes, I heard it. Scary. Guessing they know someone at the FBI."

"Run a phone trace on all calls between the DC office and Long Island. See if you get any connections," said Hughes. "Let me know."

"Roger that," said Brown, and they clicked off.

Hughes sat motionless in his seat, his mind racing through possibilities of where the killer was hiding. Maybe, thought Hughes for the first time, there were two killers. Both brothers or a man and a woman. The case, thought the agent, was now becoming more complex. Something was terribly wrong out there and Hughes was determined to track down the killer dead or alive, face to face. Whatever direction he took now, he knew that for every passing hour, the killer would strike again soon, very soon.

CHAPTER 31

GRADY BENNACK STARED fixedly at the streaming video on his GoPro drone camera while Julie gripped the wheel of her Mustang. In her rear view mirror the shroud of pine trees faded out of sight and she took in a long-labored breath of air, her heart still racing from Grady's command to escape the area with the gas pedal to the floor. What had he seen? What had he heard? To Julie, she was relieved to leave the area no matter what the reason.

A wooden shack came into view on Grady's GoPro screen. He noted it was made of gnarled knotty pine with holes made by hardened pine sap that, over the years, had popped free leaving holes in the walls like Swiss cheese. The roof was slanted and uneven. He fast forwarded the video through two more shack-like structures of similar design, the second structure the roof had fallen within the four walls. When Grady zoomed in on the ground surrounding a fourth shack, he saw three empty tin cans to the right of the slanted front door which was partially ajar.

The camera zoomed in on the three cans. Grady was able to read the label on one of the cans. In sharp focus, a red label read,

'ALPO.' Grady zoomed in closer and was able to read, '*Chop House Beef Tenderloin. Canned dog food.*'

"It's dog food, Julie." Grady said, his heart skipping a beat. "This might be it."

"What do you mean?"

"The killer's den."

"You think?"

"Yes."

"God. What do we do now?"

"We need proof."

"How do we do that?"

"We need to get inside the shack. See the dogs. Find the killer."

On the second chirp, FBI agent Hughes punched the green button on his satellite phone. "Three calls into the mother," said the FBI tracking agent, Latisha Brown.

"Did you get a fix on the location?" said special agent Hughes.

"Each call less than thirty seconds. No."

"Fuck. Send the file to my office."

"Already done."

"What's your opinion of the voices?" Hughes said.

"Two men and a woman."

"Any tonal similarity?"

"No."

"Run a biometric modality test on the voices. "

"Consider it done."

The phone silenced in one click and Hughes stood up staring at the map with four red circles. Agent Brown's voice echoed through his mind. "*Two men and a woman.*" How's that possible?

His mind raced and he drew a blank. Could three people be orchestrating the serial killings? Hughes knew that historically all serial killings were committed by one person. The Zodiak killer, Ted Bundy, the crazy necrophile, Jack the Ripper, the Hitchhikers killer, the angel of death, the beast, and the human Dracula killer. But, to Hughes, this case was baffling. Out of frustration, Hughes kicked the wooden leg of his desk so hard that the wood splintered, the toe of his left shoe was dented.

CHAPTER 32

ASHAROKEN, LONG ISLAND, is a small isolated quiet beachfront community named after an Indian chief. It is 54.6 miles from Southampton, an hour and two-minute drive, and 48.3 miles from Central Park in New York City, an hour and twenty-two minute drive by car.

For Leona Parker, living on the water off Bevin Road had been a life-long dream and she bought the $1.4 million dollar home in 2014 when she got her promotion to Marketing Director for the Estee Lauder Company in Melville, New York. She walked religiously seven days a week, even in the rain, occasionally bursting into a jog to get her heart beat up and exercise her legs.

It was a Thursday night, the third week of August and the Nor-Easterly that had pounded Asharoken Avenue at the end of Bevin Road had, two weeks ago, completely burst through and over the embankment that was rebuilt from the last Long Island sound storm by the U.S. Army Corps of Engineers. The storm wiped out any ingress and egress over the only road entering the private community. The speed limit through the village was only 30 MPH, and the police force for the private community was known to give tickets, lying in wait if the uninitiated did one mile over the speed limit.

Parker, who was openly gay and proud of it, had married her significant other, Rachel Goldstein, three summers ago with a small private ceremony in her backyard overlooking Duck Island Harbor. The Mayor of Asharoken, Paul Mandry, performed the ceremony. Parker's Rolex Gold Tone watch read 7:18 PM when she closed her front door and walked out to Bevin Road. She could smell the salt air and the gentle southwesterly breeze gave the young woman a sense of freedom and calmness from the frenetic pace of business. She loved Estee Lauder and her fast-track upward promotion had been assured after she helped with the successful promotion launch of four new brands.

Her pace increased to a brisk walk as she headed north on Bevin Road toward Long Island sound. As she looked ahead down the road, she saw a large black van parked along the road. Strange, thought Parker, the Asharoken Police were very strict on any vehicles parked on the private roads of Asharoken and so, as Parker approached the black van, she peered at the windows trying to see into the van, but they were all heavily tinted. She noted that the van had several deep dents on the rear fender and on the left rear door. As she was passing the van, she cupped her hands against the driver's side window to try and see if anybody was inside. She could not see a thing, so she moved on quickening her pace not looking back. As she reached Asharoken Avenue, crossing over the road. and over the dunes onto the Long Island sound side beach, Parker did not see the front door of the black van open as a figure stepped out onto the road. Nor did she see a blur of motion exit from the back of the van. Whatever it was, it headed for the beach following the woman.

Parker was now walking along the shore heading west and concentrating on the high tide seaweed line that marked the sandy beach. She passed an orange buoy, then an empty Tide detergent bottle, now what looked like part of the frame of a lobster pot. For some unknown reason, she stopped all forward motion and spun around to look behind her. The thought of the black van entered her mind again and she wondered how long it would be before the Asharoken police would arrive to issue a ticket.

The thought passed and she walked up from the shoreline now entering a small pathway onto the J.P. Morgan estate, a vast 400-acre swath of waterfront property that the famous banker had purchased from Cornelius H. DeLamater who owned the Brooklyn Iron Works that built the iron clad USS Monitor that fought and sunk the CSS Virginia in the Chesapeake Bay in 1862. In her spare time, Leona Parker was an avid Civil War buff who loved the lore surrounding Asharoken and the body of land that the small waterfront town connected to Eaton's Neck.

About two-hundred yards into her brisk walk, Parker stopped at the edge of the vast field overlooking Long Island Sound to enjoy the view before entering thick underbrush and the thick trees that surrounded the open field. In the distance she thought she saw movement across the field. Small dots of something. She squinted to see detail but whatever it was moving too fast along the field edge to decipher. She turned east and vanished into the thick shroud of trees, vines and brush on a thin trail heading back east. She would exit onto Eaton's Neck Road before the firehouse and walk back to her home via Pheasant Lane, a scenic and peaceful road that, for Parker, was the best part of the jaunt. As she walked deeper into the trees, she heard from behind her a tree limb snap with a loud crack. Startled, Parker spun around. Nothing. But, she thought, something was close to her. Close enough to make a haunting, terrifying sound. She continued moving east only increasing her pace. Her fast walk was now a jog. As she moved along the path, she heard something else, heavy breathing, too close for comfort. Her head snapped around to the left, then right. Still nothing and yet something or someone was gaining on her. She broke into a run but tripped on a vine. Her body rolled over twice and she lept to her feet and burst into a frantic run. Something flashed to her left, now right confirming in one agonizing fear gripped thought that she was surrounded. Then it happened. Coming at her from the front, was a large airborne dog coming at her face. For a brief unbridled moment, Parker was relieved. She could assuage a dog. Somehow escape or talk the animal into some sense of control. But as the dog impacted her forward movement, the sheer speed of the collision sent Parker sprawling to the right. As she landed, another dog attacked her legs, another lept onto her midsection and she screamed a guttural cry. She felt pain immediately as the dogs tore into her flesh. She rolled over onto her stomach and, with all the strength she could muster, she lifted herself up shrieking a high-pitched terror laden sound that echoed through the dense trees of the Morgan estate. She pulled herself up through the jaw ripping massacre and pitched forward toward a thick vine that was hanging only five feet from her. She grabbed the vine and started to shinny herself off the ground, the pack of attacking dogs leaped up at her, one grabbing her left ankle and shaking her leg. She looked down and counted four dogs and then she saw it, forcing her to scream repeatedly in short spasms of terror. Something so frightful that her body froze six feet off the ground forcing her to release her grip on the vine and collapse into a feeding frenzy of animals so wild and vicious that all hope of surviving vanished as her body turned pink, then red and now covered the brush around her in a sanguine pool of bone, viscera, and torn clothes. Suddenly, the attackers vanished and all that remained was scattered parts of what was once a thriving successful woman who had suddenly ceased to exist.

When Asharoken police officer Clark Dove approached the black van on Bevin Road, he parked his police car in front of the it and got out to inspect it. He reached for the driver side door handle but it was locked. He tried all the doors. They were also locked. Dove got back into his police car and entered the license plate number. A minute and a half passed before the plate number details popped up on Dove's screen. The officer was distracted when he saw movement in his rear-view mirror coming towards him. It was a person accompanied by several dogs, but he couldn't make out the details. He opened his car door and stepped out onto Bevin Road.

"This your—Dove didn't get to finish his question. The appearance of the individual was so shocking Dove grabbed for his gun, which instantly triggered a simultaneous attack by the four dogs.

Dove was dragged to the ground and his pistol was knocked from his grasp. He felt the sharp pain of multiple bites, especially on his right arm and shoulder as the four dogs pinned him to the ground. Dove could not speak, could not move, and what he saw hovering over him terrified him. He heard a loud shrieking command and the dogs pulled back. Officer Dove lay on the ground rigid— eyes wide open in fear. Dove heard another command, and a door open. Whatever it was, entered his police car, a moment passed, and then the doors to the black van opened and the van pulled out from behind the police vehicle and sped off onto Asharoken Avenue.

Officer Dove lay on the ground for what seemed like ten minutes, but was only two or three. Slowly he sat up dazed and looking around, trying to comprehend what had just happened.

He stared at his right hand. There was no blood, no puncture marks except for a fading red, then pink, then skin colored imprint that was, to Dove, an obvious jaw mark from sharp teeth. Dove rolled over onto all fours then slowly stood up. Instinctively, he reached for his holstered weapon, but it was gone. He searched the ground around him. Nothing.

The officer walked back to his patrol car and opened the driver side door and slid onto the seat, his heart still pounding from the unmitigated dread that was surging through his mind. He looked at the screen on his dashboard where he had just entered the black van's license plate number for a state check on the vehicle. The screen was blank. Dove punched in a series of numbers and pressed, '*enter.*' The sound of the computer fan whirring filled the air in his cabin and then a message scrolled across his screen.

"*NO VEHICLE IDENTIFICATION EXISTS.*"

Dove sat back staring through the windshield across Asharoken Avenue at the sand dunes as four minutes ticked away. His mind was trying to process what had just happened. He picked up his hand mike and said, "Officer Dove here. We have a 10-11 and 10-38 case. Black van, Asharoken Avenue. Stop the car. I'm coming in." Dove, like all police officers, was required to memorize all police 10 codes used to describe all incidents happening out in the field so as not to alarm the public or provide information to criminals. He surprised himself that he recalled the codes that he never had used before.

"Roger that, Officer Dove," said the officer manning the Asharoken police station headquarters desk. Officer Gary Clark looked out his window staring at Asharoken Avenue and saw nothing.

Clark said, "Don't see a black van. We'll put up a barricade. What's the dog problem?"

"Attack dogs pinned me down and stole my Glock."

"10-4."

Clark could hear Dove's siren in the distance and by the time he barricaded Asharoken Avenue with his police car, Dove's vehicle screeched up beside it to form a solid block in the road. A van approached the police cars, but it was green. Dove said, "Not him. Let him pass." They let the van pass through and another car approached. It was a BMW which passed the barricade. The black van in question had passed the police station four minutes before the officers barricaded the road, and it had rounded the left curve vanishing up the steep hill leading out of the beachfront town.

Officer Dove ran back into the police station and ordered an APB on a black van. The 10-35, major crime alert, raced through the system and moments later special FBI agent Greer Hughes saw the APB stream across his screen. First the 10-32, (person with a gun), then Hughes saw a 10-38, (stop suspicious vehicle), a black van, but it was the 10-11 that was now streaming across the agent's screen prompting Hughes to sit bolt upright in his chair, his heart racing. A 10-11 was a dog problem and that, coupled with a 10-32 and 10-38, meant to Hughes that this could be a hot lead emanating from the police office in Asharoken, Long Island. He picked up his satellite phone and punched in a number.

The phone rang twice before a voice said, "Asharoken police, Officer Clark speaking."

"Officer in charge, please," commanded Hughes.

"Speaking."

"FBI special agent Greer Hughes. I saw your APB. Who issued it?"

"Officer Dove."

"I need to speak to him immediately."

"Hold on." Clark put the phone down and called out to Dove. "Clark. Line one. An FBI agent on the line."

Dove picked up the phone and said, "Officer Dove here."

"Agent Hughes. I saw the APB, officer. Talk to me. What happened?"

Dove said, "Got attacked by dogs."

"How many?"

"Four."

"Was there somebody controlling them."

"Yes. Some weird guy. A man, I think. But not sure what it was."

"Was anybody else around the dogs? Another person?"

"I don't think so, but I'm not sure. This thing, whatever it was, controlled the dogs. Attacked me on command. Took me down. Took my Glock from me, then they vanished. Whatever it was, it got into the van with the dogs and took off."

"How long ago?"

"Thirty, maybe forty minutes ago. Scared the shit out of me."

Hughes was writing notes rapidly into his log book. He looked up and studied the map now appearing on his screen. It was a map of the Village of Asharoken. He circled the main road and said, "Officer Dove."

"Yes."

"I want you to listen to me carefully. I want you to shut down the road leading in and out of Asharoken. Asharoken Avenue. Next, I want you to alert the local police forces near you, Northport, Centerport, and Huntington. Have their forces converge on the area."

"Not necessary agent Hughes. The van's long gone. What's the point?"

"Right now, officer Dove, I'm not worried about the van. We have an APB on it. I'm worried that somewhere within Asharoken is a serial killer's fifth victim."

CHAPTER 33

THE CALL CAME into the Asharoken police station at 7:28 P.M. and Officer Clark picked up the phone to answer it. Outside the police station, eleven police cars were parked waiting impatiently for more edification on why they had been summoned to Asharoken. A major crime alert had been issued. Officer Dove gave them a brief report and was waiting for agent Hughes to arrive and provide more details.

The Asharoken Police station phone jangled. A frantic voice sounded in officer Gary Clark's ear and his first words were, "Slow down. I can't understand you. You're talking too fast."

"Rachel Goldstein. It's Leona Parker. She went for a walk an hour and a half ago and she's not back. I'm worried, officer. Something's wrong."

"I'm sure she's okay," said Clark trying to reassure the woman.

"It's not like her, officer. She's meticulous about her time. Her walks normally last for thirty, tops forty-five minutes."

"Where does she normally walk," pressed Clark.

"Down Bevin Road. To the beach. Sometimes to Eatons Neck. Other times she circles out to the mouth of Duck Island Harbor, the west side. Or she'll walk out to the sluice. Officer," Goldstein pleaded, "Something's wrong. Terribly wrong. You have to help find her," and she burst into tears.

FBI agent Hughes sped around the bend in Asharoken Avenue too fast and skidded into the sandy curve on the left then he corrected the spin pulling into the police station in a screeching stop, the smell of burnt rubber scenting the air. Hughes stepped out and walked swiftly into the office. He spoke briefly to officers Dove and Clark then walked into the large conference room where eleven patrol officers were impatiently waiting. Hughes scanned the assembled group and was surprised to see Southampton police Chief Tom Bennack sitting at the end of the table. He nodded to Bennack, having met with him last Tuesday to review the case and the murder of his daughter Judy.

Agent Hughes did not sit down. Instead, he pulled out a map with four red circles on it and said, "We have a serial killer on our hands. Four people have been stalked, tracked down, and killed since June. Hughes looked over at officer Dove and said, "Officer Dove, I believe, just confronted the killer two hours ago on Asharoken's Bevin Road which is why you're all here. Officer Clark has just received a frantic call from an Asharoken resident who reported that her wife, who went for a walk two hours ago, has not returned which means we need all of you to canvas the surrounding area in hopes of finding her."

Hughes reached into his briefcase and extracted a white book tossing it on the table. "This is the high school yearbook from Freeport High School, class of 1994. All four of the killer's victims are from that class. Officer Clark just gave me the name of an Asharoken resident who's missing. Name is Leona Parker. I hope to God she's not in this book." Hughes leafed through the yearbook to the senior class and scanned the alphabetical photos and profiles. He looked up and said, "Son of a bitch." He held the book up pointing to the photo of Leona Parker. "I'm afraid Ms. Parker might be the fifth victim. For the first time, we have someone who confronted the killer who's still alive to tell us about it. Officer Dove, enlighten us about your experience this afternoon."

Officer Dove held up his right hand. It was trembling. "I was checking out a black van parked on the side of Bevin Road. Doors locked so I concluded someone was walking on the beach. I returned to my patrol car and was entering the van's license plate for a vehicle check. As I was waiting for a response, I saw movement in my rear-view mirror. Somebody was approaching my car. I got out and immediately reached for my Glock."

A patrolman said, "Why the gun?"

"Because whoever was approaching me had some kind of mask on his face. I'm not sure it was human."

"Hypertrichosis," said agent Hughes.

"Werewolf ," Chief Bennack added. "It's also called Ambrose , a very rare disease. The gene controlling hair growth is missing and hair grows all over the body. The Centers for Disease Control got a sample of blood from the second corpse, and they confirmed it."

"So, how do you know it's the same guy who attacked officer Dove today," asked officer Clark.

Bennack said, "Four dogs attacked officer Dove. I suspect it's the same serial killer. The final proof is if we find a body tonight— Leona Parker. She's missing so we start a search now." Bennack held up the yearbook and closed out the conversation with, "Our missing person was a Freeport High School graduate, same year as my daughter. I'm afraid our fifth victim is lying out there somewhere in your village."

The police officers all looked up at a map of Asharoken pinned to the bulletin board. Officer Dove used a pointer to identify hiking trails that Parker might have taken. "Let's split up into three search parties. It's dark out there now, no moon. Be careful. Use your two-way radios to report any discovery."

"Whatever you find tonight, is not going to be pretty. If we find a fifth victim, that pack of attack dogs will have made mincemeat out of them."

The squadron of police officers got into their patrol cars and drove back to Bevin Road where officer Dove was confronted. When they arrived, they got out with their flash lights. Beams came on in an eerie penetrating show of light and force. A K-9 unit had arrived, and three dogs were released, their trainers issuing commands for direction and scent. The dogs sniffed the road area where the confrontation occurred, and they issued guttural snarls confirming scent. Upon command, the dogs tracked the scent toward the beach, over the dunes onto the shoreline and headed west. The rest of the patrolmen fanned out, each group vanishing in a different direction. A half-hour passed and nobody had reported a sighting. Another half-hour passed and still nothing. It was almost two hours into the search when one of the K-9 handlers said over the two-way radio, "We have a scent. Dogs are tracking something leading onto the Morgan estate."

"Keep us all posted," said Bennack.

"Roger that," officer Dove said.

Dog handler Jon Schmauss' voice interrupted the silence. "We're onto a strong scent, east side of the Morgan field. Now into heavy underbrush.

Everybody could hear Schmauss was breathing hard as his pace quickened, following his dogs. Now they were barking and snarling. Their K-9 handler, Schmauss, knew he was onto a fresh trail that promised to deliver results. His flashlight beam pierced the pitch darkness searching for any telltale clues. The barking and yelping intensified and Schmauss left his two-way on so that the other policemen could get a sense of the hunt. Suddenly, Schmauss gave out a guttural shriek that triggered the squelch on his hand-held radio phone. He let out a sudden cry as his flashlight beam rested on the torn remains of a body, blood soaking the ground, clothes torn free of flesh, and arms and legs splayed at unnatural angles. Schmauss said, "Bloody Christ. I found her. What's left of her."

Schmauss gave his coordinates and within twelve minutes, the crime scene was encircled by thirteen officers, each one expressing horror at the massacre their lights revealed. Asharoken officers Dove and Clark confirmed that the face of Leona Parker, screwed up into a mask of terror, was her, the fifth murder victim of the serial killer.

Officer Bennack said, "We'll find this sick son-of-a bitch."

Special agent Greer Hughes stared at the shredded remains of Leona Parker whose grotesque face stared back at him in the middle of his spotlight beam, her eyes wide open, bulging from a terror she witnessed defying description. Her tongue lolled in an open mouth, agape from her last terrified breath. The agent's heartbeat was pounding in his chest as if trying to send a Morse code message of warning. He looked up at the circle of officers and said, "Whatever's driving this killer to murder members of his high school class is something we must stop before he gets to his next victim."

CHAPTER 34

THE APB SENT out across Long Island, New York, New Jersey, and Connecticut with the description of the black van turned up eleven vans that matched the profile. Three of them had a dog in the car, one had two dogs, but they were mothers picking up their school children with a pet or two in the car.

Police Chief Bennack had seen the report and sat in a Lazy Boy chair in the den of his home trying to piece together anything that would provide a lead to tracking the killer. His son Grady entered the den and sat down.

"Any leads, Dad? I read about the fifth victim."

"A black van and the killer's first confrontation with the police. He's getting careless."

"Maybe he wants to be caught," Grady said.

Bennack hesitated before answering. "Maybe," he said.

Grady sat in his chair rigid, thinking. He was debating sharing with his father what he had discovered in the pine barrens. But he had no proof that the killer was hiding in the dense Long Island pine forest. Only a hunch based on the photos he had just taken with his drone. He decided to wait until he had proof. Then

an idea came to him and he rose suddenly from his chair and
exited the den.

The day after the fifth murder victim was discovered in Asharoken,
special agent Greer Hughes had driven back to the police station
and was engaged in a detailed investigation interview with patrolmen Clark Dove.

"Describe the confrontation you had with the killer on Bevin
Road yesterday. I want to know every detail."

Dove cleared his throat and quaffed another swig of Dr.
Pepper, coughing twice, his eyes watering from the fizz. "It happened so fast,"

"Tell me again what you saw."

"Four dogs approaching me . . . from Asharoken Avenue . . .
onto Bevin Road. My police car was parked in front of his black
van. I heard some kind of command. Somebody was behind
the dogs moving with them as if part of the pack. Fast. Very fast
toward the black van. There might have been another person
behind them, but I couldn't see detail."

"Did you speak?"

"Hell, I pulled my Glock from my holster and before I could
raise the gun and take aim, the first dog was in the air locking onto
my wrist in its jaws. The gun fell to the ground."

"Did you get a look at the perpetrator?"

"Everything was a blur. Shit no. Four dogs were on me, and
I fell to the ground. They were all over me. The sound of their fury
scared the hell out of me. I was paralyzed."

"You must have seen its face," said Hughes.

"A brief glimpse of something, a man, I think. Looked like it was wearing a mask. Whoever it was moved so fast that by the time I sat up they had vanished in the black van."

"When did you call in to report this?"

"Whatever it was, they took my car keys. Luckily, I had a second set. They also took my two-way and wiped out my license plate search."

Hughes said, "When it took your cell phone you must have seen a face."

"I was on my gut protecting my face from the dogs, so I couldn't see anything," Dove replied. "Only got a very brief look at the face when it approached behind the dogs."

"What about the dogs. Someone was shouting orders at them, right?"

"Yes."

"Describe the voice," pressed Hughes.

"Sing-song like. Eerie. High-pitched. Demanding. The dogs were at his command. When the guy went back to his car, he opened the van's back door then issued one command."

"What happened?"

"The dogs took off back to the van and it drove off."

"What did you see," Hughes said.

"Whatever it was, was hunched over."

"You refer to the guy as 'it.'

"Yes. From what I saw of its back, whatever it was didn't seem human. Eerie, scary shit. Freaked me out. It never looked around at me. Focused entirely on the dogs."

"And it never said a word to you?"

"Not a word. Only shouted something to the dogs."

Agent Hughes stood up and said, "Thanks officer. Appreciate your time."

Dove looked up at him and asked, "No leads yet?"

"Only the black van and your testimony. Did you see the make of the car? You're the first person alive who has come into contact with the killer. A mistake made by the killer, no doubt, but maybe it was intentional. If so, whoever or whatever it is, it's playing us. We'll nail him soon."

"Hope so, 'cause this thing was scarier than anything I've ever seen. I mean this dude was animal like, hunched over and swaying back and forth when it walked back to the van. It was a Chevy, by the way."

"And you didn't see anybody else?"

"It all happened too fast."

"Thank God you didn't graduate from Freeport High School."

"Why do you say that?"

Hughes walked toward the door to exit. He stopped and turned around. "It's a long story."

CHAPTER 35

THURSDAY WAS AN overcast, gloomy day with dark clouds and a threat of rain hanging over Long Island's Pine Barrens. Grady Bennack sat in Julie's red mustang studying a detailed map. Julie drove the car in silence. She turned left onto a dirt road and drove over the washboard surface. The road dead ended, and she pulled over to the right side approximately twenty yards from where she had parked three days before when Grady first launched his drone into the pine forest.

"I still don't understand why you didn't tell your dad, Grady," her voice demanding an honest answer.

"Because I don't have enough vital information yet. That's why. I'm hoping to find a track with this." Grady held up a dragonfly drone no bigger than the living insect. He held it in the palm of his hand. Pretty cool, huh?"

"What is it," said Julie, eyebrows furrowed.

"Miniature drone."

"You're kidding, right?"

"No," said Grady. "It clips onto the mother drone."

"Cool. What does it do?" Said Julie, eyes wide.

"I fly the larger drone into the Pine Barrens with the dragonfly piggybacking on it. When I get the drone close to something I want to explore in detail, on command the dragonfly drone takes off and is able to fly down chimneys, and through open cracks in doors and windows. It flies undetected because it looks like a real insect in flight. Then I land it and I can take close up pictures and video without being detected," Grady said, his voice confirming his excitement.

"Where did you learn all this stuff?" Julie said.

"My passion for the technology, I guess. Plus, it enables me to go places safely and acquire evidence."

Julie looked at him, leaned over and kissed him. "I'm impressed. You really are going to be a great detective." She hesitated and added, "that's if you don't get us killed in the process."

"Not to worry," said Grady. They were alone and isolated on a secluded dirt road. He opened the car door and said, "Stay here like last time. I'll be close by flying the drone."

"Be careful, Grady. I love you," Julie said. "Don't be long."

Grady walked toward the pine tree forest about one hundred yards from Julie's Mustang and spread a map out on the damp ground preparing his drone for liftoff. Four minutes passed and Grady looked back at the Mustang and waved at Julie with a thumbs up gesture. Julie smiled and waved back through the windshield.

The drone rose off the ground, hovered above the edge of the thick pine barren forest then vanished out of sight above the trees. Grady watched the screen on his drone control board for six minutes and suddenly his heart skipped a beat. Something appeared on the screen in a flash of motion then vanished. Grady's eyes widened and were riveted to the control board as he flew the drone dropping down into the thick forest, hovering in place, then flying in and out and around trees as if it were homing in on a target that only the teenage pilot could find.

The Southampton police chief, Tom Bennack sat around a large conference table that he used daily to give orders to his team of patrolmen. Sitting across from him sat FBI special agent Greer Hughes and three of his agents assigned to the case. Agent Hughes said, "Since the black Chevy van sighting and the Asharoken murder, we're not any closer to finding the killer."

"It's the killer's first mistake though," said Bennack, "and it won't be his last. At least we've got a hot lead."

"The APB will find that van," Hughes said. "The reason I wanted to meet with you, Tom, is that I know you ran the K9 unit in this region and I want to understand how our perpetrator is able to control his attack dogs to murder his victims. None of us have any dog training experience, especially using them for killing humans. I also want my agent team to understand what kind of serial killer we're tracking. The discussion will help all of us zero in on our suspect hopefully before he kills his next victim."

"Understood," Bennack said. "This has been extremely difficult for me since the first victim was our daughter Judy. Admittedly it's been tough trying to abstain from taking matters into my own hands. If I ever confronted the bastard, I'm afraid I'd shoot first without question, but I know taking the law into my own hands is out of the question so I'm glad your FBI team is spearheading the hunt and not me."

"So, we know the killer is driving his pack of attack dogs using a black Chevy van. The APB sent out is having all black Chevy vans pulled over in the northeast region. How the hell does the killer control these dogs to attack and kill?"

Chief Bennack had three files in front of him. He opened the first file and said, "When I controlled the K9 attack dog division, we used Schutzhund training. It's the German word for, '*Protection Dog*,' and the Germans developed it in the early 20th century for tracking, obedience, and protection work. The Germans used Schutzhund training primarily with German Shepherds to send their attack dogs behind enemy lines to track, attack, and kill the enemy. They were very effective in the first and second World Wars."

"So you think the killer is using this Schutzhund training method to attack and kill its victims?"

"Without question. You heard Asharoken officer Dove tell us he heard some kind of command shouted before the patrolman was attacked and disarmed," replied Bennack. "The most common breeds used in attack dog training are the German Shepherd, Rottweiler, and the Doberman Pincher, all German bred dogs. We know from the DNA testing that CDC did on the attack scenes that the killer is using those dogs, probably two German Shepherds, a Doberman, and a Rottweiler. These three breeds were used by the Germans as killing machines during all wars engaged by the Germans. And our Army used them to track and kill the Japanese after Pearl Harbor. We know that thousands of soldiers were killed by these Schutzhund trained dogs. The attack commands that the serial killer is probably using are track, hold, drag, and kill. Our killer obviously has these dogs extremely well trained. The fact that the killer commanded the dogs to attack and disarm officer Dove confirms that the killer can instruct the dogs to do his wishes. The CDC thinks our killer might be dealing with different personalities and, if so, the killer might identify himself as one of its pack, actually thinking he is a dog. If that's true, then the bond between the killer and its family of attack dogs proba-bly is tight. They call it the werewolf syndrome and the bond is unbreakable. A human with this syndrome will perform the same functions as a dog. The human will sniff out something of interest, follow a track, attack a victim just like a dog on attack."

Agent Hughes cupped his chin in thought. "So, if we're out in the field hunting the killer, we should have attack dogs with us to follow the scent, right?"

"Having attack dogs track scent in the field," said Chief Bennack, "will definitely help you lock onto scent a lot faster. A dog's nose is one thousand times more sensitive than a human nose. Dogs have 220 million olfactory receptors in their noses while humans only have five million. It's been proven that dogs can smell scents underground up to forty feet deep and can pick up smells over a mile away. So, yes, having a dog or two when you're in the field will increase your odds of finding the killer if he is, or has been, anywhere near your location. I'll call my K9 unit and ask for a couple of good trackers to accompany you when you're in the field. When the dogs join you, take them out to the killing sight in Asharoken which is still fresh with scent and have them smell the killing site. Once they get the scent of the other dogs and the blood of the victim, that will instill the scent to track and lock it into their minds."

"Thanks, Chief. We'll take two trackers," said Hughes.

Bennack said, "You'll need a handler. Someone to control and direct the dogs on the hunt."

"You know of a good handler?" pressed Hughes.

"Yes. Me. It was my job training and handling attack dogs in the K9 unit I managed. The bastard killed my daughter and I'll handle them."

Agent Hughes' phone chirped a loud ring and startled the assembled group. Hughes punched his phone and the speaker came alive. An excited voice said, "We've found the black Chevy van."

Hughes said, "Where?"

"Long Island Pine Barrens, southeast of Flanders, Route 24."

Hughes killed the call, stood up and looked at Chief Bennack. "How fast can you get the attack dogs?"

"We'll pick them up on our way to the Pine Barrens."

CHAPTER 36

THE MINIATURE DRAGONFLY drone flew out from behind a large Scotch pine tree, stains of dried sap clinging to its bark while the mother drone sat motionless on the ground next to the tree trunk waiting for Grady's next command.

Hovering four feet above ground, the large insect stared purposefully at the thick stand of trees ahead. Then it flew toward a fifteen by thirty-foot wooden shack. The shack's roof was at a sharp slant due to a rotten roof beam. The drone inspected the roof and walls, looking for an opening. There was a broken glass window in the back of the shack and the insect peered inside. Nothing, so it flew back into the thick stand of trees and vanished behind a wall of pines, with the mother drone following it. Another shack appeared in the distance and the insect flew up to it and hovered around it, six feet off the ground while the mother drone nestled near a small sapling. Then, the insect drone flew around the shack twice stopping to hover at the front door. It rose to the top of the door and discovered a four-inch crack. It backed up and then flew up over the roof looking down for other options. Nothing, so it flew back to the front door and buzzed up to the open crack of the door perching atop it and peered down inside.

Grady stared intensely at his screen and motioned for Julie to join him by his side. She left the car and hurried over to kneel down beside him. They both stared at the screen showing a stream of sunlight piercing through one of the shack's side windows.

Grady worked the controls with precision and the insect flew down into the small shack. It hovered for a brief moment until it spied a crossbeam running wall-to-wall and flew up landing in the middle of it. Next, it looked down at the floor scanning the small enclosure. Grady and Julie sat motionless studying the shack's interior through dragonfly eyes. They could see multiple empty dog food cans, two rickety chairs, one leg missing on the chair in the left corner of the room, and a flat table. About six feet behind the table, two mattresses lay on the floor with a clump of blankets. The teenagers could see something on the table but the insect's vision was not good enough to make out the details. The shack was empty of life, so Grady deftly flew the dragonfly down from the crossbeam and skillfully landed it on the tabletop. Grady and Julie stared at the screen eyes wide in shocked surprise. The insect rose from the table and hovered in flight giving a crystal image of what lay atop the table. Newspaper articles and photos. The headline of one of them read, *"JOGGER KILLED BY SHARK."* Then they both saw the photo of the victim mentioned in the article. It was Grady's sister, and the copy below the photo said, *"JUDY BENNACK KILLED IN SHARK ATTACK."* Grady caught a compulsive sob, and Julie put her arm around him.

To the right of the newspaper articles was a small notebook which lay open on the table. The insect flew over it and hung motionless in flight like a hummingbird, its wings batting in a whir of motion hardly perceptible to a human.

Grady said, "It's a list, Julie."

"I see it," her voice trembling in excitement. "Get closer."

The dragonfly flew downward, now hovering in flight a foot above the open notebook. Grady said, "What is it?"

Julie squinted at the screen and said, "Oh my God."

"What?" And then he saw it too. "It's got the names of the victims."

"And look at the notes beside the names, Grady."

"Dear God," Grady said. "He's killing all the people who made fun of and bullied him at Freeport High School."

Julie counted the names on the page. "Eleven names and the comments they each made to him."

"He's killed five so far. Six to go."

"Let's get out Grady, before they come back!" Julie cried frantically. "Get the dragonfly out now!"

The dragonfly flew up and out of the shack's front door crack and back to its awaiting mother drone, attaching itself successfully atop its mother drone's back. The small craft lifted off the ground and flew above the Long Island Pine Barrens back to its pilot.

Grady and Julie looked up at the sky and above them the drone appeared, descending to his outstretched hand, where it landed perfectly. "How quickly can we get a printout of those names and comments?"

The teenagers ran back to Julie's car. Turning the key, the engine surged to life and they hurriedly left for home with their new trove of information.

Chief Bennack got out of his police car and opened the back door on the driver's side. A German Shepherd and a Rottweiler jumped out and were greeted by eight FBI agents. Special Agent Greer Hughes, stood in front of them, engaged in a strategy discussion. One of the agents turned toward the dogs and said something.

The Rottweiler strained on its leash growling, displaying his large tooth-filled jaws. The startled agent backed up as Bennack shouted a command and the dog leash went limp. "Keep your distance," said Bennack. "They're trained to kill."

One hundred-forty-yards from the assembled group sat a black Chevrolet van matching the description of the killer's vehicle. It was empty and parked beside the Pine Barrens on the south side hidden partially by a small circle of pines. The agents and officers spread out surrounding the vehicle keeping just out of sight. The plan was to wait for the killer and capture him when he returned to the van. They were instructed to shoot to kill the killer's dogs only if they threatened an attack, but Bennack said the likelihood of a dog pack attack was remote in that the serial killer was only focused on specific targets. He knew that trained attack dogs would only attack on their human's command.

They waited thirty minutes, then forty, then fifty. Nobody came out of the woods. An hour passed. After another ten minutes a faint bark sounded from deep within the pine forest. Two-way radios came alive and the alerted force was ready. The intent was to capture the serial killer alive. "Shoot him only if necessary," Agent Hughes had commanded. Bennack was determined to kill the perpetrator, but he kept silent.

Another bark sounded. Closer this time, then another, still another. More than one dog, at least two, maybe three. Weapons drawn, the force was well concealed behind pine trees and thick brush. Two marksmen were lying down, rifles at the ready, aiming at the black Chevy van. Somebody's voice sounded in the distance. Bennack thought it was a command. Another dog barked. Hughes could hear his breath. His heart was pounding in his chest. This serial killer was his and he was determined to add a big notch in his CV. His promotion would be clinched. Bennack was kneeling behind a fallen tree, his dogs flanking him, awaiting his command.

Bennack heard a stick snap in the forest followed by more rustling. They were close, and his trained eyes scanned the trees and beyond looking for motion. There to the left! Something appeared. It was a dog, then two now three. A human appeared behind them, then another. Bennack's heart skipped a beat. The plan was about to launch. Everybody waited in silence for Bennack's command. As two humans appeared well back into the pine forest, moving toward the black Chevy, Bennack stood up rigid and shouted the Shutzhund command, "Fass," which he had told the agents was the German command to attack and take down victims. The German Shepherd and Rottweiler burst into an attack run toward the edge of the forest just as their victims came into view behind three dogs. The air was full of snarling sounds as Bennack stood up with eight FBI agents converging on their target.

A blood curdling scream sounded in the distance as six men, one woman, and Chief Bennack ran full speed toward their targets. Bennack's two attack dogs hurled their bodies at a man and a woman taking them both down to the ground. Three other dogs attacked Bennack's two dogs and the vicious sound of dogs attacking each other and the two people on the ground filled the air with chaos.

Bennack arrived at the scene first and shouted the command, "Aus," and the two attack dogs released their victims. Bennack's 38 Special pointed at the man, while the woman stood up holding her wrist and crying out in pain.

The man lay on the ground holding his bleeding wrist. He stared at Bennack's gun and shouted, "What the hell is this, man. We're out walking our three dogs and we get attacked. Look at my wife, goddam you! You attacked us! I want to know why?"

Bennack held his gun steady aimed at the man's head. "Let me see your identification."

The man started to get up and Bennack shouted, "Stay down. Identification."

The man reached for his wallet, pulled it out and handed his driver I.D. to Bennack. Agent Hughes stepped closer to the man and woman and studied the couple's three dogs, a Golden Retriever, a Doberman, and a mixed breed of Boxer. Their three dogs hovered over their owners, licking their hands and faces, wining as if out of sympathy. The woman looked up at Bennack and said, "Why? We did nothing wrong. We were just out walking our dogs."

Her husband looked at Bennack and Hughes angrily and said, "I'm going to sue your asses."

"Easy, young man. I'd check your words. There's a serial killer that's driving a van like yours. He's killed five people and is using attack dogs to track and kill his victims in this area."

Bennack ran a background check on the man confirming that he and his wife lived in Islip. He called Hughes aside and whispered, "Clean slate. Mistaken identity. Let's close it out, fast."

Hughes took in a frustrated sigh and walked back to the couple who were surrounded by their dogs. "Sorry. Our mistake, but I would not walk your dogs again in the Pine Barrens. There's a serial killer out there somewhere and you're risking your lives . . . and your dogs."

"I'm going to sue you," the man repeated. "Mistake or not. You had no right to attack us."

Bennack walked over to the man and offered him his hand to help him stand up. The man refused, already plotting his revenge. "I wouldn't waste your time," Bennack said. "You're both lucky to be alive."

CHAPTER 37

I T WAS SIX minutes after three o'clock on Thursday
afternoon when Grady and Julie pulled into the Bennack
driveway. They both ran inside, Grady clutching his drones
as if he held a million dollars in cash that someone was about to
rob. They sat down on the love seat in the den of Grady's home,
both parents out working. Grady carefully placed the drones on
the coffee table in front of them and removed the dragonfly from
the mother drone. He extracted the small camera from the mother
drone, found an outlet behind the sofa and plugged in the charger,
his heart racing.

"Grady, we've got to get the video to your dad as soon as we
finish reviewing the tape."

Grady did not respond.

"Did you hear me?" Julie demanded.

"I heard you, Julie."

"Okay. Then you agree."

Grady did not answer. He set the video camera down in front
of them and pressed *play*. Both of them leaned toward the small
screen and watched through the small insect's eyes the first broken
down shack appear in the thick pine barren forest. Soon after, the

second shack came into focus and the teenagers both sensed the terror as the dragonfly flew through the small crack in the door and landed on the cross beam above. The rickety chairs, the mattresses, and rumpled blankets piled atop it and now the dragonfly focused on the table. The newspaper headlines came into view, and then the newspaper photo of his sister, Judy Bennack. Grady said, "I can't believe this." He hit pause on the camera and sat back on the couch, his hands covering his face.

Julie watched him and saw tears streaming down his cheeks. "My sister was so young. Why? Why did he have to kill her, Julie?"

Julie held his hand between both of hers and said, "I . . . I'm sorry—Play the rest of the video. Maybe it will have some answers. We've got to print out that list we saw and get it to your father."

Grady sat up, wiping the tears from his face, and leaned forward pushing the *play* button on the camera again. The open notebook came into view through the eyes of the hovering dragonfly camera, Grady and Julie squinting to see detail. There it was. A list of names. Beside the names were comments but they could not discern the detail enough to read the contents.

Julie said, "Freeze the frame. Now."

Grady punched the *pause* button and the photo on the screen froze. "Can you enlarge the notebook page and print it out?"

"Yes," said Grady."

"Where's your printer?"

"In Dad's office."

They both stood up and walked swiftly into the office. Grady connected his camera to the Epson printer and punched *print,* pacing back and forth while the printer spewed out the page. The printer stopped and Grady and Julie stared at each other before picking it up.

"I'm scared, it's the killer's list of victims."

Grady hesitated then looked down at the list. His sister, Judy Bennack, was the first name appearing on the list. Grady counted the names before him. "Eleven names," he said, his heart pounding in his chest. "Randy Zand, victim number two, Rance Matthews, victim three, Alejandro Garcia, number four, and victim number five, Leona Parker."

"Oh my God, Grady. He's killing them off, one at a time in the same order that's on the list." She peered down at the list to the sixth name. "Laquan Williams. He's next. We've got to get this list to your dad now."

Grady held the printed paper in his left hand, which was visibly shaking, ignoring Julie's demand. "Look at the comments beside each name, Julie."

Julie stared at the list and read aloud the comments appearing beside each name. "He's killing each victim who bullied and made fun of him in high school." Beside Judy Bennack's name the word, '*Chewbacca*' appeared. "Judy must have called him, *Chewbacca*, that was Han Solo's copilot in *Starwars*. They called him *Chewie*." Julie said.

Grady began to cry. "She didn't mean to hurt him, Grady," Julie said. "*Chewie* had a kind heart. I'm sure she meant it as a loving compliment."

Grady wiped the tears from his eyes. "Maybe, but he was covered in hair, so it was taken as an insult, making fun of him otherwise she'd still be alive."

Beside each name appeared a derogatory name or comment. Randy Zand: '*Ape man. Hairy ass hole.*' Rance Matthews: '*Threw dog biscuits at me. Called me his pet doggie.*' Alejandro Garcia: '*Perro peludo malo.*'

"What does that mean?" asked Grady.

"Bad dog," said Julie who had taken two Spanish classes. She Googled peludo and said, "Hairy. Bad hairy dog."

"Jesus. The poor guy. Everybody made fun of him and now . . ." Grady paused in thought.

"He's getting revenge," said Julie. "How sad. They drove him crazy. Killing anybody who made fun of him. Six more on the list. We've got to save the others before it's too late."

Grady read aloud the six remaining names on the list and the comments appearing after their names . . .

Leshawn Williams . . . *Dirty dog.*

Juan Lopez . . . *Una miereda de perro.* (A piece of dog shit).

Rashona Smith . . . *Hairy ape. Gave me a banana.*

Bobby Dorsett . . . *Little werewolf. Wuff wuff.*

Charlie Hamilton . . . *King Kong.*

Betty LaGrange . . . *Called me a freak and gave me a dog leash.*

Julie burst into tears. "Those kids were so cruel. In addition, high school is the age when children begin to have serious romantic feelings toward the opposite sex and eventual marriage and family. It's doubtful any girls would consider him." she said. "No wonder he cracked. I feel so sad for him."

"I'm surprised he didn't kill himself," Grady said. "How much can a person take before they break."

Julie shook her head as if to clear the thought and said, "Yes, but he's killed five people, Grady." She handed him her cell phone and said, "Call your dad now. This is a crisis, Grady. We've got to save the six people on the list before it's too late."

Grady held her cell phone in his hand staring at it without action.

"Now, Grady. For God's sake, Now. Lashawn Williams is next. Save him. Call your dad."

CHAPTER 38

WHEN CHIEF BENNACK picked up his phone, he heard heavy breathing and an excited voice fill his receiver. "Dad. Dad, It's Grady."

"Yes, son?"

For the next seven minutes, Grady Bennack spilled out what he and Julie had discovered. Using the drone, the Long Island Pine Barrens, exploration of hidden shacks deep into the tree pack, the list of victims and comments beside each name, empty cans of dog food, and newspaper clippings of each victim.

For a moment Bennack was silent as his son's frantic message took hold. "How long ago did you discover this, Grady?"

"About forty-five minutes maybe an hour ago, dad, but nobody was in the shack. It was empty."

"Can you pinpoint exactly where the shack is in the Pine Barrens?"

"I think so. It's deep in the southeast sector."

"Where are you now?"

"Home with Julie."

"And you have the drone video of all this?"

"Yes."

"Good job, son. Stay put. I'll be there in ten."

"What are you going to do?"

"We'll talk when I get there."

By the time Chief Bennack arrived home, four police cars were in front of his house including FBI special agent Greer Hughes. As Grady prepared his drone camera, four cops and Hughes hovered over the large television screen, eyes riveted on the moving landscape. The pine forest canopy now appeared and then the drone flew down between tree branches and around tree trunks until the first rustic shack came into focus. The drone explored the outside walls of the shack then found entry. Special agent Hughes looked at Grady and said, "You're really good at this stuff, Grady."

Grady did not look up. His focus was on the screen. "Thanks," he said. "Nothing in this shack."

The drone moved swiftly, exited the shack, and flew in and around trees until, in the distance, another shack came into view. "This is the one," Grady said. The officers leaned in closer as the small dragonfly drone lifted off the mother drone and flew toward the shack. They saw the empty cans of dog food and now, in through a small crack in the front door, the dragonfly landed on a cross beam. Suddenly they were looking down on the makeshift table where the newspaper clippings came into focus.

One of the police officers said, "Shit, Grady. You are good. How the hell did you pilot through that crack in the door?"

Grady said one word, "Carefully."

His dad put his hand on his son's shoulder and patted it thrice. "Well done, son."

The list of names now came into view and Grady held the printed list in his hand giving it to his dad as the dragonfly lifted from the beam and flew back to the awaiting mother drone for the flight back to Grady.

FBI agent Hughes didn't hesitate. He took the list and scanned down to the next victim. "Lashawn Williams."

"They all graduated from Freeport High School. Julie and I already checked the year book," said Grady.

Hughes barked an order to another FBI agent. "Get Williams' current address if he's still alive."

"I'm on it," said Nancy Dunham as she punched in a phone number and held the receiver to her ear.

Hughes made two quick calls and Chief Bennack heard him give a command about blocking off and surrounding the Long Island Pine Forrest, Southeastern sector. Hughes pulled out a detailed map of the forest plot and Grady studied the map along with the officers. He pointed to a heavily wooded section and said, "The two shacks I saw were in this section, here." Grady rewound the drone video and both shacks reappeared. Agent Hughes circled the area with a red magic marker and said, "Are there any roads or paths leading to the shacks?"

Grady said, "The drone didn't see any. It's really thick in there. I could barely fly the drone in and around the trees."

Hughes said, "Chopper. We can helicopter in there and drop an assault detail of troopers to secure the perimeter surrounding the shack."

Bennack said, "We'll need a pack of dogs to pick up scent and engage, drop them by air."

"How many would you need?" Hughes said.

"Two, maybe three. I'll control them," Bennack said.

FBI agent Dunham punched off her third call and said, "We've located Laquan Williams. Calverton, just outside the Pine Barrens."

"What's his profile," Hughes said.

Dunham looked at her screen and said, "Married, two children, employed by Brookhaven Labs as a technician, African American, wife Caucasian. Twenty-eight."

Agent Hughes looked down at his watch. It read 4:53 PM. "He probably gets off at 4:00 PM. Dunham, get over there now with an officer."

"Roger that," Dunham said, and she vanished out the door with officer Tom O'Malley.

Hughes and Bennack reviewed plans to encircle and contain the southeastern sector of the Long Island Pine Barrens containing the shack that Grady's drone had shown. Hughes looked at Grady and said, "You did an incredible job finding the killer, Grady. Someday you'll make a hell of a detective." Hughes reached into his wallet and extracted a card and gave it to Grady. "When you graduate from College, I want you to call me. I'll have a job waiting for you and we'll talk later about a summer intern job."

Grady shuffled his feet in place and shook the FBI agent's hand. "Thank you, sir. I will for sure."

Bennack placed his hand on Grady's shoulder and said, "I'm proud of you son. We've got it now thanks to your efforts. Incredible drone work."

Julie Harned stared at Grady admirably and sidled next to him touching his hand. She smiled. He returned the smile.

As the officers and agents walked toward the front door, Grady called after them, "What if he's not there. Then what?"

Nobody answered his question. Julie said, "I'm more worried about Laquan Williams and will they get there in time to save him."

The front door had already closed before Julie's question was heard. It was still three hours before sunset and what Laquan William's FBI profile did not mention was that Laquan was a disciplined jogger.

CHAPTER 39

T HE MEXICO-UNITED STATES border, Frontera
Mexico-Estados Unidos, separates Mexico from the United
States and from the Pacific Ocean on the west to the Gulf
of Mexico in the east. The border crosses urban and rural areas
to deserts, 1,954 miles, and is the world's most crossed border
allowing over 350 million documented crossings annually. There
are forty-eight U.S.-Mexico border crossings with 330 ports of
entry. The San Ysidro Port of Entry is located between San Isidro,
California and Tijuana and it is where, twenty-eight years ago,
Santiago and Camila Anguilera entered legally with the dream
of starting a family and getting meaningful jobs to support
themselves.

The Anguileras entered the United States legally. They first
settled in New Burn, New Mexico and Santiago worked as a
short order cook at a small restaurant on the east side of the
small town, population 787. His wife Camila was a nanny to a
family with seven children. They made enough between them
to rent a small apartment just outside of New Burn and life was
good until Camila got pregnant and gave birth to twins, Hector
and Mauricio.

Mauricio was born first and seemed normal, six pounds eight ounces. The second baby followed, and Camila heard the assisting nurse exclaim, "Madre de Dios." *Mother of God.* Camila remembers her heart racing when she heard the nurse. The doctor held the baby by the feet giving it three slaps on the butt and the baby's lungs filled with air and it sounded an eerie cry of angst.

Camila's eyes bulged in disbelief as the four-pound, three-ounce baby filled her vision. She said, "Que es?" *What is it.*

The doctor said, "No lo se." *I don't know.*

Camila lay atop the birthing bed embracing the first twin in her left arm. The doctor offered the second baby to Camila to hold. "Aqui," he said. *Here.*

"No," the mother said. "Que tine de Malo." *What's wrong with it.*

The doctor repeated, "No lo se," and the baby, rejected from its mother, let out a plaintive cry that caused the assistant nurse to reach out and take it from the doctor, holding it close to her breast. The baby stopped crying immediately. "Esta cubierto de pelo," she said. *It's covered in hair.*

The doctor said, "Es uno especial de mutante."

"Se ve tan triste," *It looks so sad,* the nurse said, as she patted the baby's back gently.

It took Camila three weeks before she agreed to hold the second twin, whom they named Hector, and to breast feed it along with Mauricio. To Camila, she told her husband Santiago that the baby looked like an overgrown guinea pig, hair covering its entire body. At times, Camila thought she heard Hector purr when she was breast feeding. Over time, she grew attached to the child and felt terribly sad for his plight in life once it was confirmed that their twin son had the very rare disease, hypertrichosis, werewolves syndrome. The Anguileras researched the disease and later learned that it was also called Ambrose . The gene controlling hair growth is missing and hair grows all over the body continually, Santiago confirmed, and found that it was first mapped to chromosome Xq24-q27.1 and that it was first found in a Mexican family which confirmed that Hector Anguilera was the second Mexican to acquire the disease. Santiago, in his research with the CDC out of Atlanta, confirmed that the cause of his son's disease and genetic defect remains unknown.

The moment Hector entered kindergarten, the incessant teasing, belittling, and bullying began. He would come home sobbing into his mother's waiting arms telling her how mean his classmates were to him. They called him names, pushed and shoved him, and pulled his hair. It was the reason that the Anguileras moved eight times across the country searching for a peaceful home where discrimination might be less than where they had lived. They were unsuccessful and finally settled on Freeport, Long Island, New York because the school they researched in Freeport seemed to highlight a diverse student body that they hoped would offer their son, Hector, a reasonable chance of equal opportunity where he could receive an education with the least amount of trauma because of how he looked. Hector was now twelve and in sixth grade at Freeport elementary school and Camila and Santiago had met with all the counselors to review the sensitivities of their son Hector's disease. They assured them that, while they could not guarantee a biased free environment, they felt that the Freeport school diversity of Black, White, Hispanic, Native American,

Shinnecock Nation, and Asian students collectively had been dealing quite reasonably with accepting their differences.

On the fourth day of Hector's first week at Freeport elementary school, it began again. Hector, yet again, came home dissolved in tears over comments made to him about his appearance. The name calling, pushing, pulling his hair and public bullying began in earnest and was wearing down the young boy's confidence and self-esteem. He began thinking about ending his life and googled the many ways it could be done. Opioids, jumping out a window of a tall building, a knife to the wrist, a gun, or hanging himself. But each time the terrible thought entered his mind, the quest for a way to survive the constant discrimination against his appearance kept overtaking the depressing thoughts of suicide. It was his mother and father's constant love and reassurance of how wonderful a son he was that saved him each time from suicide.

Over the next five years, suffering, continued harassment and bullying, Hector Anguilera's mind began to change. At times, his vision would blur, other times he would hallucinate, and then it happened. He began to develop different personalities in order to cope with the torment and torture from his high school peers. One personality was passive aggressive, another more aggressive, and yet a third personality began to emulate a wolf where his bodily habits began to change, and his eyes seemed to change in shape. In his bedroom at night, he would get down on all fours and sniff the bed and furniture like a dog or wolf. Then his mind would snap out of the trance and he could not remember who or where he was.

His mother and father noticed the personality change and were very concerned. They sought counseling for Hector. It seemed to help at first, but with continued harassment and bullying at school, his personality would shift in order to protect his inner self. Then on a Wednesday, in March, sixty-seven days before Hector's graduation from Freeport High School, he vanished along with his twin brother, Mauricio.

CHAPTER 40

LAQUAN WILLIAMS ARRIVED at his home in Calverton from Brookhaven Laboratories at 4:18 PM. It was 4:43 PM when he left his home jogging toward the north sector of the Long Island Pine Barrens, seven minutes from his home on Picnic Court. The weather had changed rapidly from an eastern front off the Atlantic Ocean and a mist now hovered like a paste in the late afternoon air. The temperature had dropped twelve degrees in less than an hour and was seventy-two degrees.

FBI agent Nancy Dunham and officer Tom O'Maley arrived at Laquan Williams home at 5:19 PM. They both got out of the car and approached the front door. A young woman opened the door and Dunham said, "Sorry to bother you, but we're looking for Laquan. Is he here?"

"I'm his wife, Phoebe. Is there something wrong?"

"No," said officer O'Malley, "But it's very important that we talk to him."

"Why?"

"Because he might be in danger. Where is he?"

The look on Phoebe's face changed to one of dread and she said, "He just left the house to go jogging. He always does when he comes home from the Lab."

"How long ago?" Said Dunham urgently.

"About twenty minutes ago. What's wrong."

"It's a long story. We'll tell you the details later after we locate your husband. Are you familiar with the path he normally takes in the Pine Barrens?"

"It varies each time, but he normally enters at the Calverton property sign on the Barrens entrance way."

"What's wrong officers? At least tell me what kind of danger he's in. We have two children and this . . ."

"I'm sorry ma'am. We don't have time. We'll circle back when we have him and explain." They spun around and jogged back to the car, Phoebe staring at them as her two children encircled her legs in an embrace. The youngest one, a girl of seven, said, "What did they want, mommy."

Williams did not answer. She just stared at the patrol car as it sped away leaving a two-foot swatch of burnt rubber. In the distance she heard sirens fill the air and they were in the direction of the Pine Barrens. It was then that Phoebe Williams felt her heart racing in her chest and her eyes filled up with tears.

Laquan Williams was on his favorite path deep within the Pine Barrens when he looked down at his watch. It was 5:09 PM and the mist from the falling barometer hung thick in the air now. He was a powerful runner and in good physical shape. Not quite in the shape when he held the 100-yard dash and 220 yard hurdle records at Freeport High School, but he knew that his records still held up eight years after he graduated. His 100-yard dash record at Howard University was broken two years ago, 9.8 seconds.

In the distance, Williams thought he heard sirens, but he wasn't sure. The sound was muffled by the thick tree pack of gnarly pine trees. Suddenly he heard a helicopter fly overhead. It seemed to be low to the ground, very close. It flew above him, hesitated then veered off to the left, but Williams didn't break stride. He pressed forward deeper into the Pine Barrens forest.

Outside the pine barrens a string of patrol cars encircled the forest entrance, eleven in total, and a stream of cops and FBI agents entered the park in a sweeping orchestrated thrust that FBI Special Agent Greer Hughes controlled. He had radio contact with police Chief Tom Bennack who was up in the chopper with his pack of three K-9 tracking dogs. Both men were confident they had triangulated the position of their serial killer, Hector Anguilera, and the noose was now tightening. It would not be long now, Hughes had told Bennack. They would save Laquan Williams' life just in time and apprehend the serial killer.

From above the pine barrens, approximately two hundred yards from where Williams was jogging, Chief Bennack and his three tracking attack dogs were now being lowered down through thick branches of the pine forest from the helicopter as it hovered fifteen yards above the vast arboreal landscape. As he pressed forward, Williams could still hear the faint sound of chopper blades drumming in the distance. His path veered sharply off to the right, away from Bennack who had just touched ground and was now commanding his pack of dogs to hunt and track scent. He moved fifty yards from the landing sight and stood rigid, listening. The three trackers held their noses up high, sniffing the air. The lead tracker, a German Shepherd suddenly jerked its head to the right and the other two did the same. A scent had filled their noses and the German Shepherd set off at a fast pace to the right, the

Rottweiler and Doberman close behind. Bennack followed in a slow jog commanding his pack.

It was 5:52 PM when Williams was aware that something was following him. He looked over his shoulder and saw nothing, yet he heard the break of branches behind him triggering him to pick up his pace. Now 5:58 PM and the sound was closer. He heard heavy breathing, but no sirens, no chopper blades, just the deafening forest silence that punched adrenaline through his veins. He had read the headlines in Newsday about the serial killer from Freeport High School who was killing classmates so on each jogging mission, Williams was acutely aware of his path and the need not to be alone for more than ten minutes. He was still a fast runner and two weeks ago began carrying a club with him. At 6:03 PM, Williams darted away from the path thinking he would cut in half the time to circle back to the pine barrens entrance.

Chief Bennack was now one hundred thirty yards from Williams and his dogs, nose to the ground, were tracking a thick scent. He tried to see through the thick pine forest, but the pine boughs provided no break in the view. Bennack knew from his dogs tracking that they were close to something but there was no way of telling whether or not it was Laquan Williams in front of him or something else.

At 6:07 PM, Williams panicked when he saw the shadow of two creatures moving off to his left. Now he heard breathing, saw they were heading him off, and when he exploded into a dash through the underbrush and thick pine forest, he was suddenly encircled by a pack of dogs, four of them. The large one, he thought was a Rottweiler, lunged into the air from his right side and he swung his club with a thrashing slice that caught the attacker on its shoulder blade. It gave a gnarled deep throated growl and that's when they all attacked. Williams was now swinging his club for his life. He felt pain grip his left calf, then his

PART III: The Confrontation | 240

right, but it was the Rottweiler that had him by the throat trying to bring him down. Williams was strong, and he thrust himself up and out of the melee with a lurch that gave him enough momentum to grab hold of a large pine tree trunk. He heaved himself up the trunk, clawing his way upward out of reach. Below him was the sound of dogs on the attack and the Shepherd had his left foot, the Rottweiler leaping into the air trying to snag his right leg, but Williams' powerful strength pulled his body up out of reach, and he climbed swiftly up the tree out of reach, the German Shepherd falling to the ground.

Agent Hughes had his strategic force now swarming through the pine barrens forest, combing every section on the Northside just south of Calverton. No sightings yet, but Chief Bennack had just communicated to Hughes that his dogs were onto a strong scent and he was moving northeast from where he was dropped off into the forest.

Bennack's pace had quickened. He sensed he was getting close to his target based on the frenetic action of his three trackers. Then he heard it. In the distance. The faint sound of an attack. Dogs fighting. He did not know if they were attacking each other or attacking something else. He quickened his pace, bounding around thick trees, leaping over fallen logs, and the sound of an attack somewhere ahead of him. Then he heard a muffled scream. It was human and Bennack pulled out his Glock, safety off.

Laquan Williams was twenty-two feet above ground in the pine tree when he saw it. It was climbing up after him. When it reached William's feet, it looked up at him staring through eerie haunting eyes. Williams' heart fluttered in his chest, and he said, "Jesus Christ. It's you."

It did not respond but climbed higher into the tree, now knee high to Williams who desperately was trying to pull himself out of reach. In one thrashing slice, it drove a dagger sharp knife into Williams, severing his femoral artery. Blood now sprayed like a fountain atop the ground below and Laquan felt his life slowly ebbing away. It lowered itself out of the tree and waited. Above, Williams' feet slipped off the supporting pine branch as he hugged and clutched the main trunk of the tree. Two minutes passed. His grip loosened. Four minutes passed and he released his grip, his body cartwheeling limb over limb to the ground landing on his head. Immediately four dogs tore at his body until the ground became a pool of red.

Chief Bennack and his tracking dogs broke into the circle of carnage, and he emptied his Glock at the escaping killer who faded into the thick stand of trees. Bennack walked up to what remained of Laquan's body, and tears welled up in his eyes. He shut his eyes and all he could see was the anguished face of his daughter, Judy.

Agent Hughes had heard shots ring out in the forest and directed his men in the direction of the sound. A helicopter now hovered above Bennack. Within minutes, he was surrounded by FBI agents and the police. They all stared at what lay on the ground before them.

Bennack heard one of the officers exclaim, "Mother of Christ."

One of Hughes agents, a woman, asked, "Who could do something like this."

"One sick bastard," said agent Hughes, "and we're going to smoke the hell out of him when we get him."

"It better be soon," said Bennack. "They're five more on his list."

Hughes said, "Spread out and we'll encircle him to the east. I want the entire parameter of the Pine Barrens sealed off. We've got him now."

CHAPTER 41

THE ROOM WAS dark save for a candle that flickered against the moist walls with an eerie glow. On the floor lay four dogs that had just consumed six cans of Alpo dog food. Newspaper clippings were affixed to the walls in no particular design. Each had photos of the deceased. On the opposite wall were six other photos. Anguilera spoke first as he removed one of the six photos from the wall and tore it to shreds.

"Laquan Williams recognized us."

"What did he say," a low angered voice filled with rage queried. It was Mauricio, Hector's twin brother.

"It's you. That's all he said. It's you,"

A woman answered in Spanish. Her voice was soft and reassuring, "*Esta bien, Hector.*" It's okay, Hector. "*Fue muy malo contigo y se merecia lo que tenia.*" He was very mean to you and he deserved what he got. "*La genre es tan cruel el uno con el otro. Me allegro de sue se haya ido. No te molestara mas hijo mio.*" People are so cruel to each other. I'm glad he's gone. He won't bother you anymore, my dear son.

"Why, mother? Why were they so mean to me?" Hector asked, his voice filled with grief.

"*Porque eras diferente a ellos, hijo. A la gente no le gustan las diferencias. Solo les gusta la gente de su propia clase. Es muy triste que no podamos excepto el uno al otro y apreciar nuestras diferencias. Eres muy especial a mi y tu hermano.*" Because you are different than them, son. People don't like differences. They only like people of their own kind. It is very sad that we can't accept each other and appreciate our differences. You are very special to me and your brother.

Hector began to cry. At first, he wept silently, tears streaming down his hair covered face. Then he began to sob in a wrenching, soulful sound of grief and despair. The four dogs encircled the grieving man licking his hair covered arms and legs.

Mauricio, his brother suddenly stood up and screamed a deafening cry of rage, his voice low and guttural, filled with anger, and resentment. "Why, mother, why did this happen to my brother. He was so innocent. He never hurt anybody. They bullied him, made fun of him. They picked on my brother constantly. The bastards," he shrieked. "The sons of bitches." Mauricio's voice rose to an angered pitch and he shouted, "They all deserve to die."

The dogs began to snarl, jaws snapping at the air, rubbing up against Hector protectively.

Hector's mother sat motionless now, taking it all in. Her warm and loving voice now softened the darkened room with affection that seemed to calm Hector, Mauricio, and the dogs. She said, "*Ahora esta en manos de dios, mi hijos de mi querido. Dios te hizo un hermoso, Hector. Cada Vida es hermosa. La gente no puedo evitario. Olvidan lo que significa el amor.*" It is in God's hands now, dear sons. God made you beautiful, Hector. Each life is beautiful. People can't help themselves. They forget what love means.

Her voice silenced the room and the candle suddenly snuffed out from a faint motion of wind as if a window or door had been opened. The silence was palpable. Hector looked out into the darkness and heard movement. He sat motionless as did his brother Mauricio and their mother, Camila, all staring into the darkness.

CHAPTER 42

T HE EASTERN PERIMETER of the Long Island Pine Barrens had been sealed off tightly with patrol cars and a phalanx of police officers and FBI agents was now triangulating the shack that Grady Bennack had discovered with his dragonfly drone. Chief Bennack and special FBI agent Hughes were now converging on the shack that they could now see in the distance through the thick pine forest. A helicopter hovered above the treetops directly above the shack providing directions for the ground force.

Bennack led the squadron of fourteen patrolmen and agents on the left flank while agent Hughes swept the right flank circling around behind the shack. Bennack's dogs arrived at the shack first sniffing the side walls and back of the decrepit aged wood structure and were now snarling and clawing at the rickety front door to get inside.

Gun drawn, agent Hughes heeled the front door, and it swung halfway open with an eerie creaking sound. Bennack's three attack dogs leapt through the door and covered the small space, noses to the floor, growling and pawing the floor. Hughes and Bennack entered, pistols drawn.

Bennack said, "Shit. Nothing. No newspapers. No blankets. Nothing."

"Maybe this isn't the right shack. There were no empty cans of dog food outside or inside the shack that the drone video showed."

"Maybe not," Hughes said.

The two men came out of the shack and Hughes barked a command. He pointed, "That way. Nothing's here. We've got the wrong shack."

Bennack radioed the chopper above and it shifted its position to the northeast and hovered, its infrared camera locking onto another structure. The force spread through the tree pack heading to where Grady's video showed another shack. Bennack was convinced it was the next shack. All they had to do now was find it.

In less than fifteen minutes, they saw the second shack in the distance. It was larger than the first shack and there were empty dog food cans scattered outside the front door. Bennack's Schutzhund trained attack dogs were in a frenzy and they were barking outside the front door which was ajar. Paws scratching against rough pinewood. Hughes and Bennack flanked the front door. Bennack shouted, "Fass," the Schutzhund command for attack and hold. Three dogs leapt at the front door. It swung inward with the grinding sound of rusted hinges. Snarling guttural growls filled the air. Guns drawn, Hughes and Bennack swung around and leapt into the shack expecting the worse. The Doberman was ripping at the floor carpet and the German Shepherd tore at the other end ripping the small carpet to shreds.

"Jesus," said Hughes. "Where the hell is he?"

Bennack spun around the room looking for blankets, newspaper clippings, a list, or any trace of the crime, but everything in his son's drone video had vanished except for the empty dog food cans still scattered outside and inside, seemingly untouched. The carpet was clenched in the attack dogs' jaws.

"Goddamit!" Bennack screamed. "The son of a bitch just vanished. Not even a trace, except cans of dog food."

"There are probably many more shacks in the Pine Barrens where we could look," Hughes said.

"But this is the shack in Grady's video. No question about that," said Bennack and he looked up toward the ceiling at the cross beam and pointed. "Grady's drone rested on that crossbeam and I recognize the room. Whatever was in here was removed purposefully."

"I agree," Hughes said. "Cunning bastard."

"Wolves are cunning, like humans," Bennack added.

"Creepy," Hughes said. "If it's got that werewolf disease and thinks it's a wolf, the serial killer will be impossible to find."

CHAPTER 43

GRADY BENNACK WAS alone with Julie Harned in a passionate embrace in the back seat of her red Mustang. They were parked on a dead-end street just off Dune Road in Southampton. It had been a safe quiet place they had frequented many times, but it was the first time Grady was able to clear his mind of the jogger killings. He was confident that his father was now, with the aid of his drone information, in a position to apprehend the serial killer. Besides, he had promised Julie to let the police and FBI handle the case. Nevertheless, he felt left out not participating in the final events.

The scent of Julie's lavender lipstick filled the air and Grady crossed his left leg atop Julie's thigh as he sought to remove her bra. The hook unsnapped and his hand gently cupped her left breast. She moaned and Grady responded with urgent ardor. Maybe this was the moment, he thought.

He had fantasied about having sex with her for over a year now and the moment had finally arrived. Yes, this was the moment, he told himself. Grady's mind rushed as he fumbled for the prophylactic in his wallet. His wallet fell to the backseat floor, and he desperately tried to find it without losing the pace and excitement of the moment he had dreamed about since puberty.

"What are you doing, Grady," her voice whispered.

His mind was at a loss for response. Finally, the fingers of his left hand found the wallet and he clutched it trying to extract his protection.

"What are you doing," she repeated.

"Protecting myself," he said, his heart pounding in his chest.

Julie closed her legs and said, "No."

Grady's mind froze as he lay in the back seat rigid with expectation, his pants down to his knees. Finally, he gasped, "What?"

"No. I said no. I told you I want to wait until we get married."

"You can't be serious," he said, his voice cracking into a high-pitched finish. "We're sitting in the back seat of your car and you don't want to do it?"

Julie held up her fidelity ring on her left finger. She poked it into his face to emphasize her commitment. "I know it's hard."

"It sure is," Grady exhaled in a puff of frustration.

"I mean hard to resist," she said. "I want to do it too, Grady, but I promised myself and my parents that I would wait."

Grady's groin ached with anticipation, and he sat up on the seat wriggling back into his pants.

"Are you mad at me?" Julie said softly.

Grady exhaled trying to catch his breath. "Everybody's doing it, Julie."

"I don't believe that, Grady. A lot of my girlfriends tell me they've never had sex."

"And you believe them?" Grady said incredulously.

"Yes. I do," Julie said earnestly.

"They're lying, Julie. All the guys, my friends, have all had sex except me."

"That's bull shit, Grady, and you know it. Do you think they would admit that they never had sex?"

He hesitated to respond, thinking about all the times he lied to his friends that he had had sex many times before. He held his silence in check.

"See . . . it's a testosterone thing. They would never tell you, never. Besides . . . what difference does it make. We're talking about us, not them. I love you, Grady Bennack and someday, I hope we'll get married. And when we do . . ."

"When we do, what?" Grady said, his testicles now in a knot of pain.

"When we do have sex, on our wedding night, I'm going to fuck you silly and you'll thank me for waiting for that special moment."

Grady looked into her emerald-green eyes and repeated, "Fuck me silly?" He actually grinned then burst into laughter, the thought titillating his aroused mind.

Julie held his head between her hands and kissed him hard. She broke off the kiss and said, "Yes . . . fuck you silly. Now let's go home."

Chief Bennack drove into his driveway thirty-nine minutes after Julie had dropped Grady off and the look of frustration had washed over his face. He had just reviewed the serial killer's profile again with FBI special agent Greer Hughes and they both concluded that they were no closer to finding the killer than before. The dragnet employed over Long Island and New York City, New Jersey, and Connecticut had not provided any more leads since the confrontation with the Killer in Asharoken. The shack sighting from Grady's drone failed to produce any reasonable clues except that the killer had struck again with an intensity that left the police and FBI in a dark place. For the first time, they had proof that the killer had used a knife to kill his prey. After studying the crime scene in the Pine Barrens, they concluded that Laquan Williams had climbed the tree to escape the dogs and the killer had climbed up after him plunging a dagger into his femoral artery. The knife was still in the corpse when Bennack arrived.

Hughes and Bennack agreed on the killer's motive. He was motivated to track down and kill his victims because of what each of them had done or said to him at Freeport High School. The comments beside each of the victims that the killer had listed on the sheet of paper Grady's dragonfly drone had photographed said it all. Bullying, belittling, teasing, pushing, and shoving him all his teenage life slowly, over time, wore Hector Aguilera down to the point that his self-worth and confidence had vanished. They both reasoned that Hector's personality had morphed into actually believing that he was a werewolf and had attached and identified himself with a pack of dogs that he was now controlling to kill his victims. The case, Bennack and Hughes agreed, was eerie and rare and what bothered them the most was how elusive the killer had become, almost taunting them. They both agreed that most of the killer's victims being joggers was shear chance or coincidence since some of them were not joggers but instead had a habit of walking for exercise and not jogging. Bennack had told Hughes that any motion for a pack of attack dogs would heighten the chase.

The photographs taken by Grady's drone was proof that the killer had been in the shack. But now he had vanished with no sign left behind but five empty dog food cans scattered inside and outside the rickety shack's front door. Bennack's tracking dogs had circled the shack numerous times and Bennack knew from their excited pitch that they were onto the scent, but the moment they worked the pine forest territory a quarter mile away from the shack, the scent had vanished and his attack dogs backtracked to the shack in renewed frenzy.

Hughes and Bennack instigated orders to comb the Long Island Pine Barrens with the largest man hunt ever assembled on the island. Over fifty police officers, and eighteen FBI agents, four teams of K-9 dog trackers and three helicopters now swarmed over the pine barrens hoping to flush out the serial killer who had now killed six victims. Bennack and Hughes were both at a loss as to where the killer was hiding and his black Chevy van that the APB had failed to locate added frustration to the hunt. But they did agree that the most important thing to do now was locate each of the people that the killer had on his list that were still hopefully alive and put a tail on each of them with the hope of catching the serial killer before he killed his next victim.

Bennack got out of his police car and entered his home. The first thing he said was, "Grady?"

"Yes, Dad."

"No sign of the killer. The shack in your drone video was empty. Everything has vanished, including the newspaper photos and all the blankets. Nothing."

At first, Grady stood rigid in silence, arms at his side. His mind was consumed with one question: how could the killer and his dogs vanish from the shack without a trace. Finally, he said, "How could that happen, Dad?"

"We don't know, son. We've got a dragnet search through the entire Pine Barrens now."

"They've got to be in there somewhere. You had the perimeter sealed off, right?"

"Tight as a drum."

"Then they're still in there, dad. They have to be. No place else to go."

"If they are, we'll find them. But I want you to stay out of this, Grady. We're dealing with a sick mind and a serial killer who's very cunning and dangerous. "

Grady did not move. He was looking at his father, but his mind had already shifted beyond his father's voice and a strange excitement was now surging through him. If the authorities could not find the killer what were the chances that he could find the killer again as he had the first time with his dragonfly drone.

"Grady?"

The teenager stood in silence staring over his father's right shoulder, his vision blurred with possibilities.

"Grady. Grady. Did you hear me?"

"Yes, Dad. I heard you." He lied.

CHAPTER 44

THE SERIAL KILLER had vanished into thin air and FBI agent Greer Hughes had already decided to take a different approach to better understand the killer's thought pattern.

Hoping to get inside Hector Anguilera's mind, Hughes had assembled research on clinical lycanthropy, a rare psychiatric syndrome with the delusional belief that one is a werewolf. The disease, also known as Ambrose S, first appeared in 1852, and described a man admitted to an asylum in Nancy, France. He was convinced that he had turned into a wolf. He parted his lips with his fingers to show his alleged wolf's teeth, and complained that he had paws with long nails, and that his entire body was covered in long hair. He said that he only wanted to eat raw meat, but when it was given to him, he refused it because it was not rotten enough. Hughes felt a gnawing, sick feeling in his gut. Suddenly, he realized his entire body had broken out into a cold sweat.

On the wall in front of Hughes' desk, he had affixed photos of a grey wolf and several photos of people who had contracted the rare disease. He also had a photo of the serial killer. He posted photos of the four breeds of dogs that DNA samples at the killing site proved had committed the slaughter. If Anguilera's mind had morphed into lycanthropy as the Centers for Disease Control had hypothecated from the blood samples taken from the crime scene of the third victim, then Hughes could assume that the perpetrator had taken on the thought process of a wolf and that with Chief Bennack's knowledge of K-9 attack dogs, the killer was controlling dogs in his pack as the alpha male to carry out the killing of each of his victims. Hughes had also thumb tacked onto the wall a photo of the six victims who had been killed and photos of the five remaining victims on the list who were still alive.

According to the list of victims that Grady's drone had captured in the video, each of the eleven victims had maligned Hector by bullying him in such a hateful way that, over time, Hughes concluded, Anguilera's mind finally snapped. The justification for killing his victims, based on the comments that the killer had documented, seemed all the justification that Hughes needed as to why Hector was singling out and hunting down each victim as a wolf would do in its search for prey. Some kind of suppressed subconscious hateful revenge on those who had tormented him with such evil intent when he attended Freeport High School.

Hughes studied the habits of the grey wolf noting that The first gray wolf, Canis Lupis, probably appeared in Eurasia sometime in the Pleistocene period about a million years ago. Around 750,000 years ago, the wolf was thought to have migrated to North America. Dogs were just a loose category of wolves until 15,000 years ago when people tamed and began managing them. People fed them, bred them, and spread them from continent to continent. While other descendants died out, dogs grew into new species. Although around the world many families kept dogs as pets, the majority of the world's dogs were free-ranging. The total population of dogs in the world, Hughes noted, was estimated at 900 million with 89.7 million living in homes in the United States with the world's gray wolf population at nine million. But Hughes was noticeably frustrated because his research did not probe into the Wolf's mind other than he knew it hunted in packs, tracking and hunting its prey. They would choose den sites and establish the pack's territory developing strong social bonds within their packs. Then he found what he was looking for, a clue.

Wolves have a complex communication system ranging from barks and whines to growls and howls. Hughes was making notes in his log as fast as he could write. He noted that while wolves don't actually howl at the moon, they are more active at dawn and dusk, and they do howl more when it's lighter at night, which occurs more often when the moon is full. So, Hughes reasoned that Hector probably spent his time at night tracking the next victim and then once discovering where the next victim lived, he lay waiting with his pack until the time was exactly right for the kill which in all six killings happened in the light of day when the eyes of the wolf could see his victim and plan the exact sight of the kill.

Hughes' mind was spinning. Where was the killer's den. How did he successfully evade the dragnet and where was the black Chevy van being stored. Was someone helping him? Hughes stood up rigid and stared at the wall of pictures. And then, in one defining moment, he saw it. He picked up his phone and made one phone call.

CHAPTER 45

H ARNED'S FORD MUSTANG was parked almost in the same spot that it had been before the first probe of the Long Island Pine Barrens.

"I don't feel right about this, Grady. You agreed with your father that you were going to stay out of this mess. The killer is deranged and very dangerous. He's killed six victims, Grady, and we have no business involving ourselves in any way."

Grady sat in the front seat holding the drone in his lap, lost in thought.

"Did you hear me? Grady, I'm talking to you."

No response.

"Grady?"

"What."

"Did you hear what I said?"

"No."

"I said that you promised your dad that you would not get involved in the killings."

"I didn't promise him."

"You agreed to stay out of it."

"That's not a promise."

"Whatever, Grady. I'm staying in the car. You're being impossible and it's going to get us both killed."

"I'm not going into the woods. I'll be on the outside like last time. But keep the car running just in case."

"Just in case what?" Julie's heart skipped a beat.

"In case we need to get the hell out of here fast like last time."

"I don't like this, Grady."

"Don't worry. We're safe."

Grady opened the car door and exited closing the door behind him, his mind focusing on the mission of finding the killer. When the police and FBI failed to locate the killer, Grady was almost relieved because it was an opportunity for him to reinsert himself back into the situation. The fact that the killer's evidence had vanished from inside the shack peeked Grady's resolve to find him. When the police and FBI failed to find the killer within the thick pine forest, Grady spent two days researching the Long Island Pine Barrens. What he discovered ignited an idea of what might have happened to the killer and his pack of dogs within the boundaries of the vast pine barren forest. If it was true, Grady Bennack could be onto a major breakthrough in the search for the killer. Now, his resolve was set. Nothing could change his mission or determination of finding the den where the killer was hiding.

Grady walked up to within forty yards of the thick tree pack and set up his drone. He stared at the thick forest looking for movement. Nothing. Then something moved on his right. His eyes pierced the thick pine forest and he saw a young fawn suckling from its mother. Such a peaceful sight, thought Grady, was an oxymoron to the lurking serial predator that might still be hidden deep within the Pine Barrens.

The drone lifted off the ground as Julie watched through the windshield and flew high over the edge of the pine forest then vanished over the treetops.

Grady had punched in the coordinates where the second shack was found and the drone flew to the exact location, hovering above its target. It was 3:48 P.M. on Thursday when it descended between the tree pack and circled the shack twice then, behind the shack, landed to the left of a large moss covered stump of a pine tree near where it had landed before. Grady could see nothing unusual about the shack. It looked the same as before, sagging roof, timbers punctured with pine knot holes, and a rusting old tin pipe chimney jutting from an unsteady roof where somebody, Grady thought, once cooked and kept warm in front of a crooked hearth from within. The front door seemed to be in the same position, slightly ajar, as it was last week when Grady first discovered it.

The dragonfly drone lifted off gently from its mother drone and whirred atop the roof then hovered motionless facing the front door inspecting its point of entry. Slowly it flew toward the small open crack in the door and carefully entered inside. Now it hovered halfway between the ceiling and the floor before flying up and landing on the same cross beam as before. Once there, its eyes scanned and studied the small room. Grady's eyes were riveted on his video screen. There were no newsprint copies on the small table within the room nor were there any blankets or dog food cans outside or inside the shack. The room was vacant. The dragonfly left its perch and flew down atop the table and sat still, its eyes moving left to right, right to left, then straight ahead. Was anything different about the room, Grady pondered, his heart racing in his chest with expectation, but there seemed to be nothing visually different other than the missing objects that had been there before so vividly one week ago. The insect lifted off the table, hesitated, then flew down to the floor. Now it looked up then studied the walls, then the floor. Something was different, Grady thought, other than the missing objects, but he could not identify what it was. The dragonfly wings stopped whirring and the insect sat quietly on the floor. Suddenly, something moved within the room and it startled Grady's fix on the opposite wall. The wings came alive and the small insect lifted off the floor back to the beam and landed. Its eyes were riveted on the floor below. There was a filthy dark brown swath of torn rug that began to move. Slowly at first, but now something was moving it and Grady, hands trembling, watched in fixed astonishment as the rug slowly slid away from the center of the room as if an unseen hand was magically pulling it aside. Then it happened. A red light flashed on Grady's control panel and the screen before him went blank. The Dragonfly battery was dead! Grady said aloud, "Oh my God. No! It can't be!"

CHAPTER 46

BY FBI SPECIAL agent Greer Hughes' order, FBI agents
had located the five remaining names of the Freeport High
School graduates who were still alive and on the serial killer's
list. They had contacted each one of them to warn them that they
were each being tracked and hunted down and that each of them
had been assigned an FBI agent to protect them until they caught
the killer.

Hughes' plan was to set a live trap using the next victim as
bait. The only problem, concluded Hughes, was that if the killer
switched the order of his attack other than the order appearing on
the list that Grady Bennack's drone had captured, it would present
a challenge of coordinating the trap. That aside, Hughes had
already decided that the only way of capturing the killer was to use
live bait, a human. He chose Juan Lopez.

For three consecutive days, at 5:00 P.M. each day, Juan Lopez was
instructed to jog from his home in Greenport, Long Island into a
dense farm field a quarter mile from his home in the North Fork

farm belt. His path was secured by five FBI agents who tracked Lopez's path with heat seeking thermal cameras. Lopez insisted he carry a baseball bat in case his protectors failed to reach him in time. On the fourth day, nothing happened. No sightings of anybody suspicious. So, the trap was called off and Rashona Smith, the next victim on the killer's list was asked to repeat the process and the trap was set. Again, after three days, nothing happened until the fifth day. It was Bethpage, Long Island, and Charlie Hamilton who lived alone, was supposed to report to work at Harris GSSD Corporation. The FBI agent watching Hamilton's house was parked a third of the way down the block from his house on the opposite side of the street. The FBI agent, Sally Bromfield, reported no activity from the house. She had seen Hamilton leave his home each of the last four days and return about the same time each day. This morning, Bromfield reported not seeing any activity and it was 8:39 AM Hamilton was religious about leaving his house by 7:45 AM since Bromfield knew he was due at Harris GSSD by 8:00 AM. His car was parked in the driveway and no sign of Hamilton.

She held up her hand mike and said, "Bromfield here, No sign of Hamilton. Something's wrong. I'm going inside."

Greer Hughes' voice sounded immediately. "You need back up."

"Not yet. Let me check it out and I'll report back."

"Roger that," said Hughes. "Nothing here either."

"10-4."

Bromfield opened her car door and slipped out onto the street. She palmed her weapon for comfort and walked toward Hamilton's house. She stopped at his car parked in the driveway and peered inside. She tried the driver's side door, it was locked. The silence now gripped her. Something didn't feel right. She thought about calling for backup but hesitated long enough to check the thought. Slowly, Bromfield approached the front door and knocked. No answer. She knocked again, using the door knocker this time. Louder. No answer. She tried the front door and it opened.

Bromfield took a deep labored breath, drawing her weapon, and stepped inside listening. The silence was palpable.

Her eyes scanned the foyer, then the living room. Nothing. She looked up the steps and said, "Charlie?"

No answer.

Louder this time, "Charlie!"

Again, no answer.

Her heart was pounding in her chest as she slowly walked into the kitchen. Nothing. She circled around back into the living room towards the stairs approaching the front door. Slowly she advanced upstairs one step at a time, her Glock at the ready. She reached the top step and thought she heard heavy breathing. Slowly she searched the first bedroom at the top of the stairs. Empty. She sidestepped to the next bedroom, gun pointed right, left, then straight ahead. She could hear her own breathing but was it hers or someone else. Almost whispering, again she said, "Charlie?" Suddenly, from behind her, something took her down in a single sliding motion that knocked the breath out of her and she gasped. Her head hit the floor, hard, and she blacked out for thirty seconds. When she opened her eyes, something was hovering over her and there was no gun in her hand. Its eyes pierced down at her. She opened her mouth to scream but nothing came out but a rush of thin air. And then it happened. Four dogs surrounded her snarling with gnashing teeth. Whatever hovered above her was beyond her ability to cope. It uttered some kind of animal command, and she closed her eyes tightly expecting to take her last breath. Instead, in a flashing moment, she heard a flurry of motion and whatever had assembled around her had disappeared down the steps and out of the home. When she opened her eyes, they had all vanished including her Glock and her two-way radio which had been in her chest pocket. She lay on the floor paralyzed. All the FBI special forces training she had aced had not prepared her for a confrontation like this. She blinked her eyes in disbelief as if willing away what had just happened.

Rising slowly from the floor, she stood stiffly staring at the third bedroom door. She moved in slow motion toward the bedroom, a half step at a time, no gun. The door was closed. She opened it slowly and stood at the center of the doorway taking in a sight that caused the blood flow to her brain to cease. Her eyes blurred and the ringing sensation pulsating in her ears confirmed she was in the process of fainting. Her knees buckled and, in full uniform, FBI special agent Sally Bromfield fell forward onto her face knocking her right front eye tooth back into her throat. Eleven minutes later, a strong hand rolled her body over onto her back. It was FBI agent Greer Hughes who guessed there was trouble when she did not respond to his repeated calls.

Four other FBI agents encircled her. On the floor in front of them lay the bloodied remains of victim number seven, Charlie Hamilton. His face was unrecognizable, except for the mask of terror that was visible to Hughes in one gaping opened eye. Agent Bromfield slowly sat up and put her right hand to her mouth and swallowed hard. It was then she realized she had just swallowed a tooth. Greer had spied the gaping black hole in her opened mouth when he rolled her over.

CHAPTER 47

THE VIDEO SCREEN on Grady Bennack's mother drone glowed brightly on the coffee table in the den of his home. Hovering over the screen, squinting to see every detail, Grady and Julie stared at the dark brown carpet as it moved slowly across the small room as if an unseen hand was guiding it. It was the fourth rerun of the video that the teenagers watched and what they saw was unmistakable. Something was somehow moving the carpet, but they could not identify what it was.

"This is really scary, Grady. We've got to show it to you father. The killer has to be beneath that rug. That's where he's hiding," said Julie, her voice trembling.

"Not yet, Julie," Grady said. "We don't have proof that the killer moved that rug."

"Grady, for God's sake. Less than a week ago, that room was filled with evidence that the killer was there. The newspaper clippings, the list of victims, cans of dog food, blankets and two chairs. Now the shack is empty. Nothing's in there but a dirty old rug. That's all the proof you need to prove to your dad that the killer's still there." Julie closed her eyes tightly and sighed. "If you don't tell him now, I will."

Grady hesitated in a long thoughtful stare. "Not yet. Because
. . ." Grady said, not finishing the sentence.

Julie sputtered a response. "Because why?"

"Because we don't have any proof that he's there. Dad and the
FBI were all over this shack and found nothing."

Julie leaned into the video screen again and punched the
replay button. Staring at the screen, she watched the brown rug
move slowly across the floor yet again. When it moved about
three inches, she pressed the *freeze frame pause* button. Grady
now leaned in also and both of them stared at the bright screen
unblinking.

"Can we blow this up on your TV screen," Julie said.

"Yes," said Grady, and he took some wires from behind
the Smart TV screen and attached them to his video camera.
Suddenly, the five-foot TV screen showed the brown rug up close.

"Jesus, mother of God!"

"There it is," said Julie.

"What is it?"

"Can you blow it up more?"

"Yes."

The screen now displayed a close up of the rug's edge.

Julie and Grady studied the image for a minute before Grady
said, "I think it's a hand."

"Fingers?" Said Julie. "Good, God."

"It's his hand," said Grady. "Covered in hair. Looks like a paw.
Look at the finger nails. They're huge claws."

"This scares the hell out of me, Grady."

"Hair covering all of them. It's him," Grady said. "The killer."

"See the floor?" Julie said to Grady.

"What about it."

"The crack. The small crack in the floor. "Is it a trap door?"

Grady leaned in closer staring at the big TV screen. "Maybe. Where do you think it goes?"

"I don't know."

"Probably its den down below the trap door."

"That really bothers me, Grady."

"What?"

"You referred to Hector as an *'it.'* As if he's not human. I feel so sorry for him. Picked on and bullied all his life. It's not his fault he turned out this way. The people who made fun of him drove him crazy." In a burst of emotion, Julie started to cry, tears streaming down her cheeks. "I don't want to see him die, Grady. It's so sad. It's not right."

Grady felt a brief pang of sadness too and he stood rigid staring at the screen than he spun around and stared at Julie's face. The sounds of her grief filled the air. His mind raced for some possible response that would help assuage the pang of tragedy and sadness that Julie was feeling about the killer. But the loss of his sister and how she was tracked down and tragically mauled to death by this violent serial killer consumed his mind. It would have to be killed, Grady thought. But how and when? That was the troubling challenge. If the killer was hiding below the shack, underground, thought Grady, in some kind of den with a pack of wild attack dogs, how could they possibly coax him out of the den to capture him.

Trying to comfort her, Grady embraced Julie, still thinking about what they had discovered. He would tell his dad, he decided, but he hesitated about the timing. Then an idea came to him. He broke the embrace startled in thought. "Julie . . ."

She looked up into his eyes, tears still spilling down her cheeks. "Yes?"

"I have an idea."

"What?"

"Before telling my dad about our discovery, I want to study the Long Island Pine Barrens."

"What are you talking about? What for?"

"I have a hunch."

Julie wiped the tears from her cheeks and sniffled. "What hunch?"

Grady did not respond. He stared into her searching eyes and then leaned in to kiss her soft lavender scented lips. It was a soft and reassuring kiss, one that to Julie was filled with compassion and unanswered questions.

For almost ten minutes, Grady shared with Julie his idea about what might be beneath the Long Island Pine Barrens. When he finished sharing his thoughts both of them opened their laptops and began the search. Grady discovered that by 1200 AD a Native American tribe, the Lenape, had settled in the Long Island Pine Barrens. The Lenape tribe, also called the Delaware, were an Algonquin speaking people who lived in the Delaware Valley and across New Jersey to the Atlantic where they eventually migrated to Long Island.

Julie was now absorbed with the research and discovered that the Europeans arrived in the late 1600s and were received by the Lenape tribe as friendly and welcoming. They shared information about finding wild foods that grew in the Pine Barren forest. But Julie read that the Dutch settlers were very cruel to the Native American Lenape. She was relieved to find that the Swedes, Quakers, and Scotts were much kinder to the native tribe.

Julie looked up from her laptop and saw Grady punching the keys frantically. She said, "Grady."

He didn't respond. Louder this time, "Grady."

He looked up. "What?"

"I don't see anything relevant here that could help us find the killer."

"Wait."

"Wait for what?"

"I'm onto something."

"What?"

Grady held up his left hand in a frustrated stopping motion.

He stared at his computer screen and read aloud, "When the European settlers landed in America, they brought diseases. Smallpox, malaria, and tuberculosis ravaged the Lenape tribe. They had no immunity. By the mid-18th century, the Lenape population was reduced to a small splintered tribe."

Julie interrupted Grady and said, "Stop, Grady. This has no relevance to the search for the killer. Enough already."

Grady looked up from his computer and said, "Except for this one fact. In order to escape the plague of these diseases and to avoid Dutch settlers, a singular band of the Lenape tribe went underground and created a vast underground system of tunnels and living quarters beneath the ground . . ." Grady looked up hesitating.

Julie sat frozen in front of her computer concentrating on every word spilling out of Grady's mouth. The silence between them was palpable.

She said, "Yes? Beneath what? What are you hesitating for?"

Grady looked at her and grinned. "I found it."

"Don't tease me like that."

"Grady repeated the sentence leading up to the pause in his voice. "The Lenape tribe went underground and created a vast system of tunnels and living quarters beneath . . ." Grady looked up again staring at Julie.

"Stop it," she demanded.

Grady finished the sentence, "beneath the Long Island Pine Barrens."

"Jesus," Julie said. "I can't believe it."

Grady sat back away from his computer and stared at the ceiling. Finally, after a two-minute pause, he said, "Somewhere in that underground maze of tunnels is the den of our serial killer."

Julie stood up and walked over to Grady. She leaned over and kissed him hard. When the kiss broke, she said, "I love you, Grady Bennack. Now call your dad and let him know what you've found."

Grady corrected her, "What we've found together."

"Whatever. Call your dad."

CHAPTER 48

FBI SPECIAL AGENT Greer Hughes and police Chief Tom Bennack stood in front of a twenty by forty-foot map of the Long Island Pine Barrens affixed to the wall of the large conference room. Red arrows pinpointed twenty-three outbuildings, most of them rickety aged shacks, lean-to structures, and abandoned sheds spread out over 100,000 acres of land in Suffolk county, long island's Pine Barrens. It is Long Island's last natural area and its last remaining wilderness. Almost all of the Peconic River and Carmans River, two of Long Island's biggest rivers, including much of their watersheds are in the Barrens, Hughes told the assemblage.

Facing the map sat seventeen police officers and nine FBI agents who were about to conduct the largest manhunt ever launched against a serial killer in the northeast United States.

Agent Hughes approached the podium with a thick file tucked under his left arm. In his right hand, he held a laser pointer which he now flicked on. A bright red dot illuminated the position of a shack in the southeast quadrant of the Pine Barren forest. He looked out at the audience and said, "First, kudos to police Chief Tom Bennack's son, Grady Bennack. With his drone, this young lad has somehow managed to find our killer's location and a complex underground labyrinth of tunnels. At least we have a suspicion that he might be hiding underground in one of the tunnels created by the Lenape Native American tribe hundreds of years ago. This young man Grady is outstanding and I've already offered him an FBI internship for next summer. Good men and women are hard to find, and this lad is God dammed good."

Bennack sat to the left side of the map upfront and he looked at Hughes with a thankful nod for the compliment. "Thank you, Greer. I'll tell him," Bennack said in a crisp but appreciative tone.

Hughes' red light now circled a spot on the map with the shack where the drone landed.

"We suspect that the killer is hiding somewhere in the underground tunnels. Note on the map the tunnel system beneath the ground is superimposed atop the map in red. The question is where's the killer's den? So, here's the plan. We're going to use motion sensors which alert you with a low beeping sound when the motion tracker picks up any motion. If that does not work in locating the killer, we'll smoke him out. Fill the underground system of tunnels with smoke and cover every possible exit. With gas masks, we'll enter the tunnel from this shack because we know the killer used the shack to plan his attacks. Simultaneously, from the western entrance into the tunnel system, another force will enter the tunnels from the east. Both forces will converge toward the center where there's an exit. If we are forced to smoke him out because we can't find him with the motion detectors, then we'll be waiting there for the killer to exit when the smoke fills the tunnel system. We are going to blow smoke into the tunnel system from the east and west entrances simultaneously. Each agent and police officer will be equipped with a bright spot light capable of piercing thick smoke. You each will wear a gas mask so you can breathe in filtered air without a problem. But I'm hoping we don't have to revert to smoke and that we can find the killer's den by using the motion sensors and K-9 tracking dogs."

Hughes looked up. "Questions?"

A woman officer sitting in the back raised her hand. "When we confront the killer, what's the order?"

Chief Bennack stepped in front of Hughes and said, "Shoot to kill."

"What about the dogs?"

Without hesitating, Bennack said, "Shoot to kill. This predator has killed seven victims and has a list of four more who are still alive. We have a tail on each of them. My daughter Judy was the first one killed. When you confront the killer, take him out, including the dogs."

Hughes seemed hesitant. He interrupted Bennack and said, "If there's a chance to take the killer alive, make it happen; otherwise, if there's no other option . . ."

Bennack interrupted Hughes in mid-sentence and said, "Take the predators out."

Hughes thought about disagreeing with Bennack, but he knew the emotion Bennack was dealing with and stood in silence. He held up a device in his left hand and said, "Infrared imaging device. On the small screen, you will see the tunnel configuration. Do not stray from your assigned path shown. Your motion detector will alert you if it senses anything in front of or behind you. Use both devices."

"What about communication with the force? We'll have twenty-six agents and officers down in the tunnel. How do we not shoot each other," said a woman FBI agent with a butch haircut and a thin line of lipstick. "Especially if you're blowing smoke up our asses."

The room broke out in a quick burst of laughter, but Bennack said, "Not funny. Nothing's funny about this case. I want this killer found by the end of this week."

Bennack stood up and said, "Use your judgement. You each have two-way so when your motion detector picks up movement, alert the force."

"We're all underground in a tunnel. What about the signal," a younger policeman queried.

"Should not be a problem," Bennack said.

"What if it is," the same woman persisted.

"Deal with it," Bennack barked. "Change your position to capture the signal."

Hughes said, "Any other questions?"

Nobody responded.

Bennack pointed the red light at two points on the map and said, "You each know your entry launch coordinates. Be at your coordinates in the Pine Barrens at 0800 hours tomorrow locked and loaded. Dismissed."

CHAPTER 49

THE SCENT WAS pungent and dampness hung in the air. The hair covering Hector's body was moist and covered in dirt and grime as was the fur on the four dogs that lay on the ground around him. A candle sputtered in the faint cool breeze that surrounded them.

The woman spoke first, her soft voice offering assurance that they had nothing to fear. Her left hand reached out and gently touched the large head of a Rottweiler. It lifted its massive head and licked her fingertips. In Spanish, she said, "*Se acaba el tiempo*." Time is running out. "*Saben que estamos en los pinos*." They know we are in the Pine Barrens.

Hector said, "Yes, mother. They do. But they'll never find our den."

An angry voice shattered the silence with rage. The four dogs stood up, snarling encircling the man. It was Mauricio, Hector's twin brother. "Tonight, Bobby Dorsett dies," he snarled. "He called you a werewolf and threw dog biscuits at you. I should have killed him in high school."

"*Te amo*," the mother said. I love you. "*Eso es todo que importa*." That's all that matters.

"Thank you, mother," Hector said, and he hugged the German Shepherd that stood next to him whining appreciatively upon his touch. Tears filled Hector's eyes trickling down into the thick hair covering his cheeks. He rose from the damp floor and said, "Shhh. Listen."

Faint but discernible, the sound came from above and the den ceiling trembled from the movement of something big.

Mauricio's body began shaking. His mouth opened wide and the sound of his raging voice filled the small dark space. "Kill him. Kill him. Kill him."

Suddenly, the small door protecting the den opened and they vanished into the dark tunnel system. Clutched in Hector Aguilera's hairy fist was a note prepared by his brother, Mauricio. It was the profile of Bobby Dorsett. Address, life habits and the timing of his everyday activity.

The Long Island Pine Barrens' 105,000 acres, in central and eastern Long Island, New York is a vast terrestrial and aquatic environment and Hector Aguilera knew his territory the way the wild wolves of Yellowstone National Park know their hunting grounds. The ponds, streams, thick tree packs, and rare man-made structures within the Pine Barrens became the trail markers of Aguilera's survival like cairns leading one on a mountain overpass.

Thick pine tree branches slowly parted in an abandoned rarely visited or known section of the 900 square mile Pine Barrens and a dirty black Chevrolet SUV van emerged into the thick pine forest. There was no visible path for the vehicle to take nor was there any sign that any car had ever driven this path before. The van threaded its way in what seemed to be uncharted territory and yet Hector Aguilera knew every tree, every shrub, and land marker as if he had commuted this way a thousand times. Mauricio, his brother, was now breathing hard, anticipating the hunt, anxious to find and destroy their next victim. After twenty-seven minutes, the black van exited the Pine Barrens on the southwestern perimeter. There would be no detection from outside forces. Just as a wolf knows how and when to attack prey, Hector and his brother Mauricio were now in synch, and they would not fail to take out their eighth victim.

They would encounter Bobby Dorsett in nineteen minutes. In the back compartment of the van, four canine attack dogs awaited command. Their breath came in short, unified spasms of anticipation for this was what they had been trained for. The command from their master would launch them into the hunt and kill, a frenzy of action. Now, fourteen minutes closer. Then nine minutes. The tension inside the black van of death was rising. Seven minutes to target.

CHAPTER 50

BOBBY DORSETT LIVED in Syosset, Long Island on the border of Cold Spring Harbor with his wife, Mary Lou, a son, Bobby 3rd., and a forty-two-pound black and white potbellied pig named Dexter. The pig enjoyed leftovers, but eight days ago, he consumed a large bowl of pulled pork and developed the runs so badly that they had to take him to the vet and ply him full of Kaopectate.

Unfortunately, Dexter's diarrhea ruined Dorsett's Persian rug, a wedding gift from his grandfather, with a stream of digested pulled pork that stained the center pattern including the initials of the Iranian rug designer. When Dexter closed the front door to jog, he left Mary Lou with the fat pig rolling on the kitchen floor in acute pain not having evacuated in eight days since being plugged with Kaopectate. Before the door shut, Dorsett, highly pissed from the ruin of his family heirloom, suggested they have a pig roast this weekend.

Dorsett was an internet website developer with American Internet Technologies, AIT, and, at twenty-seven years old, life was good. No debts except the $250,000 mortgage on his four bedroom colonial with a market price of $825,000.

He was jogging downhill on the south side of Route
25A heading east toward the Cold Spring Harbor Fish Hatchery.
When he reached the dirt driveway of St. John's Episcopal Church
abutting the fish hatchery, Dorsett took a hard right and jogged
past the church on his left then vanished into a small pathway
surrounding the church lake. The weather was clear, sun against
high cirrus clouds, and Bobby Dorsett was in his element and at
peace with his career and family life. He began jogging only two
months ago to stay in shape and lose weight.

Two months and a week ago, Mary Lou announced she was
pregnant with their second child. The ultrasound test she had done
just forty-eight hours ago confirmed the baby was a girl. They cel-
ebrated by opening a bottle of Dom Perignon champagne. Mary
Lou lifted her full glass to join Bobby in the toast, clicked glasses,
but she abstained from even a sip. Bobby gleefully consumed the
entire bottle and Dexter ate the cork.

As Dorsett rounded the far end of the lake, he heard a stick
crack in the thick forest surrounding the lake and his head
snapped to the right. He saw something flash in between the thick
underbrush. Dorsett was warned about seven of his classmates
being killed by a serial killer, but he was not concerned about jogging alone as he knew he was being tailed by an FBI agent whom
he knew was not far behind him.

FBI agent, David Ottaway, had accepted the protective order from
special agent Greer Hughes two weeks ago and Dorsett felt secure
knowing that Ottaway's only job was to keep him safe and alive.
After the fourth day, Dorsett complained that he had no privacy,
and that Ottaway was being obsessively intrusive and a pain in
the ass about tailing him everywhere. The agent assured Dorsett

that it was for his own good and to be thankful he was still alive. The comment from Ottaway sent a surge of fear through Dorsett's body and he chose not to bitch about the agent's protective custody. It seemed that everywhere Dorsett went, he was conscious of Ottaway's presence especially now that he had entered the thick tree pack surrounding the southeast side of the lake. Maybe the shadow he had just seen was Ottaway.

Agent Ottaway was not a jogger, so he told Dorsett to keep his pace to a slow jog, preferably a fast walk. It was frustrating to Dorsett, but the agent told him not to ever lose site of him. Dorsett kept his pace and looked back over his shoulder to insure he could see Ottaway. He saw something that he thought might be the agent in the far distance but wasn't sure, so he jogged in place while squinting to see detail through the thick woods. Something was moving towards him and getting closer, so he was reassured, but then something flashed to his left, closer. Then motion to his right. A sudden strike of fear coursed through Dorsett's heart and he sprang off diagonally toward the lake in a fast jog. As he did, he shouted, "Ottaway." No answer. Again, "Ottaway."

A louder yell, almost a low guttural panicked shout, "Ottaway. Dave Ottaway."

The FBI agent heard Dorsett's first shout and responded with a loud answer that got muted in the tree pack. But Ottaway quickened his pace now, puffing frustration from losing sight of his charge. He shouted, "Dorsett," as he entered deeper into the lakeside green density of shrubs, vines and deciduous trees, mostly sugar maple and oak. The agent did not see Dorsett, nor did he hear his shout for help. Instead, out of the dense forest, coming at him at an alarming speed were two charging dogs. Ottaway heard the snarls and heard something else, a loud inhuman shout of something he had never before heard. A spike of fear shot through his body, and he yanked his holstered Glock out firing three shots at the approaching dogs but failed to hit the fast moving targets that were veering off at different angles. As the last of three shots cleared the chamber, Ottaway felt a hard thrust into his back that sent him sprawling forward onto the ground. The agent's face hit the ground hard and in one motion, he felt his Glock being wrested from his right hand and he lay rigid with dread, now unarmed. He tried to peer upward but the sound of attack dogs surrounding him kept him motionless. He had only one thought . . . save Bobby Dorsett, and then they just vanished into the dense tree pack leaving Ottaway breathless, rigid, and unarmed. He waited only moments before springing to his feet. Now he was running through the woods as fast as he could not even registering that he was without protection. On the run, he reached for his two-way and shouted,

"Agent Ottaway here. Need backup. Been attacked. Lost Dorsett. Southeast side of lake on St. Johns Church property, Cold Spring Harbor. 10-4."

Ottaway heard a woman's raspy voice. "Roger that. On the way. 10-4."

Bobby Dorsett knew he was in trouble when he did not hear agent Ottaway respond. He determined that his only choice for survival was to reach the lake. Now he heard the sound of angry dogs, one on his left and three to his right. Something else was behind him as he had seen a momentary flash of motion running through the woods in a strange gait that he could not discern if it had two or four legs. Whatever it was, sent Bobby Dorsett's heart into a spasm of fear. But in the distance, he heard something reassuring. It was the sound of sirens and they were close. Very close. Now Dorsett could see the lake clearing in the distance and he was in a full sprint through the woods, jumping over fallen trees, leaping over shrubs, and zigzagging his way closer to the lake's edge. Behind him and gaining was the pack of dogs that were thirty yards away, now twenty-five, then twenty. He tore off his shirt, now fifteen yards, he unbuckled his pants, thirteen yards, squirming free of his pants and jockeys, at ten yards then, just as the lead Rottweiler sprang into the air, lunging toward its prey, Bobby Dorsett took a high arching racing dive into the church lake speeding away from shore towards the center of the lake, stark naked.

Two of the dogs dove into the lake after him yet Bobby Dorsett was now in his element. He was the New York State champion of the 100-meter freestyle swim beating the national record of 47.05 seconds in 47.02. He would have gone on to the Olympics were it not for breaking his ankle when he dove off the high diving board. Dorsett had already reached the center of the lake and the two dogs swimming after him had already turned back to shore.

What now frightened Dorsett was the salvo of gun shots coming from the far shore in back of the St. John's Episcopal church that were piercing the lake and ricocheting off the water's surface in an effort to kill the dogs in pursuit. Eleven agents and police officers were now circling the lake, guns drawn, but none of them heard the wheels screeching from a black Chevrolet van that had been secreted uphill above the church and fish hatchery parking lots in a shroud of low hanging tree branches. The van vanished just as Bobby Dorsett had exited the lake standing naked dripping wet surrounded by five officers and two agents. Thankful to be alive and in a state of shock, Dorsett didn't even bother to cover himself. Agent Ottaway came running up to Dorsett, out of breath and exhausted. He looked at his charge and said, "I told you to do a fast walk, not a fast jog. Thank God you're alive."

Dorsett hesitated for a moment before saying, "Where the hell were you?"

Ottaway stared at Dorsett without response.

"I shouted for you several times."

"I heard you the first time."

"I got taken out."

"What the hell does that mean," Dorsett said, pissed that the agent couldn't keep up with him.

"Four attack dogs took me down and disarmed me. You're dam lucky to be alive, Dorsett," Ottaway snapped, and he turned abruptly and returned to his government issued black SUV, still out of breath from the chase.

Dorsett accepted a young woman's police jacket to cover himself, and as they escorted him to police Chief Bennack's patrol car, Bobby Dorsett realized how close to death he had come. He also decided he would have Dexter on a spit for Saturday night's dinner for ruining his grandfather's Persian rug.

CHAPTER 51

JULIE HARNED HAD every intention of not getting further involved with the serial killer and Grady's obsession with solving the case. It had become too dangerous and there was no question in Julie's mind that Grady was getting closer and closer to finding the killer perhaps before the cops and FBI agents. But something Grady said two days ago suddenly changed her thinking. "They're going to kill him, Julie, and the dogs too." It was an emotional moment and Julie had burst into tears. "It wasn't his fault," she had argued. "He was born with that terrible disability and has lived with it every day of his life. He deserved their understanding and help—not derision and rejection. It's not fair. His life was never fair. We can't let the cops and FBI agents kill him, Grady. And the dogs. They shouldn't kill the dogs. They're just following his orders."

Grady stood rigid shaking his head. "How, Julie? How the hell can he be saved? It's too late. He's killed seven people, almost an eighth. We have no choice. It's up to the cops and FBI. And if the dogs get in the way they'll kill them too."

"No," Julie cried. "We've got to save them. Your dad can save them, Grady. You're going to let your dad kill them all?" Tears streamed down Julie's cheeks yet again.

"Whatever," Grady said in resignation.

"What do you mean, 'whatever'? I hate that word. It means you don't give a shit."

"Yeah, well maybe that's how I feel, Julie. You didn't lose a sister and you don't know the pain of what it's like to lose someone you love. Our whole family has suffered enormous pain because of that killer."

Julie stared at him, thinking in silence. "You're right, Grady. I don't know what it's like to lose someone. But I do know what's driving Hector Aguilera to kill his victims. He was tortured and felt worthless. You and I don't know what it would be like not to ever feel loved. To feel worthless. We have lots of friends, Grady, but Hector suffered enormous rejection at school and then one day his mind cracks and his mission is to kill all those kids who made him feel miserable. But it's not Hector the kids made fun of in school. It's the monster they created by picking on him constantly. They drove him crazy, and we've got to save him."

"It's too late, Julie. We don't know where he is now."

"It's never too late, Grady. He's in the tunnel. We saw the hand."

"That doesn't mean he's still in there."

"He's in the tunnel somewhere," Julie stated forcefully.

"If he's in there, how the hell do we find him before my dad and the agents get to him? And what do you suggest we do when we confront him if we can even find him?"

Julie said, "I don't know."

"He'll kill us, or the dogs will before . . ."

"Before what?" Julie persisted.

Suddenly, Grady's eyes widened, and he said one word, "Drone."

CHAPTER 52

THE BLACK CHEVROLET van sped through the back streets of Syosset leading east to the edge of Long Island's Pine Barrens near Manorville. The point of entry was not marked by any sign, dirt road, or path. It was an ancient overgrown zigzagging trading route used by descendants of the Unkechaug Indians before the Lenape settled in the area around 1200 A.D. The entrance was concealed by a mass of low hanging pine branches clumped together in an overgrown mass of green. The pack's den was deep within the pine barrens and the alpha male now realized he was being hunted down and his time was running out. The Native American underground tunnel system, hidden seven feet beneath the Long Island Pine Barrens, provided his pack the perfect den secreted from those he hunted. But now, things were changing fast and his senses told him he would have to keep moving the den inside the tunnel system that was hiding his pack.

Within the dark damp den, which had shifted to the southwest quadrant within the tunnel matrix, they all huddled together. Suddenly, Mauricio's voice broke the silence in a shrieking torment of violence. "You should have killed him before he got to the lake."

The dogs snarled in response.

Camila's voice was soft and reassuring. "*Hiciste todo toque purist, mi hijo.*" You tried your best, my son. "*No nos emcontrarian ahora.*" They won't find us now.

"Bobby Dorsett is still alive. You failed to kill him," Mauricio screamed, his voice cracking with the strain of emotion.

Sitting within the circle of the four dogs, a flickering candle gave a haunting specter of light as Hector Aguilera burst into tears and wailed an anguished response that his pack responded by nudging him with sympathetic whining. Then, in a voice punctuated with grief, Hector said, "They hated me. Made fun of me. I was nothing to them. Even when I pleaded with them to stop, they laughed at me, like I was a piece of shit."

Mauricio leapt to his feet, pounding both fists on the den wall causing shards of ancient dirt and clay to fall to the den floor. The dogs began barking, growling, and snapping their jaws. Mauricio shrieked at the top of his lungs a guttural rasp of rage. "They will die. We will kill them all and Bobby Dorsett will be dead by sunset tomorrow."

Her voice filling with restraint and compassion, Camila said, "*Te amo, Hector. Recuerda que siempre amare.*" I love you Hector. Remember that I will always love you.

Light brown matted hair tangled in knots and threads thickly covered Hector's face. He looked up squinting at the flickering candlelight in front of him and began a wrenching sob that tore at his gut. Four Freeport High School classmates on his list were still alive and his brother Mauricio's rage was building. The only person who brought peace to their underground den was the soft voice of their reassuring mother, Camila. But that peace promised to be short-lived.

CHAPTER 53

EILEEN LANGLEY WAS emptying her Tesla Model 3 of the last bag of groceries from Lewis Supermarket when her cell phone rang. It was 3:46 PM, Friday, and a dark sky was spitting rain. She punched a button to answer the call.

"Hi, Eileen. Grady Bennack."

"Hi, Grady. What's up?"

"We've got a problem and I need your help."

"Go ahead."

"Remember our discussion about Hector Anguilera? The guy from Freeport High School you remembered befriending?"

"Yes."

"The police and FBI are going to kill him."

There was a noticeable gasp into the phone and Langley said, "Why?"

"He's the serial killer. The same guy from your class. The guy who killed Judy and six others in your class at Freeport High. All because they bullied and made fun of him. Called him a freak."

"How awful. I didn't know it was Hector. I read about the killings. Are they sure it was him?"

Langley flashed back to Freeport High School and the vivid memory of Hector Anguilera whom she befriended. It was Hector and her experience with him that was the flashpoint of her decision to pursue a career in psychiatry. When she received her PhD from Cornell, she had tried to contact Hector to inform him that he was the motivation for her decision to devote her career to helping people in distress with disorders and mental challenges. Witnessing the sadness of Hector's life left an indelible mark on Langley. So now, as she was listening to Grady declare Hector's demise, she pressed her cell phone close to her ear listening intently.

"As far as we know, yes. He's the killer. You mentioned you befriended him."

"Yes. And he sent me an email not too long ago that I told you about. Asking me to meet him."

"Yes," said Grady thinking about how he was going to continue the conservation. "And you drove out to meet him and he never showed up. It was all was very strange, you told me."

"Yes. It was so sad how many people made fun of him and bullied him. I tried many times to assure him that I was his friend. He really was responsible for changing my life, you know."

"How's that, Eileen?"

"Knowing him and witnessing his life of agony, prompted me to get my PhD to try and help others adapt to life. I wish I knew him now as I know I could have helped him."

Out of curiosity, Grady said, "How?"

"Convince him how special he is. How many other talents he has and to learn how to focus on appreciating himself and how to feel sorry for those less fortunate people who try and feel better themselves by belittling people around them like Hector. It is those people who bully and make fun of other people who are the tragic ones. Pathetic, actually. That's what angers me about them.

I know I could have helped Hector feel better about himself if I knew then what I know now."

"Makes sense to me," said Grady taking in a deep breath before speaking. "My girlfriend, Julie Harned, and I, we have you on speaker, Eileen. We want to try and save Hector before the cops and FBI agents get to him. They'll kill Hector and we know they'll kill all the dogs too. If you were with us, we think you could talk to him and convince him to surrender before he gets killed."

There was a long silence on the phone. After a minute, Grady said, "Eileen. You still there?"

"Yes, Grady. I liked Hector and I loved your sister, Judy. I still mourn her loss, but the answer is no, Grady. No way. Hector's not the boy I knew at Freeport High School. If he's the killer, he's obviously been driven insane, and I pity what was done to him and what he has become. But we obviously would not be able to reason with him. He's a serial killer, Grady. You just confirmed that to me."

"Yes, but you were one of the few people who were nice to him," persisted Grady, "and the fact that he reached out to you not too long ago, proves he would remember you if we met. He obviously trusted you enough to try and contact you. And, you just told me you wished you could know him today and be able to use your PhD to work with his mind. Think of that challenge, Eileen,"

Langley paused for a minute, maybe two, before answering thinking about the one challenge of her career that might pass her by that she just might be able to resolve and rehabilitate Hector. "I don't think so," Langley said half trying to convince herself otherwise.

Julie Harned had listened intently. She suddenly blurted out, "I agree with you, Eileen. But . . ." she hesitated in emotional thought, "Hector might not be who he was at Freeport High, but nobody ever fought to save him like you did. You were probably the only person who reached out to him to offer him any kind of friendship or any chance of building his self-esteem. Everybody except you beat him down so he had nobody to reach out to except maybe his family and I don't know his family, but from what I understand, you were his only hope. He tried to reach out to you, Eileen. Nobody else. Now, unless we can get to him first, before the cops and FBI agents, he'll be dead by tomorrow night, and we've got to . . ." Julie couldn't finish the sentence. She burst into tears and pleaded, "please help us save him."

"Please," Grady added. "Please, Eileen. Judy would have done the same thing. Do it for her."

"But Hecter killed your sister, Grady. I doubt, if she knew who the killer was, she would have tried to save him," Eileen reasoned. "As teenagers, most of us don't think about the harm we do to each other with comments we make. And, knowing Judy as I did, I know whatever she said to Hector was made without hurtful intent."

"Maybe so, Eileen, but so many people belittled him, the damage to his self was probably already done before Judy said something to him. Fact is, time is running out and unless we do something now, he'll be dead tomorrow. Help us, please."

"What can we possibly do to save him?" Eileen asked.

"Hector, we believe, is somewhere in the tunnel system beneath the Pine Barrens. We're going to use my drone to locate him," Grady said.

"And if you locate him, what then?" Eileen said, her voice filled with tension.

"We go into the tunnel after him and hopefully reach him before the police and FBI agents do," Julie said.

"You do realize that the three of us could be killed when we confront Hector, if we find him."

"We think Hector would listen to you, Eileen. And we believe the three of us could save him together. With you being a doctor, a psychiatrist, you would know the right words to use to convince him he is safe with us, especially with you."

"That's one hell of a leap of faith. And if you're wrong, we'll never get out of that tunnel system alive."

"There's only one way to find out," Grady said. "Are you with us?"

"Is it just Hector and the dogs? Anybody else with him besides the dogs?" Eileen pressed.

"We think it's only Hector."

"How many dogs?"

"Four."

"What's your source?"

"His dad, Chief Bennack," Julie said.

"My dad and FBI agent Hughes are leading the search," added Grady.

"Does your dad have any idea you two are involved in the serial killer search?" Eileen said in disbelief. "I mean, you realize this is one hell of a crazy thing you both are suggesting. You're both teenagers for God's sake. Your father would panic if he knew you were suggesting this plan."

"Probably, Eileen," Grady said, "but I've provided a lot of the clues that have helped the police and FBI thus far."

"Grady wants to be a detective when he graduates from college."

"I can't believe what I'm hearing from you two," Eileen said but now she was more than curious about the outcome and started thinking if they actually could save Hector and whether or not she could actually reason with him in an effort to save his life if they came face to face. It would be the crowning testimony of a burgeoning career in psychiatry, and she was already making great strides at The Creedmoor Psychiatric Center, Queens Village, New York, but this was a lunatic leap of faith, she thought.

"Eileen, please join us. Help us save Hector," Grady said.

"It would be the first time in Hector's life that somebody cared enough about him to try and save his life," Julie added in a pleading hopeful voice.

The phone went silent, and Grady and Julie could hear Eileen breathing hard. They listened and the tension was palpable. Then in one word, Eileen Langley said, "Okay."

"Thank you, Eileen," Grady said. "We'll be in touch soon."

"We're crazy to do this, you understand."

Julie said, "I can't thank you enough, Eileen."

Eileen's pensive comment gave impact to the call. "Pray that God's with us. Because if He isn't, we're all . . ."

Langley did not finish her sentence. Instead, Grady and Julie heard a decisive click on the end of the phone terminating the call.

CHAPTER 54

AROUND AN OVAL conference table at the Central Long Island FBI office in Melville, Chief Tom Bennack and FBI special agent Greer Hughes stared at a topographical map identical to the enlarged wall map of the entire Pine Barrens area. Beneath the surface was the red outline of the underground tunnel system built by the Lenape.

Bennack took a magic marker and circled the area surrounding the small wooden shack that Grady Bennack had discovered with his drone where the serial killer was spotted.

"So if he's still in this area, this should be a quick search and destroy mission," said Bennack. "But if he's moving his den around within the tunnel system, it's going to be tough as hell to find him."

"We've issued motion detectors to the force and instructed them on use and communications within the tunnel," said Hughes. "If we can't locate the den after our search, we're going to blow smoke into all the entrances."

"I hope to hell we don't have to use smoke especially when we don't know the tunnel system."

Hayes circled the known tunnel entrances with a green magic marker. "We've got our teams all poised to enter the tunnel system tomorrow morning at 0800 hours sharp. Tom, I don't agree with the order you made this morning regarding confrontation," Hayes said firmly.

"About killing them all?" Bennack said.

"Yes. If we can save Hector, I believe we should do so. Why kill the dogs too?" Hughes questioned. "Factually, it's important to get inside this guy's mind. Find out what triggered these hateful killings and caused him to crack. As for the dogs, Tom, they were trained to attack and kill on command so why smoke them?"

Bennack put his magic marker down on the table and looked Hughes in the eye, an intimidating glare. "You ever been attacked by a dog, Greer," said Bennack. "Without anything to defend yourself?"

"No."

"They can rip you apart in a heartbeat. Tear your flesh to shreds, eat your organs while you're still alive."

Hughes started to drum a pencil on the table, a sign of discomfort.

"And then when you still think you might have a chance to survive because it's only a dog for christssake, it lunges at your throat and rips your trachea and esophagus from your throat in one decisive blood thirsty second."

"What the hell's your point, Bennack?"

"That's what happened to my daughter, Judy. She was utterly helpless and alone."

"I'm truly sorry, Chief, for your loss, but it wasn't the dogs' decision to kill your daughter. They were commanded by a sick person to kill her so you can't blame her death on the dogs. If possible, we should try and save at least the dogs."

Bennack's voice rose to an angry response. "I headed up the K-9 unit for all of Long Island, Greer. I understand and know that dogs are trained to attack and kill on command better than anybody. I trained them to hunt, attack and kill, but I also know that dogs are innately pack hunters and it's in their DNA to run down and kill prey."

"If they're wild dogs, yes. You're right, Tom. But how do we know they weren't rounded up by the killer from owners who just let their dogs run free at the end of a summer never to retrieve them again."

"These four dogs were trained by the killer to stalk and run down his victims and they sure as hell weren't house pets like Goldens, Pugs, Spaniels, Labs, or Chihuahuas. Once trained, the killer knew what he had. They were the same dogs that the Germans used in World War II to go behind enemy lines and attack and kill the enemy, Dobermans, German Shepherds, and Rottweilers. Our serial killer knew that his dogs, once trained, were killing machines on command. They're all guilty of murder. And when I confront them, I'm taking them out."

"Our serial killer, Tom, deserves a fair trial."

"Bull shit," Bennack snarled. "He's killed seven people."

"If we take him alive, the court will decide, Tom. Not us."

Bennack stood up and looked down at agent Hughes. "He won't be taken alive. Tomorrow at 0800."

"I hope I get to him first," agent Hughes said.

Bennack grabbed his file off the table and walked briskly toward the door. When he reached the door, he spun around on his heel and said, "You won't," and closed the door behind him.

CHAPTER 55

GRADY BENNACK HELD two lithium batteries in his hand then inserted the larger battery in the mother drone, the smaller one in the dragonfly drone. Both batteries promised one hour of flight time within the tunnel system.

"Do you think we can find the den within an hour inside the tunnel," Julie said hopefully.

"We better or they'll all be dead."

"I hope Eileen doesn't bail," she said.

"Me too. Without her, we don't stand a chance of saving Hector and the dogs . . ." He hesitated in thought . . . "or us."

"So, when do the drones go into the tunnel," Julie said, her heart skipping a beat. "I'm spooked by this whole thing, Grady. We're way over our heads and we have nothing to protect ourselves. If Hector gets violent, he'll kill us."

"Saving him was your idea, Julie."

"Yes, I know, Grady. Nobody else would. It's so sad. We've got to try. Even with the risk. What do you think our chances are?"

"Of saving him?"

"Yes."

"It's going to be a tough challenge. If my father gets to Hector first, I know he'll kill them all. But if we get to him first, I think we have a good chance of saving him. Agent Hughes wants to save them all."

Julie said, "Assuming Eileen's with us."

"Yes."

"You have to trust me on this, Julie," Grady said. "My father told me about the plans for tomorrow at 0800. An invasion of the tunnel system."

"I'm surprised he told you."

"He told me because he wants me to stay the hell out of it. I got the big lecture about staying alive. And its police and FBI work, way above my head."

"So, he knows nothing about us entering the tunnel, the drones, and Eileen?"

"Nothing."

"When do the drones enter the tunnel."

"Tonight."

"What time tonight?"

"After dark."

"Does Eileen know the entry point where we're meeting?"

"Yes, I texted her."

"Did she answer?"

"Not yet."

"I don't like that, Grady."

"She'll be there."

"Hopefully."

"She'll be there."

"And if we confront your father and the force in the tunnel?"

"We'll be in the tunnel system well before 0800 tomorrow."

"Grady . . ."

"Yes."

"I'm scared."

"So am I."

"No, I'm really scared."

"So am I."

"This is crazy bizarre for us to do, you know."

Grady said, "Yes. I know. Crazy stupid."

When the Lenape Indian tribe built the underground tunnel system beneath the Long Island Pine Barrens, they not only thought of multiple ingress and egress points surrounding their territory, but two secretive tunnel offshoots that, should they get trapped underground by the British, there was always an exit that only the tribesmen knew about. Grady Bennack discovered one of the exits by accident when he discovered the tunnel system.

The point of entry and exit for this special tunnel offshoot is midway between the Carmans and Peconic river juncture running through the Pine Barrens. The secret tunnel entrance is disguised by a dense tree pack and overgrown bushes and shrubs that Grady missed on his third trip into the area.

Once inside the entrance, Grady found two tunnel switchbacks disguising the fact that one of them would lead into the massive tunnel system somewhere hopefully containing the den.

Shortly before 8:45 PM, headlights lit up a pothole laden dirt road and moved slowly northeast toward the Long Island Pine Barrens. The washboard road made it difficult to navigate, but Julie Harned gripped the wheel with tight fisted determination, her heart racing with fear of what they were about to do.

"Do you think she'll be there," Julie said squinting to see the curving road ahead. A white tailed deer leaped out of the dense tree pack from her right side and she swerved sharply to avoid it. She and Grady flinching in unison.

"That was too close," Grady said, the tension in his voice was palpable. "She'll be there."

"I hope she can find her way in here. This place is hard to find."

"The Lenape knew what they were doing. I'm sure the British had no clue about this secret entrance."

The dirt road swerved back and forth, left to right, then right to left, leaving behind them a thick cloud of dust. The road straightened out, curved to the left once more, then right, then cut diagonally toward what appeared to be a dead end.

"How in the hell did you find this," Julie said pulling her car into the shrubs on her left. She turned off the ignition and pitch blackness surrounded them.

"Research. I studied the tribal tunnel system looking for all openings. There are six clearly marked, two of the tunnels leading to an offshoot that looked like it would be a strategic exit in case of attack. My hunch was on the mark."

"You're amazing Grady Bennack." Julie peered out into the darkness and flashes of light lit up the darkness.

"Fireflies," Grady said.

"What do we do now?"

"We wait for Eileen. It's 9:06."

"You told her 9:00 o'clock sharp."

"Patience, Julie. She'll be here."

"Should we call her cell?"

"There's no signal out here. I have zero bars."

"Jesus."

"Turn the car light on."

Julie punched the light switch on, and the cabin lit up.

"I'll ready the drones."

"How far from the car to the tunnel."

"About 200 yards."

"Is there any kind of path leading to it?" Asked Julie.

"No."

"Then how can we find it?"

"Markers."

"What markers?"

"You'll see."

Out of the darkness, a head poked through the side window and Julie screamed. Grady jolted forward in his seat smacking his head against the dashboard. A voice said, "Sorry I'm late."

"Jesus Christ, Eileen. You scared the hell out of us."

Langley said, "This place is really in the boonies. Leave it to the Native Americans to baffle the hell out of the British. No wonder they never conquered the U.S. You ready guys? Drones ready?"

"Yes," Grady said.

"Julie?"

"Yes. I hope so."

"Then let's go save Hector."

Three flashlights flipped on, and Grady lead them into the dark thick tree pack. There was no moon. The night was pitch black save for the beams of three flashlights and occasional flickering lights from fireflies. Eileen Langley, ten years their senior, tried to disguise the gush of fear that spread through her body the moment she exited her car which she parked discreetly fifty yards behind the two teenagers. The sadness and empathy she felt for wanting to save Hector Anguilera's tragic life overrode the fear she had about risking her own life. This, she knew, would be a career changer, if she was successful. Now, as Langley plodded almost blindly through the thick pine forest following two teenagers bordered on disbelief to the young woman. But now she was committed and there was no turning back. She hoped that Grady and Julie shared the same conviction.

In a whisper, Grady stopped and turned around for the other two to catch up. "Stay close to me. We're almost there."

"How much farther," Julie asked.

"About a football field, a hundred yards, maybe less."

Eileen didn't like hearing, 'maybe,' and for the first time, she questioned in her mind how accurate could Grady Bennack, an eighteen year old teenager, be in finding the den of a pack of attack dogs controlled by a sick mind who had already killed seven people. She willed the outcome out of her mind and trudged forward into utter darkness broken only by the three small beams of light.

CHAPTER 56

I T WAS 9:38 P.M. Thursday night and Tom Bennack had just made passionate love to his wife Andrea. He rolled over stark naked onto his back staring at the ceiling while Andrea slipped out of bed and went into the bathroom. Still out of breath from undulating in urgent ardor, Bennack tried to gather his thoughts.

Something had been bothering him since noon today and his heartbeat shifted in pace from his explosive orgasm to a deep-seated dread. The confrontation tomorrow morning, starting at 0800 with the serial killer who snuffed out the life of his daughter, Judy Bennack, hung in his mind like a nightmare still unfolding.

Andrea fell into bed, her nightie back on, and lay on her back next to her husband. "Did you enjoy it?"

Bennack blinked twice to change his mindset and said, "Ten out of ten."

'Good. I'm glad."

"How about you," he said.

Andrea remained silent for thirty seconds, maybe a minute, thinking.

Her thought caused her heart to skip a beat. The image of Dave Pritchard, owner of the Cobblestone restaurant, flashed through her mind like a nail splintering wood, and the image of this hulk of a man kissing her forced a labored response.

"Do you want to do it again," she offered smiling in the dark.

Bennack rolled over on his side facing Andrea, five inches apart.

He seemed to push out the words from his mouth. "You serious?"

"Yes," she said. "Of course, I'm serious."

"You've never offered to do it twice before."

"There's a first time for everything," she teased trying to disguise the rush of a vivid flashback of guilt. "You surprised . . ."

"Kind of . . . So yes, I'm surprised. I appreciate the offer, darling, but I have a big day tomorrow. I'd love a raincheck."

"Sure." She rolled over atop him and kissed him hard. She felt his response. "You sure?"

"Yes." Bennack paused in thought and then said, "I'm very troubled about tomorrow."

"Talk to me," she said, rolling off him onto her back.

"When I confront that bastard . . ."

"Yes . . ."

"I want to blow his brains out."

"He's a sick man, Tom. You don't have to kill him?"

"Yes, I do. He killed our Judy."

"I know, and I'm trying to live with it every day. Very painful, but maybe they can rehabilitate him."

"Fuck that. It will never be over."

"Think about it. That's all I'm saying."

Bennack rolled onto his back again thinking. "Is Grady in bed?"

"I think so," Andrea said.

"Did you see him come home?"

"Earlier, before dinner. He had something to eat. Why?"

"He's been possessed with this case, and I'm worried about him."

"He'll make a great detective someday."

"He already is," Bennack said. "Agent Hughes, FBI, has already offered him a summer internship."

"That's great, Tom. You told me. I'm so proud of him."

Bennack slipped out of bed and stood up, his shadow silhouetted on the wall from the hallway light.

"Where are you going."

"Grady's room."

"He's asleep, I'm sure. Let him be."

"I want to make sure."

The tunnel was pitch dark and smelled of damp dirt when Grady, Julie, and Eileen entered the south eastern orifice shrouded in thick, overgrown vines and pine trees. "It's a miracle you found this hole," Eileen said with a shiver from what seemed to be a constant cool breeze now wafting through the tunnel system to the outside.

"Modern technology," Grady opined.

"He never gives up," Julie said proudly palming his jacket from behind.

"I forgot to ask," said Eileen. "Do either of your parents have any clue where you are right now."

"Hopefully not," said Grady. "I stuffed a number of pillows between the sheets to disguise my absence."

"I'm supposed to be at Karen Walden's home for a sleepover. We're best friends so they'll never question it," Julie said.

"Hope you're right," Eileen said.

Two flashlights and a lantern gave off an eerie glow against the oval tunnel walls. From the tunnel ceiling, root systems hung like ganglia from above and the silence filled their senses with building dread.

"Let's get on with it, guys. My nerves are wearing thin," Eileen said. "It's beyond spooky. Like it's haunted down here."

Grady led them deeper into the tunnel which switch backed four times before it straightened out. "We set up the drones here," Grady said as he pulled the mother drone from its sheath and coupled the dragonfly drone to the underbelly of its carrier. Grady was punching in a complex flight pattern that he had worked on from the tunnel schematics from the Lenape tribe's ancient mapping records. "Okay. We're ready. All systems go."

Eileen stared at the teenager's face, amazed at his fixation of concentrated effort. "You're pretty amazing, Grady Bennack."

"Save the compliments until after we locate the den." Grady pressed a lever and the whir of four propellers lifted the drone off the tunnel floor and it hovered in mid-air, at the center of the seven-foot-high tunnel, four feet from the ceiling, three feet from the floor. Grady viewed the screen and, as if it were human, said, "Go find them. Find the den."

The drone sped off into the tunnel and vanished around a sharp turn to the right responding to the GPS program, its small headlights lighting up the tunnel ahead. Grady stared at the screen and took in a deep breath confirming tension. Around each corner was a new tunnel vista and the drone headlights were doing their job of lighting the way. The three sat on the tunnel floor in silence waiting for some discovery that they hoped the drone could find. All were staring at the drone screen which shown a clear path except for the occasional root system that hung unevenly from the walls and tunnel ceiling.

Three minutes passed, then four, now another two. Grady said, "Nothing yet."

The drone flew through the first tunnel matrix in eleven minutes and was approaching what appeared to be the end of the first quadrant of the mapping schematic when Julie's voice screeched, "Back up. Back up the drone. What was that?"

"What," Grady said, his heart pounding in his chest.

Eileen stared at the screen. "What was it?"

Julie pointed at the screen. "That."

At 10:27 P.M., Agent Greer Hughes sat at his desk hunched over in thought as he reviewed the plans for invading the Pine Barren tunnel system at 0800 tomorrow. What occupied his mind was the difficulty of how to capture Hector Aguilera alive, contain the dogs without snuffing out a life, and prevent Chief Bennack from interfering. Troubling to Hughes was Chief Bennack's ultimatum to, *'take him out at all costs, including the dogs.'*

As one of the FBI's top special agents, Greer Hughes had entrapped many suspects in his career, two of them on the *most wanted list*. He had killed six deadly assailants since he joined the force eleven years ago. The closest he came to losing his own life happened in Weehawken, New Jersey. Hughes and Charlie Dickson (another FBI agent) had chased an escaped convict, serving a life sentence at Bayside State Prison in Leesburg. He had butchered his mother's third husband with a meat clever and stuffed his body parts into her freezer, hidden beneath five-gallon containers of vanilla and mint chocolate chip ice cream. The report said that when his mother went into the freezer to pull out a gallon of vanilla ice cream for her peach cobbler dessert, she found herself staring at her husband's eyes which were frozen in terror. It took the medics forty-eight minutes to revive the woman from shock.

Hughes found the escaped con the hard way. As the FBI agent was sweeping through dense forest growth, Glock pistol drawn, safety off, the man, like a puma, fell from a tree branch atop Hughes slicing his left shoulder muscle to the bone with a box cutter he had secreted from the prison mail room. Hughes rolled to the ground sideways, blood spurting from his shoulder. The ex-con sprang to his feet to flee. He got fifteen yards away from Hughes before the agent drilled a 45 slug into the back of his skull. He fell forward like a yule log thrown into a Christmas hearth.

Now, Hughes was torn over the hunt for a serial killer who had killed seven former classmates using trained attack dogs.

Hughes had studied the entire profile of Hector Anguilera. Hector was born with a tragic, disfiguring condition for which he was ridiculed and tormented by children from first grade until he finally left school in high school. He correctly assumed that an adult life for him would be no better, maybe just a bit more subtle.

Hughes had read the comments that Hector's classmates had called him that appeared in Grady Bennack's drone photos. Over time, Hughes concluded, the constant persecution drove Anguilera crazy, and revenge ultimately struck in a vicious killing spree that Hughes supposed was the killer's way of getting even. Either way, Hughes pitied the killer and the thought of killing him plagued him with guilt. If Greer Hughes had a choice for a verdict, it would clearly be life in prison pleading insanity rather than snuffing out his life. The thought of what he would do when confronting the killer, tore at his conscience. The six people Hughes had killed on duty, in his mind, deserved to be extinguished. But Hector, with Ambrose and werewolf disease, Hughes believed he was dealing with an enormous challenge and the hair covering his body was a genetic disorder not of his own doing. Hughes had dealt with suicides, people taking their own lives from bullying and teasing in person and on the internet, but this was different, thought Hughes. Hector had been tormented by his peers beyond anything Hughes had ever witnessed.

Agent Greer Hughes knew one thing for certain. If Chief Tom Bennack confronted the serial killer before him, Hector Anguilera would be stone cold dead by the time the FBI agent reached his body.

CHAPTER 57

THE MOTHER DRONE hovered in place and then backed up ten feet, did a clockwise turn to face the right wall. Its small headlights lit up a squatting figure scrunched up against the wall with a small dog at his side. He looked puzzled at the small hovering object, his eyes squinting. He reached out to touch it, but it pulled away and vanished deeper into the tunnel.

"It's not him," Grady said starring at the screen.

"A homeless man and his dog," Eileen offered.

"I agree," said Julie. "The tunnel's probably full of them. Perfect place for shelter and safety."

The drone passed three more people sheltered in the tunnel. A teenage boy with a black cat, the other seemed to be a mid-twenties young woman, needle marks dotting both arms with tattoos, and the third was an old man, tattered with a gnarled white beard, shirtless and no shoes.

"Sad," Eileen said. "I wonder how many homeless the tunnel's housing?"

"I'll bet hundreds," Julie said.

"We need to find only one . . . Hector," Grady said.

The drone flew deeper into the tunnel, pausing as it passed more homeless people then it probed further seeking out corners and hesitating in flight to inspect what might be a hidden door or structure that might secret a man and four dogs. Nothing. The drone explored two more tunnel systems as programmed and was now into the fourth tunnel, the largest. Grady peered down onto the control panel and saw thirty-eight minutes of battery power remaining. As the drone sped down the tunnel, two-thirds of the way to the end, Grady saw something and the drone stopped in mid-air and approached slowly. He saw, what appeared to be a piece of two-by-four built into the top of the wall. *It could be a door—or not.* There was only one way to find out.

The drone landed on the tunnel floor and Grady, to preserve battery life, turned his flying machine off. Now the team of three was moving through the tunnel system at a fast pace to check out what the drone had found. Their flashlights cast bouncing patches of light on the tunnel's walls. and the sound of their footsteps were magnified by the close confinement of the tunnel system. According to Grady's configuration, they were eleven minutes away from the drone's location.

But eleven minutes passed, then fifteen and now twenty minutes and there was no drone. They had turned left at a fork in the tunnel and then took a right at another fork. Thirty minutes passed, and Eileen said what the others were afraid to utter. "I think we're lost, Grady. What's the GPS say now."

Grady studied his GPS map and it confirmed they had taken two wrong turns. They doubled back and picked up another tunnel system, one not identified before. This tunnel was larger than the others and Grady, for the first time, felt fear. Fear that he was lost and that quite possibly they might not find their way to the drone or out of the tunnel.

Tom Bennack rolled over on his side and stared at the clock. It read 5:18 AM. Quietly, he sat on the edge of the bed rubbing his eyes. He stood up and walked out of his bedroom toward Grady's room. He cracked the door and peered into darkness. Entering, he approached his son's bed, looked down at him, and whispered, "I love you," then turned and exited the room without awakening him. He started to close the door then hesitated. He cracked the door and listened. The room was silent and Bennack quietly closed the door and walked toward the bathroom.

He dressed, toasted a sesame bagel, and sat in silence at the kitchen table, his mind filled with angst and the confrontation he hoped to have today with the serial killer. A sick mind, Bennack thought, of someone who had killed seven people and who thought he was a werewolf. Bennack shook his head in thought. He wondered how a werewolf's mind processed thought. Did it think like a human or like a wolf. And, thought Bennack, if it did think like a wolf, that was more concerning to him because wolves were cunning. Wolves could track and hunt probably better than humans and today promised to test that theory which sent a jolt of concern through Bennack's mind. Conscious of his heart beat now racing in his chest, brought the Southampton police chief back to reality. He looked down at his watch and it read 6:57 AM. Bennack stood up and walked over to the Keurig® coffee machine. He normally would have two cups of French roast to start his day, but he had downed three cups and his heart beat and alertness confirmed that the caffeine had taken hold. Now 7:12 AM, the police chief exited his home and he slid into the driver's seat of his cop car. He thought of his son Grady and how helpful he had been in cracking this case. He was glad to see his son sound asleep in his bed. Bennack promised himself to tell him again how proud he was of his detective and drone work.

The car engine turned over and the chief pulled out of his driveway heading for the rendezvous point at the Long Island Pine Barrens. The only thought entering his mind now was that he would be glad to confront and kill the person who murdered his daughter. It wouldn't bring her back, Bennack knew, but it would bring closure to the hate that plagued his mind since Judy's passing and perhaps extinguish the gruesome memory that kept flashing through his mind of her contorted face and twisted body that lay on the beach when an angler had foul hooked her torso. He pushed the flashback out of his mind, palmed his Glock and turned left at the corner.

CHAPTER 58

AFTER AN EXHAUSTIVE search of the tunnel system, Grady was able to put a fix on the drone's location and they found it at 4:46 AM Once at the location, Grady, Eileen, and Julie searched the tunnel wall where the two-by-four board had been sighted by the drone. It was nothing more than an abandoned single piece of wood that somehow, years ago, had been dug underground from an abandoned wood shack above the location. They had encountered seven more homeless people who had each asked for money, and they encountered three more dogs, all strays probably released by their owners at the end of the summer. They all agreed how sad it was that humans and dogs were forced to somehow survive underground in an abandoned tunnel system.

The drone lifted off the tunnel floor and Grady sent it out of sight into another chamber in the vast underground tunnel system. According to Grady's GPS calculations, two more tunnel systems remained to be explored. Time was running out as they were exhausted, hungry, without water, and now covered with a thin vail of dust laden dirt.

Two thirds of the way through the second to last tunnel, Grady saw movement on his screen. It was a fleck of a streak of motion that caused his heart to skip a beat. Julie and Eileen leaned in peering at the screen and had also seen it. But when the drone backed up to take another look, whatever it was had vanished. To save battery life, Grady grounded the drone and turned it off yet again. The team of three advanced toward the tunnel and reached the location in nine minutes. Now they turned right and stood rigid at the tunnel entrance.

"He might be down this one," Grady said.

"What do we do again if we confront him," Julie said.

"Let me do the talking," Eileen said.

"What will you say?" Grady added.

"I'm not sure," Eileen said reluctantly. "I have to get him to recognize me and talk to me."

"That doesn't sound very promising," Julie said, her voice laced with doubt.

"I mean, it depends on what Hector says when we first see him."

"What if his dogs attack us," Grady said.

"I'm hoping Hector will remember me," Eileen said.

"And if he doesn't?" Julie asked.

"We all pray to God."

"You serious?" said Grady. "He better remember."

"That was ten years ago," Eileen added. "Remember, let me talk first."

"Okay," Grady said. "Let's go for it."

"I'm really nervous," said Julie.

"Not as nervous as I am," Grady said.

"When we confront Hector, you guys stand behind me. Remember that," Eileen commanded.

Simultaneously, Grady and Julie said, "Yes."

The threesome vanished into the tunnel and a cold silence gripped them as they advanced toward the drone's grounded location. Whatever had flashed across Grady's screen had bulk to its body and it seemed to move in a purposeful gate before it vanished. They would find out soon enough as they were now only two hundred yards from the drone. They stopped only once to reassure themselves that they should continue, and it was now Eileen that was walking ahead of Grady and Julie with purposeful momentum. She was desperately trying to hide the growing fear that was now gripping every nerve ending within her body, but she was also remembering the strategies she utilized in the case studies with her clients and the imperatives needed from a psychiatric application. One hundred fifty yards to contact, now one hundred. Seventy-five, then fifty yards. Now they stood rigid again, huddled in the middle of the tunnel path, flashlights probing the pitch-black darkness.

Grady said, "This is it."

Julie said only one word, "God."

Something moved in the distance. "Did you hear that," Eileen said.

"Hear what." Grady said, his heart thumping in his chest.

Eileen whispered, "Turn your lights off and listen."

Suddenly, the lights extinguished and the three stood in silence, utter darkness surrounding them.

In the distance, they heard movement.

"What was that?" Julie whispered.

"I heard it too," Grady said.

"Shhh," Eileen said. "Whatever it was is very close. Don't move."

At 7:58 AM, all tunnel entrances were populated with a force of FBI and police officers numbering fifty-eight. Chief Tom Bennack stood at the northeast tunnel entrance with a force of seventeen men and women officers and agents while FBI special agent Greer Hayes stood at the tunnel entrance at the southwestern opening with a force of fourteen. The balance of the force numbering twenty-four were split at the two remaining tunnel entrances.

"We're ready here, Chief," said Greer Hayes. "Remember the drill."

"All set at the northeast entrance," Bennack said.

Two other forces at the remaining tunnel entrances responded affirmatively.

"You all have motion detectors. Turn them on when you enter the tunnel and don't turn them off until you're out of the tunnel system," agent Hughes said. "If you confront the suspect, try and take him alive. That includes the dogs."

"We will not use smoke in the tunnel unless we fail to engage," Bennack said.

At 0800 hours, the force of fifty-eight men and women officers and agents vanished into the tunnel system. It was now only a matter of time before engagement.

CHAPTER 59

T HE SMALL TEN by twenty-foot den-like compartment
was well hidden from detection from the outside, but
there was a small opening at the top of the removable door
designed to let air pass into the chamber that only swung open
from the inside where it was locked shut with an iron latch that
slid through a u-shaped opening bolted to the door. From the
outside, the door blended into the tunnel wall with no perceptible
indentation or outline, totally camouflaged from the human eye
by natural root systems, packed clay and earthy stones scattered
throughout the mix.

Inside the den, four dogs lay in silence, panting softly, and
their master stroked their heads in gentle circles trying to keep
them calm. A small candle flame flickered up and down giving off
shaped shadows against the den wall.

"They know we're here, mother. I just saw them. They're close.
Very close," Hector Anguilera said.

"They will never find us," Mauricio, Hector's brother, said.
"Never." His voice was full of rage, and he was now standing up
in the den looking down at the four dogs. "They all deserve to
die. They made fun of you, Hector, and ridiculed you. You never

harmed any of them. I'm glad they're all dead. We have four more to kill and, my brother, I promise you we will kill them all. They will all be dead when I'm finished." Mauricio's voice filled the den with terror, but the thick door locked from inside muted his cry into silence not heard beyond the door's threshold.

"*Calla, hijos mio,*" said their mother. Be quiet my sons. "*No sabian nada major, Mauricio. Dejalos ir y estar en paz.*" They didn't know any better, Mauricio. Let them go and be at peace.

"*Nunca, mi madre. Nunca. Han arruinado a mi hermano. Me desquitare con todos ellos. Todos estaran muertos pronto.*" Never, my mother. They ruined my brother, and I will get even with all of them. They will all be dead soon.

Hector crouched on the den floor, like a wolf about to spring atop prey, hair covering his body in a shroud of head-to-toe fur. His head hung down upon his chest and he suddenly burst into tears wailing in grief and the pain of torment. Then silence. Total deafening silence. Something outside the den had stirred and Hector heard commotion outside the thick door.

The tunnel system was now swarming with officers and agents moving methodically deeper through each one of the tunnels, their motion detectors sounding a high-pitched repetitive beep upon detecting movement.

Chief Bennack was the first to report. "We've got a lot of homeless people down here. Four encountered so far. Over."

"We've seen seven in our tunnel," said Hughes.

"When we kill this son of a bitch today, we'll have to clean out the tunnel system of all the homeless including the dogs."

An officer said, "Where will we put them? There's enough dogs down here to fill a kennel."

"Back on the streets," Bennack said. "Stay focused on the mission. We'll deal with that problem later."

At 9:48 A.M, the underground force of agents and officers had swept through three tunnel systems without incident and, coincidentally, agent Hughes and Chief Bennack came within two hundred yards of each other after sweeping through separate tunnels. Bennack arrived at the fourth tunnel system first and he entered the tunnel pressing forward. When Hughes arrived at the same tunnel, Bennack was already seventy-five yards in front of him. According to the tunnel system chart, this tunnel was the longest and the schematic showed no exit at the end of it. When Hughes began walking swiftly into the tunnel, he could see lights ahead of him streaking the tunnel walls in an eerie glow. Hughes knew someone was ahead of him and he hoped it wasn't Bennack.

As Bennack and two officers moved deeper into the tunnel, the chief sensed danger. He pulled out his Glock unlocking the safety and held up his hand in a stopping motion. Three officers behind him stood rigid, listening. Bennack heard a muted sound in the distance. He had heard it before. It sounded like the whirr of a drone. Bennack's heart skipped a beat. He knew his son Grady was asleep in his bed. He saw him lying in bed at home. If it was the sound of a drone, it must be flown by someone else in the tunnel system. But who?

The chief looked behind him and saw distant lights approaching. He clicked his hand mike and said, "Identify yourself."

A voice answered immediately, "Agent Hughes and three agents."

"Roger that," said Bennack, and he picked up his pace leading deeper into the tunnel toward the whirring sound.

Grady was deftly flying his drone back and forth inspecting the tunnel walls, ceiling and floor and had spotted nothing unusual until seven minutes ago. The drone was flying ahead of them when Grady saw on the drone screen that he only had three more minutes remaining on the mother drone's battery pack life. He took in a deep labored breath and focused intently on the screen. The drone almost missed it, flying by it before circling back to inspect an irregularity in the right tunnel wall six inches below the ceiling. When the threesome approached the area, Eileen Langley saw a small vent-like opening toward the ceiling, twelve inches long by four inches wide. But with all three flashlights shining on the wall surrounding the vent, they could not detect any outline or indentation of a door, only the small vent.

Grady leaned over his mother drone and extracted the dragonfly drone. He sized up the vent above and said, "It will fit. If it's the den, we can fly her through that vent. If this is Hector's den, we will know soon enough."

"If he's in there, how do we convince him to come out?" Julie asked.

Grady looked at Eileen and nodded.

"I'll talk to him," said Eileen.

"I hope to God it works," Grady said.

As Grady fired up the miniature dragonfly drone, Julie said, "Oh my God."

"What," Eileen said.

Grady's heart thumped in his chest, and he coughed reflexively, catching his breath.

"Somebody's in the tunnel. I saw a flash of light in the distance, behind us," Julie said.

"It's them. The police force and the FBI," Grady said.

"Your dad, Grady. It's got to be your dad," Julie said.

"Hurry, Grady," Eileen said. "Get the dragonfly inside."

The small insect-like flying machine lifted off the ground and climbed up, now even with the vent. Grady, Julie, and Eileen stared intensely at the drone screen as the dragonfly approached the entrance. In the distance, flashing lights were moving closer to them. Slowly, the small insect flew into the vent and vanished.

Grady said, "Oh my God."

Eileen let out a gush of breath that would have extinguished a candle were she five feet away from it. Julie just stared at the screen in shocked surprise as Grady landed the dragonfly on a cross beam in the upper left back corner of the den, its two black beady camera eyes focused on the scene below.

CHAPTER 60

C HIEF BENNACK COULD barely make out the small
speck of light well into the distance, but he knew it was
light coming from somewhere deep into the tunnel he was
now one third of the way through.

Special agent Greer Hughes was not far behind Bennack
now and he was gaining. He knew that if the suspect, Hector
Anguilera, had any chance of survival he would have to at least
catch up to the chief to arrive at the same time, if the den was
somewhere within this two-and half-mile long tunnel, the perpetrator would be found.

The rest of the force had streamed through their assigned tunnels without incident and were now closing in on the last tunnel
system where Bennack and Hughes had arrived.

Eileen stood rigid staring at the screen trying to think of what she
would say as Grady and Julie faced her, waiting. For the first time
in her life, Eileen Langley stood speechless, tears now streaming
down her face confirming all the tortured memories of the boy

she knew and befriended at Freeport High School ten years ago and who was responsible for her chosen career along with her brother Robert Langley who had Cerebral Palsy and walked with a dragging left limp leg and jerky motion. Seeing both of them teased and tortured with comments about their disability clinched over time her determination to be a doctor of psychiatry. Both of them were so sweet, so innocent and smart, and so tormented by their peers. She opened her mouth to speak through the drone and burst into tears, trying desperately to get the first words out of her mouth. "Hector. Hector. It's Eileen Langley," she cried. "I'm so sorry for what happened."

His brother, Mauricio, spoke first and it was a rage of emotion. "They all deserve to die," he shouted. "They tortured my brother until he broke. I will kill them all."

Four dogs circled Hector protectively snarling viciously at the intruder's voice that filled their den. She thought she saw a shadow of somebody else in the small room but wasn't sure. She saw movement but not a definitive shape.

Grady, Julie, and Eileen stared at the screen, extreme concern on each of their faces as Mauricio continued to rant. "Where are you hiding," he screamed. "We will find you." Mauricio was staring around the den trying to find out where the voice was coming from when suddenly a woman's voice filled the den.

"*Es una voz amistosa, Mauricio. No le hagas dano.*" It is a friendly voice, Mauricio. Don't hurt her. "

Grady whispered to Eileen, "Who is she?"

"I think it might be their mother,"

Eileen spoke into the drone speaker. "Hector. It's me. Eileen Langley.

I'm here with my two friends, Grady Bennack and Julie Harned. We want to help you. Talk to you to save you from all this torture. Please come out and talk to us. We won't hurt you,

I promise. Please hurry. Open the door so we can talk. We're here to save you."

"No," screamed Mauricio. "You'll kill us. We'll kill you first."

Hector stood up and, for the first time, spoke. "Is that you, Eileen? Really you? Eileen Langley?"

"Yes Hector. It's me. Eileen Langley. I was always your friend, remember? I'm still your friend. I'll always be your friend. Please open the door so we can talk. I want to help you. To save you. Please. Hurry."

Hector was staring at the ceiling corner toward the voice coming from the perching dragonfly. He pulled matted hair away from his eyes, staring at the small insect. He reached out to touch it and retracted his hair covered hand. "I want to see your face, Eileen. Before I open the door."

Grady's eyes widened. "Oh my God no," he whispered.

Eileen said, "What's wrong."

"Hector will have to turn the dragon fly around to look at the small screen. It's tiny."

"But could he see me if the mother drone transmitted my picture to the dragonfly," Eileen whispered, looking away from the mother drone screen to Grady.

"Yes, but Hector would have to touch the dragonfly and turn it around."

"Do it," commanded Julie. "We're running out of time. They're coming closer. Do it now."

"Hector. Can you hear me."

A hesitant voice said, "Yes."

"Listen to me. I want you to look up into the left corner of your den."

They watched Hector looking around the den. Then he saw the little insect perched on the beam that he had just seen before.

He reached out to it barely touching it. "That's it, Hector. Now I want you to pick it up in your hands carefully."

Mauricio shouted in a terror laden scream. "No. Don't touch it Hector. Don't touch it. It's a trap."

Suddenly, Hector's mother's voice broke in. It was a soft and loving voice. "*Estan tratando de ayadarte, Hector. Dejalos hacerto.*" They are trying to help you, Hector. Let them do so.

"Did you see that," whispered Julie. "Jesus."

"Yes," Grady said. "Three people in the den, but I only see one."

"It's Hector. Only Hector," Eileen said in shocked surprise. "He's got multiple personalities. Schizophrenic. I can deal with this. I have many patients like Hector." she whispered. "Three people inside him. His mother, brother, and himself."

"No," demanded Mauricio. "No, Mother." His voice was violent and full of rage.

"Eileen . . ." Hector said.

"Yes, Hector. I'm here for you. Here to save you from this torture. I've always been your friend. Take the insect off the beam and turn it around. You will see a little tiny screen. Look at the screen and you will see my face. I'm waiting outside to help you. Please do it now. Hurry. Please open the door and let us help you."

Hector looked down at his four dogs, nudging his right leg for reassurance. A sharp command filled the den, and they laid down surrounding him. He reached up to touch the dragonfly.

"That's it, Hector. Now, turn it around. You will see my face."

Hector gently turned the small insect around and stared at what appeared to be a small screen. He stared at it intensely.

"That's me, Hector. Eileen Langley. Please."

"I see you," he said. "It's you."

"And I see you, Hector."

Hector hesitated for a half minute then said, "If I open the door, where will you take me . . . and the dogs? They are my only friends."

"No!" shrieked Mauricio. "No!"

"*Abre la puerta, Hector. Abre la puerta*," his mother said in a soft reassuring voice. Open the door, Hector.

"Hector, trust me. I will make sure you are safe," Eileen said. "Trust me."

Agent Hughes finally caught up with Chief Bennack and now they could both see lights flashing more clearly far into the tunnel, maybe 300 yards further, maybe less, but they were gaining on the light source and their pace had quickened.

Hughes and Bennack and their small force now numbered seven, five men and two women. Bennack said, "I want your weapons drawn, safety off and ready to kill upon contact."

"If we can take the perpetrator alive, try to do so. And the dogs, but if the dogs attack us, shoot to kill," Hughes commanded.

For the first time, Bennack did not contradict Hughes in his order to try and save the suspect, but the chief had already decided what he would do.

The police and FBI force was gaining on the light in the distance. When they were close enough to see flashlights and silhouette outlines of people in the distance, Hughes counted three of them. He said, "Douse the lights. We move in the dark from here to point of contact, weapons ready."

Suddenly, part of the tunnel wall moved outward with the sound of rusted hinges squeaking eerily as the one-foot-thick door swung slowly open.

Behind Eileen stood Grady and Julie, their hearts beating wildly in terror for fear they were about to take in their last breath of life. When the door was half opened, a figure appeared slowly from within the den and stood motionless. Four dogs exited the den and surrounded Hector, each one of them snarling and bearing their teeth. A shadow moved behind him to the left and vanished. Only Julie saw motion. Before them, Hector was hunched over and appeared to be about five feet tall at best. Hector Anguilera, to the three people standing before him, looked like a wolf on his hind legs, completely covered in hair and crouched as if ready to spring at them. The four dogs snarled at the intruders, but a command to stand down had already broken the silence. The sound to Grady seemed to have come from behind them, but he wasn't sure.

Eileen stepped forward and opened her arms to embrace him, but he hesitated, stepping back toward the den. Then he stood erect and topped six feet tall, staggering Grady and Julie's mind, both cowering in his presence. But Eileen had remembered him and stood rigid in place. "It's me, Hector. Eileen Langley. Your friend from Freeport High School. I'm here to help you. To save you. Please. I beg of you. Let us help."

Three personalities hidden deep within Hector's mind suddenly emerged.

"No!" Mauricio shouted. "No!"

"*Ella esta aqui para ayudarte, Hector. Esta bien,*" said another personality, his mother in soft reassuring tones. She's here to help you, Hector. It's okay.

The dogs surrounded him protectively. He turned toward Eileen who again opened her arms to embrace him and as he stepped forward to accept her embrace, Chief Bennack shouted, "Freeze."

"Hector Anguilera you're under arrest for the murder of seven people including my daughter." Bennack raised his Glock pointing it at Hector's head.

"You're a sick bastard," Bennack shouted as his finger touched the trigger.

Suddenly, Grady Bennack jumped in front of Hector and said, "Don't kill him, Dad. He needs help and we can save him."

Chief Bennack stepped back in shocked surprise trying to comprehend who it was. When his light beam flashed across Grady's face, he said,

"Get out of the way, son."

"No, Dad. No. Please don't kill him, Dad. We can help him get better. He's sick and he needs help, but he's never had it."

"Move out of the way, Grady. He killed your sister and six others."

"No. Dad. I'm not moving."

"Grady. Step aside." Bennack ordered. "Now."

"No, dad. I'm not moving," Grady said resolutely.

"Don't shoot, Chief," said agent Hughes. "We've got him covered."

Julie Harned stepped in beside Grady. "Me, too, Mr. Bennack. Hector needs help and we can save him. Please listen to your son. Don't shoot."

Eileen Langley joined Julie and Grady. "Judy was my best friend, Mr. Bennack, and Hector Anguilera was also my friend.

He was tortured in high school. I saw it all. It was awful what they did to him. We must save his life. He was driven to this, and he desperately needs help. I'm a doctor in psychiatry and I can help him. Please put down your weapons."

Chief Tom Bennack held his Glock pointed at Hector's head and suddenly, Hector fell to the ground sobbing in wrenching tortured cries from the pain he had suffered all his life, the four dogs surrounded him, licking the hair on his face and body, echoing his anguish with their own cries.

Slowly, Bennack lowered and holstered his weapon, shaking his head. Agent Hughes took in a deep labored breath and exhaled in relief that the suspect was still alive. He stepped toward Hector and cuffed him, both hands in front. One of the four dogs, the Rottweiler, lunged at agent Hughes and dug its jaws into his left thigh. The German Shepherd came at Bennack's crotch with gaping jaws and Bennack shouted, "Platz. Bleib." Again, he screamed, "Platz. Bleib."

The two dogs immediately went down and froze rigid in silence, as if Chief Bennack was their master.

"Shit," agent Hayes said gripping his thigh in pain. "How the hell did you do that."

"Shutshund training. That's what he used to control his dogs," said Bennack.

Grady approached his father and hugged him with a loving embrace. "I'm sorry, Dad. I had to do this. I love you."

"I love you too, son, but you were supposed to be home asleep. Before I left home, I looked in on you. You were sound asleep."

"Pillows, Dad. Stuffed the bed with pillows."

Hugging his son again, Bennack said, "I should have known better."

Agent Hughes overheard Bennack's comment and said, "Your son is already a hell of an agent. He figured out the whole fucking plot before any of us."

Julie sidled up to Grady and kissed him on the lips, the scent of lavender filling his senses. "I love you, Grady Bennack. You're awesome."

Grady held her tightly and said, "I'm going to marry you someday, Julie Harned. And when I do . . ."

"I haven't forgotten my promise, Grady."

Grady smiled in the dark and said knowingly, "What promise . . ."

Julie nuzzled close to his right ear and whispered, "That I'm going to fuck your brains out," and she kissed him again hard in the darkness of the tunnel.

"Hey Chief," said agent Hughes. "What the hell did you say to those dogs."

"Down and stay. German commands in Schutzhund attack dog training" Bennack said.

"How did you know Hector's dogs would understand the language," agent Hughes queried.

"I didn't, but I heard one of the commands when you told everybody to freeze," Bennack said.

"What was the command?"

"Packen fass."

"What the hell's that," said Hughes.

"Attack and bite."

"Shit. We're fucking lucky to be alive."

"You got that right, Greer," said Bennack. "But it wasn't Hector that issued the command."

"What do you mean," Hughes said.

"It was somebody else. Another voice."

"Who," persisted Hughes.

"Another personality. I don't know," Bennack said, but it wasn't Hector's voice."

"We'll find out soon enough. Thanks, chief, for not pulling the trigger. Your son saved Hector's life."

"I know, and he also found our perpetrator."

They both turned toward the tunnel exit and slowly walked out in silence with Hector Anguilera walking between them, four dogs trailing behind them.

CHAPTER 61

Four Months Later . . .

B Y REASON OF insanity, Hector Anguilera, was found
not guilty and assigned to a captive life sentence at The
Creedmoor Psychiatric Center located at 79-26 Winchester
Boulevard in Queens Village, Queens, New York. The center
occupied 300 acres including fifty buildings that once housed
over 7,000 patients. The site was named after the Creed family
who farmed on the site from 1870 to 1892. In 1984, the violent
ward of Creedmoor Psychiatric Center was downsized and, with
the development of antipsychotic medications, developed a trend
toward deinstitutionalization. A series of dramatic budget cuts
and smaller patient populations led to the closing of psychiatric
centers across the nation. Today, due to under budgeted and staff
challenges, Creedmoor now houses less than 300 patients.

It was November 17th, a Tuesday, when the front doors to
the Creedmoor Psychiatric Center swung open and patient 297,
Hector Anguilera, entered, accompanied by police chief Tom
Bennack, FBI special agent, Greer Hughes, and Linda Zollar, a

Creedmoor psychiatric counselor specializing in psychiatric disorders, including schizophrenia.

Hector Anguilera, after all paperwork for admittance was completed, was taken by elevator to the third floor on the west wing, the tightest security floor of the complex. From his small bedroom through a double iron bared window, Hector could see the New York City skyline.

After three weeks, the antipsychotic medication was starting to work, and Hector's three personalities now consisted of only episodic personalities emerging when confronted by his counselors who tried communicating to his mother, brother Mauricio, and himself. While progress was slow, it was deemed successful now and the terror filled personality of his brother Mauricio was beginning to fade. But the most positive news for Hector Anguilera was that Dr. Eileen Langley had requested and been granted psychiatric care of Anguilera at Creedmoor. Her positive results in helping Hector find and cure himself became the prescription for all future split personality psychotic patients across the nation.

The news media picked up and promoted the capture of the serial killer, Hector Anguilera, and his entire life story of how he was bullied in Freeport High School and driven insane developing multiple personalities was spread around the world including all social media. All the networks, CNN, Fox News, CBS, NBC, and ABC covered the story with interviews with Chief Bennack, FBI Agent Greer Hughes, and they probed deeper to include interviews with Grady Bennack, Julie Harned and Eileen Langley. They even got the names of four of the hunted prospects that were still alive. Fox News convinced two of them to appear on Tucker Carlson's nightly news broadcast and talk about bullying and the impact of name calling and social media allowance of verbal attacks on teenagers and adults causing suicides. It was not a pretty story, but it got consumer attention across the nation and people began lecturing their children about bullying and the need to report it if they witnessed it in action, and both schools and colleges added special courses on bullying and teasing and consequential torment and how it impacted the victims.

Out of the news coverage on Hector Anguilera's life came the startling facts of suicide. Over 4,400 deaths per year occur according to the Center for Disease Control. Out of every suicide for young people, there are at least 100 suicide attempts. Bully victims are between two to nine times more likely to consider suicide than non-victims according to studies at Yale University and a study in Britain found that at least half of young people's suicides are related to bullying.

According to statistics reported by ABC news when covering the Hector Anguilera case, nearly 30% of students are either bullies or victims of bullying and 160,000 children today stay home from school every day because of fear of being bullied.

It was the intensity of news coverage and profiling the tragic life story of Hector Anguilera that convinced all four victims that were slated to be killed, but somehow were still alive, to visit Hector Anguilera at Creedmoor. Perhaps out of extreme guilt, but also for seeking hopeful forgiveness from Hector for what they had said and done to him at Freeport High School, all of the victims sought forgiveness for their actions.

Of the four victims still alive who visited Hector, it was Betty LaGrange who felt most remorseful for what she still remembered doing to Hector in the ninth grade at Freeport High School. When she entered his room on the third floor, Hector was sitting with his back to her staring out the window at the New York City skyline. As was Creedmoor protocol with all patients committing violent crimes, an armed guard sat inconspicuously in the far corner of Hector's room to accompany all visitors.

LaGrange cleared her throat to announce her presence. Hector wore a white gown and, when he swiveled his chair around, a flashing memory tore at her emotion.

"Betty LaGrange, Hector," she said and burst into tears, sobbing the broken words, "I'm so sorry for what I did to you at Freeport High."

Hector did not respond immediately. Instead, he stared at her trying to remember who she was ten years ago.

"I gave you a dog leash and called you a freak. What I said and did was so awful," she sobbed. "Can you ever forgive me, Hector. I apologize."

Hector stared at the young woman standing before him asking for forgiveness. He remained silent, sitting rigid in his chair, his eyes glazed over from his medication.

LaGrange stood in front of him, now looking into his eyes. Looking for some acknowledgement. Some glint of recognition of who she was.

She began weeping again as she talked. "If I could roll back the hands of time, Hector, I would have realized how immature and mean I was. Making fun of you gave me the feeling that I was much better than you, but I was so wrong. You were so much better of a person than I ever was or will be. Please, Hector, forgive me. I was so wrong for what I said and did to you."

Hector sat rigid in his chair staring at her without movement.

LaGrange took three steps closer to Hector. She leaned over staring into his eyes, her body shaking, but determined to somehow break through to him.

"Do you remember who I am, Hector."

He moved for the first time, sitting erect, but still staring at her without emotion.

"Betty LaGrange, Hector. Freeport High School. I desperately want to reach you. To apologize to you and tell you how wrong I was. Hector . . . Can you hear me?" She was still weeping between each word she uttered.

She moved closer, close enough to touch him, but she restrained from doing so.

For the first time, Hector nodded and LaGrange smiled at him. "You can hear me, Hector. Can you talk to me?"

Hector nodded again but remained silent.

"Talk to me, Hector. Say something. Anything."

Hector stared at her pleading face. He leaned forward and his entire face and expression changed. A bellowing angry voice shouted one word, and it punched Betty LaGrange in the gut as she fell backward trying to catch her balance from the shocking angry shout. This was a different person. An angry person and the voice shouted, "Why?"

LaGrange backed up and buried her face in her hands and burst loudly into tears. She came closer now, touching his shoulder. She had read about Hector's multiple personalities, but which one was this, she wondered, then, at the risk of being hurt, she leaned over and kissed his hairy forehead and said, "I don't know why, Hector. I wasn't thinking."

"I'm not Hector," the voice shouted in a rage. "I'm Mauricio, Hector's brother, and you and others ruined his life making fun of him."

LaGrange stood up in front of the man sitting in the chair staring down at him then, gathering all of her courage, she pulled up a chair and sat down facing him, three feet apart.

He leaned forward in his chair and stared deeply into LaGrange's eyes. His mouth opened to speak and then closed without word.

"Yes," she said hopefully. "You were going to say something, right. Hector, are you there?"

His mouth opened again to speak, and he pulled his chair closer to her. They were only two feet apart. "If you looked like me . . . If you were me . . ."

"Yes . . ."

"If you looked like me and I said to you . . ."

"Yes?"

"How would you feel if I called you a freak and gave you a dog leash. That's what you did to me in high school."

LaGrange bent over in her chair, her head touching Hector's knees, and cried convulsively as the thought of what he said tore into her soul and every conscious nerve ending with profound simplicity of what Hector had just said. "I'm so sorry, Hector. I never thought about it that way. Please forgive me. I beg of you. Please. I was so cruel. So, mean. I'm so very sorry."

Suddenly, his face morphed into another personality and a woman's voice spoke in Spanish. "*Perdona a su, Hector. Perdona a su.*" Forgive her, Hector.

The facial expression completely changed again, and Betty LaGrange now saw a different countenance. It was Hector, she thought, and he slowly reached out and touched her damp face and held it in place for a long time, maybe two minutes, maybe three. She stared at him, tears of regret and emotion pouring down her cheeks. Finally, he said, "I forgive you."

LaGrange stared at him then got down on her knees as if to pray and hugged Hector, wrapping her arms around his legs, she sobbed hysterically, it seemed, for five minutes. She looked up into his eyes and forced the words out of her mouth, "Thank you, Hector. Thank you."

Betty LaGrange stood up, said goodbye, and walked slowly to the door. A woman's voice said, "*Gracias por venir, Betty.*" Thank you for coming, Betty. *Significa mucho para mi hijo.*" It meant a lot to my son.

For Hector Anguilera, it was the first time he could remember feeling appreciated for simply being human. He stood up and walked over to a mirror and, staring into it, seeing himself for who he really was, hairy face and body included. Hector Anguilera smiled into the mirror for the first time he could remember. Suddenly, in the mirror, he saw two people standing behind him at his doorway. He thought it was a mirage and he shook his head. It was his mother, Camila, and brother, Mauricio, who had come to visit him for the first time at Creedmoor. He turned around to greet them and decided this would be a good day. No, he thought again. This would be a great day. Perhaps the beginning of a new life with hope, love, and acceptability. He smiled at them and held out his arms, his mother embracing him first, then his brother. They laughed and cried together, but it was for Hector a new day, a new life, and the memories of the past lingered only faintly in his mind as a very bad nightmare that hopefully, he thought, would never surface again.

A nurse appeared in the doorway and said, "Time for your meds, Hector."

Hector nodded and she said, "I'm sorry but visiting hours are over."

His mother and brother disappeared, and Hector walked slowly over to the window staring at the 1,776 foot high One World Trade Center tower built in 2006. The setting sun gave the massive building a golden glow in the distance, almost surrealistic. For the first time in his life, Hector felt a tingling sense of hope. Tomorrow was a new day and as the medication took hold, his mind seemed clear of all else but himself. He looked down at the thick hair on his hands and stared at them slowly turning them around with appreciation. His lips parted and he smiled then laughed for the for the first time he could remember. He thought of the Grinch, then Chewbacca, the Wookie. They were both funny characters, he thought, but they were also strong, intelligent, and seemingly invincible. Maybe, just maybe, Hector thought, he would rise to their level someday. Just the whimsical thought forced another smile and expanded into a broad grin, and he laughed yet again then yawned. It had been a long arduous day and he was tired. He turned away from the window and walked toward the bed and lay down.

Dr. Eileen Langley entered his room and walked over to his bed tucking him in tightly. He looked up at her and said, "It's you," and he smiled.

"Yes. It's me and I love you, dear friend. You are an amazing person, Hector." He smiled and said, "Thank you, Eileen. So are you."

In moments, he was asleep dreaming that he was Chewbacca, the Wookie, in *Star Wars* exploring a distant planet. He was in charge of the expedition, and everybody looked up to him and respected him and, most soothing in the dream, was that nobody bullied or made fun of him.

CHAPTER 62

FBI SPECIAL AGENT Greer Hughes met police Chief Tom
Bennack twice after the verdict became official to commit
Hector Anguilera to Creedmoor on insanity charges for the
murder of seven victims for the rest of his life.

Agent Hughes had already stamped his seven open files on
Anguilera '*CLOSED,*' but Chief Bennack still had one open file
that he was uncomfortable in closing. Something bothered him
about the case in deposition. Hector Anguilera was incoherent
during part of the trial, and it happened when he was asked
questions about the four dogs that tracked down and killed each
victim. He did not recognize any of the commands in Schutzhund
dog training that were asked of him. Nor, did he acknowledge any
direct contact with his mother, Camila, or have any memory of
being with his brother Mauricio since he vanished from his home.

Hector Anguilera was unanimously convicted of murder by
insanity by a jury of nine people. And the evidence supplied at the
trial confirmed that Hector used four dogs to carry out the killing
of each victim. The prosecutor was relentless in proving that
Hector was the serial killer without question. They profiled each of

Hector's three personalities and determined that it was Mauricio, the third personality, who gave the orders to kill the victims.

Still, to Bennack, the troubling part of that prosecutorial conclusion was that if Hector's third personality was truly responsible for the killings, then the Hector personality must remember something about Schutshund dog training commands. But maybe not, Bennack wrote in his closing notes on the case.

Not being a psychiatrist, Bennack wasn't even sure how people with multiple personalities maintained any relation or communication between the various personalities who emerged from their minds. If Hector was not behind any of the orders to kill his victims then he could be proven innocent, or worst case scenario, an accomplice. A wild theory, thought Bennack, but then the entire case was surrealistic so Bennack noted in his log, '*anything is possible without proof*,' and since Hector could not remember anything about the special words to control attack dogs, maybe somebody else controlled the dogs to attack and kill upon command.

And, there was something else troubling Bennack. In the tunnel when they confronted Hector, Bennack definitely heard the Schutzhund word for attack, '*Fass*'. It was too dark in the tunnel to see who issued the command, but it came from Hector's direction. Maybe it was him—maybe not. And if Hector did not shout the command, '*Fass*', then somebody else commanded the dogs. But who, thought Bennack. The other missing link was the black Chevrolet SUV. Where was the car now and who drove it? In questioning, Hector could not remember anything about a car—which was troubling to the jury.

Bennack extracted the files of all the people whom he taught K9 Schutzhund training dating back eleven years. Most of them were potential trainees hoping to join the police force K9 unit after completion of the course and Bennack was the only person on Long Island responsible for all K9 training. He kept all of the trainee names on his laptop. He hoped the file was still in his ICloud. He flipped through the open file and examined the notes he had taken. The notes did not appear relevant to his search, so he opened his laptop and entered, Schutzhund Training. A list of 324 names filled the screen and the police chief stared at the screen. Helka sidled up to Bennack and nuzzled his right arm for attention.

"Good boy," said Bennack, and he had a painful flashback to his daughter Judy, but the dog provided the Bennacks assurance that their daughter was somehow present in spirit.

The dog looked up at Bennack and seemed to be trying to tell him something. Helka nuzzled his arm again and tilted his head from side to side then gave a distinct bark.

Bennack said, "I know, Helka. I miss her too."

Helka barked again, louder this time as if commanding him to do something.

"I'm checking, Helka. I'll get to it."

Helka whined.

"Okay, okay." Bennack looked at the laptop screen and scanned the first five names on the list. No recognition. He stared at the screen then clicked the search bar and slowly typed in 'HECTOR ANGUILERA'. The computer responded, and it was negative. So, the chief concluded Hector had not taken the K9 training course. He typed in another name, 'MAURICIO ANGUILERA', and the screen suddenly began filling up with a profile. Bennack's heart skipped a beat, his hands on the laptop began to shake. He looked down at Helka and put his hand atop the dog's head. "We found the killer."

Helka began barking and would not stop until Bennack commanded, "Nein," The dog silenced and Bennack's heart was still pounding in his chest.

CHAPTER 63

TOM BENNACK'S CELL phone chirped thrice and he clicked to receive the call.

There was no voice on the call. Only silence. He pressed the receiver tightly to his ear.

"Hello," he said.

Silence.

"Hello. Who is this?"

Silence. Then he heard it. Breathing. Heavy breathing. No voice.

"Who is this?"

More silence then the phone went dead and Bennack clicked off. He tried calling the number back, but it rang busy prompting a flashback to FBI special agent Greer Hughes and the anonyms calls he had received before they captured the serial killer. Just an unrelated call concluded Bennack or wrong number, but it was unnerving and Bennack stood rigid in place waiting for another call. It never came.

Bennack's police car pulled up in front of Camila Anguilera's home and he exited and went to the front door and rang the doorbell, knocking the door hammer twice. The door opened and Camila stood in the doorway.

"What do you want?"

"To ask you a few questions."

"You've ruined my son Hector's life. I have nothing more to say," and she closed the door on Bennack's left foot.

Bennack persisted, pushing the door inward. "I want to ask you a few questions about your son Mauricio."

"He's not here."

"Where is he?"

"I don't know."

"You and Mauricio visited Hector at Creedmoor recently to see Hector so you know where he lives."

The woman tried to shut the door again and as Bennack resisted pushing back, he saw a sudden look of fear in the woman's eyes as she looked over Bennack's right shoulder. He heard a car behind him and spun around.

The chief saw a white SUV slowly drive by the home. The moment the car passed the police car, its wheels screeched, and the car sped down the road out of sight. Bennack said, "It's him isn't it. Mauricio."

Camila's face was ash white, mouth open, eyes wide.'

"Answer me," Bennack demanded. "It's him."

The woman stood rigid in the doorway, tears now streaming down her face. The chief twisted to his left and leaped off the door step sprinting across the front lawn to his car. The engine sprung to life and the patrol car squealed down the road, red lights spinning, siren blaring. Helka, paws on the dash, sensing the excitement of a chase, leaned forward barking in pursuit.

In the distance, the SUV careened to the right in a hard turn at the corner and took another hard left, wheels topping the corner curb in a rubber burning puff of smoke. Bennack was gaining and his daughter's German Shepherd was now into the chase, pacing back and forth in tight quarters in the front seat staring at the distant car through the front windshield, a deep guttural growl now emanating from its throat confirming he sensed an eminent chase, lips flared showing jaws at the ready. The chief gripped the wheel in a tight-fisted clutch, his mind focused on the chase, yet thoughts of his once cherished daughter flashed through his mind. But he was troubled by the fact that the serial killer's suspected car was black, not white like the one he was chasing. If Mauricio Anguilera was innocent, why was he now in a full throttle escape. Bennack looked at his GPS and he had a fix on the white SUV's position. They had exited Baldwin, the home of Camila Anguilera, and were now speeding toward Hempstead, back roads that Bennack had no familiarity with.

Eight minutes passed and the white SUV was speeding up to fifty-two miles per hour on side neighborhood roads, the trailing police car now losing ground. Bennack turned onto Southern State Parkway heading south and the SUV was doing over ninety MPH, now three miles in front of him. The chief's new high-tech GPS was spitting out options for the chase. Either the SUV was heading toward Malverne or North Valley Stream where the GPS flashed a park and pond, or it would take exit 18 off Southern State into Hempstead Lake State Park. Bennack pushed another GPS locator option button and an enlarged map appeared on the dashboard screen. A red star flashed brightly, and the GPS fixed on Hempstead Lake State Park. Bennack's speedometer read 101 MPH and he was two miles from exit 18. As he approached the exit, he braked to take the sharp exit curve and saw in the distance the white SUV speeding toward the Hempstead Lake State Park entrance.

The SUV did not stop at the entrance gate to pay the $3.00 fee. Instead, it crashed through the yellow wooden gate leading into the 737-acre park and sped off into the distance taking a sharp skidding curve to the left passing a sign that read, *"NORTHWEST POND . . . 1/4 MILE"*. All the intricate pieces of the serial killer's strategy now raced through Bennack's mind in one searing vivid flash. It was Hector's brother, Mauricio, who was the serial killer using the Schutzhund K9 dog training that Tom Bennack had unknowingly taught him in his training classes, who had trained and controlled the dogs to attack and kill seven people, his daughter Judy being the first victim. Bennack concluded from the trail of facts that Mauricio's brother, Hector, was only an accomplice in the killings and not the perpetrator. Hector had nothing to do with planning and executing the commands to the dogs to track and kill seven victims. Mauricio's objective, Bennack reasoned, was to even the score with all the Freeport High School students who had teased and bullied his brother by intercepting and killing each one of them. To Hector's tormentors, that Mauricio painfully witnessed them torture his brother and cause him to snap, it would be his ultimate revenge of insuring that each of Hector's tormentors would never ever bother his brother again.

Helka was now in a frenzied attack mode, sensing an impending chase.

The police chief raced through the park entrances' broken gate and saw the white SUV zig zagging in the distance around sharp narrow dirt road curves leading to North West Pond. The SUV vanished around a distant curve and Bennack, foot to the floor, sped after him. He reached the curve, and a billowing cloud of dust filled the air obscuring his vision up ahead. He braked the patrol car and Bennack waited for the dust to settle so he could see the road. When the dust settled, he could not see the SUV in the distance. So, he floored the car and sped to the next sharp curve in the road up ahead. When he negotiated the next curve, he could see the North West Pond shoreline in the distance but no SUV. He sped up to the lakeside shore and slammed on his brakes. He got out of the car and frantically looked around for movement. Nothing, so he got back into the car and raced back to the point of the last SUV sighting, about 450 yards back. When he arrived, there was a dense tree pack on both sides of the road, but no sign of Mauricio's car.

Bennack pushed the car door open and jumped out onto the dirt road. The German Shepherd leapt out of the car and circled Bennack snarling and barking.

In an emotional command, Bennack shouted, "*Judy's killer, Helka. Voran, Helka, Voran.* Go on . . . Blind search. *Judy's killer. Fass. Fass.*" *Attack and hold.* The German Shepherd held its nose high in the air taking in scent. Suddenly, Helka's head snapped to the left, its nose taking in a long purposeful scent. Its lips flared showing glistening white teeth and the guttural snarl changed into a deep throated rattling sound of terror.

"*Judy's killer. Voran. Fass.* Find the killer, Helka. Find your master's killer." The dog looked up at Bennack, gave a prolonged yelping cry, then barked repeatedly before vanishing into the thick woods heading away from the lake in a lunging run.

CHAPTER 64

THE GERMAN SHEPHERD lunged through the thick tree pack following a swath of broken branches and crushed bushes. In the distance, Helka could see an SUV stopped before a line of birch and maple trees. The dog raced up to the car, encircled it then pounced up on the hood staring through the windshield, nose sniffing frantically for scent. It jumped down on the ground, nose to the air, and veered off to the right following a strong scent in pursuit.

Behind Helka, the police chief held a tracker in his hand, a yellow arrow pointing toward the dog's direction. The tracking device had been affixed to Helka's collar and assured Bennack that he could track and find Helka at any point in the search.

Nose to the ground, the German Shepherd raced through the dense underbrush, the killer's scent now firmly imprinted in her mind. Mauricio Anguilera was running wildly through the woods on the north side of the lake seeking the underground den he had first built before deciding on the Pine Barrens because they are vastly larger and thicker in tree pack and underbrush then the Hempstead Lake State Park. He was approximately four hundred yards away from his target when he heard behind him the guttural growls of a dog on the hunt. He knew the sound intimately and he hoped that the dog would respond to the Schutzhund commands he had learned in his K9 training classes that Bennack had taught him eleven years ago. Mauricio knew that the same police officer who had taught him those commands was the same man that was now hunting him down and was the father of Judy Bennack, the first victim that he had hunted down and killed.

The police chief was running frantically through the dense woods, leaping over fallen trees and swerving around twisted vines and clumps of bushes. When he ran around a thicket of bushes pursuing the yellow arrow on his tracker screen, up ahead he saw the white SUV and he drew his Glock pistol and clicked off the safety, his heart pounding in his chest. He raced up to the SUV and keyed a three-inch swatch of white paint on the shot gun side of the front door of the vehicle. As his car key scraped the white paint away, his suspicion was verified. Black paint now shown beneath the shiny white coat of fresh paint that had been applied only three weeks ago. Proof to the police chief that Mauricio Anguilera was the serial killer. All he could think of now was that he was about to confront the man responsible for killing his daughter and he was prepared to extinguish his life with one bullet to the head.

Helka was racing toward his target, only forty yards behind him and gaining. Mauricio looked over his shoulder and knew that the dog might overtake him before he could reach the den door which was hidden by a thin mat of mossy green earth marked by two birch trees flanking either side of the door. The den would lead the killer into a large twenty by ten-foot earthy underground room, but Mauricio still had fifty yards ahead of him to make it to safety. It would be close. He pulled out a 22 pistol and clicked off the safety. The German Shepherd's leaping gate had now put him only thirty yards behind its target, now twenty, then ten yards. At five yards, Helka was in the air. But Mauricio had already turned around to face his attacker and he pulled the trigger point blank as the dog's jaws were gapping only five feet from the killer's face.

Bennack heard the shot in the distance. He also heard a blood curdling human scream, "*Aus, Aus, Aus,*" Schutzhund training for 'Out, let go'., and "Nein, Nein,". The police chief knew Helka had engaged and it forced Bennack to lunge forward in a desperate attempt to save his daughter's dog and confront the killer.

The bullet had struck and lodged on the right side of Helka's chest, missing his lungs, heart, and vital organs by a half inch. The dog's leaping ninety-three-pound momentum had knocked the killer on his back, pistol jared loose from the fall, only two feet from his side. Mauricio was screaming Shutzhund commands to release him and stop the attack, but Helka was atop Anguilera now and his jaws had found the attacker's throat.

Bennack could now see the German Shepherd atop its victim and as he ran up, Glock at the ready, he now stood over the victim who was writhing on the ground, screaming at the dog commands to stop the attack. The chief shouted several commands to the dog to stop the attack, but Helka's jaws dug deeper into the man's throat as if the dog knew that he had his master's killer in its jaws. Bennack stared down at the blood-stained ground and watched the life of the killer slowly expunged in one terror enraged twisting and snapping motion of his windpipe and esophagus. Mauricio's eyes stared blindly up at Bennack as he heard the killer's last breath squeeze out from a collapsing chest through a gaping mouth.

The German Shepherd released its grip on its victim's throat and suddenly the dog collapsed atop the man it had just killed. Bennack fell to his knees embracing the dog. It was then that he realized Helka had been shot in the chest, blood now covering the chief's hands. He lifted the dog's body up and into his arms and walked swiftly out of the woods back to his patrol car. He radioed in for backup giving the coordinates to take Mauricio Anguilera's body out of the park and Bennack now frantically drove to the nearest veterinarian clinic in Hempstead in hopes of saving Helka's life.

CHAPTER 65

SIX WEEKS HAD passed and Tom and Andrea Bennack sat on a couch in their living room home. They held hands and talked softly above their Sonos® which was playing Enya's *Caribbean Blue*. On the floor in front of them, curled in a comfortable sleep, lay Helka. While bandages still covered her chest, the German Shepherd was making a healthy recovery from the gunshot wound, the 22 long slug had been successfully removed surgically from the dogs chest.

"She's with us, you know," Tom said squeezing her hand gently.

"I know," Andrea said looking down at Helka. "She never left us."

Bennack leaned over and kissed Andrea on the lips. "I love you, Andrea."

"I love you too, Tom," returning the squeeze. "What do you think will happen to Hector, now that his brother is dead, and we know he was the killer?"

"First, Hector has to get mentally well. And I think Judy's friend Eileen Langley will help expedite that with treatment. He's still an accomplice to the killings but considering his plight, the court could grant him leniency once he's healed."

"I hope so, Tom. Hector's had such a tough life."

"Yes, he has," Bennack said.

Grady Bennack walked into the living room from the den holding Julie Harned's hand.

"Mom and dad . . ."

"Yes," Andrea said smiling.

Grady said, "Can I tell you something?"

"Of course," said Bennack.

"Julie and I want to get married."

Andrea and Tom suddenly sat up in the couch, eyes wide.

"Really?" Andrea said. "That's wonderful, dear but . . ."

"I love your son, Mr. and Mrs. Bennack," Julie said.

"And I love Julie," Grady said.

Tom said, "What about college and a job?"

Andrea said, "Maybe you both can wait until you both finish college and have a job. I mean I think it's wonderful that you both love each other, but it might be a little too soon . . ."

Grady looked at his mother and father and hesitated in thought. "Mom, you were my age when you married dad. And dad you barely had a job when you both got married and you never went to college. I have a summer job as an intern with the FBI this summer. I think that's a good start."

Andrea squeezed Tom's hand and they both looked at each other smiling.

"He's right, Tom. We were about the same age."

Bennack thought for a brief moment and said, "Have you asked Mr. Harned for Julie's hand in marriage?

"Yes, he has, Mr. Bennack," Julie said grinning broadly.

"And what did he say?" Andrea asked.

"He said, yes," Grady responded with a big smile.

"I guess that clinches it, Bennack said. "So have you already asked Julie?"

"No."

"What are you waiting for?" Andrea said, tears now streaming down her cheeks.

Julie looked at Grady with a hopeful smile.

"I was going to wait until we're alone," Grady said.

Bennack encircled his arms around Julie and Grady and pulled them into a circle with Andrea facing him. "Ask her now," he said.

"Dad," Grady said. "Not in front of you and mom."

"Your dad never bowed to protocol, Grady. It certainly would be a first."

"It's okay with me," Julie said.

Grady stood in the circle awkwardly without word.

"I suppose it would help to have an engagement ring," Bennack said.

Julie smiled. "He has one."

"You do?" Andrea said in shocked surprise.

"Yes," Grady said. "When I asked Mr. Harned if I could marry his daughter, Mrs. Harned offered me Julie's great grandmother's engagement and wedding ring."

"That's beautiful," Andrea said, wiping the tears from her eyes. Looking at her son, she said, "Where's the engagement ring?"

"In my pocket," Grady grinned nervously.

"Well . . . now's the perfect moment to ask, son," Bennack said.

"Dad . . ."

"Grady . . ." Julie said.

Standing in a tight circle, Grady reached into his pocket and extracted a small black box. As he opened the box, he stared across the circle at Julie.

Suddenly, Helka squirmed her way into the center of the circle and sat down, tail wagging. He looked up at each of the four faces staring down at him and let out a small squeal of emotion. Tom Bennack said, "She's here with us in the circle." All of them immediately knew what he meant. Grady's eyes welled up in tears. He looked across the circle at Julie and knelt down beside Helka who started licking his face. Grady put one arm around Helka and looked up and said, "Julie Harned. Will you marry me?"

"Julie stared back at him, tears in her eyes and said, "Yes, Grady Bennack, I will marry you."

Grady took the engagement ring and reached up to her left hand and placed the ring on her finger. The moment he did, Helka let out a squeal of excitement and Tom Bennack said, "Congratulations."

Grady stood up and they closed the circle tighter in a loving hug, Helka standing up on her hind legs within the circle licking Grady's and Julie's face.

ACKNOWLEDGMENTS

Thanks to David Brown, movie producer of *Jaws*, *Sting*, and *Chocolat*, who encouraged me never to give up on the 'dogs attacking joggers' theme and who walked Central Park to study how he might film one of the attack scenes. He requested "First Option" on the movie rights of *JoggerKill* when I sold the hardcover.

Also, thanks to Tom Congdon who, Senior Editor at Doubleday who edited Jaws who had me do two rewrites of *JoggerKill*. While he eventually rejected publishing the novel, when he left Doubleday to start his own imprint, he told me he could not get *JoggerKill* out of his mind.

Finally, thanks to all my family members who positively reinforced my journey to share, through the impact of *JoggerKill*, the hazard of—and instilling fear about—jogging alone.

ABOUT THE AUTHOR

J OCK MILLER COMES from a strong publishing background. His great grandfather, George Terry Dunlap, was founder of Grosset and Dunlap book publishers; his grandfather, John R. Miller, Sr., was president of West Virginia Pulp & Paper Company (Westvaco); his father, John R. Miller, Jr. was President of the Hearst Corporation; his uncle, Dunlap Fulton, founded the first Pennysaver on the east coast. Miller founded his own publishing company at the age of twenty-eight, EOP, Inc., and it became the nation's first interracially owned and staffed company.

Jock received a BS degree in Zoology from Ohio Wesleyan University. Focus of study: paleontology, ornithology, and comparative anatomy. He attended Harvard Business School to participate in a case study publishing management program sponsored by the

American Business Press. Before starting his own publishing company, Miller served as Director of Marketing and Sales Service for Billboard Publications, Inc, then Director of Circulation for the twelve-magazine publishing company. Miller has appeared on cable TV talk shows, been interviewed on numerous radio talk shows, and interviewed live on the "Today Show" with Barbara Walters. He has been a guest lecturer at C.W. Post College and C.W. Post Brentwood Campus, lecturing on industry's responsibility to society and its community.

Miller is Director Emeritus of The First National Bank of Long Island where he served on the Board for twenty-three years. He is currently serving on the Board of Directors of the Middleby Company (A $4 billion dollar manufacturing company), as Chairman of the Compensation Committee. He is past President of the Boards of The Cold Spring Harbor Whaling Museum, The Huntington Arts Council, and served on the Cold Spring Harbor Fish Hatchery Board of Directors. He has served as an Elder and Deacon of the First Presbyterian Church of Huntington and as president of his Co-Op board in New York City.

Miller received the Pericles Award for his work promoting people with disAbilites, Wounded Warriors, Minorities and Women into the workforce through the company he founded, EOP, Inc. (www. Eop.com) now in its 53rd year of publishing. He is also the recipient of the Valley Forge Honor Certificate recognizing his contribution to a free society.

His 4-star best-selling novel novel, *Fossil River*, has received over 300 reviews.

Jock's hobbies are fly fishing, writing novels, and playing the bag pipes and piano. Miller is an amateur radio operator, K2MUS, if you are so inclined.

OTHER WORKS BY
JOCK MILLER

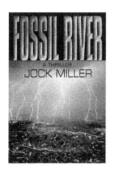

PREDATORS vs. U.S. MARINES!
Publisher: Fossil River (September 27, 2012)
Print length: 296 pages
ISBN: 978-0983605843 (pbk)
Also availble in digital and audio

Fossil fuel has an ageless affinity with dinosaurs. To create it, dinosaurs died. In this riveting, action packed thriller, the tables are turning! The perfect energy storm is sweeping over the United States. Japan's Fukushima nuclear plant meltdown has paralyzed nuclear expansion globally, BP's Gulf of Mexico oil spill has stalled deep water drilling, Arab countries are in turmoil causing doubt about access to future oil, hurricanes hitting the Gulf's oil rigs and refineries have increased due to global warming, and the nation's Strategic Oil Supply is riding on empty.

As the storm intensifies, the nation's access to Arab oil is threatened, causing citizens to panic for lack of gas, stranding cars across the country, and inciting riots. Those in charge must find new sources of domestic fossil fuel or face an energy crisis that will plunge the nation into a deep depression. At the last moment, a U.S. petrolium geologist discovers the world's largest fossil fuel deposit. Located in a remote mountain range, it is revealed by glacier thaw within Alaska's six and a half million acre Noatak National Preserve. The only thing standing in the way is a colony of living fossil dinosaurs that will protect its territory to the death.